hardscratch row

Also by Anne Cameron

Fiction
Sarah's Children
Those Lancasters
Aftermath
Selkie
The Whole Fam Damily
A Whole Brass Band
Escape to Beulah
DeeJay & Betty
Kick the Can
Bright's Crossing
Women, Kids & Huckleberry Wine
South of an Unnamed Creek

Traditional Tales
Daughters of Copper Woman
Tales of the Cairds
Dzelarhons

Poems
The Annie Poems
Earth Witch

Stories for Children
The Gumboot Geese
Raven Goes Berrypicking
Raven and Snipe
Spider Woman
Lazy Boy
Orca's Song
Raven Returns the Water
How the Loon Lost Her Voice
How Raven Freed the Moon

Stories on Cassette (Audio Book)
Loon and Raven Tales

hardscratch row

ANNE CAMERON

HARBOUR PUBLISHING

Published by
Harbour Publishing Co. Ltd.
P.O. Box 219
Madeira Park, BC Canada
V0N 2H0

www.harbourpublishing.com

Printed in Canada.

Cover design and page layout by Martin Nichols
Front cover photograph by Rick Blacklaws
Author photograph on back cover by Peter Robson

We acknowledge the financial support of the Government of Canada through the Book Publishing Industry Development Program for our publishing activities. We further acknowledge the support of the Canada Council for the Arts and the Province of British Columbia through the British Columbia Arts Council for our publishing program.

THE CANADA COUNCIL | LE CONSEIL DES ARTS
FOR THE ARTS | DU CANADA
SINCE 1957 | DEPUIS 1957

National Library of Canada Cataloguing in Publication Data

Cameron, Anne, 1938–

   Hardscratch Row

   ISBN 1-55017-290-5

   I. Title.
PS8555.A51871H37 2002   C813'.54   C2002-910769-5
PR9199.3.H75H37 2002

*For my children, Alex, Erin,
Pierre and Marianne,
and their children,
with love.*

one

THE SQUEYANX SAT ON THE HOOD of the new pickup, leaning against the windshield and occasionally turning to look inside, then wink and grin at Noel, who winked and grinned back. Kitty concentrated on driving, and on making sure not to tie herself up in the idea that a supernatural spook of some kind was accompanying them, a spook whom they accepted, as anyone else would accept kindly old Uncle Ralph or dear sweet Grandma.

The pickup was a pleasure to drive, the CD system was wonderful to listen to, and if you had to have company, Noel was the kind to have. He didn't chatter or yap or blither on about wanting candy or ice cream or chips or pop, he just sat, his seat belt properly done up, watching out the windows, his little fingers with their gnawed nails tapping with the music or feeling the fabric of his new jeans.

City driving may not be boring, but it is not interesting either. There are too many kamikaze drivers coming from all sides, too many people jay-walking, too many lights flashing, blinking, distracting you, and no time at all to actually *look* at anything. The good thing about it—perhaps the only good thing—was that the downtown crush petered out, stores gave way to urban residences, which eventually gave way to suburbs and finally ex-urbs. Stay on the main street long enough and it becomes the highway, and then, with no seam or boundary, the on-ramp to the freeway, and the city, with its nose-stinging exhaust-laden air is behind you; you could see the first fields, and not long after, the first of the dairy farms, with black-blotched cows standing in clover, jaws working, bags hanging and swollen, teats taut like the fingers of inflated rubber gloves.

"I could eat," she said quietly.

"I could too," Noel agreed.

He didn't look at her when he spoke, and she wasn't sure what that meant, if anything. Always someone ready to hop up and give you the

Reader's Digest condensed version of the deep psychosocial meaning of the wotzit of whozit and how it related, or didn't, to the price of rice in China.

If he wasn't in shock, deep shock, it was only because he had been so ill-used, misused and abused that he'd grown as tough as old boot leather. Well, she'd known other kids who grew up that tough, and on the whole, more or less, so to speak and all things considered, they'd done okay.

She took the access road that curved gently to the right, then curved again and became the parking lot of a huge Freeway Service, a glittering, gleaming temple to something, with eight double-hosed gas pumps, a soft-ice-cream pit stop, a small twenty-four-hour convenience store with shelves full of empty calories, and a huge restaurant where it looked as if you could get anything, from automat-style sandwiches and sticky buns to a full meal.

She parked in an empty stall near the front door, and she and Noel stretched, looked at each other and grinned.

"Well," she said softly, "this must be the place."

"I have to pee," he confided. "And, you know, the other too."

"Immediately, or do you have a minute or two?"

"Two minutes."

She locked the pickup and they headed for the door. Noel reached up and took her hand, as easily as if he'd been doing it most of his life.

"Do you like mashed potatoes?" he asked.

"Love 'em. You?"

"Yeah. And gravy. And I like hamburger steak better'n that other kind, you know, the all-in-a-chunk kind?"

"Hamburger steak, eh? Some people call it minute steak. Some call it Salisbury, I think."

"Yeah?"

"I like liver and onions."

"Yeah?"

"Yeah. And hot turkey sandwiches. With peas."

"I hate canned peas."

"Ah, but frozen ones? Or better yet, fresh ones!"

He shrugged, and Kitty knew that he'd never eaten fresh ones. Probably never had fresh green beans, either. Carrots, maybe—even exhausted addict basement dwellers grab a plastic bag of baby carrots from time to time and take them home with a container of chip dip so the kid could gnaw his way through some shoot-'em-up blow-'em-up special-effects nightmare.

"I can order for you while you go to the john if you tell me what you want."

"Mashed potatoes." He let go of her hand and headed for the washroom with the supposedly male figure painted on the door. She wondered whether it was the stylized drawing or the Squeyanx standing by the door, beckoning and grinning, flapping his skeleton fingers.

She slid into a booth and reached for the menu. "There will be two of us," Kitty told the waitress, almost absently. "I'll have liver and onions with double mashed, and he'll have the Salisbury. We'll have the house salad with the house dressing, and I don't know about dessert."

"To drink?"

"Coffee for me and, uh . . . oh, apple juice, I guess."

"Small, medium or large?"

"Medium."

"Salad with or before?"

"Right away, but don't hold up the real food until he's finished his salad or we'll be here all week," and Kitty smiled, although what she wanted to do was snap, Quit the dithering and just bring the bloody food, will you! But it was no use ripping off the waitress's head, it wasn't her fault.

The salad arrived before Noel did and Kitty took a taste. The house dressing was a mistake, it was too sweet. And there you have it, some places go for heavy garlic, some don't, and at this one they seemed to think the travelling public wanted dessert sauce on lettuce. Which was basically what the house salad was—iceberg lettuce. It also had two, count 'em two, slices of red pulp that must be tommy-toe in disguise, also a dark green slice, possibly green pepper, and some white slices, cucumber. One sliver of onion. Jeez, let's not go overboard on this one, an entire slice all to myself! I'm touched.

Noel slid into the booth across from her, looked in the plastic-pretending-to-be-wood salad bowl, nodded, then dipped his finger into the little paper cup of dressing and tasted it. He nodded again and started to eat, but he didn't pour the dressing on the salad. He took forkfuls of salad and dipped them in the little cup.

The waitress brought their plates and Noel grinned. As quickly as that he was finished with his salad. Kitty took his slice of onion and winked at him, and he grinned.

"You got more mashed than I did," he pretended to whine, not meaning any of it.

"You shut up and eat what you have or I'll pour it all down the back of your neck," she told him. The waitress grinned.

"This is *good*," he blurted, stuffing meat into his mouth. "Boy, this is real good."

"Must have the world's second-best cook working back there, eh?"

"Would you like a booster chair?" the waitress asked.

Kitty looked at Noel, who sat back on his heels, chewing. He was more or less kneeling on the plastic-covered bench, and Kitty might have said yes, please, but JimmySpook was leaning over the back of the booth, shaking his head, twisting his bones into a terrible frown.

"No thank you," Kitty said, making eye contact with the waitress. "Booster seats are for little kids. This guy'll do fine the way he is."

"Good mashed potatoes," he decided. "What's yours like?"

"Real good. Want to try some?"

"I never had any of that before. What is it?"

"Liver."

"What's that?"

"It's meat. Everybody and everything has one."

"Do I?"

"Sure do. It's inside you, tucked up here." She tapped herself in the general area of what would have been her wishbone if she'd been a hen.

"Guts?" he gaped. "You're eating guts?"

"Sure am." She cut herself another piece. "You've probably eaten it too and just didn't know. You ever eat a thing they call pâté?"

"You mean that, like, party stuff, you put it on a cracker? Yeah, I had that."

"Well, there you go."

"Can I try?"

"Sure." She chose carefully and cut him a small piece. He opened his mouth like a baby bird and then chewed, carefully, as if it might blow up in his mouth.

"Doesn't taste like party stuff," he declared. "Doesn't even feel like it. But it's good. I like mine better, though."

"I like *mine* better."

"Well, I like *mine* better."

"You going to eat your vegetable?"

"I had salad."

"True enough. Don't you like mixed peas and carrots?"

"I had salad," he repeated.

"You already said that. All's I'm trying to do is find out what you do and what you don't like. I'm not going to push it in your ear, you know."

"I don't like it. I only like broc'li, and then only if it's crunchy. I *hate* slimy stuff!"

"Me too. I don't mind soft, and I can manage mushy, but keep that slimy stuff away from me."

"What's that?" He pointed at her plate.

"They say it's bacon."

"You gonna eat it?"

"No."

"Can I?"

"Sure. You want some of my extra spuds?"

"No. You want these bejubbles?"

"Christ, no, I'm not eating my own, am I?" She laughed, and so did he.

She sipped the last of her coffee and the waitress materialized at the end of the table, pouring a refill, smiling. "Dessert?" she said, chirping like a canary.

"You got strawberry shortcake?" Noel asked hopefully.

"No, but we've got a pineapple upside-down with whipped cream."

"Real whipped cream or that other stuff?"

"The other stuff."

"Maybe I'll just have ice cream."

"Cone or dish?"

"Cone."

"Soft or hard?"

"Soft." He squirmed, got his legs out from under him, and sat so that he was suddenly lower, the tabletop just reaching his armpits.

They finished their meal and stopped at the twenty-four-hour, where Kitty bought two packs of Players filter, a package of bubble gum, two bags of chips (one salt and vinegar, one ketchup), some chocolate bars and fruit gums, and a few cans of chilled pop, as well as a small picnic cooler and a bag of ice cubes. She poured the cubes into the cooler, nestled in the pop and closed the lid.

"I can carry that," Noel said confidently.

He took it to the pickup, then waited while she unlocked the door. He handed it to her while he got himself into place, did his seat belt, then pulled his feet out of the way so she could put the cooler on the floor.

"You can rest your feet on it if you want." She locked his door and got behind the wheel, putting the bag of gum, chips, and candy bars on the seat between them.

"That wasn't very nice apple juice," he told her. "It was that kind that tastes like it's got smoke in it. Not real stuff."

"I know the kind you mean. I think they make it from powder. Smoke, eh? I never noticed that. I thought it tasted like old bruised apples."

"I didn't drink it."

"I noticed."

"You did?" he seemed honestly surprised. "You never said nothing. You never made me drink it."

"Why would I? If you aren't drinking it I figure you aren't thirsty or else you don't like it. If you aren't thirsty, why should I make you drink it? If you don't like it, why should you drink it?"

"I'll probably be okay with pop," he said.

"Right. Probably will."

Half an hour later he was asleep, his head resting on her jacket, which she had stuffed against the side window. JimmySpook was in there too, the jacket looking to rest more or less on his shoulder, although she wasn't sure a bunch of strung-together bones could really be said to have a shoulder. If you turned your head and looked straight on, you saw Noel, sleeping with his head on her jean jacket, but if you snuck a glance from the corner of your eye you saw JimmySpook with the kid's head resting on him, one bony arm draped around Noel's thin shoulders.

"I don't suppose you enter into conversations." She turned the music up a tad. Maybe it would soothe the kid, keep the bad dreams at bay.

JimmySpook just looked at her, which can't be easy when you don't have eyeballs.

"How come *this* kid? How come, out of all the kids on the face of the earth, *this* is the one you choose? And why *me*? I don't know how much of this you set up and made happen, but did it ever occur to you that all you had to do was send a welfare worker around to that roach palace? You just had to fix it so the cops bust in on one of those sick parties and pulled the kid out, and he'd get placed with some nice people who *don't* act tacky."

The Spook did the same thing with his bone fingers that he'd done in front of the men's washroom—he sort of wiggle-waggled them, as if he were brushing lint out of the air in front of him.

"Yeah. Right," she agreed. "Because they're nice, right? And nice people get all upset and squirmy inside when they're around a kid they think is crazy, right? So they'd send him to the diplomas, right? And by the time *they* were done, he'd be a total head case, right? Like what they'd have done to Jimmy except for the fact they were scared stiff of Gran."

The creepy-crawly SpookThing laughed soundlessly, ugly face agape, white trim-or-whatever creasing and folding upon itself.

"So what am I supposed to do here?"

She waited, but there was no answer. She sighed, lit a cigarette and had the satisfaction of seeing the Spook lean toward her. If he'd had nostrils they'd have twitched eagerly. She took a deep drag and blew the smoke in his direction, and without seeming to move he was sitting in-on-under-part-of the bag of treats and goodies, right next to her. She took another drag, then let the cigarette burn down in her fingers, the blue smoke trailing in the draft from the open window, moving to the Spook head and maybe through it.

Savannah knew there would be no arguing, not even about the kids. Everything was so . . . so . . . so bloody civilized! One by one they spoke, she listened, then she spoke, and they listened. Everybody nodded. Only Savannah wept, and she couldn't have explained why. The weeping knocked them for a loop, they were up and moving immediately. She got a roll of toilet paper for her tears, she got a pot of tea, she got her hand patted, she got her shoulders rubbed, she even got held and cradled. "I'm going to miss you," she managed, but that was only part of why she was weeping, a little part.

The very next day they went to the same lawyer who handled all the legal work for the construction company, the same lawyer who had handled the purchase of the house, who had set up the trust funds for each of the kids when they were born, who had dealt with the BS that the welfare tried to bring down on her. That first visit was brief, and not very businesslike; they had tea, they talked, mostly in the language she could be polite in but had never managed to learn. They explained to the lawyer why they were there and the lawyer explained why they would have to come back, told them it would take time, a lot of it, to make sure all the arrangements were fair for everybody, especially the children.

"You know," the lawyer said carefully, "that on paper, at least, you are half owner of the company."

"We did that for tax reasons," she reminded him. "I don't expect to hold them up for it." The tears started again and she reached for a tissue. "I'm not mad at anybody," she said, and never knew how dignified she looked, tissue and all. "And I'm not looking to hurt anybody. We're friends."

"One thing about it," the lawyer sighed, "their parents will be overjoyed."

"Yeah." More tears came. "Yeah, they sure will be."

She knew their real names, knew how to spell them and even to write them in their own cursive, curly-toes language. But for all those years they'd been the Three Wise Men, or Larry, Shemp and Moe. Even in the dark, even wrapped in passion, this one was Larry, this was Shemp, and the youngest one, with the curly hair and the shy smile, was Moe. It was Moe who took away all the photo albums to get duplicates made, who returned a week later to give her the originals and who, as damp-eyed as she was, put the copies on the shelf in the living room.

"Will we be allowed to visit?" he asked, and then they were holding each other, their tears mixing.

"Oh, God, Moe, you can visit any time you want, you can pick them up for holidays—hell, man, you can move in with us for however long at a time."

And, eventually, all the ins and outs were finished, all the wherefores and why-ofs were satisfied, most of the kids' stuff was packed and put in storage until they were settled. Savannah herself took only her clothes, the photo albums and one cookbook.

She knew it would only take a hint and Moe would tear off, get the marriage licence, buy a different house, do back flips and probably burst into song, but she wasn't going to drop that hint. Not only because it would be the start of trouble between the brothers, not only because she wasn't sure she wanted to be married, but because everything else had been carefully thought out and marrying him hadn't been.

They did manage to surprise her, though. They bought her a brand-new van to replace the much-used station wagon. And when the day came, not one of them went to work. They stayed and helped load the backpacks, then hugged each kid, one at a time, in bunches, and all at once.

Savannah kissed each of them, got behind the wheel, checked to make sure the kids were settled in, seat belts done, doors locked. And then she put the new vehicle into gear and drove slowly to the street. She stopped, checked both ways, then pulled out, turned to the right and headed off through the familiar neighbourhood. The kids were very quiet for all of five blocks, and then it was just another trip, like dozens of others they'd made, out of the city and off to see Uncle Jimmy.

She didn't have *all* the kids, of course, only her own. So why did it feel as if she'd left bits and pieces of her heart behind, why did it feel as if there ought to be more shiny black heads in the van, why did it seem as if there was only half the crowd there should be, only half the number of voices, only half the teasing and whining and laughing? What makes a kid "mine"? What makes a kid "yours"? And damn it, if this sniff sniff sniffing didn't stop, she was going to pull over to the side of the road, park the new boat, get out, bend over and kick herself in the butt.

"You okay, Momma?" Victor asked.

"I think it's probably hay fever or something," she lied.

"You never had hay fever before."

"I'm fine, darling, just fine. How's Victoria?"

"Sucking her fist. Got the whole thing in her mouth. And she's drooling all over herself."

"Teeth." She concentrated on her driving, made the turn from the street to the on-ramp, found her place in the heavy stream of traffic, then dared to relax. Not much, though—get too relaxed in this mess and you'll wind up in traction. Just enough to get some of the rock-hard stiffness out of her shoulders and neck.

"Will the dads really visit us?" Victor asked, a thin quaver in his voice.

"Darling, listen to me, and listen good. I am not having a fight with any of your dads. Things are changing, yes. But nothing is *over*, okay? Yes, each and every one of them will visit, maybe one at a time, maybe all-of-a-bunch. And they'll phone. And you'll phone them. And there will be letters. And you can send cards and pictures and presents. And they're going to set it up so that any time you absolutely cannot stand to be away from them any more, *if* you have school holidays, you can come stay with them. I'll drive you to the airport and see you on the plane, and when it lands here, well, there they'll be—or one of them. But someone."

"Why are we moving, Momma?" he dared. The other kids stopped yapping and nattering. They wanted to know too.

"Can we wait until we're out of the city for this?" Savannah felt as if she were pleading, and maybe she was.

"But you will?"

"So help me God, Vic. I thought I already had, but hey, we'll do it again and again until it's enough. But not with bad manners, okay? I'm sure you want to know, but—*fuck!*" She hit the brakes and the horn at the same time. The fat man who was trying to fudge in ahead of her hit his own brakes, his eyes wide, his face shocked. The driver behind him braked, more horns sounded, and the fat man's car stalled.

"Now there's a big mess behind us," Elaine said, dripping satisfaction. "Everything is snarled up and two guys are out of their cars and yelling at Porky. Good move, Momma."

Jimmy was in his glory hole, his eyes bleary, his hair rumpled where he'd scratched his head. There were bits of wood and shavings on top of his head, but he didn't know they were there. He could smell himself, not just sweat, but that other tang, a more personal one, a pong that came from his skin, his hair, even from his breath, maybe especially from his breath. He held his latest creation in his hands, cradling it, stroking it, his scarred fingers moving gently over the apple wood. It felt complete. Not just finished—a table can be finished, a chair or a milking stool can be finished, but Jimmy was searching for that other thing, the one that didn't happen very often, the one that meant he'd managed, briefly, to go where he needed to go to do what he so desperately needed to do. The carving was complete, he could feel through the wood the awareness inside the figure. He knew he wasn't going to sell this one, even though he'd get an incredible price for it if he did. This one had never been intended for sale. This one was personal, this was a part of the family, this was a part of *him*, and he'd made it knowing that he was going to share it, to give that part of himself—as close to an explanation as he would ever get.

Even he didn't know what he was trying so hard to explain. Maybe it was just another way to show off. He hadn't had much to show off when he was a kid, not like Glen, who was good-looking, and smart, and always one step ahead of anyone else. Not like Kitty, who could move—God, she could move, as if every muscle in her body had been in prime condition and fully trained before she even came out of the oven. The first time she swung a softball bat she looked like someone who'd been playing for years, and the first time she rented a pair of ice skates and stepped out on the ice she moved like someone who was trying out for a hockey team. Kit could climb trees, walk the roofline, you name it and Kit just up and did it. Easy for her to show off, she could probably have skipped while doing handstands. And Seel, well, all she had to do to show off was pick up a crayon, or a pencil stub or probably a burnt matchstick. Flowers came from her fingers with everything except the perfume, and if that wasn't enough, she was as cute as a button, big big *big* brown eyes, and blond hair. That if nothing else proved that the absent parent wasn't her dad. Kit—well, Mom had said she was, but the old man, wherever he might be, had insisted no way, and looking at Kit didn't give any answers, she looked so much like Savannah she could have popped out of a photocopier. The face, anyway. But their bodies were totally different, and Kit didn't have the hair, probably nobody else in the world did. Gran said her sister had hair like that, said the old man would have had it too if he hadn't had a crewcut all his life—well, until he started losing his hair. No need for any crewcut now. The old fart was as bald as they come, just that goofball little fringe, but he kept it shaved off. Odd thing, that. What would it feel like, get up in the morning, have coffee and rah rah, then into the bathroom for a quick shower and shave and while you're doing the face, lather up the old head, too, get 'er all done, then rinse, dry, and off to conquer the world.

Savannah could have shown off on any of probably a dozen fronts. Not just the looks of her, although you'd spend days and weeks of your life looking to find someone who looked as good, let alone better. She was tough, she was smart, and she was good at heart. Even Gran, the old biddy, had known that under the smart-mouth, under the wise-ass, under the round-heels and easy-make that everybody saw, under all that was the real Savannah. Jimmy hadn't been as good-looking as the others, still wasn't, never would be, and school had been hell from the first day. He hadn't done well and after a while he didn't even try. He hadn't even known he could find faces until he was into his teens. That was when he finally had something to show off.

The best of his work didn't get shown off, however. The very best work he'd done was here, on shelves, in his glory hole, seen only by himself and the very few who were allowed in; and fewer of them every year. Seely's kids knew he'd raise holy old hell if they went anywhere near. They weren't even allowed to come down into the basement. Seely could come in, and she often did. Sometimes Jimmy would look up from his work and good old Seel would be there, in the big ratty chair that had been Gran's, just sitting, sometimes with a little bit of a smile, listening to the CD music that was turned low, so low it was really like background sound, not really like music at all. Jimmy could not abide loud noises. Or sharp ones, either. The sound of knives, forks or spoons just tossed into the drawer cut into his ears, into his head, like sharp jagged knives, a phone bell could make him wince, a doorbell was agony and the sound of trail bikes or those three-wheeled all-terrain jobbies sent him into a fury. No thought, no reason, just reaction. But at least the bastards had quit bothering him, asking if they could zip around the field or go rattle-tattling around in the bush. He hadn't even been polite, he told all of them the same thing: no. Fuck off and leave me alone. Some of them had been insulted by his words, his tone, his expression, as if they had the right to show up at the door, ringing the bell, knocking knocking knocking until he answered, as if he were under some obligation to be sweet and kind just because they showed up with their wants and their smarmy pretences. Hey, Jimboh! Remember me, we were in school together, I was one row over and two seats behind you. And I was wondering if...No, fuck off and leave me alone. Well jeez, Jimboh, no need to get shirty, I was just...

Yeah. Right. As soon as you *want* something you "just." You didn't "just" when all hell had bust loose and a word or two might have helped, you didn't "just" when the old biddy was lying in hospital, but now that you've got yourself another toy and you need a place to burn up gas, well, you "just." So "just" fuck off and leave me alone.

But not Audrey. She knew what it was like, she'd been judged, classified, slipped into the slot they'd decided she should occupy. And then she'd been criticized for daring to occupy it with a measure of contentment. That's what really stuck in their craw. If she'd suffered somehow, if she'd rambled around drunk all the time, or stoned, or if she'd stuffed herself with chocolate until she was a ten-ton tub they might have hated her less, but she did none of that, she just lived her life as best she could. And yes, she was a whore, if only part-time. So? The town was full of married women who lay limp beneath the humping bodies of men they despised, two or three times a week, for their meal ticket, their house, their TV and their car and their clothes, and what was that but another kind of whoring? At least Audrey had her regular job, afternoon shift at the convenience store. Minimum wage, of course, no union benefits, no tips, no bonus, no security, and the boss as miserable a shithead as you would ever find. Thirty-five hours a week because if you work forty hours it's a full-time regular job and then you have rights, but if you work less than that, well, you're on your own, kiddo.

She was plain looking, a pleasant face, but nothing you'd notice as you passed her on the street. Strong body, but not spectacular, just a strong body with good-sized tits and comfortably wide hips. A guy could just cradle himself in there—comfort, not speed, was what they said. You could just look at a person and know if they'd come from poor, from workie or from middle class. The teeth were a clue—if they were crooked or bucked or yellow or false, well, that told you a lot about diet, about expectations, about environment. The upper crust kept their own teeth, got them straightened, even got them whitened.

Audrey had her own teeth. Well, except for that one at the front, it wasn't her own. She joked about it, of course it's mine, it cost me damn near three hundred dollars. Car accident, she said. They had to build up the one next to it because it was so badly chipped, whap on the old knee. Oh well, she shrugged, a tooth and a half isn't all that much, the guy driving got a crushed chest and the other two got scarred up from glass and such when the car rolled over and over and over. But by then Audrey wasn't in it, she'd been thrown out the passenger door on the first or second flip. She couldn't remember any part of it, but she knew she'd landed in a huddle that slammed her knee against her mouth, because they found a chunk of broken tooth there, in the bump at the edge of the big bruise.

But that was before she moved here. Jimmy suspected it might even be *why* she had moved here. But he didn't ask. None of his business. He met her when he met her, and anything prior to that didn't count, didn't matter, didn't exist.

He had met her when he was just coming out of a big spell in the glory hole, where he'd been for weeks, and he looked it. Thin and no tan left, and what Gran called fusty-looking. He'd cleaned himself up, shower, shampoo, shave, even had himself a good meal, but he still looked like someone who hadn't been brushing his hair or eating often enough, someone who was maybe coming off a bender. He was driving around, not going anywhere, just easing himself back into what they called the real world, not ready to enter it yet, but observing it. He pulled in for gas and thought about getting a coffee, but something about the whole set-up at the gas station made him angry. You'd think the entire world was lined up for the chance to hold up the place, the poor damn attendant in this kind of a booth thing, might as well be in jail. You put your money in this tray and it moved back and forth so you couldn't get a knife or a gun anywhere near the cashier. Your change came back the same way, in the moving tray. If you wanted coffee, you got it from a machine, and there was another machine beside that one with sandwiches, God knows how old *they* were, and next to that another machine, chips or chocolate bars. Anything you wanted, even cigarettes, was there in a machine. And it pissed him off.

Across the street the twenty-four-hour store was all lit up, with plenty of room on the parking lot, so he got in his car and drove over there for his coffee. Paper cup, same as from the machine, but a smile with his change. He sipped the coffee in the two-four and got himself a couple of glazed donuts. And there was Audrey, and she talked to him, same as if he looked presentable and normal. He was unwrapping a deck of smokes when the cops came in for their coffee. They didn't pay for it. Jimmy was ticked off but he didn't say anything. Having the cops in there was probably worth more to the management than a couple of cups of coffee. Nobody's going to waltz in, gun in hand, if the constabulary is there filling its pot belly with sticky buns and bear claws.

The cops looked at Jimmy with that we-know-who-you-are-asshole look on their faces and he smiled his widest and cheeriest smile. Anyone who didn't know, or who couldn't see the cops' eyes, would have thought everything was fine, just hunky-dory, couldn't be better.

He leaned on the counter, sipping coffee, finishing his donut, listening. Boy, what you can get away with when you're in uniform. Anybody else talked like that and it'd be time for the cavalry charge, but Audrey just fixed her face in this polite look that told Jimmy everything he needed to know.

The midnight-to-morning clerk showed up, and the cops had a very different attitude to her, so obviously different that Jimmy got insulted on Audrey's behalf, even if she showed no sign of feeling that way herself. The whole business hit him the wrong way, or maybe the right way. No sooner did the midnight clerk have her jacket off than Jimmy was turning to Audrey and smiling his wide smile, only this time it was totally sincere. "Your ride home awaits you, ma'am," he told her.

"I've got my own car," she blurted, caught off-guard.

"Yes, ma'am," he agreed. "But I can follow you, then wait until you get out of your work duds and into your fancies, and we can go to the Dine'n'Dance and catch us a steak supper. Please?"

"My pleasure," and she was laughing, but not at him. They were both stuffing it right up the cops' noses.

He did look fusty, in fact he looked half-wasted, but he was clean. And who would have noticed him, anyway, with Audrey standing beside him? She told him later that she had stood under the shower trying to decide whether to dress up or dress down, and decided down simply because she wanted to save the dressed-up look for the next time, if there was a next time. If there wasn't, why waste it?

Black slacks, and the quietest white blouse in the world, no rings, no necklace, just one silver bangle-bracelet. But when they walked into the Dine'n'Dance, she made all the others look faded. It wasn't her face, it wasn't her body, it wasn't anything you could point to. It was the kiss-my-arse tilt to her head, the up-yours look in her eyes.

Jimmy didn't try to kiss her goodnight. He wasn't far enough out of the glory hole even to think of it. The company was enough, it was better than sex and far, far better than romance. By the time they made it between the sheets they were as easy with each other as any two people could be. Yes, there were other guys got into that bed, but they paid for the chance. Audrey didn't give anything away free of charge, as if it were worthless. You pay for the chance to sit in some stinking theatre for an hour and a half watching bullshit in technicolour but not to spend a few hours with some-one who makes you feel like a million? You pay who-knows-how-much to go to a massage therapist, who is considered a professional, a pillar of the community, a member of the healing profession, but Audrey is a hooker, a whore, a shameful thing? Well, not in Jimmy's book. Who could expect anyone to pay rent, food and all the rest on the wages from the two-four?

Anyway, what happened when Jimmy wasn't there wasn't any of his business, and she never ragged on him about the times he wasn't there, or railed at him that the least he could do was phone once in a while, or bugged him about making sure he never, ever, no matter what, forgot her days off and always stayed available for a cozy dinner or some other damn thing.

He'd known her about six months when he showed her the glory hole. By then she knew about the art galleries and the fuss and all that, but it didn't make any difference to her. She knew him, the person, not that other one.

She moved to the ratty old chair and sat in it, letting herself loosen up all over and looking at the things he had on his shelves. "Jesus, Jim," she said softly, "this is incredible." She didn't ooh or ah, she just sat quietly and looked, and after a while she patted the arm of the chair and he sat on it, and they weren't touching each other but they didn't have to.

He'd given her a key to the house and told her she could come into the glory hole any time at all. He didn't have to tell her not to talk to him if he was wrapped up in his work. She knew.

He put the finished carving on his worktable and stood up, trying to stretch out the kink in his back. His hands were tired, his wrists were sore and swollen, and when he walked to the door his legs were stiff and he moved awkwardly. What he needed was a proper chair. That old kitchen jobbie had about had it.

He found clean clothes and put them on his bed, then grabbed the deep-maroon-coloured housecoat Savannah had given him for Christmas and took it to the bathroom. He stripped off, got in the shower with his tooth-brush and toothpaste and stood under the hot spray, brushing brushing brushing. He rinsed his mouth in the shower spray, then reached for the mouthwash. Mouth full of minty-tasting something, he shampooed his hair and rinsed it, then spat out the minty stuff and stood in the shower yawning. He was starting to feel tired now, really tired, deep-in-the-bone belly-full-of-it tired, and drowsy, and relaxed and smooth. If he didn't get out of there and into bed, he'd fall asleep on his feet, under the hot water.

His bed felt so good. Soooo good.

The nurse checked the technology before she checked Glen. He thought that was funny, but didn't say anything about it. Talking was such hard work. Even thinking was becoming a chore. What he wanted to do was sing, but he knew he couldn't do that. There wasn't enough breath in his lungs or strength in his throat. But he could *think* the songs, and that was every bit as good.

He had no idea where he'd been for the past little while. Oh, his body had been here, no doubt about that. Even he knew that this was the last place on earth *he* would be, there would be no pick-up-thy-bed-and-walk for him, final destination, no forwarding address. Well, there must be worse ways to go. He didn't like the idea of fungal infections, it was too much like growing mushrooms in the dark. And he didn't like the ugly taste in his mouth, what they called thrush, even though he'd grown used to it. It was old and tired and blah blah blah.

He himself was tired and blah blah blah, although he'd never get the chance to be old. But he didn't really care. That's one of the side benefits of being terminally ill. After a while a kind of laziness takes over and you just stop minding. You lose interest. It's all just too much trouble. The breath-ing in and breathing out, the beat beat beat and pump pump pump. Sometimes he'd lie and listen to the sounds of his body and wonder, in a distant way, how long the mechanics of it all could continue. He'd hear his own voice in his head, calm and more rational than he'd ever been when he was healthy, and the voice would tell him what he already knew. Not as strong today, I'm getting weaker, the same thing that happened to Greg is happening to me, only not as quickly, my God it was no time at all and that dear man was gone, but I seem to be setting some kind of record.

He knew that Fred still came to visit, but it must have been like visiting a stump or a punky log on the floor of the bush. Glen tried, but he couldn't manage much more than a smile. Or, with enormous effort, to reach out and take Fred's hand in his. He had so much to say to Fred, but none of it really needed to be said, and Fred knew it.

There wasn't much left. House gone, car gone, money gone, everything gone, really. Even friends, most of them had gone where Greg had gone. It was like watching a scythe go through a patch of long grass, leave no blade standing. But then nobody had ever managed to avoid dying, some just took longer to do it than others.

Nice to be in two places, even if he was only half in each of them. He wished he could tell the others what it was like, but as soon as they came, especially if Savannah was with them, he got yanked, not roughly but firmly, all the way into this place. Maybe that was how it was supposed to be, maybe the ones who were vibrantly alive weren't supposed to know or imagine what was on the other side of the door. When he was by himself, he drifted, he floated, he went back and forth, never completely here, never completely there; aware of much, unaware of most. He was at ease in both places, he felt at home. Very much at home.

All he'd have to do is reach out and remove the IVs. Wouldn't take long after that. But he didn't. If the time came when he was supposed to, he would, but for now, if this was what he was supposed to be, supposed to do, supposed to not do, fine. He was up for it. As long as all he had to be up for was dozing off and waking, or partially waking, and dozing off again.

He felt closer to them than he had when he was healthy. Closer, too, to Gran. She and he had never been easy with each other. She couldn't understand why he was such a mean son of a bitch, probably because she wasn't mean herself. But now it was all okay. Maybe the fever had burned the ugly out of him. Maybe he just didn't have the energy any more. But he and Gran got along just fine now. Mom, too, but in different ways, although Phyllis, now, she was more of a pain in the arse than she'd been when she was walking around and braying and popping beer cans. The rug rats— well, they were rug rats, busy with their own stuff, just too different for him to understand. Even if they weren't snivelling and whining and fighting and bitching and being downright miserable any more, they were still rug rats.

The nurse was shining that light in his eyes again. He blinked, he smiled, he even lifted his hand. "Hey, sweetheart," he whispered. "Anybody ever tell you what a gorgeous creature you are?"

"One or two, once in a while," she answered. "Give me a hint, Glen. What can I do to make you feel better?"

"Popsicle," he managed. "Peach flavour."

"You've as good as got it. I wish there was more . . . it's an awfully helpless feeling, you know, when here I am, useless."

"Hubris." He felt himself slipping back into sleep.

But he pulled out of it, briefly, when she came back with the popsicle. She held it, and he swallowed the juice. He wasn't aware of time going by, and maybe he went back to sleep at some point. In one blink he was enjoying the taste and in the next blink only the stick was left and she was taking it from his mouth.

"Thank you." He felt himself drifting off again, back to that other place, where all he had to do was float.

"Here," she said, tucking the sheet over his shoulders. "Here, we'll just get you comfortable, and then I'll buzz off and leave you be so you can have a good snoozy before lunchtime. Now you *be* here when I come back, you hear? No sneaking off when my back is turned."

"Yeah." He wanted to tell her he wasn't going to die until—whatever—but he didn't know what that whatever was, and he was so sleepy that he wasn't sure he'd be able to tell her anyway.

If he could just drift into sleep he was sure he'd get a chance to visit, maybe with Savannah. He never got to visit with Seely. He'd given up hoping, they'd all made it plain that maybe it would make him feel better but it wouldn't do anything good for Seel. So he just let it go, he'd done enough already, no need to hurt her any more. Some stuff doesn't get settled. Or if it does, it happens in ways other than those we recognize.

Seely sat in the comfortable chair by Sandra's bed, reading to her from *Comanche Moon*. God, it was a long book! Maybe not as long as *Lonesome Dove*, but long enough that she was sick of reading it. If they're going to pass laws, why don't they pass one that no book can be any longer than three hundred pages? After that it gets tiresome. How do those silly-ass writers do it, hour after hour every day, reading their own stuff, reading the same writer, listening to the same voice, page after page of it? Look how much you can get into a three-page letter. Entire months of your life summed up and put out for someone else to read. If a person who isn't a writer can do that, then why can't the ones who claim to be writers do the same, get the story told, for crying in the night? Get it done, let the rest of us get on with our lives. If you can't say it in three hundred pages, el tough-oh, you'll have to write another one, pick up where you left off, like those TV mini-series.

"Would you like a drink?" She put the book aside, swallowed, licked her lips and wished her tongue didn't feel numb. "I need one. There's orange juice, there's cranberry cocktail and there's my own special mix." She winked.

Sandra couldn't wink any more but she could still use her fingers. She held up three of them and Seely nodded, got out of the chair and headed for the kitchen. Her special mix was a can of beer. Sandra would be able to manage maybe half, or almost half, and on a good day she could even get a full can into her. The daily visiting nurse would go tsk tsk and wonder what kind of people they were, giving alcohol to a woman who was barely alive. Or maybe not, maybe she'd be a real human person. If it was Dora, she would be real. Dora had shown Seely how to flush the catheter so Sandra didn't have to wait for the nurse. Dora would have shown Seely how to remove the damn thing and insert a fresh one too, but Seely's face went all white and her hands started to shake so Dora just patted her on the arm and let it go. A person can only do so much, especially when she's doing it to the woman she considers to be her real mother. Pulling out rubber tubes and putting in other rubber tubes was over the limit.

"Hey," Seely had blurted, "I'd recognize her face in any crowd, okay, but let's not go overboard," and Sandra had laughed. It was dangerous when she did that, she could choke as easily as not, but the risk was worth it that time, all three of them laughing, Seely sitting on one side of the bed holding Sandra upright, Dora on the other side, her arm behind Sandra, her hand warm on Seely's shoulder.

They shared the beer. Sandra didn't manage half a can, she barely managed a third, but you could tell she enjoyed it. Of course, it made her sleepy, and that meant, oh woe is me, oh woe is you, oh woe is all of us, Seely didn't have to read any more of the book. Not right then, anyway.

You could buy audiotapes with voices reading stories. Some of the voices were famous ones—maybe that's how the stars got charity write-offs, read a book onto tape and then donate the reading fee, and tell the tax man the fee would have been a million dollars. Some of the stories were good, some of them you wondered who had made the decision to go to all that time and trouble, but it takes all kinds and all tastes. She taped CBC radio dramas, she taped *22 Minutes* and *Royal Canadian Air Farce* because you could listen to them a few days later and laugh all over again and hear punchlines you'd missed first time around. Jimmy taped stuff too. He had a radio setup, my God, you'd think he was going to open a studio, and his satellite dish could pull in programs from other places, good drama from England that Sandra really enjoyed.

It didn't bother her that sometimes the tapes had already been up to the hospital to that other one, she wasn't worried about catching anything and Seely wasn't worried about it, either. She'd learned what she could and she knew you wouldn't get it from a toilet seat or a sneeze or a mosquito bite. They'd given up yapping at her about it. Fred, your friendly neighbourhood faggot, the social workers, the hospice workers, the Compassionate Friends, the whole lot of them had given up. She was sure Jimmy had had a talk with them about it. Jimmy, who didn't really understand, but who accepted. Glen was the one who had taught her to not mind one way or the other what came down on him, Glen was the one who had set things up the way they were, and just because Glen was dying and wanted her to forgive him didn't mean she was under any obligation to unlearn what he had taught her so often and so hurtfully. He could die on the lawn of City Hall at high noon with the whole town watching and she wouldn't bother turning on the TV news to see the report about it.

People thought she hated him. Wrong. She didn't give a hoot about him. She was like one of those people who live near a river, and as long as the thing stays in its banks it's just there, you don't have to be running out every hour to check on it, you don't have to zip off with a picnic lunch every day and visit with it. Time enough when it's in flood, trying to swallow your porch and carport and maybe even the entire house.

And now that Glen was closer to dead than alive, he wasn't going to come flooding over her life, popping the lock on the bedroom door, or, worse, already in there, hiding under the bed until she was in her pyjamas and lying down, the baby of the family, first one to bed at night, all alone in the room except Glen. Kitty thought the reason she so often came to bed to find Seely weeping was that Seely was a suckybaby who wanted an excuse to crawl into bed with Kit. Well, they knew better now. Now. Why hadn't she told them before? To what avail? That's what Sandra would say. To what avail?

She went to the kitchen and once again read the instructions in the cookbook Savannah had given her for Christmas. She carefully gathered the things she would need, then, uncertain, uneasy, anxious and nearly convinced she was going to goof it up, she started what Savannah called whomping it up. Oh, Savannah said, sounding as if there was nothing in the world easier or less bothersome, oh, just toss it together, whomp it up and pop 'er in the oven, nothing to it. Sure, Savannah, sure. And if you goofed, there was all that food, fit only for the dog. Except she didn't have one, there'd been one too many sad stories in that area.

The visiting nurse parked her car, got out and waved. Oh good, it's Dora after all. Some things just make life easier, no doubt about it, and Dora was one of the angels God sent to earth disguised as an ordinary person. Sandra enjoyed Dora's company, enjoyed her ministrations, and Christ, all things considered, it was small enough comfort for her. Not fair not fair not fair. The words chanted in Seely's head and she almost lost her place in the cookbook. She was willing to bet that the chant never distracted Savannah. How is a person supposed to do anything, do new things, complicated things, with that friggin' voice going Not fair not fair not fair?

Maybe there wasn't much in life that *was* fair. The alternative, however, was grim. It wasn't that she was afraid to die, she just had a whole bunch of stuff to do before she packed it all in.

The girls, for example. What was that old joke? Take them, for example—oh please, dear God, *take* them... Or maybe they weren't all that bad. Sandra seemed to think they were the best thing since sliced bread, or unsliced for that matter. Bread, the staff of life, right.

So you put up with it, because it makes Sandra happy. All it took was for Seely to give one or the other a whap on the arse, and no matter how much the little bugger deserved it, Sandra was weeping. When she'd told Savannah as much, she shook her head and said Seel, for criminy sake, maybe the woman is weeping with relief because somebody finally did something about the little bitches. But no, Sandra adored them both. Of all the people who'd asked questions like Who is the father, Do they have the same father, as if it was anybody's business, Sandra had never once—not one time—asked. Well, neither had Jimmy, or Kit or Van, but everyone else seemed to think it was their business. It wasn't. It wasn't even Darlene and Lizzie's business as far as Seely was concerned. Just hers.

Lots of things were nobody else's business but Seely's. No way she was going to pay money to join one of these groups where people sit around telling each and every little thing about themselves, their lives, their hopes, their fears. Jesus, next thing you know they'll be building hives and moving into them, learning how to make honey or something, not one single solitary private moment left. No thank you.

"How is she?" Dora asked quietly.

"She's real quiet today, real tired. She's sweating too, but I can't figure out why, it's not a hot day. I've got the air conditioner going, I've got the quiet fan going, I've given her two sponge baths with alcohol in the water to cool her off." She could hear the tears in her own voice and didn't care. If she couldn't be honest with Dora what was the point of any of it? "I've been pouring fluids into her, putting ice chips in her mouth, got a half can of beer into her. She seemed to be following the story when I was reading to her, but—I don't know, I just don't feel easy about it."

Dora put her arms around Seely and held her. She didn't pat her on the shoulder, she didn't stroke her back and say there, there, dear, she just held her and she was ready to hold her for however long it took.

"Oh, Dora," Seely mourned, "it's so hard on her. I'd give anything..."

"I know, dear. And I know it would be different if there was anything that seemed to give her some joy, but the way it is, especially right now, the most we can do is try to keep her comfortable."

"She didn't eat any breakfast at all, not even her yogurt. Supper last night she seemed to like her broccoli, I mean it looks like green goose shit by the time it's gone through the blender and all, but it tastes like broccoli, and I put on some of that cheese sauce you showed me how to make. I kind of spooned up some mushed broccoli and then dipped the spoon in the cheese sauce, you know, so all she had to do was suck it off and swallow. And she didn't choke or anything, but—"

"Did she eat anything else?"

"Pudding." Seely relaxed suddenly, the stiffness gone from her back and shoulders. "Butterscotch pudding. Not instant or even that ready-in-a-minute boil-it kind, I made it from scratch, the old way. Then I put a layer of whipped cream in a bowl, then a layer of pudding, then the whipped cream, and like that. I hid some vitamin pills in it and she didn't even notice. She really liked it."

"Nobody could do more, Seely."

"Yeah. In a way that makes me feel a bit better, but still, it's not much compared to what she did for me."

She concentrated on the recipe book, but heard every sound from the bedroom. She heard the gasp, not so much pain as impatience, exasperation, and a kind of fatalistic Oh God, here we go again. Dora must have rolled Sandra on her side, propped her up with pillows and gone to work on the bedsores.

Seely couldn't handle the bedsores. They'd been out of control for a while, spreading and oozing and spreading. The ones on Sandra's ankles were the worst. And then Jimboh showed up with a thieving great bottle of cod liver oil. Vowed up and down and sideways that he'd read about it on the Internet, but couldn't seem to remember where or how he'd found it. By then Dora was just about desperate enough to try lawn clippings if someone said it would work. Jimboh had papayas with him too. Lots of them. And so, with Dora watching, Jimboh soaked the bedsores with cod liver oil, then made a paste of the papaya and put it right on the oozing patches. He soaked bandages in cod liver oil, put them over the papaya stuff, then put plastic wrap over top so the oil would stay on the poor thin buggered-up skin and not soak into the sheets. No change for a few days, but you could tell Sandra appreciated Jimmy's concern. She'd reached for his hand and he sat on the chair beside the bed, letting her hold him even though she had a grip like an alligator's jaws and not enough control to be able to release it. Sometimes you had to pry her skinny fingers off and there'd be marks on you. Seely made sure she kept Sandra's fingernails clipped real short, otherwise she might put holes in you without meaning to, and no matter how hard you try you can't always keep the nails as clean as you'd want them.

A week and a half, maybe two weeks later, the oozing and seeping stopped. As soon as it did, Jimboh stopped with the fruit, and put on pads soaked in cod liver oil, with cotton batting over top. Okay, so the damn things hadn't healed shut, so there was no big miracle, but even a fool would know the sores had grown smaller, and they didn't weep and stick to the bandages any more, and there weren't any new ones.

It seemed weird. Worse than weird, it seemed wrong to be tootling off down the highway like this without Caroline, without Jason, without Brandon and Brittany. But Carol and Betty had their rights, even if Betty probably wasn't any more interested in such things than she was in taking over the SPCA. She hadn't stayed with them all that long, a couple of years and she was off down the pike, leaving the twins behind, thank God. And yeah, for sure, Savannah had as much claim to them as Carol did, and for sure she loved them as much as Carol did. But Savannah had five kids, Carol only had two—well, three if you counted the pumpkin growing under her shirt. Not fair, really, that Savannah should wind up with seven and Carol with two-going-on-three, and no one in their right mind would split up the twins. God help them if they tried! What a pair.

There was satisfaction in knowing that Larry was going to defy the old bitch and her yitter-yatter. Sometimes you'd like to be a fly on the wall, just to see the look on the old harridan's face when she found out her first-born had up and married, not only without her permission, but without her approval and in spite of her loudly declared opposition. Some things you can't understand unless you grew up with them. Everyone said that women were subservient and men were the bosses, had the power of life and death over their wives and daughters, could beat them or out-and-out get rid of them, toss the body in the garbage dump, and just about the time you started to believe some of that, *poof*—you run up against someone like old Bindi. And don't anybody ever believe anything but that she pulled the strings, she gave the orders. Oh, the old man might crack the whip, but only in those areas where the old girl didn't care to bother. And when it came to her sons, the old woman bothered. Bothered everybody!

Well, Larry could stand up to her. Of the three of them he was the hardest, the toughest, the most rigid. Poor little Moe, he wouldn't have a chance, he was too soft-hearted, too gentle. She was pretty sure Moe was Victor's dad, they had the same great big eyes, the same long, long eyelashes. Elaine had the lashes, but not the eyes, and Vic's hair was wavy, not really curly, but gorgeous all the same. Elaine had the curly hair—except for the colour it was like Savannah and Kitty's all over again. Bobby had hair like that, and Alan, well, he had the waves, same as Victor, but no chance little Moe was involved there. That hyper, skinny, zip-zoom-zip-again, that was Shemp.

"So, Mom?"

"Yes, Victor?" She knew what he wanted.

"Mom?"

"Why don't we pull in at that place up ahead there? Get ourselves a whack of burgers and fries? We can eat in the car, *if* somebody promises to hold my drink for me, because I've only got two hands, right? And then," and she patted the steering wheel as if she was looking forward to the chance, "then I'll explain the whole thing, the move and all."

As far as Jimmy was concerned, if that goddamn noise didn't stop soon, he was going to head out with a sack of rocks and start chucking 'em. Bang bang bloody bang bang bang, Christ, was there no end to it? A person couldn't bloody die around here, let alone roll over and sleep!

Glen didn't seem surprised to see him. It was almost as if he had been expecting him.

"Okay, butt-head," Jimmy said softly, "here we go, arms around the neck, you know how to do it, don't be such a lazy fart."

"Hey."

"Don't waste air talking, you got nothing to say anybody would want to hear anyway. Attaboy, we got 'er all set up here, even got two nurses ready, willing and able to do the trick with the damn bottles'n'jars. Okay, you ready? Here we go."

Glen didn't even feel it, and there he was, out of bed and in the big wheelchair. IV hanging here, IV hanging there, tube draining here, tube draining somewhere else, but none of that mattered, it was nothing much to do with *him*.

"So, you ready? Now, don't you start blubbering on me or I'll just tip the chair and dump you out on your scrawny ass. And don't think you're getting any kind of treat in *here*. If you don't let me take you to hell and gone outside, then it's back into bed for you."

All Glen could do was smile, and nod, and then—*zip*—so he must have fallen asleep again. God, it was hard not to be asleep, hard to stay here, even with Jimmy talking non-stop, trying to focus him. And they were outside. He could feel the breeze against his face, and he would have shivered but couldn't quite bring it off. Jimmy knew, though, and tucked the blanket all around Glen, took off his own jacket, put it back-to-front so that it covered Glen's chest.

"Sniff in, butt-head," and there it was, the wonderful smell of coffee, the rich black stuff Jimmy made. "How's that, then? She's a bit hot, yet, so don't dip your beak or you'll get burned. Just sniff at it and . . . here, see if you can suck on this."

Dear God in heaven, thank you. Amazing how much peace there was in one little puff on a cigarette. If they knew, really *knew* how much it meant, what it tasted like, what it felt like, what it signified, if they had even a hint of it, they'd lift the No Smoking restrictions on the terminal wards. The last thing Glen had to worry about was addiction, and so what if he got lung cancer? He had just about every other kind a person could get. Take away the tumours and he'd weigh half what he did. Maybe less.

"Attaboy," Jimmy said approvingly. "You're smoking the shit out of that cigarette, guy. Want to try some of the brew?"

Nobody expected him to swallow it. And he was long past the point of politeness or icky-yucky. He sipped and held the coffee in his mouth, flooding all three or four of his remaining taste buds, the ones that hadn't been destroyed by the thrush.

When the stuff cooled off, Glen nodded. Jim put the kidney basin under his chin and he let it dribble out, didn't try to spit, didn't have the oomph or the co-ordination for it. The coffee spilled out. He took another puff on the cigarette, then another sip of the coffee.

"Savannah's coming down," Jim told him. "Should be here by about— oh, ten tonight, something like that. You hang on, okay? Don't croak until after she gets a chance to see you."

"Early," Glen warned.

"Yeah, I know. If we can work it we'll sneak 'er in tonight, but if we can't, well, you just keep suckin'er in and blowin'er out again and I'll have her here as early as they let us inside."

"Vic . . ."

"Yeah, I think we can manage that. Nice kid, that Victor." Glen heard the chuckle behind the words. "Maybe it's just that the first one to arrive is always special. Better looking, smarter, more talented, nicer—"

"Poof."

"Poof? Is that the best you can do? I was expecting you to leap up outta your chariot and holler Fuck that, Jimboh, and fuck you too. God, Glennie, do you remember the time I sent you halfway around the bend?"

Glen laughed, and knew it sounded more like a cough. He remembered.

"Jeez, the old lady didn't know whether to sit down and cry or stand up and shriek. You can yap all you want, you dumb shit, I said, but everyone in the world knows that when I was born, Mom and Dad and Gran and everybody took one look and said, This is perfection, never do better than this one, from here on in it doesn't matter what kind of scruffy pups we have. And my God, didn't you just about go into orbit! Nearly frothed at the mouth."

"Ah, Jim."

"Yeah, you got it, you creep. Not much else to say, is there?"

Another puff, another sip, another dribble down the chin, and then Glen only had time to shake his head as a warning and Jimmy pushed the kidney basin out of the way and let Glen's head loll to one side. He was asleep again, or in that on-again, off-again coma again. Nobody knew exactly what was going on when he did that. Face pale except for those awful purple welts and patches. Teeth all gone, just up and fell out, no gums left to hold them. Mouth open, tongue swollen, the thick coating of thrush stained brown by coffee. Jesus, if a person has to croak, couldn't they at least go out looking *okay?*

He emptied the last of the coffee onto the ground, emptied the kidney basin, put the paper cup in the isolation bag—Jesus, you can't even toss the damn thing in the trash, not because the virus is that contagious but because people are that scared and ignorant. Take it all back. Why not, none of it mattered. You could tell Glen was long past feeling shamed or diminished by all the careful disposal.

Jimmy pushed the chair back into the room, and the nurses were there lickety-split to help with the plastic pouches.

Jimmy lifted his brother to the bed, settled him gently. "Ah, you poor son of a bitch," he said. "If I'd'a known it was going to be like this, I'd'a taken you out and shot you, so help me God."

He scrubbed up, then sat for a while by the bed, just in case Glen woke up, but when the breathing deepened, almost into groaning, Jim got up and left. That sound might have been snoring, who could tell. Might have been him choking to death, who could tell.

He had a huge pot of sauce ready, and a salad just about big enough to feed a hippo, and Seely brought over an array of desserts. It would have been nice if she'd left those two whining wimps at home. When the headlights swept through the big front window and across the living room wall, both Darlene and Lizzie started screeching as if they were really happy to see their cousins. The glee would last about as long as it took for any of Savannah's kids to get some attention from Jimmy or Seely, and then the jealous green-eyed monster would surface in both of them and the whining and nagging and showing off would start up. Whatever you do, don't take the spotlight off either of 'em.

He turned the heat on under the big pot of water. It had already boiled once and was still blistering hot. By the time Savannah got herself parked and all the so-good-to-see-yous were finished, the water would be hot enough to boil the pasta. Everything would be fine. Just fine.

And the best part of all was when she came in the kitchen you could tell she hadn't yet noticed, probably wouldn't notice until the next day. It would be hard to overlook then, by God. The damn noise was almost worth it. He could feel himself smiling, not just outside but inside.

Savannah was shocked when she saw Glen. Nothing about him reminded her of who and what he had been before he lost the lottery. He was bald, all his lovely thick hair gone, not even fuzz to soften the shine from the tight-stretched skin. Without the hair his entire face had changed. But it would have done anyway, as the weight dropped away and the dehydration set in, impossible to stop even with the IVs. And the purple patches, they didn't add anything to his appearance. If Jimmy hadn't been with her, if he hadn't been talking to the ghoulie in the bed, calling him by her brother's name, even managing to get a little bit of a smile from him, she wouldn't have known who he was.

The fright turned toward her. She supposed the eyes were focussed on her but she didn't know for sure. "Hey," it rasped.

"Hey yourself."

"I'm Victor." The boy stepped forward. "Remember me?"

"Love you, Vic."

"This is Elaine, she's next in line, then this is Alan. We didn't bring Bobby because when he's tired he gets cranky, and we didn't bring Victoria because she's just a baby. Auntie Seely has them at her place. But Bobby looks a lot like Alan, just a bit shorter is all, and Victoria, well, she just looks like a baby."

"Hi, kids." The words were barely audible, but the kids moved closer.

"We're moving up here," Elaine said. "We only brought some of our clothes right now, the rest is in storage, but our dads said no problem, they'll make sure it all comes. We're gonna go to school here and everything."

"I didn't want to come," Alan admitted. "There prob'ly isn't much to do here. I was in hockey at home. I was in soccer too."

"We've got a hockey league," Jimmy answered, "and a soccer league. Our kids took the district last soccer season, and some of our hockey players were on the BC team, so things aren't too tacky here. And gymnastics," he added, "and swimming, and volleyball and basketball and chess."

"See," Elaine soothed, putting her arm around Alan's waist, "I *told* ya it would be okay."

"He didn't want to leave our dads." Vic let the kitten out of the bag. "He's really sad about not being with them."

"Yeah," Jimmy nodded. "That's actually a good thing. It shows that he has real loyalty, and lots of love. Tell you what, Al, and this is a promise. When you can't stand it, I'll drive you to the airport myself, get you a ticket and fire you on down for a long weekend. You can ask anybody,

Jimmy doesn't tell lies. If Jimmy says a thing is going to happen, it happens, okay?"

"Our dads are like that too," Elaine told him. "When our dads give a promise, boy, you can count on it."

"Is there a temple here?" Vic asked the wraith in the bed.

Glen nodded and moved his hand, waved weakly at Jim.

"They just built one out on McRae road." Jimmy looked uncomfortable. "It's not very big, but... why, you religious?"

"My dads want me to keep up with the language." Victor looked at Elaine, then at Jimmy again. "I don't 'spose you know many people who speak it, eh?"

"Not a one," Jimmy agreed.

"Uncle Glen is falling asleep." Elaine noticed first. "I guess we'd better go."

But the googly eyes jerked open, and Glen tried to smile again. Elaine leaned forward, kissed him on the cheek. Savannah hated herself for the rush of relief she felt when she saw that Elaine hadn't touched any of the discoloured parts.

"We'll come see you again," the girl promised. "You can count on it."

"Night night, Uncle Glen." Victor leaned forward. He did not kiss Glen, but he did manage a half-hug. Glen's eyes flooded, and they all heard the sob. "See you tomorrow." Vic patted the scrawny shoulder, then stepped aside.

Alan didn't hug or kiss anyone, but he did pat Glen's hand. "See you," was all he could manage.

He was very quiet in the car, and he sat pressed close to Elaine. "You okay?" Savannah asked him. He nodded, but he sniffled. "You sad about Uncle Glen?"

"He's nearly dead," Alan blurted.

"Yes," she agreed.

"I don't even know him. Not really."

"None of us did," she shrugged. "He kind of kept to himself. And the rest of us were busy."

"Why wouldn't Auntie Seely go?"

"Seely hates him." Savannah just laid it out on the table. "He wasn't always very nice, and he was especially ugly to Seel. She's the youngest and she's the littlest, so it was easy to push her around, and he did."

"But he's her brother!" Alan was shocked.

"Not everybody gets along good like you kids. Not everyone knows how to love."

Darlene and Lizzie were in bed, thank you dear God for the mercy you show us. Bobby was conked out on the sofa with a blanket over him, and Victoria was just finishing her bottle of supplemental formula.

"She's wonderful," Seely beamed. "She didn't even play strange! She knew I wasn't her momma, but she was willing to give me a chance. Weren't you, angel? Oh, *look*, she sees her mom!"

"Come see me, baboo." Savannah lifted the baby and rocked her. "Would you like to go in and see if Granny Sandra is awake before we leave? Would you like one more snuggle and cuddle? Oh, she likes you!"

"Does she ever." Seely seemed more relaxed than she'd been at supper, maybe because she didn't have to be on edge waiting to see what kind of crap her girls would pull. "They had a great old visit."

Sandra was in a half-sitting position, propped up with pillows, her head turned toward the doorway. She was as thin as Glen, as gaunt and as detached, but at least she wasn't bald, didn't have thrush or those purple stains on her skin. When she had first become ill, and was first diagnosed, her sense of humour had cushioned the ugliness for the rest of them. "What a crock," she had said, "at least the guy they named it after got to play major league baseball. Do I get that chance? No. Just my luck." The sickness had as good as robbed her of her voice and if she kept on choking when she swallowed, they were going to put a tube in her and feed her that way. She already had the catheter and bag.

Savannah had never had any particular horror of dying, but that damn bag had given her one. Whatever else, she did *not* want to have to go around with a bag of her own shit strapped to her side. When we hit that point, guys, we're pulling the plug, okay?

Most of Sandra's communication came from her eyes. The rest of her was quite effectively frozen. She had partial use of one hand and the arm on that side, but it wasn't controllable so it wasn't dependable. As often as not, it jerked at exactly the wrong time, sending a food tray flying or a basin of water tipped onto the floor.

They put Victoria on the bed, then sat around it chatting, drinking tea and eating Seely's soon-to-be-world-famous Nanaimo bars. The kids got a bad case of the yawns and Savannah took the hint. "I think we should be thinking of hitting the road," she warned, "or we're going to be carrying them out one at a time."

"Oh!" Seely gasped.

Savannah turned. Sandra was wide-eyed with surprise and a one-sided small grin tugged at her face. She looked as if an unexpected visitor had come into the room. And then the smile was gone, the eyes were staring, and the phlegmy breathing stopped.

"Oh. Oh no." Seely sat frozen, staring.

"Betcha it was Glen came for her," Jimmy said, his face chalk white, his eyes staring past the dead woman as if he could see someone or something else in the room.

"I never saw anybody die before," Elaine said clearly.

There was no going home then, no leaving Seely alone to handle all the details. Alan lay down on the sofa with Bobby and fell asleep quickly, but Elaine and Vic stayed awake, wide-eyed. First the family doctor arrived, then the police, and finally, the coroner. Questions were asked and had to be answered, a couple of forms needed to be signed, and then the ambulance arrived, without siren or lights, and finally, finally Sandra Grainger was taken from her bed and moved to the funeral home. As the ambulance pulled away, another car parked in front of the house and a woman in jeans and a long-sleeved pink sweatshirt with a unicorn on the front hurried to the house. The unicorn had a rainbow wrapped around its horn.

"Seely, dear." The woman moved to where Seel was sitting on the chair, looking lost. She put her arms around the too-stiff body, and the starch dissolved. Seel sagged, leaned her head against the woman's belly and sighed.

"I don't know what to do," she admitted.

"Take these pills, for a start." The woman handed her two small white tablets and Jimmy hurried to get a glass of water. "And in a little while, you're going to go to bed and just let go. Just let go . . . I'll be here, I'll stay with you. When the girls wake up, I'll tell them and give them breakfast. All you have to do, dear, is let go."

And after a while, Seely did. Maybe it was the pills. Jimmy picked her up as if she didn't weigh any more than Alan, and carried her to her bedroom. He pulled the covers over her, patted her, then stroked her hair.

"Go to sleep, Seely," he said, and she closed her eyes obediently.

They left. There was nothing more they could do for a while. None of them wanted to deal with Darlene or Lizzie, and Seely would be out for hours.

The first light was struggling against the night darkness as they pulled off the highway and started up the driveway.

"What is *that?*" Savannah blurted.

"Oh, that." Jimmy tried to make it sound as if it were no big deal at all. "The three wise men arranged for that."

The house stood just back of where the old house had been. The ground around it was bare and beat-up, all those work boots and machinery wheels and all the to and fro had pounded the dirt down as hard as concrete. Bits of sawn wood lay around, and sawdust, snippets of electrical wire, bits of cut flashing and other mess had been raked into small piles.

"Three floors," he told her, as smug as if he'd done it himself. "No basement, so nothing to flood. Half a dozen bedrooms, a games room, a kids' TV room. Kitchen will knock your eye out. They were going to put in a garage sort of under the living room, there at the bottom right side, and I said no way, she can use mine, you don't want gas and stuff stored right in the damn house! So it's a laundry room, with the freezers and such in it too."

"Not word one," she breathed.

"No, they said they wanted to surprise you. Guess they did."

"I'll be damned."

"She's not finished yet," he went on. "No furniture in it. I've got the living room door just about done, and I finished the fireplace mantel but it isn't installed yet. It will be, though. By the time you've chosen your furniture, there you'll be. All set up as fine as fine."

He thought she'd go bombing over right away to have a look at it, but she was more interested in getting the kids into the house and into some beds. Even Vic was more asleep than awake, and Jimmy had to carry Elaine in. Savannah herself looked just about ready to lie down on the concrete walkway and sleep. She'd been driving for how long, and then all the rest of the excitement, supper, and people dying, and you could just about name it. One thing about it, life is seldom boring. If it isn't one thing, it's another.

Some people in town were surprised, some were shocked and a few were appalled, but the memorial service was a double-barrelled one, with Fred the friendly faggot saying a few words about Glen, and about how much love and support there had been from the family, and Seely saying some words about Sandra and what she'd meant to her, which everyone pretty well already knew. A few guys nobody but Fred knew came up from the city, and they sang out loud and clear when the music started. Other people had nice things to say about Sandra, and then there was more music. Lucy and Debbie helped look after Savannah's kids, and Kitty and Christie took over with Seely's brats. The little guy with them, Noel, seemed overloaded with so many cousins, but he behaved. He blew a few minds by taking one look at Jimboh, grinning from ear to ear, going over to him and holding up his arms. Jim picked him up as if he'd been doing it all his life.

"Hey," Jimmy whispered, "How's my guy?"

"Good," the kid said, and snuggled his face down into the curve of Jimmy's neck and held on. He didn't relax his grip on Jimmy's shirt until he fell asleep, and even then Jim held him.

A great big reception was set up in the basement of the Legion hall, with two big photos side by each. One was of Glen, all done up in a tux, when he was healthy and had all his hair and lived in the city. It was an enlargement of a publicity photo for a TV show, done by a real professional, and he looked gorgeous. Which, of course, he had been at the time. The picture of Sandra showed her in her wheelchair, with Darlene on one knee and Lizzie on the other, they were looking up at her as if she were the one who provided all the lollipops for all the children, and she was laughing. Seely couldn't remember what had made Sandra laugh like that at the time, but it didn't matter. It was an image everyone could take home with them and think of, instead of remembering what a poor little wreck she'd wound up before she died.

Savannah's three wise men showed up, and that gave the shocked 'n' appalled bunch even more to talk about. You had to give it to those guys. When they got out of their work clothes and got themselves all cleaned up, with some scented lotion or oil on their beards, and their turbans wrapped just so, wearing suits that cost a week's wages for most people—well, they were a good-looking bunch. They brought another woman up with them, obviously a real good friend of Savannah's, all those black-haired kids just glommed on to one another something fierce.

There were sandwiches until next September, salads of all kinds, buns and rolls and trays of raw veggies with dip. And desserts. You could be sure if Seely had anything to do with an event, there would be desserts. If anybody went away from the reception hungry it was their own damn fault. When the crowd had dwindled to about half, Savannah moved forward and tapped the microphone for attention. "Ladies and gentlemen . . . please . . ." All heads turned her way. "We've got *tons* of food left. Please, take a paper plate or two when you leave, and fill them up and take them with you.

Please. We're a big family, yes, and we've got a tribe of kids, but there's no way we can handle all of this. Everyone has been so overwhelmingly generous, and kind, and we appreciate it very much. You're good neighbours, all of you."

As if.

But they did what she said, and still there was food left over, lots of it, so they told the cleanup crew they could have it. Then they took the photos and the flowers and some of the untouched desserts, and they left. The desserts they took to the hospital and left for the staff who had looked after Glen. The flowers they took home with them, not because the adults wanted them, but because the kids insisted.

"They were for my Granny," Darlene pouted.

"Mine too." Liz was all set to quarrel, as usual.

"Nobody's arguing with you, so stop it," Savannah said quietly.

Lizzie looked at her with that up-your-arse look on her face, the one that made Jimmy's palm itch. Savannah just smiled, but it was enough. Up-your-arse gave way to puzzlement, then Lizzie just let it drop. Even Seely noticed. She almost said something, but changed her mind and went on about her business, which, at the moment, was putting cans of beer in Jimmy's fridge.

"Can we stay here with you, Jimboh?" she asked, sounding so much like Seely-the-kid that it was a shock to everyone. "I just *can't* stay in that house right now. I don't know if I'll ever feel...I mean...I go inside and all I feel is..." her voice broke and she shook her head. "I just feel *sad*."

"Hey, no prob," Jim said.

But everyone, even Seely, knew it was a prob, a big one. It wasn't room or lack of it, there were bedrooms, bathrooms, all the space they'd need, and the kids were all more than willing to bunk it with sleeping bags in the shed Savannah insisted on calling a cottage. The prob for Jimboh would be those two girls. They'd be a prob for anyone. Except maybe Savannah, who seemed to have the number of at least one of them.

They didn't have to worry about where Kitty, Christie and Noel were going to sleep, they had their trailer. And Lucy and Debbie had taken a room at the motel, because with Lucy's hip the way it was she couldn't just plunk down on a sofa or a foamie on the floor. And anyway, the motel was just a mile or so down the road, so they could have meals together, and with all the kids whipping around, well, you couldn't expect either of them to feel easy. They weren't used to any kids at all, let alone a whole horde of them. The three wise men stayed overnight in the same motel, but as soon as the obligatories were done they went back to the airport. Carol stayed, with her kids and a set of twins that seemed to be someone else's kids, and she and Savannah were head to head in conversation from the time they left the Legion.

"You're kidding," Savannah said, in the tone of voice that meant she believed every word of it.

"I'm not kidding. I know Larry would have gone through with it, but I went for a long walk the night after you left, and I sat on the seawall and asked myself how many years of my life I wanted to spend locking horns with old Bindi. It wasn't a very big number, if the truth be known. So I went back to the house, and talked to Larry, just him an' me, and then after a while he called in the other two. Moe cried, poor little guy. But hell, when push comes to shove, it isn't even fair to the kids. That old woman is *never* going to bend around them. Who needs that? And then, the next day, you phone and give us the news from up here and . . . " She shrugged. "It seemed like it had a life of its own. So the only part of it that sticks in my throat is that the old lady is going to think she won something."

"Her? What did she win? She lost her grandchildren. Not that any of them ever meant anything to her, anyway."

"She's got things arranged, in her own mind at least. Larry says she's already gone through the hoops, didn't tell them or anything, just push here and shove there, and there's gonna be three fully acceptable wives showing up. Sooner or later, anyway."

"Maybe she'll be happy then."

"Maybe. But only if they let her boss them around. That was your big mistake, Vanny, you never let her boss you around."

"Hell, she didn't even show up until Elaine was crawling and Alan was started! You don't just waltz into someone else's place and start giving orders."

"Different folks, different strokes, like they say."

Kitty sometimes felt downright uncomfortable surrounded by so many kids, especially now that one of them was as good as her own. Noel didn't have much experience with other kids. He'd never been to preschool or kindergarten, and it showed. He was uneasy, even awkward with the ones who were more or less his own age, although he got on fine with Vic and Elaine.

"I don't like those two girls," he whispered, pointing at Lizzie and Darlene. "And they don't like me."

"Just stay away from them," Kitty told him. "When I was a kid we called kids like that pizzmires. Jerks. Nerds."

"They said I didn't belong in the fam'bly."

"Don't worry about it. *They* aren't the family."

She waited until everyone was seated at the big picnic table Jimmy had made in the backyard, and then, with Noel seated on her knee, happily chewing on a piece of barbecued salmon, she dropped her little bomb.

"I'd like to hear everyone else's thoughts about this," she said, with no hint of a smile. "Darlene and Lizzie told Noel he wasn't a part of the family. Does anyone else feel that way?"

Darlene and Lizzie had the grace to blush beet red. The silence stretched. Seely didn't leap in and try to smooth the way for them, she ignored them and carried on eating potato salad and pita bread spread thick with humus.

"Well, he's *not!*" Darlene blurted finally. "He's just . . . a kid."

"Anyway," Lizzie lied, "I never said that, Darlene did."

"You liar!" Darlene slapped Lizzie.

Savannah reached across the table and slapped Darlene's cheek.

"Don't you touch me!" Darlene shrieked.

"You want me to get up, go over there and *really* let you have it?" Savannah's voice could have cut glass. "You keep your damn hands to yourself and so will everyone else. If it's okay for you to hit, the rest of us can do it too. And don't *you* start!" She pointed at Lizzie. "As far as I'm concerned, Noel is family. Kitty's my sister and he's her kid, same as Seely's my sister and you're her kids."

"But he isn't! Not really!" Lizzie argued. "You know . . . "

"If you knew half as much as you think you know, you'd know enough not to say stupid things like that."

"Just shut up, Darlene." Seely didn't even look at them. "You too, Lizzie. Shut up until you know what you're talking about."

"But he's *not!*" Darlene yelled.

"Either shut up about it or go home," Jimboh said, sounding bored to tears. "The rest of us are trying to have some lunch here, okay? We're having what they call a family get-together. Noel's part of it. You can be part of it too, or you can leave. And if you leave, well, you won't be part of the family get-together, so maybe you won't be part of the family."

"That's not even fair," Lizzie grumbled.

"Vic, have you got enough salmon or do you think you need some more?" Savannah asked. "There's plenty, you know."

"I think I need some more. And some tater salad too."

"You should try this," Elaine said. "You take a piece of that ham stuff? And you put some tater salad in it, then you roll it over once, and then you put a slice of dill pickle and finish rolling it up, like a burrito. It's really good."

"I like those." Noel pointed. "Those bean-y things."

"Bless you." Seely patted his head. "Those are green bean mustard pickles. I got the recipe from Sandra. You go on and pig out on them, and remind me that you're to take some jars of it with you when you go. Which better not be too soon or I'll be upset."

They waited a few days before they took both little boxes and went up into the bush, to the creek and the swimming hole. Jimmy had put benches there too, really nice ones. Not only did they look beautiful, they were comfortable to sit on. He'd planted some rose bushes at the foot of some alder trees, red climbers and yellow ones, and over where he'd put the footbridge across the creek he'd planted white old-fashioned ramblers. They followed the handrails, which meant you couldn't use them or you'd get scratched and pricked, but the flowers looked great. One entire bank of the swimming hole was planted with flowers—California poppies, ranunculus, anemones, nasturtiums, and other things.

"I should get you to fix up around the big house," Savannah teased him.

"Fix up your own goddamn yard," he grumbled.

He was doing his bad-tempered bear imitation, probably because Savannah had gone ahead and phoned Audrey and asked her if she'd like to come. Jimmy hadn't even known anybody else knew he had a girlfriend, and he was as shy and embarrassed as if he were only twelve and still pretending to hate girls.

Audrey wasn't the least bit shy, though. She and Savannah looked each other up, then looked each other down, and then they were fine with each other. Kitty didn't get the same kind of scrutiny. Audrey just smiled, nodded and shook hands, and that was that.

It was too early for the kids to go swimming, the water in the creek was still icy cold, but they had a good day all the same. Nothing fancy, nothing sentimental or emotional, just soft and easy. They let the wind take Glen's ashes first, then Sandra's. There were sure to be some people in town had things to say about that, and about how Sandra hadn't been buried in the cemetery alongside her husband, but what they said was of no concern to the ones left in charge. Up 'em. All of 'em.

When the ashes were spread and mixed, and Darlene had had herself a little weep, they walked back to Jimmy's place. They sat around for a while, sipping beer and not saying much of anything, and then, great minds think alike, they were up and heading over to the big house to start setting things in place over there.

The timing was great. They'd just finished the vacuuming and there they were, the guys from Gustaffson's bringing in the beds, and Savannah pointing at the rooms. All she needed was a big fake-fur hat and a baton and she could have led the parade.

The stuff she'd chosen was plain as can be. Jimmy said that's how you knew it cost an arm and a leg. But Gustaffson's were happy, and why not? They probably had their year's expenses paid for with the one delivery. Beds and dressers and cedar chests and living room furniture and kitchen stuff, two TVs, two VCRs and a sound system—the whole nine yards. Plates and mugs and bowls and two fridges, one in the kitchen and another in what was supposed to be a garage until Jimboh put the kibosh on it. Two washers, two dryers, two freezers. It would take all three of the wise men to pay the tab.

The thing of it was, though, Carol wasn't Savannah, and Kitty worried that there'd be hair flying all too soon. The way Carol looked at Jimboh, for example. That wouldn't be good for them, not any of them. Sure, Jimmy was famous and his work was incredible, and yeah, he was good-looking, but he wasn't someone you played with, he wasn't someone who could just flirt a bit, hump a bit and move on to someone else. Jimmy was every bit as crazy as the rest of them.

"All artists are eccentric," Carol said, fussing with her damn nails. They stuck out from the ends of her fingers like little daggers, and you never knew what colour she'd have them painted. So far, brief as their time with her had been, they'd seen everything from apple green to a shade of deep purple that was almost black. She'd just finished taking all the colour off of them and she was starting over from scratch, putting on some watery stuff. "They use this on the hooves of French racehorses," she bragged.

"Really?" said Kitty. "Haven't heard of the French horses winning any big races lately, though, have you? I mean Dances Lightly was American and Go For It was Canadian—from Ontario, I think."

"It makes their hooves last longer. Makes them stronger."

"Yeah. You going in any races any time soon? Do you use it on your toenails too?"

"Savannah told me you were funny. She said you were an awful tease."

When the French racehorse stuff was dry, she put on some clear liquid. "This is a hardener and strengthener," she pronounced.

"You shouldn't flirt with Jimmy the way you're doing."

"Jimmy's a big boy. If he don't like it, he'll say so."

"He won't. He'll just disappear into his glory hole and stay there."

"He'll come out when he's hungry."

"You're not listening to me. Jimmy's not like other guys."

"If he was, I'd keep twenty-five feet between me'n'him."

"He's got strange ways."

"We all do, Kitty. For God's sake look at *you* and how *you* live. Bad enough you sat on top of wild bulls and wild horses and got yourself bounced silly. At least when you were doing that you only had to stay alive for what, eight seconds or something, and then you could run away. Now? Oh, you'll be out there all night, near as I can tell. You trying to get yourself killed or something? I mean you *could* take a sleeping bag onto the tracks and just lie there waiting for the train, you know."

"You seen his arms?"

"So he carves himself, not just pieces of wood." She examined the nails on her left hand, nodded in satisfaction and started brushing something on the nails of her right hand.

"There's a million other men out there. Try one of them. Try all of them if you've a mind to. But not Jimmy."

"I tried 'em all, already." The challenge was there in the stiff smile on her face. "I started when I was seven. Well, I didn't start it, it sort of got started for me. Anyway by the time I was twelve or thirteen the whole thing was old hat. My uncle, my brother, next-door neighbour, dirty old man down the street, guy in the candy store—funny how they can pick the one kid in the crowd who's been as good as trained for it. When my poppa found out he beat the crap out of me. When I was fourteen I ran away because I was pregnant and afraid he'd kill me. Met a guy in the bus depot, name of Ed. He said he was going to help me, and he did, I guess. Found someone to take care of the problem, that's what he called it. Then he started bringing guys to the apartment. Jesus Jesus Jesus, a chartered accountant couldn't have kept track of them all."

"When did you meet the three wise men?"

"I was, let me see, nineteen, I think. Yeah, nineteen. Savannah was as big as a house, with Alan? Yeah, Alan. And Larry, he showed up with Ed.

Here's a special rater for you, says Ed. Entire weekend. It's the next best thing to a vacation when that happens. I mean, they think they're so horny they're just going to go one after the other non-stop the whole time, but it never happens. We actually had fun. Well, I did! He was back the next weekend. Then the one after that the three of 'em showed up. That set me back a bit. But Ed had his money, he was happy, so I wasn't going to get whipped or choked. Next thing I know they've made me an offer. Me, not Ed."

Kitty shook her head. "And you think *my* life is crazy?"

"Ed raised hell, but Larry, he's the oldest one, he's not stupid. He had it all arranged. I went into drug rehab so Ed couldn't use that to keep me tied to him."

"You were a druggie?"

"Who do you know who isn't or used to be?" Carol looked carefully through her collection of little bottles, taking her time about choosing the colour she was going to use. Finally she decided on a quiet coral pink and began to apply it.

"So?"

"Huh? Oh, the drug rehab thing. I did it six weeks, it wasn't as bad as I thought. Then they said I could leave the in-patient part of the treatment. And there was Larry, big grin on his face, opening the door of the car for me. So I moved in with them." She looked at Kitty and spoke as openly as if she were talking about her perfect attendance record at Sunday school. "I hadn't expected kids, and there they were, two of 'em whipping around. Well, Vic was whipping around, Elaine was crawling and tottering. Savannah was just about ready to pop, but she had supper ready and everything. My own room. Twice a week to the rehab counselling. Every day I went to the alternate school to fill in some of the education I'd missed. It was like a fairy story. And only three guys to take care of, instead of the whole frigging city. So you see, when you tell me to stay away from Jimmy because he's weird—well, my whole life's been weird."

"You aren't listening."

"*You* aren't listening. I don't want to hump your brother. I don't give a rat's ass if I never hump anyone again as long as I live. If I see eighty-six without having another guy squirming around inside me, I've still had way more than my share! I flirt with Jimmy because no way anything will happen. I know it, he knows it—hell, even Audrey knows it. I never got to flirt with anyone."

It sounded good, but Kitty was unconvinced. She went to Jimmy and talked to him about it while he sat with his latest bowl in his hands, sanding it with a piece of dogfish skin. Christie had given him the idea, something she'd said about the way the Lummi people used to use it. He didn't say a word, just stroke stroke stroke on the bowl, nodding his head rhythmically, sometimes chewing his bottom lip or bending forward and peering at his work. From time to time he picked up his magnifying glass and examined the curve of a carving, looking for flaws, looking for irregularities, finding none.

"I'm not going to fuck her," he said suddenly.

"Jimmy, it isn't just the—"

"No, I won't fall in love or anything stupid like that. Don't worry, Kit-Cat, okay?"

"I *do* worry. You're so fuckin' weird, Jimboh, and you've got no idea what the real world is like."

"And you do?" He laughed softly, blew on the bowl, put down the stinking fish skin and reached for a fine brush. "Kitty, really. You're more at home with bucking horses than you are with people. You've had more girlfriends than I've had! And some of 'em, I have to tell you, left a lot to be desired. This one, well, at least she's fun. When she isn't all bent out of shape, that is."

"She's what they call sensitive."

"Right. Me too, eh?" He put the bowl on his worktable and leaned back, staring at it.

"You get flirting with Carol and Savannah is apt to rip her head off and feed it to the pigs."

"Yeah, but not on Sunday."

"What does that mean?"

"Not a damn thing. What do you think?" He gestured at the bowl.

"What is it?"

"It's a fucking *bowl*, Kitty, okay?"

"I can see it's a bowl, Jimboh. A blind man could see it's a bowl. I mean that critter on it, looks like it's all tail."

"How can you be so friggin' ignorant?" But his tone was gentle and his smile was the one he wore when the two of them were sharing something only they would understand. "Remember how the old biddy used to tell us that when people called us sons of bitches they were actually giving us a compliment? Remember how she said the old goddess had these dogs, and if you were a son of a bitch you were from a family that followed the old religion? Well, that's those dogs."

"What's the snake?"

"That's dogs' tails. There's four dogs, nose to nose, arse to arse, see? And their tails...see...and in between the dogs, the tails swirl and twist and become birds, see...then become tails again, and—"

"I'll be...Show me up close, Jimboh. I missed three-quarters of it just because I didn't know what I was looking at. What's this, a half-eaten apple, then?"

"Battle-axe, you gorp. Another one over here, see? The whole thing balances. On more than one level too. See, this big one and those others, then these and...can you see it, Kitty?"

"I think so. How long you been working on this?"

"All m'life."

"Hey, this is me, eh, not one of those ditzy reporters. You got coffee?"

"No. Got beer, though. Maybe I'll have one too."

"So is it one or is it two? I'll have one-two? Why not three-four?"

"How long you been seeing them?"

She felt cold. "Few months." Suddenly there was a big knot where her stomach ought to be. "About the time I got all pranged up. You?"

"Long time. Jeez, Mike was living with us...no, I tell a lie, it was Fred living with us...not Glen's Fred, that other shithead."

"You never said a word."

"Crazy Jimmy will you get up," he chanted, "will you get up, you get up, Crazy Jimmy will you get up, it's time to go to school."

"Ah, Jimmy," she sighed.

"It don't matter. I didn't so much *see* them. Yet. It was just that I'd get these, like, pictures in my head. Probably why I couldn't draw or paint the way Seel could. I'd pick up a pencil and all's I'd see on the paper was this...well, you saw some of what I did. Ugly shit. But they didn't start showing up, in the room or whatever, until—oh, after Glen got himself a dose at the midway."

"Oh Jesus yes, and we wound up with all those damn stuffed bears."

"You got 'er." He drained his beer and tossed the can into the trash box across the room.

"I'm going to have another," he announced. "You?"

"Don't mind if I do." She finished hers and tossed it to the box, and missed. "To the showers, I guess, eh? No basket for me."

"Now *there's* an idea." He turned slowly, smiling widely. "I could carve a bowl that looked like a basket. That'd be one layer. And there'd be a design on the basket, that'd be two layers. And hidden in that design would be another...and..." He tossed the beer to her and she caught it easily. "Thanks, Kitty. I'll maybe give it a try."

"Know what I'd like you to try?" She pulled her cigarettes out of her pocket, took one and tossed the pack to Jimboh, who took one and tossed the pack back to her. "I'd like you to try making some bracelets, or necklaces or such."

"Me? Get real," he scoffed.

"I am. I'm as real as real gets. You're going stale, Jimmy. You've turned an entire woodlot into bowls and what-all, and you're scrabbling for ideas."

"I'd have to start all over again, back at square one. I don't know zip about...well, for example, I wouldn't even begin to know how to—" His voice trailed off and that inward look came over his face. "And what you'd be working on would be small, you'd have to re-examine everything you thought you knew about perspective and about negative space," and again the words went to whispers, the whisper buried itself in his throat. "There's this course at the college in the wintertime, though, and I could—" He sipped his beer, and laughed suddenly. "I know what it is, Kitty, you bitch. You're going to quit riding, and that means you won't win any more belt buckles, so you figure you can get *me* busy making them for you. As if anybody needed more than one!"

"All's I'm trying to do is find ways to keep you too busy to get yourself tangled up with Carol."

"If you was as good at running your own life as you think you are at running everyone else's, you'd be a whole lot more settled down than you are. What you going to do with the kid?"

"Noel? What's to 'do' with him? There's lots of kids move with the rodeo. You chip in to pay the tutor, kid gets correspondence. No sweat."

"He can stay here with me, you know."

"Don't be a fool. You'd crawl into this pongy old mess of a place and forget all about him. He'd wind up having to go over to Savannah's place for something to eat."

"At least she's a good cook. God, the times we wound up at Gran's, eh?"

"So you're telling me the truth about Carol?"

"From my lips to God's ears."

"Where'd you hear that? You don't even believe in God."

"Audrey said it."

"She seems like good people."

"She's a whore."

"Yeah? Well, I don't suppose they pay her enough to live on at that store."

Seely decided she didn't want to move back into the house in town. Darlene whined and grizzled and bitched, Lizzie did all that and more, and Seely just sat on the sofa, arms crossed, face turned away from the two of them.

"Tell me," Lucy invited.

"It was where I went to be safe," Seely whispered. "And now when I go in, I don't feel safe, I just feel sad. And if I go back there, those two brats will just go on being brats, because that's how they've always been in that place, and I'll just go on letting them be that way because that's what I always did."

"So what do you want to do? You can't stay in the house with Jimboh, it isn't fair to him. He'd never say a word, never drop a hint, he loves you so much he'd ruin himself trying to make it work. But it can't work. It isn't anybody's fault, it's just how it is. What solution can you see?"

"I want to sell the house and buy a trailer. Not a travel one like Kitty has. One of those other kind, the modular home kind, you know the ones?"

"Where would you put it?"

"Here, of course."

"Stay away from the swimming hole, or those two girls will get the idea it's in their backyard and they'll start bossing it."

"Send 'em to Little Flower Academy," Seely threatened. "Or Queen Margaret's School for Young Ladies. That'd show them. Other side of Savannah's place."

"You sure you'd rather a trailer than a house?"

"I could get two trailers. One of 'em for the bakery. It wouldn't have to be big, you know. I could have three or four ovens...I could...and I could!"

"You could so. It's not that far from town. Hardly at all, now."

"Used to seem like the far side of the moon. Remember?"

"Oh, I remember. I remember I hated it. I had to ride my bike nearly four miles just to get to the school bus stop."

"And a big freezer."

Lucy and Debbie checked out of the motel and headed back to their own place. Jimboh didn't want them to leave, but no sooner had their pickup turned onto the highway than he was over his pout. He'd been in his glory hole for two days and nights, and his eyes looked bleary, as if he had a hangover, or the flu.

"You feeling okay?" Seely asked, and he nodded, didn't say a word, just nodded. Well, he'd know how he felt. Maybe he'd been working non-stop, he did that sometimes. "I could make you a chocolate cake," she offered. He smiled, nodded, gave her a peck on the cheek. "With that boiled icing, like Gran made?"

"Bit of peppermint in it?" he hinted.

"Macaroni and cheese for supper?"

"You spoil me, Seel."

"I want to move a trailer onto the place," she blurted. "That okay with you?"

"It's as much your place as mine. Gran left it to all of us."

"You're the only one been paying taxes and such."

"I'm off to stretch my legs a bit. Okay?"

She nodded and he left the kitchen, his steps slow. Anyone who didn't know him would think this was the first time he'd been in the place, the way he looked around to be sure where the door was, and once he was through it, the way he stood on the top step, staring out like he'd never seen his own backyard before.

"You okay?" she called. He didn't answer, just sort of flopped one hand in what might have been a wave. Or not.

It was nice to have a goal, even if it was only supper. Seely made the cake first, and made it as rich and chocolatey as she could. Jimmy had a real yen for chocolate cake. Sometimes it seemed as if he could live on that alone for days on end. He'd even been known to come out of his glory hole in the middle of the night and go down to the two-four to get himself one of those Sara Lee ones. He'd take it and a spray bomb of make-believe whipped cream to the lookout and sit there in his car, stuffing his face. Lots of times he finished the whole thing, then locked his car doors and fell asleep, right there, as if he didn't have a bed to go home to. The cops would check on him, but not to hassle him—they'd given that up years ago. For one thing, he hadn't done anything outrageous, and for another, as Jimmy said himself, all's you need to do is get your name in the paper and you go from arsehole to artist overnight.

She took her time with the macaroni and cheese, getting it just right, the way he liked it. The girls would probably complain about it. When Sandra was alive, when they were living in the house in town, Seely made sure there was something else for supper, something the girls really liked, just to keep the grizzling and whining from getting out of hand. But she didn't much feel like doing that. If they didn't want what was put in front of them, they could make themselves a peanut butter sandwich. Jimboh loved macaroni and cheese and so did Seely. If she hated the stuff, both girls would decide that they absolutely had to have it three nights a week. Sometimes it seemed as if everything was easier before Savannah taught her how to cook. When she was getting take-out most nights, pizza or Kentucky fried or Chinese, it was easy to order something they would all eat.

Maybe it was hormones. Maybe. Or maybe they were as sad and feeling as beat-up as she was. Sandra hadn't really been like a granny at all, more like a second mother, and maybe they had grown so used to seeing her all buggered up and stuck in bed that they'd thought she'd be there forever, not up and die like that. Glen dying, well, that wouldn't bother them one way or the other. All they knew was the name, they'd never had to be anywhere near him. Still, to have both of them going that same night, it was odd. Kids don't like things to be odd, all they want is for things to be usual. So much about them is changing all the time, all that growing and new teachers every year and some kids leaving school, new kids starting. Maybe that's why they want some stuff to never, ever change. Seely couldn't remember feeling that way. She'd always prayed things *would* change. Be careful what you pray for, old girl, things changed all right, bang bang bang, nothing will ever be the same again.

And here we are, no bangs this time, but nothing will ever be the same. And if it can't be the same, you might as well change the whole thing. What was it Gran had said, it doesn't hurt the puppy any more to cut its tail right off than to snip off a little bit every night until it's short enough to suit you.

Jimmy checked on the rats, and a good job he did, too. In all the fuss and go-round of the past week and a half, he'd more or less neglected them. He hadn't so much forgotten about them as somehow not managed to get around to them. "Christamighty," he muttered, "look at the goddamn mess of you's."

But it was easy enough to fix. He checked the food dishes in the clean set-up, made sure all the waterers were full, put fresh shavings in the bottom, then slid open the divider-door. The rats in the dirty set-up were hungry. They could see the rabbit feed and the chopped apple he'd put in, and they could smell it. They hurried over to eat. Even the moms rushed to the other set-up, leaving their babies in the stinking nests. Jimmy closed the divider-door, then scooped up the wigglers, moved them to the clean set-up one at a time. The moms got upset, ran around squeaking and chittering until they figured out whose was which, but they were still hungry and thirsty and they accepted the changes quickly. With the small shovel, Jimmy got all the stinking shavings out of the dirty set-up and dumped them in a cardboard box. He cleaned out the pellets of shit, then got a bucket of warm water and lots of disinfectant and the wire brush, and scrubbed the dirty cage. Rat piss. Only thing that stinks worse is cat poop.

He took the cardboard box of shavings and crap with him, climbed halfway up the hill to the burn barrel and dumped it in. He lit a cigarette, used the paper match to set fire to one corner of the flap of the box, put the grate over the top of the barrel and stood watching as the flames consumed the whole thing, stinking shavings and all. When there was only a bit left smouldering, he dropped in the cigarette butt and sauntered off to the benches set up around the swimming hole.

He got out the plastic jar from under the bench, unscrewed the cap and tossed some fish pellets into the pool. Flash flash splash, and the pellets were gone. He threw more, and it happened again. He'd overlooked the fish too. Well, he'd give them a good feed to make up for it. They couldn't look after themselves like wild fish, there were too many of them and they were too big.

He'd like to put some koi in but that would just kick off a pond war. The koi would eat the trout eggs and baby trout, and the trout would eat the koi eggs and baby koi, and sooner or later one of 'em would wipe out the other. And what would a person do if he caught a koi? They were supposed to be just a fancy carp, and lots of people ate carp, but would you really want to sit down to supper and scoff back a glorified goldfish? Still, the ones at the nursery were incredible, the guy had great big red things had to be two feet long, weighing in at five, ten pounds each. Big whiskers on 'em, like catfish. Was that what a carp was, just some kind of catfish?

Maybe get another pool. This one was natural, but the one at the nursery sure wasn't. It had a plastic liner and everything. Shouldn't be impossible, a person ought to be able to get it together over a weekend. That'd be nice. Maybe put it closer to the house, though, figure out some way to make a cover for it, have to have something to keep the blue herons from feasting on the koi. A trout, now, it can hide itself pretty well, but not much chance of hiding when you're bright red or orange with black blotches, especially not if you're two feet long. You could add netting. Herons wouldn't be the only ones you'd have to deal with, there'd be hawks and kingfishers and ravens and probably even eagles lurking around, waiting for the chance to snatch an exotic meal.

He threw in another handful of fish pellets and put the plastic jar back under the bench. Be a damn shame if all those kids started feeding the fish too. They'd be so fat and sassy and overfed they'd hardly bother to come up for anything.

Can you believe it? A month ago there wasn't a one on the place and now, poof, there they were, five here, four there, two others and then Noel, but he'd be heading off with Kitty and Christie in a day or two. Still, a dozen of them. Even if Seely did get herself set up in a trailer, the place was going to be totally different. They'd be laughing and yelling and playing soccer around the house and this one or that one would always be dropping over in the evening.

He could always look around for another hunk of land and get a house built on it. Might be nice to have a house designed and built just for him. He might even have a real glory hole, not just a room in the basement. Maybe a big room, with lots of windows, lots of light, and not from bulbs stuck in extension cords like he had now. But, dear God, what a lot of to-do, lara-diddle and downright dog's-body labour! All that packing and unpacking. Just the idea of it made him feel tired. And what if he didn't feel easy when he got there? There were lots of places where he didn't feel the least bit relaxed, where he couldn't carve himself a set of chopsticks. What if the fright faces moved with him? Or worse, what if they didn't? And how would he visit with Gran, or with Glen, now, if he ended up seeing him more now than he had in life?

Well, Victor was okay, and Elaine was great. Alan wasn't so bad, and Bobby was too young to have a real personality, so who could say what he'd be like? Same with Jason. Caroline was a bit of a whiner, but the twins were all right. Yeah, the bunch of them were okay kids, really. It was just there was so many of them.

Then again, it was like anything else. You get your head around it and if you can't do that, find something you can get it around.

Darlene didn't say a word about there being no second choice for supper. Lizzie looked around, sniffed, got no whiff of anything like roast pork or Swedish meatballs or veal cutlets and asked, "Is this all?"

"Lots of salad," Seely smiled. "I made two kinds, a Caesar and a tossed."

"But just macaroni and cheese?"

"Yum," Jimmy grinned, oblivious to the undercurrent. "Look, she put broccoli and cauliflower in, both. God, nobody makes it as good as you do."

"Well, Savannah—"

"No, Savannah makes a good macaroni and cheese, but yours is way lots better. Hard-boiled egg in it, and...remember when you put in all those asparagus pieces?"

Lizzie wasn't about to let go of it. "We haven't had steak in ages."

"Tell you what." Jimmy passed her the Caesar salad. "We can go over to Willoughby's place and I'll get us an order of beef, how's that? 'Course, there's only so many steaks to the average steer, and it wouldn't take long for this crowd to munch their way through them, but we could have a barbecue. Bet I can pack away more steak than you can."

"Bet not." She put salad on her plate, next to her untouched macaroni and cheese.

"Bet so."

"No way!"

"Way!"

"Will they eat beef? Those Paki kids, I mean?" Darlene asked innocently.

Jimmy's smile faded. "They're not Pakis, they're your cousins."

"Well, yeah, but...you know, they've got this thing where cows are holy, don't they?"

"Not this bunch. That's some others from over there. Sure is a good supper, Seely."

For a minute she was afraid that the glow had gone off, chased away by the Paki remark, but the macaroni and cheese won out. Jimmy's good mood returned and Lizzie didn't even seem to notice she was eating the casserole as well as the salads, both kinds.

"I like the chocolate icing better," Darlene announced, looking over at the chocolate cake.

"You don't have to eat this," Jimmy said, his mouth stuffed. "I'll eat your share. You can have bread'n'jam."

"Fall on your jaw, Uncle Jim," Darlene said clearly. "The day hasn't come when I'm giving you a crumb of chocolate cake. You might not even live long enough to see that day."

"Swine." He reached for the casserole dish and refilled his plate. "Sow."

"Hog," she countered. "Boar."

Noel didn't mind the other kids, it was nice to have someone to play with. Bobby and he spent hours with trucks and cars and a heap of sand left over from when they poured the concrete for the house. He wished they were his toys, but the kids didn't mind sharing stuff and Auntie Savannah said Noel could consider them his. "Don't be shy," she told him. "All that gets you is feeling left out and lonely."

Sometimes it wasn't easy to figure out what people were saying. He had to check with Christie to find out what "consider" meant. And sometimes they said things that sounded as if the balloon was just about ready to go up, and then instead they all laughed. Boy, if his mom had ever said things like Auntie Seely said, things like Hi, idiot, figured out who you are yet? that would have been plain awful. But Kitty just laughed and said, Listen to you, twerp, as if you've got any idea.

None of the other kids could see Thingy. It was easy to find out who could and who couldn't see him, you just watched their eyes. When Thingy showed up, Kitty's eyes followed him, but not all the time. Jimmy too, quite often. Sometimes even Christie would suddenly look around, searching, but she didn't always see him, not even when he was right beside her. She must feel him, or something. Jimmy was real easy about it, but Kitty worried. Noel didn't worry. Thingy was his friend. Maybe the very best friend he'd ever had. Even better than Kitty, but not in the same way. Kitty was great.

There was an itty-bitty bathtub in the trailer house. Kitty and Christie both said the only way they could sit in it was to bend their knees, but there was room in it for Noel to lie back if he wanted. Kitty got him some bubble bath stuff that came in a doll-thing. Not really a doll, because doll's heads don't screw off like a bottle, but it was like a doll, like Minnie Mouse. The bubble bath smelled like bubble gum. There was kids' shampoo too—that was in Mickey. And some stuff that made your hair smooth, in Goofy. Kitty would wash his hair and even if the suds got near his eyes it didn't burn or hurt or make him cry.

"Now I'm gonna drown you," she'd say, and he'd take a deep breath, squinch his eyes shut, and the warm water would pour over his head, washing away the bubbles. "You still alive?"

"Yep."

"Okay, here we go, gonna get you in condition," and she'd unscrew Goofy's head and put this thick stuff, smelled like cinnamon toast, and she'd rumple it in and make his hair stick up all over the place in spikes or waves. "See the monkey?" She'd hold up a mirror with a handle so he could see himself with his hair all up in a mohawk, or a great big curl she said was like a kewpie doll. Then she'd refill the plastic bucket, a blue one, the kind ice cream comes in, and she'd wait while he made sure his hands were rinsed, and then she'd say, Okay, gonna drown you again.

When his hair was rinsed she wiped her hand over his head, squeezing out as much water as she could, then she'd wipe his face. "Hang on" meant the towel was coming, and he kept his eyes shut while she rubbed his head good. "Okay," and he bent forward, pulled out the plug, put it in the place where the soap goes and stood up. The towel went around him, so fast nobody would have seen his bum even if they'd been looking. "Up and out," and he was over the side of the tub, standing on a second towel, being rubbed. When he said he was dry, she stopped and turned her head away, holding his pyjama bottoms so all he had to do was step into them. "You decent?" she'd ask. Sometimes he had to say no, because sometimes he wasn't as dry as he'd thought and the cloth stuck to his backside. When he said he was ready, she'd start hanging up towels to dry, finding the soap, putting it where it belonged, lining up Mickey and Minnie and Goofy in their place. Then he'd put on his pyjama top. The one that pulled over his head like a tee shirt was easy, but the one with buttons down the front, well, that took time and sometimes he needed help.

Christie got him the slippers. They looked exactly like teddy bears. Even had button eyes on the front. You slipped your foot in the back of the bear and tucked your toes into its head.

And then Christie would read to him. Nobody had ever done that, not every night, not you-can-count-on-it. Once in a while his mom had read to him, but not like this. Christie sat on the couch and he sat next to her so he could see the pictures, and they talked about it while they were reading. One of the books had lift-ups. It was about a farm. There'd be a picture of a chicken house, and the writing would say, Do you know who lives in here? And when you raised the lift-up door, there were the chickens. When you closed it, they were gone. Same as with a real door. In another picture a gate opened and under it was a goat. At first they just called it "the goat," but then Christie said it was a stinky billy goat, so they started calling him that, Stinky Billy. And one of the chickens got named Henrietta the Hen, and the rooster was Henry.

When the story was finished he went to bed, climbed in and pulled his covers under his chin, and then Christie would come in to give him a hug and say Good dreams. She always gave his dream catcher a little push so it swayed, catching all the bad feelings and thoughts in the room. After she left, Kitty would come in. She'd sit on his bed and they'd hold hands for a while. "Had a good time with you today," she might say, or "Sure did have fun with you." Then she'd bend over and kiss him, one on the forehead, one on the nose, one on the mouth and one on his chin. Or maybe she'd start with his chin and work up, but always four kisses. "If you get cold or anything," she'd say, "you crawl in with us." Sometimes he had to do that. Most nights, if he woke up to go pee or something, he'd see Thingy, and he could crawl back into bed and go to sleep and feel safe. But sometimes Thingy wasn't there. Just the black. Even with the moonlight at the window, even with the little Donald Duck night light in the hall, the black would be there, and without Thingy he had to go crawl in between Kit and Christie. Even knowing Dog was at the foot of his bed, he had to go find that warm place Kitty said was like a den, with her warm on his one side and Christie warm on his other side, and he could just move his foot and feel this one or move his hand and feel the other one and then he was fine. Sometimes he'd wake up in the morning all alone in their bed, and they'd already be up, drinking coffee or doing something in the house. Other times he'd wake up alone and Kitty would be asleep on the sofa and Christie would be in his bed, and later on they'd tease him about how he kicked and tossed and knocked them onto the floor.

Dog was nice. The other kids thought so too. Sometimes Noel almost got angry watching them all playing with her. She'd be wagging her tail and her mouth would be open, and you could see her big pink tongue, like she was laughing, and they'd be kicking the soccer ball with her chasing it, or they'd be throwing a stick or something, and Noel wanted to grab her collar and yell, She's *my* dog, leave her alone! But she wasn't his dog, she was Kitty's. And anyway, they shared their stuff with him so Christie said he had to share Dog. "Anyway," she whispered in his ear, "not a single one of them gets to go to sleep with Dog in their room, and you do, every night. You don't have to share *that*. That's just for you."

They were playing with Dog now, the whole bunch of them. The whole clanjamfrie, Kitty called it. Hard to get used to when you'd never had much of anyone around. Sometimes he got tired just trying to keep track of who was where and who was somewhere else. Kitty was with Christie, up where the roses were, saying goodbye to the dead brother, and Savannah and Carol were in their house, and Seely had gone into town to see a man about a horse. Why she'd want to do that when she had said she didn't even like horses, but that's what she had said. Darlene and Lizzie had gone with her, and just as well, they didn't get along all that well with Elaine. Every time Elaine said, Oh, will you just grow up and act your age, they got mad at her. But they couldn't do anything about it, because Victor would just wade in. One day Noel would be big like Vic, and he'd make sure he didn't take any sass. Victor told everyone, Don't give me any of your sass. Noel tried it, but he couldn't make it sound the same, he sounded like a little boy. When Vic said it, he made it sound like he meant it.

There wasn't anybody in the kitchen. Well, of course not, Seely was in town and Jimmy wouldn't be in the kitchen. Noel checked the bedrooms. Nobody. He checked both bathrooms. Nobody. Then he saw Thingy beckoning. He went through the door and picked his way down the steps, careful careful careful, because if you fall you get hurt.

A basement. He'd lived in a basement with mom. Not a basement like this one, though. Look at all the stuff! Bottles and bottles and bottles of pears and peaches and cherries and what looked like sliced beets and pickles, and all kinds of stuff. A big box with some Christmas tree shiny stuff showing at one corner. And all kinds of other things too. A lamp, but not the kind you'd get in a store. It was made from a branch or something. There was writing on it, at the bottom, but Noel couldn't read. A box of books, no pictures in any of them. A great big can of some kind. What would come in a can like this? It was a little bit like the can in the kitchen where Seely kept her flour.

Noel managed to get off the lid, and then he stared in amazement. He had never, *never*, not in his whole life, seen so many crayons in one place at one time. Wax crayons, pencil crayons, full ones, half ones, little bits of ones. And water paints, and a buncha brushes held together with an elastic band, and some tube things that had ballpoint pen nibs on them, and Thingy was having a fine time sorting through and grinning and finally coming up with just about the best knife a guy could have.

"Snooping, huh?" Jimmy said.

Noel jumped, and he peed. "I'm sorry!" he blurted. "Please! Don't! I didn't mean it! I'm sorry!"

"Whoa, guy," and Jimmy picked him up, all pee wet and everything. "Hey, I didn't mean to scare you. Wow, I'm sorry. Here, hang on. Just hang on. You'll be fine. Goddamn Bones should have let you know! He's falling down on the job. We'll get us a new one if he doesn't smarten up."

"I'm sorry," Noel sobbed. "I didn't mean nothin'."

"Hey, no harm done. It's my fault. You can poke around down here all you want. It's your basement too, now." He sat down on the floor cross-legged, like an Indian. "You found the crayons and stuff, eh? Gran kept them here for us, and we had to be sure to pick them up and put them away before we left for the other place. She'd go to the Salvation Army and the Hospital Auxiliary and all the flea markets and rummage sales and stuff and pick up all the crayons and pencils and whatever, ten cents here, five cents there, and by the time she'd spent two bucks she'd have forty dollars worth of stuff for us."

"The knife..." Noel's hand reached for it.

"Ah, the knife. Well..." Jimmy picked it up and turned it over and over and over in his fingers. "Tell you what." He rummaged in his pocket. "This little knife is real special, and it's as sharp as a razor. It isn't a knife for a kid. Well, not a small kid like you." And he frowned at Thingy. "Bones should know better. You let me have the wee knife, and I'll let you have this one." He put the knife in Noel's hand, folded his fingers over it. "That's a Swiss army knife. There's more stuff hidden inside it than you can think up. By the time you get it all folded out you won't believe it all fit in the handle to begin with. You can have it, and when you're older we'll switch again and you can have the wee one."

"How old?"

"Let's just say when you're as big and as old as Victor is."

Jimmy took him upstairs and ran water in the tub, and while Noel had a quick bath, Jimmy went over to the trailer and got him some clean clothes. He had the pee-wet stuff in the washer before Noel was out of the tub and dressed again. Jimmy put his own jeans in the washer too, and pulled on clean ones.

"And we aren't telling anyone," he told Noel. "This is our business."

"Will they be mad at me?"

"Kitty and Christie? Mad? Why, because I scared the piss out of you?"

"Not supposed to pee yourself."

"Not supposed to scare a guy, either. Me and old Bones blew it. Come on, you'n'me's going back down to the glory hole."

Jimmy took him by the hand and led him right into that room nobody was supposed to go anywhere near. Noel stared. Jimmy picked him up and plunked him on a tall stool, and that put Noel at just the right height to hold the Swiss army knife the way Jimmy showed him, and to take the piece of wood Jimmy handed him.

"See?" Jimmy showed him how to scratch a design on the wood. "See, hold it like that. Then if it slips, you won't rip open your hand. Here, put this over you." He put a leather apron over Noel's lap. "Don't need you bleeding."

Thingy sat on the table and watched. Noel knew that what he was doing was nothing, really. Even so, it was real hard work. Twice he might have cut himself, but Thingy put his hand in the way and stopped the blade. Jimmy watched, and smoked his cigarette.

"You're lucky," he said quietly. "Old Bones never did that for me, put his hand between me and the blade."

"His name is Thingy," Noel corrected him.

Jimmy laughed softly, stubbed out his cigarette and made another one. He had a red box full of tubes with filters, and a pile of tobacco sticks, and he pushed the one into the other, making a smoke. "First time I ever saw you," he said, "I was sitting here, where I'm sitting right now. Didn't know who you were, didn't know what was going on, didn't know anything, just saw you. I think you were maybe sitting on a bed, but I'm not sure. You didn't say anything. You didn't really do anything, either. Just sat there. I don't know if you saw me or not."

Noel didn't know what Jimmy was talking about. Adults were like that, sometimes. And you didn't know whether to answer or not. You could always answer Mom, but you didn't dare answer *him*. But Jimmy wasn't like him. Not the least little bit like him. Still, Noel didn't answer. He could see a design, finally. Thingy helped, a lot. Thingy sort of scratched his bony finger on the wood and left a little mark, then all Noel had to do was use the knife until the mark was cut and scratched in deeper. It was fun.

"I'm glad I got to actually meet you." Jimmy lit his new smoke, coughed and hit himself on the chest. "Fuck," he grumbled, "listen to me. The things I do for you," and he looked at Thingy and shook his head. Thingy was sucking sucking sucking, his mouth in the shape of an "O," pulling the smoke in like a vacuum cleaner.

After a while Jimmy stubbed out his smoke and reached for a piece of wood. Noel watched Jimmy's hands and tried to do what he saw Jimmy doing, but before long his fingers hurt, and his wrists hurt, and he felt sleepy. He put his head on the tabletop, and then Jimmy picked him up and carried him back up the stairs, put him on one of the beds. Noel heard Kitty's voice, but he couldn't make out what she was saying. Then he heard Christie, and he thought she was laughing. Thingy was on the bed with him, lying on his back, his bone legs bent at the knees and sticking up like triangles. Kitty had told him about triangles, and about squares and circles and rectangles. Showed him the different shapes, showed how they could fit together to make other shapes.

"Hey, guy." Kitty sat on the bed ruffling her fingers in Noel's hair. "You have yourself a nap here, and I'll keep checking on you. I promise we won't drive off and leave you behind, we aren't going until tomorrow anyway. You just snooze away, attaboy."

He didn't want to waste time napping, but he was so sleepy. He rolled on his side, facing Thingy, who reached over and patted Noel's hand. Then it was nice just to drift, nice to feel the bedspread Kitty pulled over him, the fringe of it touching his chin. Touching like little feathers, like baby chick feathers, like pussycat fur, like Christie's hair next to him when he curled up beside her.

two

THEY CAUGHT UP WITH FARNSWORTH in Cloverdale and life settled down again, slipping into a new kind of routine. Kitty did well in saddle bronc and fair to middling in bareback, but she could not bring herself to dare try the bulls again. She just couldn't manage it. She was fine on foot, wearing her hillbilly clown suit, but the very thought of sitting up there and running the risk of getting caught in the hole again, made her feel like she had a watermelon-sized rock in her belly.

She knew she was a good clown. She could tell from the easy acceptance and respect of the older ones, from the way the bull riders spoke to her. She'd spent enough time on top of the bucking behemoths that the very cells of her body recognized each twist, knew what was going to follow, understood the body mechanics and primed her to move and move fast when the rider came off and needed her to distract the animal.

Christie couldn't stand to watch when Kitty was on foot, running straight at a bull, slapping its face with her hat, distracting it from the rider in the dust, challenging it to try to get her instead.

"If you even slip," Christie breathed. "And what if you trip and fall?"

"What if I fall out of bed and crack open my head?"

Noel watched. Sometimes, most times, the JimmySpook was with him, pointing, mocking, laughing, watching. Those times Kitty felt safe. She got nervous when the fright mask came out into the ring, because that meant they had a particularly feisty bull, and *that* meant she had to pay particular attention, to take extra care.

Farnsworth had a new bull working, one that promised to be ready and active in time for the Calgary Stampede. He was a black-bodied, white-faced mammoth, and he was what the old man called "active," the kind of animal that could put his rider in top spot, the kind of animal that could put a failed rider in the hospital. Old man Farnsworth called the bull Decision.

When the animals weren't in the chutes or in the ring, they were kept in corrals, well clear of spectators, onlookers, gawkers and tourists. Decision had a corral all to himself, and Kitty was one of the people entrusted with his care. She took the animals their feed, made sure they had lots of clean water, groomed the horses, checked their feet, generally fussed over all the stock. All she did for Decision at first was put his hay in the corral, but after a while she realized that without a rider, without the strap, without the damn bell clattering, the bull was actually very quiet. When she saw the JimmySpook reclining on the broad back of the bull, grinning at her, waggling his stick-bone fingers, she lost her fear. She was brushing Decision when the old man walked past.

He stopped, looked at her and shook his head slowly. "Your life insurance all paid up?" he asked in his quiet, soft voice.

"Unbelievable, eh?" she agreed. "You'd never know this pussycat was the same one put Greg Minstrel in the hospital with a smashed pelvis."

"I wouldn't trust any of them. All's it takes is a fly bite at the wrong time and they're in a freakin' fury."

"You could say the same about the average house pet," she said agreeably.

Kitty liked the old man. He'd been rodeo all his life, grew up around it, rode for years, retired to raise good stock. What he had, what he was, Kitty wanted for herself. Especially the calm part, the soft-voiced part.

She patted the animal, then backed away from him and climbed the fence. Only then did she dare turn her back. "If he was mine," she said, "I'd use him as herd bull in the off-season. Give him different kinds of cows, keep track of the calves, see what mixes and crosses make the best creature. This guy crossed with a Santa Margarita could give you a record-maker."

"You don't think *he's* a record-maker?"

"He'll set some, for sure, but there's that stiffness in his right front shoulder, and it could work against him."

"I don't notice stiffness."

"Watch for it. If he gets a day off between contests it doesn't bother him, but if he's working every day, he shortens his step on that side. I've checked—there's no scar, he hasn't been gored. But there's something. Might be that he lands on it a particular way after he turns in mid-air or something, but whatever it is, it's not good news. Twice now, when I've been brushing him, it's felt kind of warm, not hot mind you, but warm. He hasn't flinched or shifted, but...something must have happened to him, maybe when he was a calf. He might have got kicked or knocked over.

Shame, real shame if it interferes with his work, but I don't think it's an inherited weakness."

"Shouldn't be. I'm still working his dad, and his mom has given me a good calf every time, so there shouldn't be anything genetic. You're sure you're not imagining it?"

"I don't think so. Right front, you watch him. He's working this afternoon again, so it will probably show up. He had one helluva workout yesterday."

"Hasn't been rode yet."

"Ah, sooner or later there's a rider for every critter, and a critter for every rider, nobody and nothing makes it through a season."

"You got a Santa Margarita cow?"

"Me? Hell, no. This year, the way things have been, I could just about manage to feed a gerbil. I was just supposing."

"Well, it's a good thought. Where'd you get that kid you're travelling with?"

"Him?" she laughed. "Oh, he was just flying through the air and I jumped up and grabbed him down, claimed him for myself." The old man grinned at her so she laid it on a bit thicker and threw in some invention. "I've got a red-haired sister who thinks she's the goddess of fertility. By me, this one is the cream of the crop."

"You going to put him in the Little Britches in Calgary?"

"No. Noel's not keen on it. Funny little guy. It's not that he's scared, he's just not interested. He watches, but he doesn't get excited about any of it. And he isn't much interested in the animals, either. I mean, lots of kids, if there were this many horses around, they'd be underfoot, wanting a ride, wanting to pat this one or brush that one. Noel just watches them. It's like he's trying to figure something out about them."

"Quiet little guy."

"Yeah. Easy to please, too. Everything's a big deal. You give him a bag of corn chips and he's as happy as some kids are when they get a new video game."

"Right front, eh?" He looked over at the bull, standing head down, half asleep in the warm sunlight. "Okay, Decision, we'll see. Good boy. No matter what happens, you won't be freezer beef."

Decision was the last bull out of the chutes. The young rider was good, but not good enough. Three seconds into the competition, the clowns were moving, trying to distract the animal. Kitty moved in and slapped Decision on the rump. He whirled, head down, and charged. She dodged, slapped him again as he rushed past her, and he whirled again, swinging his head. She dove, somersaulted, and the crowd roared. The young cowboy got to his feet, his face ashen, one shoulder lower than the other, that arm hanging useless. Two other clowns grabbed him, one on either side, holding his belt, keeping him on his feet. He made it to the fence and started over it, and they gave him a shove. The crowd roared and screeched, and without even looking over their shoulders, they veered, and just in time. Decision hit the fence.

Kitty rushed in from behind, grabbed the bull's tail and pulled. Decision backed away from the fence rapidly and looked around, spittle flying from his mouth. JimmySpook rode on the bull's head, laughing crazily, arms and legs flailing. Kitty spun, ran, and the noise of the crowd told her Decision was right behind her. She made the fence next to the exit gate. Decision raced through the gate into the escape chute, along it and into the corral. The gate swung shut.

Kitty poked her head up over the fence, overacting, hamming it up, looking to the left, to the right, climbing slowly back into the ring, looking over her shoulder with exaggerated made-up fearfulness. The other two clowns moved toward her, clapping their white-gloved hands together. The crowd screamed and yelled and Kitty cavorted jerkily, stiffly, copying every move the JimmySpook made, while Noel laughed happily, able to see the wraith, able to see Kitty imitating the wraith, knowing what the other spectators did not know.

When the crowd was gone and her stint was finished, she went back to the corrals to check the stock. Decision lay on his side, head up, chewing his cud, his white face turned toward her. JimmySpook sat beside the bull, resting against his bulk.

"Look at you," she said softly. "Just look at you. That was some show you put on. You almost had me convinced." JimmySpook laughed soundlessly. Decision watched her, his jaws moving. "Silly old fuck." She leaned on the corral fence, watching him. "They're putting a bounty on you. First guy to ride you gets it, whether he wins the event or not. What a damn show-off you are!"

She left the corrals and went to the trailer, where Noel was brushing Dog's black fur with his own hairbrush.

"Hey, guy," Kitty said, hunkering down to give Noel a hug. "Now when you brush your hair you'll smell like a dog."

"I couldn't find her brush. I looked everywhere."

"Well, isn't that a caution. Maybe when I get cleaned up and changed, you'n'I should head into town and buy you a new brush. Then Dog will have two of them, if we can find the other one. What would you like for supper?"

"Hot dogs."

"Again? Good lord, Noel, you've been packing away nothing but hot dogs for days. You should have something else, something … something not junky. How about I put scalloped potatoes in the oven to bake while we go get the hairbrush, and while we're there we can get, oh, maybe some chicken or spareribs."

"We could get both, have the chicken tonight and spareribs tomorrow. They're better when they cook a long, long time, you know. Auntie Savannah said so."

"Did she indeed. Seen Christie?"

"She told me to wait here for you. She said she had something she had to do."

Dog sat in the old pickup between Kitty and Noel, as proud as if they were leading a parade out of Buckingham Palace. Dog adored Noel, who had changed her life. Now, instead of sleeping in the back of the truck on a saddle pad, she slept in the trailer, and when everyone was asleep she could get up off the rug on the floor and climb up on the bed, curling herself beside Noel. She dozed there, occasionally licking his hand. If one of the others got out of bed, Dog flopped back down on the floor and tried hard to look as if she'd been there all the time. And today, instead of riding in the back of the truck, here she was up front, Noel's arm across her broad old back.

"She looks like those things you see on TV," Kitty said, pulling into a small shopping mall. "You know the one, where the queen is sitting by the window, waving to the crowd?"

"Who's the queen?"

"You don't know about the queen?"

"I know about princesses. From stories. I don't know a queen, though."

"See? Who says education is a mess and a waste of time these days? Here's a guy has never heard of the queen. Things are really looking up."

Noel shook his head slightly, his baby brow furrowed in a frown. He had no idea what Kitty was talking about, and he knew the more he tried to find out, the less he would understand. They were like that. Even his mom had been like that. He could hardly remember anything else about her. Sometimes he thought he was even forgetting what she looked like. But he remembered how nice she smelled. No matter what kind of perfume she wore, the smell of it was sweet in his nostrils.

Kitty didn't use perfume. Kitty smelled of soap, of shampoo, of underarm deodorant, of toothpaste, but never of perfume. Christie did sometimes. Most times, but not always. Mom had always smelled perfumey. But he couldn't bring her face to mind. He could see individual things—her eyes, or her mouth. But not together. As for *him*... Noel didn't want to see *him*, wished he never had. Grumble guts. Cranky.

Kitty and Noel headed into the mall, leaving Dog to guard the truck, as if it needed guarding. The new one, yes, any booster in the world would try for the new one, but Christie had it today. The old one hadn't seemed old or beat-up until the new one got parked beside it, then suddenly the faithful old thing looked like a discarded can that had been kicked down the road for a few miles, then left crumpled in a ditch.

In the drugstore they got several hairbrushes. Also toothpaste—two kinds, one for the big people, one for Noel. His had pictures of Big Bird on it, and it smelled like bubble gum. Kitty also got deodorant, shampoo and some bubble bath stuff.

"What's it smell like?" he asked.

"It says it smells like vanilla."

"What's that?"

"Here." She unscrewed the cap and he sniffed.

"That's okay," he approved. "What's a banilla?"

"It's a bean. See, it's got a picture on the front of the label. A vanilla bean."

He didn't really care about beans. Just green ones. He liked the green ones. Christie did this thing for supper sometimes, she took a package of frozen green beans, the French-cut kind, and she stir-fried them with buckets of garlic, and it was so good it was all Noel wanted to eat for supper. But he had never eaten a banilla bean. It actually looked kind of yucky.

Kitty did some shopping in the supermarket, and while they were standing in the checkout line, she got three packages of sugarless bubble gum.

Noel grinned. "Thank you," he said.

"Ho, you think this is for you? No way, guy, it's mine. Nothing for you."

"Right." He leaned against her, watching other kids with their moms. He couldn't remember being like that with his mom. But he'd been very little, and there was so much stuff from being little that he didn't remember. Thingy said you shouldn't bother remembering that stuff.

There was stuff he did remember, though. Mostly stuff he wished he could forget. He couldn't remember ever sitting in the seat part of a shopping cart and getting a ride up and down the aisles, but he could remember being taken to a party, with a whole bunch of guys and some other kids, and he could remember other stuff too, and being hurt, and crying.

"Hey, you okay?" Kitty lifted him up and sat him on her hip, and he put his head on her shoulder, his face in the curve of her neck. "What's the matter, champ?"

"Nothin'."

"Yeah, right, nothing. People just go dead white in the face and sag, do it all the time. You going to throw up?"

"No."

The JimmySpook was pacing angrily, his movements jerky, his fright-face twisted in a grimace she supposed was a frown. How do you frown when you have no flesh? He was glaring at the woman in the lineup ahead of her, and for an awful moment Kitty thought he was going to aim his stick at her. Great, just what we need, a chubby woman going into what everyone thinks is cardiac arrest. Never get out of here if you do that, Bones. Just hang on. The kid's okay.

"You okay, little boy?" the woman behind her asked.

"I'm tired," Noel yawned.

"Well, if there's anything I can do, you let me know."

Kitty turned, surprised. "Thank you."

The woman smiled and nodded, her gaze fixed on Noel. "He's a gorgeous little boy," she said softly. "He's the kind you'd be afraid to let out of the house by himself."

"Yeah, if ever there was a kid the perverts would go for, eh?" Kitty agreed.

"I bet he's a good boy too."

"Good? If he was any better he'd have to be twins." Kitty patted Noel on the butt. "He's probably the best kid in the world."

The woman ahead of them finally found her air miles card, and then there was the search for the debit card. By the time Kitty's few purchases were rung up, Noel was almost asleep.

"I'll get someone to help you out with this," the cashier smiled. "Poor little guy, he looks just about worn out. It's hard on them, I see it every day, little people and shopping just do not fit each other. Too much noise, too much to see, too many people to dodge."

The bag boy took the cart out and Kitty carried Noel. Then he packed the groceries in the truck and refused the tip Kitty tried to give him. "Thank you, ma'am, but this is what they pay me to do."

"Thank you. Very kind of you." She felt awkward, something she was feeling more often now that she had Noel sidekicking with her. Go somewhere by yourself and you can be anonymous, go with a five-year-old kid and the world clusters around you. Old people materialize, really old people who probably have grown grandchildren and maybe even great-grandchildren. They'd reach out with their gnarly knobby hands and stroke the dark hair, trace the soft curve of a little jaw. Old men with rheumy eyes would dig into their pockets, come out with change and hand it to you shyly, "for the boy." The first couple of times it happened she didn't know what to do, she just stood there feeling awkward and off-balance. But now it was like a routine, and she smiled widely and said thank you, and Noel had learned to smile and say "Thank you, sir." When they went to a park so Noel could go down the slides or ride the swings, Kitty would sit on a bench with Dog sitting beside her, and nobody even looked at her. Until Noel ran to her, leaned on her lap, looked up at her, smiling, flarching, flirting, and she nodded and let Dog go with him. Then people knew the beautiful little boy was with her, and then she had company. Moms of other kids would sit right down and start chatting.

Once a mother had asked her right out whether Noel still peed the bed.
"Pee the bed? No!"

"How did you get him to go through the night? Dennis is about the same age, maybe a bit older, and every morning his bed is soaked and so is he. I get him up at ten at night and take him to the bathroom and get him to pee, and still he wakes up soaked."

"Maybe he thinks it's up to you," Kitty guessed. "Maybe if you don't drain him at ten o'clock he'll pee and wake himself up. After a bit he might wake up before he pees. You know what they say, if it isn't working, try something else."

"They've got these alarm things you know, as soon as the first drop touches them they go off. But... that's still *after*."

"Maybe he should go to bed earlier. Maybe he's so tired by the time he goes to bed that he sleeps so soundly—?"

"Oh, if we put him to bed before he's ready to go, he just about destroys the room! We gave him the right name, for sure," she laughed softly. "Dennis the Menace."

"Slap his arse," Kitty laughed.

"Oh, surely you don't—" The woman drew back in horror.

"No, I was teasing you," Kitty chortled. "I've never slapped Noel, never had to, never wanted to." She knew she sounded smug, and she didn't care. "But he's never done anything to deserve a whack. He's not a menace, he's a darling."

The bag boy took the shopping cart away with him and waved. Kitty put Noel in, he buckled himself in and leaned back, ready for a snooze. Kitty moved to the driver's side and got in. Dog whined, then licked Kitty's hand. "Hey, old pooch. Wait until you see what we got for you. Can you believe it, they have toothbrushes for dogs. Toothpaste too, and you have a choice: poultry-flavoured or beef."

They drove back to the fairgrounds and the JimmySpook rode in the truck with them. He didn't take up any room, but he was agitated, and Kitty almost thought she heard him muttering.

"What in hell is the matter with Bones?" she blurted.

Noel looked at her and shrugged. The colour had come back to his face, and the wide-eyed frantic expression was gone. "I 'membered something," he said, sounding ashamed.

"Yeah? Can you talk about it?"

He hesitated. His hand reached out and touched Dog, who moved closer to him, whined, then licked his cheek. The JimmySpook spun around, twirled like a top. Good job he doesn't take up any room, Kitty thought, or we'd be in the toolies for sure. She waited, not urging Noel. If he was ready, he'd tell, and if he wasn't ready, she'd wait.

And when Noel started to speak, Kitty wished she'd kept her damn mouth shut. She wasn't ready to hear anything like this. She wanted to stop the truck, grab the boy, hold him tight and wail. Instead, she drove the truck carefully and listened while a little boy, safe because of a very old dog and a bag of bones, told what he had remembered that practically had him fainting at the grocery checkout.

She pulled in, parked next to the new truck and sat silently, not knowing whether she wanted to puke or howl. Nobody should have to endure what Noel had remembered, let alone a small child. She almost wished the collision on the bridge had never happened, she almost wished they were both still alive, just so she could go find them, tear open their throats, reach in and pull out their goddamn hearts and feed them to the crows.

"You mad at me?" Noel sobbed. "I'm sorry."

"Hey, Bubba." She reached over, past Dog, and put her hand on Noel's knee. "Listen to me. I am not mad at you. You have done nothing wrong. You are a good boy. You are my sweet cheeks, okay?"

"You're not mad?"

"Mad at you? Hey, get real." She patted his knee. "No. I am not mad at you. Do you believe me?"

"I guess."

"You guess. Hey, boomer, do I fib you? Do I? Do I tell you lies?"

"No. You don't fib me."

"So when I say I'm not mad at you, I'm not mad at you."

He smiled. It wasn't much as smiles go, it was wobbly at the edges, and it flickered briefly and was gone. But it was a smile, and it had taken courage.

They carried the groceries into the trailer. Christie had supper going and the place was rich with the scent of Kitty's scalloped potatoes and the marinating steaks. The table was set, with a small African violet as a centrepiece, and a fresh-baked cake was cooling on a wire rack.

"About time," Christie smiled. "I thought I was going to have to sit down and eat all this stuff all by myself."

"Not a chance." Kitty put the grocery bags on the counter, kissed Christie on the cheek, then turned to Noel. "I guess we should get ourselves cleaned up a bit, eh?"

While Noel washed his hands and face, Kitty gave Christie the bare outline of what had happened in the supermarket. Christie's eyes flooded. She shook her head quickly, almost savagely.

"Fuck," she whispered. "And how in hell old was he at the time?"

Noel came back from the bathroom, his hair damp. He went to his place at the table and sat down expectantly, looking for all the world like a pampered and indulged only child who had never had a care or worry in the world.

They ate so much supper that none of them was ready for dessert. "Just as well," Christie decided. "Give it time to cool completely. I'll put the icing on later and we can have it before bed. I know someone who'll be ready by then. Some cake shark. Some guy who would live on cake if we let him."

Kitty got Dog's dish, put in some kibble, then scraped the plates on top. Before she put the dish down she took a scoop of scalloped potatoes and put that out too. Dog stood smiling, her tail wagging in short happy jerks.

Kitty put the dish outside near the steps and Dog rushed to it eagerly. "Fat fat fat," Kitty warned. "You keep that up and you'll get mistaken for a pig and turned into sausages."

Kitty did the dishes while Christie wiped surfaces and put away the groceries. Neither of them had much to say. Both were haunted by what Noel had told Kitty.

"I guess it's just about time for me to go see to the stock," Kitty said, drying her hands.

"What time are they pulling out?"

"We'll load them as they come back from their events. Ought to be out of here by one, two in the morning. Chris Higgins wants to drive the old pickup, is that okay with you?"

"Fine by me. Great, in fact! It means we can travel together."

"It also means we'll have Dog in with us," Kitty warned.

"Dog can ride in the back," Christie said firmly. "We'll open the sliding back window and she can poke her head in from time to time."

"Noel will fuss."

"Noel can go ahead and fuss. That old dog smells."

They prepared the trailer for the move, made sure everything was in its place and secured. The African violet went in the with the dishes, held in place by several strips of masking tape wrapped around the plastic pot, then stuck to the inner wall of the cupboard.

"You okay about the rest of the stuff?" Kitty asked.

"Hey, this won't be the first time."

"You taking Noel with you or do you want me to keep him?"

"He might be better off with you. It's going to be real busy over there tonight."

"Great. I'll tell him. I don't suppose we'll need much by way of activity books or anything, he'll probably be asleep."

"I thought I'd put a sleeping bag on the crew seat. Be sure he's got his pillow and his bear. That way, if he gets too tired and cranky he can go to sleep before we pull out. Boy, it sure is a whole new thing with a kid, eh? Not the actual work—you cook for two people or you add a spud and cook for three, and a load of wash is a load of wash no matter what size the clothes are. It's the other thing that's so exhausting, the always having to be aware of where he is, how he is, what he's doing . . . some nights, honest to god, Kitty, I could just about fall asleep on a rock! And you're the one who 'does' just about everything for him!"

"Yeah, but the thing I have trouble with is..." She looked around quickly. "Is this. Even talking about it, I have to look to see where he is. We just don't have any private time any more. You know?"

"I know. Sure, he goes to sleep and sex is possible. And good. It's just...not the same."

"Remember what it was like?" Kitty teased. "Can you remember those long, slow, sexy mornings? Remember just lying there, stark naked, feeling all soft and lazy..."

"Waiting for you to bring me coffee..."

"Ah, you *do* remember. Good. Hang onto it. That way, if we ever get the chance again, at least one of us will remember how to do it."

Old man Farnsworth was in a sweat. Anyone who didn't know him would think he was just a busy old man, but today, he who was usually the personification of calm was anything but, and the stock wranglers were off balance because of it.

"You're late," he snapped.

"I'm not late," Kitty laughed. "You've just got your boxers in a twist."

"I say you're late."

"What's wrong?"

"Go see." He waved. "Go take a look at Decision. He can't go out there tonight, that's what's wrong. Jeezly aitch!"

Decision was still lying on his left side, his head up, watching the fuss and furor. He seemed calm and well, but when Kitty went into the corral and finally managed to get him up on his feet, she could see he was taking most of his weight on his left front leg, favouring his right. She walked up to him, talking softly, and felt his right shoulder. She didn't feel any swelling, she didn't feel any knots or charley horses in the muscles, and when she checked the leg and hoof she couldn't see anything that would cause him discomfort, but it was obvious he was off balance.

"I'll get him some butazole," she suggested. "At least make him more comfortable. I guess we could get a vet."

"Vet doesn't know any more about it than you do. Or me, for that matter. I can't see them bringing a bloody X-ray machine out here, and if they did I can't see him standing quiet while they use it, and if he did what in hell good would it do? It's probably muscular and not in the bone at all. Damn!" He glared at her. "If you hadn't said anything to me I wouldn't have thought anything about it when I saw him just lying there. Look at the others! Look at them! They're priming themselves, see, they know what the lights mean, they know what the music and noise mean."

"Maybe he's just super calm." She looked at Decision. "Maybe he'd be fine."

"This afternoon you said he shouldn't do two in a row. Now you're saying something else?"

"I'm just saying that maybe you and I are both making more of this than we ought to. Okay, look at him, he's not limping. Once he starts moving he looks fine."

"So what do you think? I put him out or replace him?"

"It's not my decision, you're the one who—"

"Bullshit!"

"I told you this afternoon, if he was mine I'd retire him to herd bull."

"Yeah, well, that's what'll happen. But when? Right here and now or after Calgary? I have to tell you I was really counting on Calgary. TV cameras and everything. And him with a bounty on him."

"Well, why not load him now, bed him down, keep him separate from the others, give him the night off, let him rest up, and bring him out for Calgary. Maybe with three or four days' rest he'll be readier than ever. Don't you bother swinging that goddamn head of yours in my direction, fuck-face, or you'll be hanging out with the steers and I'll have your bag for a backpack."

She waved the stock truck into place and opened the corral gate. Decision moved through the gate, up the ramp and into the back of the truck. Kitty waited until he was all the way to the front, then she moved as quickly as she could and swung the metal gateway shut, effectively isolating Decision. He snuffed and snorted, pawed at the fresh sawdust on the truck floor, and shook his head, the slobber flying. "Oh, calm your damn self down," Kitty muttered. She got four flakes of alfalfa-hay mix and stuffed them into the manger, reaching through the access window, watching the bull, ready to jerk herself out of the way if he got proddy. Decision watched her, shook his head, then moved to the manger, grabbed a mouthful of alfalfa and chewed, snorting impatiently. "Shut up, eat, then lie down and chew cud until we get where we're going." She closed the access window, then hurried to help with the other stock.

By the time the bull riding event was announced, Kitty was damp with sweat. But she was wearing her clown outfit and she moved into the ring with the other two. They were busy, the crowd was excited and loving the performances, no people or livestock had got injured, none of the animals were harder to handle than usual and everything went smoothly. Kitty did her job and did it well. And as soon as the winner was announced and the presentation of the cheque was underway, she was stripping off her costume, pulling off her bright orange wig, once again helping load the stock. The other bulls were loaded onto the truck with Decision. They had enough room to move a bit, to lie down if they wanted, but not enough room to work themselves into a sweat and charge the gates or walls.

Old man Farnsworth checked and rechecked everything, then waved his hat. The driver sounded his horn once, a short beep, and the stock truck pulled away from the corrals and chutes. By the time the crowd was cleared out of the stands, the corrals were taken apart and stored in the gear truck. This truck would bring up the tail of the convoy, and would be the first one unloaded at the other end. When the corrals were set up again, the stock trucks would be unloaded and the animals would be fed, watered, and checked to ensure they had survived the trip unscathed. Sometimes it felt like a massive juggling act.

She headed to the parking area with her clown suit. The trailer was hitched, Noel was sound asleep in the crew seat, everything looked ready and Christie was leaning against the passenger door, sipping a mug of coffee.

"You go wash your face," she teased. "I'm not driving through town with Clarabelle the Clown at the wheel."

"Jeez, aren't you hard to get along with! I need more than my face washed, I can smell myself."

"I wasn't going to mention that."

Kitty wanted a long shower, she wanted a full bath, but she made do with a good wash at a basin in the public washrooms and some clean clothes. Then she pulled on her third-best boots, stuffed her dirty clothes and her work sneakers into the plastic bag, and used one of the new brushes on her hair. JimmySpook watched, fascinated, as she tried to tame her mop. He was agitated again. Kitty took a break from her cleanup to light a cigarette, take two drags on it and lay it on the glass shelf just under the mirror. JimmySpook moved close, pursed his mouth and began to suck in the smoke. She grinned at him, gave him a wink and went back to work on her hair. When she left the washroom, the cigarette was finished. She held the butt under the cold water tap, just to be sure, then tossed it into the wastebasket.

When she got back to the pickup, Dog was curled on her saddle pad in the back, her nose on her front paws, her tail moving slowly. "Good girl," Kitty told her. "Good old girl." She closed the tailgate, then the canopy window, and climbed into the driver's seat next to Christie, who handed her the coffee mug. "Thanks," Kitty said, and sipped. JimmySpook leaned forward, breathing in the aromatic steam, grinning widely. Kitty handed the mug back to Christie and put the key in the ignition. "I guess we're set," she said.

"You're sure you're okay to drive? You've had a helluva day."

"I'm so nerved up I might as well drive. If I just sit here I'll probably jump out of my skin. How's Noel?"

"Fine. I let Dog in until he fell asleep, then I moved her into the back. He probably thinks she's still there with him."

"Dog's fine. Curled up on her pad, seems happier'n hell."

"Another sip?"

"Yeah, I think so. Look at that asshole Henderson. Honest to God, you'd think there was some kind of prize or something. Does it matter if he's third in line or fourth? But no, he has to push in ... if Cormac hadn't braked they could have wound up bending fenders."

"Oh, Henderson, he's a total pill. I don't know why Florry sticks it with him."

"Maybe he's a good fuck or something."

"Kitty, look at him. How could he be?"

"Yeah, you wonder about women who stay with guys like that."

"Florry was better off on her own."

"You'd think she'd have figured it out. He's had how many women move out on him? Two wives taking off with what, three or four kids? Then all the squeezies and honeys and not one of them sticking around for long. Florry knew all that. And still ... "

"Maybe she was lonely, who can tell."

"Couldn't be that lonely!"

Kitty took another sip, checked her mirrors and her blind spot, then put the new truck in gear and moved toward the big gate that led out to the highway.

Just past Hope she saw the old pickup ahead of them. There appeared to be three, maybe four people riding in it. "Looks like Chris Higgins got himself some company," she said.

"Good, they can chip in on gas. I'm about ready for Peepee-ville, I have to tell you."

"It's all that coffee. My back teeth are floating too."

"You know what I find funny? People ask, What do you do? and we tell them and they say, Oh, that must be *so* exciting! So I want to know why I feel bored as hell right now."

"That's two of us."

Kitty opened the small door, reached in, lifted Noel from the crew seat and carried him to the washroom with her. He wakened enough to realize where he was and do what he had to do. His aim was a bit off, but he took some toilet paper and wiped up the splatters without needing to be told to do it.

He yawned and stood in front of the wash basin, dribbling water onto his fingers, staring at his reflection in the mirror. Kitty came out of the toilet stall, washed her hands, looked at him and winked, and he held up his arms.

"Lazy boy." She lifted him to her hip. "You need anything?"

He shook his head no. His breath was warm on her shoulder. Kitty stroked his back, felt him relax and begin to slip back into sleep. She took him back to the truck, got him into the sleeping bag, made sure he was comfortable. Then she locked the small door and went to the back of the pickup, opened the canopy window and let down the tailgate. "Come on, old girl," she said.

Dog moved slowly, jumped carefully to the ground, then headed for the grassy verge to squat. A whining sound drew Kitty's attention back to the truck. Sitting on Dog's saddle pad, looking small and puzzled and totally lost, was a terrier-mutt puppy. Kitty gaped. JimmySpook capered, cartwheeled, flipped and pointed his bone finger at her. There was no sign of his power stick, and for once he didn't look grim or threatening. Dog came back to the truck, jumped in and went to the saddle pad, then began to settle herself, nuzzling the puppy, whining softly.

"I'll be gone to hell," Kitty breathed. She reached in, lifted out the pup and took it out. Then she set it down in the grass where Dog had just widdled. It sniffed, turned in circles, sniffed some more, then lowered its rear end and peed.

"What in hell is *that*?" Christie asked. "Where did you get that?"

"It was in the back of the truck with Dog."

"Where did it come from?"

"I told you, all's I know is it was in with Dog. I have no idea at all where she got it."

Kitty carried the pup to the truck and put her in the bed. The pup hurried over to Dog and pressed against her, whimpering. Dog whined and licked the pup's face, and it snuggled close.

"She seems to think it's hers." Christie sounded as if she were accusing Kitty of something. "Are you sure you didn't—"

"Hey, cut me some slack here, okay? All's I did was open this up so Dog could pee."

"What do we do with it?"

"Well, I guess you could haul it out and just leave it here. Someone's sure to run over it before morning."

"Damn it, Kitty!"

"Why be mad at me? If you want something done, then do it. The damn thing isn't in *my* way, it isn't caught in *my* throat. When we get stopped and set up again I'll ask around, see if anyone's mislaid a pup. What else can I do?"

"Don't you bother bitching at me!" Christie stomped over to the passenger door, got in, slammed the door and sat glaring out the windshield.

Kitty sighed, so angry her hands were shaking. She closed up the back of the truck, got back behind the wheel and started the engine. Christie pointedly ignored her. Kitty checked the mirrors, then pulled onto the highway, picking up speed, feeling the weight of the trailer dragging behind them. If Christie wanted to sulk and bitch, fine, she could do it on her own. Jesus! As if there was some kind of big plot coming down, spies and counterspies and who knows, maybe the pup had a goddamn microchip imbedded in it, with NATO plans for the defence of Europe.

Sometimes, when Christie was in a mood, Kitty imagined all sorts of resolutions to the problem of the emotional roller coaster. Like she could sign over the old truck—hell, the truck *and* the trailer. Here you go, darlin', she's all yours, you go your way, I'll go mine, and don't worry about Dog, she comes with me. So does the kid. There you go, you've got your stand and your knickknacks, you've got the trailer so you've got a place to live, you've got a truck you didn't have to pay for, but that's okay because I didn't pay for the other one, either. Now see how happy you are with nobody else to blame for your on-again off-again moody bullshit.

"Want a sandwich?" In Christie's voice there was no trace of whatever it had been. "I made a whole bunch. I've got salmon, I've got devilled egg, I've got lettuce, tomato and green onion. All in pitas instead of bread, they're easier to hang onto."

"I like the sound of the lettuce, tomato and onion," Kitty said, keeping her own voice agreeable.

She not only liked the sound of the sandwich, she liked the taste of it. "You didn't mention the avocado," she teased.

"Hey, a woman has to have *some* secrets. Didn't they tell you?"

They shared a mug of thermos coffee, finished their sandwiches and settled in for the long drive. After a while, Christie folded Kitty's jacket for a pillow. Kitty put Reba McIntyre on the CD, turned it low so it wouldn't disturb Christie, and undid her belt buckle. She cracked her window open just far enough to feel the breeze on her face, then took her wallet out of her right hip pocket and laid it on the seat beside her. JimmySpook was lying on his back on the hood of the truck, waving his arms in time to the music. Kitty lit a cigarette, and like *that* the little bone-rack was beside her, mouth pursed.

"God, I wish he wouldn't do that," Christie said sleepily. "It's too weird. He sort of—blinks, or something. He doesn't move, he just, you know, *is* in a different place."

"You saw him?"

"Sometimes I do. Not as often as you do or Noel does, I think. Just once in a while."

"You comfortable?"

"No. I'm chilly." She sat up and reached into the crew seat for a blanket. "Ah, good." She draped it over her shoulders, slammed Kitty's jacket back in place as a pillow and plopped her head on it. "Now if you can just keep the goddamn Squeyanx from zizzing around like a wasp, maybe I can get some sleep."

"The mood you're in, maybe you *should* sleep. Snarl snarl snarl."

"Oh, shut up. You aren't exactly sweetness and light yourself, you know."

But she wasn't snarling. Kitty could hear the smile in her voice, could tell that whatever had made her so snappy had passed. She wondered about the mechanics of glands and hormones and chemicals and what is and isn't a balance. What got pumped too hard or not hard enough to make a surge of nastiness? Sometimes it seemed to be just another way for Christie to indulge herself. Why try for self-control when you can flog people into line by being mean? Who said that Love means never having to say you're sorry, and was it true? Even a small, occasional apology for the unwarranted explosions would go a long way. Or maybe not. No way to know when you've got no experience with it. However many times she'd gone up like a balloon, however many times she'd yelled or snapped or sulked or accused or flared up, there was never an apology. All of a sudden, it disappeared, it was finished, and let's all go on with life and pretend that it never happened, or that it made sense.

She tossed the cigarette stub out the window, checked the speedometer and eased off on the gas. Best watch it! The new truck drove so smoothly and so quietly it was all too easy to wind up going faster than you should, faster than you meant to go, faster than you could control.

The next time Kitty lit a cigarette, Christie was sound asleep, and Reba had been replaced by Itzhak Perlman. She glanced at the back of her hand, at the lump she got when the bull rope pinned her and smashed all the small bones. It seemed bigger than it had been, even at the time of the accident, when it swelled up black and blue right to her elbow and hurt so bad she wanted to weep. Maybe get it checked over, see if there was anything she should be doing for it.

JimmySpook was in the crew seat with Noel, lying on top of him, looking to be asleep himself, although how and why a spook would need to sleep was a mystery. But at least Kitty got to smoke her cigarette herself and enjoy every puff. When Bones was awake, the cigarette was gone in no time flat, burned down fast by his insistent hunger. Even Christie was starting to nag her about how much she smoked, but *she* wasn't, not really. She was lighting a lot of the damn things and holding them, but she wasn't getting very many. The bones took the smoke, sometimes right out of her own mouth and throat. Intrusive bugger.

She wasn't going to keep driving much longer. So what if they weren't the first ones to arrive? They'd as good as broken the back of the drive, and there was no way she was going to stick to it just to prove a point. She'd find a good place to pull off, get out the foamie and the sleeping bags, and maybe move Christie into the back too. If Dog came up front with Noel, the kid would be fine, safer than in his mother's arms, no joke intended.

"Getting too damn old for this," she muttered. She had never before felt anxious about going through the mountains, but tonight she'd do just about anything to avoid making the trip in the dark. The truth was she was tired, more tired than she'd ever been when all she had to concentrate on was staying on an animal, staying alive, and maybe winning some money. Now she was busy with the stock, and being in the ring in her dumb-ass suit was a lot more physically demanding than riding a bull for eight seconds. She wasn't even sure she wanted to keep on doing what she was doing. It had never before seemed like a *job*, but now that's what it was. A job.

When she pulled off the highway and parked on the blacktopped lay-by with the picnic tables, she was so tired she could have gone to sleep sitting behind the wheel. Getting the foamie unrolled and the sleeping bags spread out seemed like the hardest chore she'd finished in days.

"Hey, Chris," she whispered. "I've got the foamie ready."

"Hmmph."

But Christie moved, still nine-tenths asleep. She got out of the truck and went to the back. Dog jumped into the truck and settled herself on the front seat. Kitty locked the doors, then climbed into the bed of the pickup and closed the tailgate and the canopy window. When she stretched out on the foamie, the pup moved to snug against her, whimpering slightly.

"You hush now," she whispered. "You just hush up. If you waken Chris she'll barbecue you for breakfast."

"Chris will barbecue the bastard for breakfast whether it wakes me up or not," Christie's voice said, heavy with sleep. "And you'll be dessert, I'm warning you."

Kitty wakened slowly, lulled by the movement of the truck, the sound of the tires on the pavement. She lay, dull and sluggish, looking out the back window of the canopy at the top half of the passing scenery. Finally she sat up and rapped on the window. Noel's face appeared almost immediately, his small hand moved to the catch that held the window shut.

"Sleepyhead," he said, sliding the window open. "We could hardly hear the CD for the snores, right, Christie?"

"Terrible snores. There's a picnic site about a mile ahead. I'll pull over there. We've got coffee in a thermos up here, don't we, guy? Should we give her some?"

Dog was on the crew seat, impersonating royalty again, and the little mutt puppy was on the front seat, curled up on Kitty's jean jacket, pressed against Christie's hip. Kitty almost said something about it, then had a better idea and kept quiet.

Noel handed the mug through the window. Kitty took it, sipped, and smiled at him. "Maybe you just saved my life."

"You saved mine," he replied solemnly. "I'd'a died, you know."

"Ah, but you didn't."

"I was lucky, huh?"

"Were you? I thought it was me was the lucky one."

"I'm luckier than you."

"Nah, I'm luckier than you. Because I've got you and you've only got me."

"Yeah, but I got you and you're bigger."

"*I'm* the lucky one," Christie laughed. "I got the both of you."

"Yeah, but *we* got *you!*" Noel pulled his head back out of the small window and turned to slide back down to the crew seat.

Kitty sipped coffee and yawned, leaned against the side of the canopy and wished she was someplace where she didn't have to get up, didn't have to do anything but roll over in a comfortable bed and dive back into sleep. But this was why she'd set up the foamie in the back of the truck—first one awake could start driving. They could have slept in the trailer, in real beds, but they would have had to haul Noel out of the truck, carry him over to the trailer, probably waking him up. In the morning, everybody would have had to get out of bed at the same time, enough sleep or not, because it was against the law to ride in a moving trailer and anyway life was risky enough without going to silly extremes.

One of these days, maybe a week full of frosty Fridays, she was going to make this trip without any deadline. For years she'd driven past Viewpoint and Scenic Lookout and Tourist Attraction signs and longed to check them out, see the sights. But she'd just kept driving. Gotta get here, gotta get there, gotta get somewhere else. One of these days, and real soon, she was going to stop and actually see some of that stuff. One of these days she'd up and sell the old truck, and the trailer too. Put the foamie in the back and bye-bye, blackbird. The only destination she'd have would be Lucy's place, and the only time frame would be eventually.

Darlene had her back up. Darlene with her back up was so much like Gran with her jaw set that angry as she was, Seely had to leave the kitchen and go into the bedroom, bury her face in a pillow, and laugh it out. Darlene thought Seely had stalked off because she was angry enough to give both kids a good swat. Lizzie sat on the edge of Jimmy's kitchen table, ready to be backup if it was needed. Seely came back from the bedroom, still looking just about ready to split heads.

"I do *not* want to live in a sardine can," Darlene said. "It's about the dumbest idea you ever had. That thing will fall apart inside of ten years. You saw the doors on the kitchen cabinets! That's not even real wood!

The hinges will be off in no time flat. By Christmas the front door will probably die."

"I know it's not a *house* house, but it's way cheaper. Way cheaper. And quicker."

"How do you figure cheaper? The place will be in shreds and either you'll have to pay someone to keep coming and fixing things or you'll have to junk the damn thing and buy a new one. Those aren't walls, Seely, they're just dividers. You put your hand on them and push and they wobble. The thing is crap and I will *not* live in it."

"Then find someplace else to live and move there."

"I'll just stay here."

"No you won't," said Jimmy, looking up from the book he was reading at the kitchen table. "That's why your mom is looking at trailers. I can take a very *very* small dose of you two, and then you'll wind up on the endangered list."

"What an awful thing to say!" Lizzie blurted.

"It's the truth. Each of you, both of you, pick my ass."

"What do you mean?" Lizzie slid off the table, grabbed a chair, pulled it over and sat down face to face with Jimmy. "What do I do that picks you?"

"You argue all the time." He put his book aside, got up and took his mug to the coffee maker for a refill. "Doesn't matter what gets said or who says it, either or both of you has to argue about it. You're both of you like babies, like spoiled rotten babies. Nyah nyah want this, nyah nyah don't want that, grizzle and bitch and whine and it just goes on and on. This one won't eat broccoli, that one won't eat cabbage, this one won't touch meat loaf, that one wants to live on pork chops, Christ a'mighty will you just one meal sit your asses down on a chair and bloody *eat?*" He brought his coffee back to the table, sat down, and reached for the sugar bowl. "It's like you go around with little rulers or measuring cups. She got more than I did, I had to do more work than she did, it only took her ten minutes to do her chores and I've been at it for half an hour. And you will *not* mind your own business. Where you goin' Uncle Jimmy, where you been Uncle Jimmy, what you working on Uncle Jimmy, can I come see your work room Uncle Jimmy, will you show me this, will you teach me that. I don't need all that yammer yatter yammer. So you're not staying here."

"Maybe so," Darlene said, so agreeably that it surprised Seely. "But that doesn't mean I'm moving into some kind of aluminum can. If *she*," and she pointed at her mother, "wants to waste a whack of money, well, I can't stop her. But I don't have to encourage her by moving into her stupid idea and then pretending it's anything but ridiculous."

"So you're kicking up this big stink on moral grounds, is that it?" Jimmy jeered. "Here I thought you were just bitching because you always bitch."

"And I do *not* want to live way out here. I was born in town, I've lived my life in town, and this is not town."

"So see if they'll let you move into, oh, maybe the furniture store or the back of Wing Fu's Chop Suey House. They're in town."

"We've got a house in town!" Darlene yelled.

"There, see? Yelling. Next it will be a baby tantrum. Fling herself to the floor, kick her feet, flail her arms, bite holes in the 'noleum. Baby!"

"I already told both of you," said Seely. "I can't live in that house. It makes me sad."

"Well, it doesn't make *me* sad!" Lizzie whined.

"Then move into it by yourself," Jimmy shrugged. "You'll last about a week, then the welfare will come scoop you up and put you in a foster home. If you're lucky it'll be in town, but it might be to hell and gone up a back road somewhere with people who have a chicken farm, and you'll be picking up two thousand eggs a day, or shovelling shit. Or maybe you'll be the one who catches the meat birds and rams 'em into cages, two dozen to a cage, five hundred cages to a truckload and only four hours to get it all done."

"*You* could move," Lizzie suggested. "This house is way big for only one person. You could have six people living here and they wouldn't get in each other's way. We could just stay here and you could move."

"I'm not moving. My grandma left me this house. *Me*. Not the whole damn buncha us. The house is *mine*. The land, well, it's for everyone, but this is my house and I'm not movin' out of it just because a couple of teenaged bitches have decided I should." He slammed his hand on the table, palm flat. The noise was incredible. "Who'n fuck d'ya think ya's are!" He was so angry he'd gone white around the mouth. "You come in here swanning like you were some kind of special thing, you just take over everything, your noise fills every corner, your bad temper floats around in here like skunk stink, you take it all for granted, like you got born with the right to go anywhere, do anything and never have to say thank you or gee I hope I'm not in the way. Selfish, self-centred, greedy and out-and-out nasty! You presume. Both of you presume. Oh, I'm the great I-Am and that means everybody has to just bend over backwards to be nice to me. Well, not here!"

"Jimmy, calm down." Seely moved to stand behind him, put her hands on his forehead and stroked, easing his head back so that it rested against her belly. "Come on, now, you'll make yourself sick if you don't calm down. They aren't going to be up your nose much longer, Jimboh, I promise. If I have to I'll move back to the house in town. I only thought trailer house because . . . well, because."

"Seel," Jimmy sighed. "It's going to take just about as much work to set up a damn tin box as a house. You've still got to run in the hydro, you've got to get the perc test and then approval for a septic tank, you've got the concrete pad . . . I bet if you asked Savannah she'd get those three guys of hers to send one'a their crews down here and you'd have your house in about no time flat."

"If I have to live way out here, then someone better buy me a car or something."

Jimmy was out of his chair and had Darlene by the hair in a flash. She yelled. Seely rolled her eyes and sat down quickly in Jimmy's chair. Lizzie stared, amazed.

"You've got a goddamn mountain bike must have cost your mom two thousand bucks," he gritted. "And look at you, you're packing a good twenty-five pounds more than you should. You look like the Goodyear blimp girl. You want to go to town? Peddle your ass in on that bike. You don't give the goddamn orders around here, understand? Now shut the fuck up!"

"Momma!" Darlene hollered. "Make him stop!"

"Darlene, be quiet," Seely almost whispered. "You asked for it."

Jimmy released Darlene's hair and she leapt away from him. She looked at Seely, who was sitting with her arms on the table, her head resting on her arms, like a tired child, tears slipping from her eyes. "I can't stand it!" Darlene yelled. She ripped out of the house, slamming the door behind her, and raced up the hill to Savannah's place.

"You?" Jimmy looked at Lizzie.

She shrugged. "Personally, I think this entire family is out to lunch big time. I mean *major* dysfunction, Uncle Jimmy."

He burst out laughing. Lizzie stared. He pointed his finger at her and, still laughing, chanted, "Miss Lah de Dah, Miss Lah de Dah." He turned his back on her, went to Seely and easily lifted her in his arms. "Ah, Seel," he crooned. "It's okay, babe, it's fine, come on now, Jimboh will take you to bed and you can just cuddle down and have a good cry. There's a girl.

You know Jim loves you. Savannah loves you. Kitty loves you. We all love you. You're our little baby sister. Come on, now, Jimmy's got you."

"What are you *doing?*" Lizzie breathed.

"Why don't you just shut up?" he said pleasantly. "Do you ever stop to think about anyone else? Have you ever looked at what your mom was dealing with? Never mind you two pains in the ass, but what a treat that's been. Did you ever notice how much work there was to making sure Sandra was comfortable? Maybe you think it's easy running a catering business. Maybe you think all the customers are real nice people. Maybe you should pull your head out of your ass, wake up, and look around."

Lizzie didn't even try to argue with Jim. "What's wrong with her?"

"What's wrong? It's called exhaustion, you selfish little shit. Go tell your Auntie Savannah that I need her. Please."

Lizzie was gone, no more questions, no argument. Jimmy put Seely on the bed that had been Gran's, tucked her under the covers and sat stroking her head, talking softly, assuring her things would be fine, just fine. Seely listened to the sound of his voice, gripped his hand and let the tears come.

Savannah came in and Jimmy grinned. He couldn't help it. Since age twelve the sight of Savannah running had been enough to make every male within eyesight smile and sigh.

"Jesus Jesus Jesus," Savannah breathed. "Oh, Seely, baby, it's going to be all right. Come on, now, you just let it all out. You bawl your damn eyes out and when you've cried all your tears, I'll have chicken soup and eggnog. Remember eggnog? That's how we knew we were sick, the old biddy would whip up a quart or two of eggnog and we'd get to drink as much of it as we wanted. And when we were starting to feel a bit better, she'd have her special chicken soup. And I know how to make it. You know how to make it?"

"First," Seely whispered, "you steal a chicken."

"You got it."

Carol came in and closed the blinds. She went to get a cool washcloth and put it on Seely's forehead. "I'll go steal the chicken, pet," she whispered.

Seely tried to smile but the attempt failed, and she began to sob.

"That's better," Savannah crooned. "That's much, much better, I won't relax until I hear you howling, okay?"

They left Seely with a roll of toilet paper, the cold cloth for her face, her comfortable bed in the darkened room, and the rest was up to her. Only she could sob it all out. Seely tried her best.

Darlene sat in the kitchen looking frightened and on the verge of tears herself. Jimmy ignored her as he moved through the room, filling the kettle, putting it on the gas stove to heat. He got the brown Betty teapot, rinsed it, filled it with hot water and set it on the drainboard. Then he got the canister of teabags and stood holding it in his hands, looking suddenly helpless. "I can't do a thing until the water boils," he muttered.

"Darlene wants to move in with us," Savannah said conversationally, as if Darlene weren't right there in plain sight.

"Yeah?" Jimmy sounded bored. "She bit off more than she can chew down here a little while ago."

"I heard."

Carol appeared in the kitchen with two big frozen hens in her hands. Savannah took the birds and put them on the counter, undoing the twist-ties and peeling off the plastic bags. "We've got a big house up there," she said. She might have been talking about something she saw on TV. "But none of the kids wants to share a room with her. I sure as hell don't, and Carol won't. So that would mean the only place we'd have for her to sleep would be in with the washing machines and the freezers in that place that was supposed to be a garage only wound up a spare room. But Darlene doesn't want to stay there. She's pretty insulted, in fact."

"Tough," Jimmy agreed.

"Her next idea was that Carol and I should move in together and give her Carol's room."

"Bullshit."

"For sure. So the idea following that one was that all the boys should move into my bedroom, because it's bigger, and she could have Alan's room."

"She's sure good at deciding how everyone else should live."

"Well, none of it's going to happen, see, because we've got no reason to do it. I mean it was the kids' dads built and paid for the damn house. Had nothing to do with Darlene at all. She even suggested we all move into the house in town. Now what in hell would any of us want in town?"

"I guess maybe Darlene is going to have to stop and think about how she's managed to get stuck in everyone's throat. You know, in lots of ways she reminds me of Glen, when he was the same age. Remember? It had to be his way or else. And all of a sudden she's up against a whole whack of people who aren't at all interested in her way."

"So what should we do, Jim? You got any ideas?"

"Well, there's the woodshed," he suggested. "It's snug. I built it myself. I could move my wood into the drying shed, I guess—*if* I got some help. Then a good sweeping out and maybe some, oh, I don't know, insulation and wallboard or something. Fix the floor. Might take a couple of weeks."

"The *woodshed?*" Darlene was horrified. "I'll live on the street first!"

"That's up to you, of course, but don't ever forget we made the offer."

"You're hateful. All of you! Hateful!"

"In which case why would you want to live in our house with us?"

Savannah put the big soup pot on the stove, then dumped the frozen birds in. "I guess these buggers can thaw as they cook, or cook as they thaw or something." She drizzled a bit of vegetable oil onto the bottom of the pot. "Guess they don't need to stick to the bottom, though."

"That's gonna be one helluva soup." Jimmy moved closer and peered into the big pot.

"You know how it is, if a thing is worth doing, it's worth overdoing, right?"

Darlene wasn't used to being ignored, and she didn't like it one little bit. She huffed out of the kitchen, went to the bedroom she shared with Lizzie and threw herself on the bed. The more she thought about things, the more frustrated and angry she became.

About the time everyone else was setting the table, taking a tray of soup in to Seely, pulling pans of hot rolls out of the oven and bustling around like ants, Darlene went out the bedroom window. She could as easily have walked out a door, but going out the window seemed more defiant.

She didn't even look at her mountain bike. Hell with that idea! She walked to the highway, and stood, thumb out, hoping for a ride. About ten minutes later a van stopped, and Darlene went to open the door. A middle-aged woman smiled at her from the driver's seat. "I'm only going to town," the woman said.

"That's fine, it's where I'm going too." Darlene made herself sound much more pleasant than she felt. "Thank you for stopping."

"Oh, I've hitched a few rides of my own in my time." The woman laughed softly, but didn't elaborate.

The ride into town was quiet, neither of them in the mood for conversation. The van stopped two blocks from the house and Darlene got out, said her polite thank-yous and waited until the van drove off. When it was out of sight, she walked to the place she considered home, got the key from under the big flowerpot and let herself in.

Soup for Chrissakes. Soup? No thank you. She went to the freezer, dug through it until she found a casserole dish of frozen lasagna. She turned on the oven, put the lasagna in to warm and went into the bathroom to run herself a hot tub. She lay in the tub feeling very hard done by and sorry for herself. Well, she'd show them! Sleep in the garage. Sleep in the woodshed. Why should she, when she had a perfectly good bed in a perfectly good house?

She had almost fallen asleep in the tub when the dinger went off and roused her. She pulled the plug, stepped out and pulled on her robe, then went to the kitchen to get her lasagna.

She ate it sitting in Seely's big recliner, watching TV. She'd show them, each and every one of them. They could all go straight to hell. The woodshed, indeed.

She didn't finish the lasagna—it had been made as supper for four people. But without salad and garlic bread and dessert, she was able to eat more of it than she ordinarily would have. She put what was left in the fridge.

She checked the channel listings and couldn't work up any interest in anything that was on. She looked through the video collection and only felt boredom. Finally she went to bed, her mouth still greasy with lasagna juice. She fell asleep easily enough, but wakened in the middle of the night. She went to the bathroom to pee, and when she glanced in the mirror she saw that she had tomato stain around her mouth. She soaped the face cloth, washed herself and checked the mirror again.

She froze. She wanted to scream, she wanted to shriek, she wanted to yell for her mother, and she couldn't make even a squeak. Behind her face in the mirror she could see another face—a skull, really—no body, no arms, no legs, just the skull face, empty eyeholes and all. Darlene whirled. In the movies the character would whirl and see nothing at all, just walls. But Darlene didn't see just walls. The face was there, and no matter where she turned, it stayed in front of her. She was so frightened she had to run to the toilet and pee all over again. Then she ran for her bedroom. If she could get in there fast enough, and close the door hard enough, maybe the skull face would be locked out.

Except it wasn't. It just drifted through the door. Darlene dove for her bed, pulled the covers over her head and squinched her eyes shut. She felt the skull settle itself on the bed beside her. When she peeked out from under the covers, there it was, turned toward her, eyeholes staring.

She hid under the covers again, her breathing shallow and rapid. She wanted to get comfortable but couldn't move her arms or legs. This, she realized, is what they mean when they say "scared stiff." She wondered if her hair would go white overnight. Or what if her heart couldn't take it and she died? What if her throat closed so tight she suffocated? With these cheerful thoughts in the front of her mind, she fell asleep. She wakened to a room bright with sunlight. And the skull was still sitting beside her on the bed.

Darlene fainted.

Lucy got up a few minutes before five, her hip on fire. The stiffness and cramp in her low back was bad, the pressure was on the sciatic nerve and she could almost see it, like a band of red hot anger through her buttock, down the outside of her leg to her knee, starting a bonfire in her knee, then crossing to the inside of her lower leg, cramping and searing, then to the sole of her foot, where it just ached and cursed, the fire reduced to glowing embers. Each step hurt the bottom of her foot, as though she were walking on nails.

She managed to get out of the bedroom without making enough noise to waken Deb, then closed the door carefully and, with one hand on the wall, made it down the hallway to the kitchen. She turned on the coffee machine and got her medication bottles. Leritine, you sign for that, it's on the restricted list, just like the better-known narcotics. Morphine, for example. The label said one or two a day as needed. She took one. She put that little bottle back on the shelf, took down another and shook out two of the pink pain pills, the ones with codeine in them. One every four hours as needed for pain. Fuck it, let's take two, right now. Breakfast of champions. A red estrogen pill because her physician was worried about bone density loss caused by her age and by the constant problem with the back and hip. People warned her about breast cancer, about this cancer, about that cancer. As if she had a frigging choice. And, to top off the little heap in the palm of her hand, Prozac. One a day to combat depression. My my, and once I've swallowed them all will I be the same person I was when I woke up? Do I care? Would anyone notice? If they did, go back to the first question: Do I care?

She washed down the pills with cold water from the tap, then went to the living room to get a cigarette. She opened the drapes, looked out the big window at the place and sighed with satisfaction. Much much easier to make hay here than near the coast. Not a sign of fog. Only the barest hint of dew. Fine, then. Good enough. She turned on the TV, tuned it to the weather channel, hit the mute button so the sound wouldn't disturb Deb. The map showed the maritime provinces. Great, good luck to them all, good folks every one, it gives me time to go get my coffee. And my cane.

When she came back, the map was focussed on Alberta. Sunny and clear. Good, just the kind of weather Kitty would need for Calgary. About the worst thing that can happen to a clown is rain. You need to have your footing firm, you don't need to be sliding in the mud with a ton of large animal hot on your tail.

The map changed again. Ah, fine, then—the coast. As always it was "unsettled," but it looked like a good bout of weather for her area. When the weather number flashed she went for the portable phone, dialled, and waited for the meteorologist to answer. You had to pay for the service, but so what, when you're talking acres and acres of hay worth a minimum of $5.50 a bale?

Her next phone call was to the air base met section. No charge there. And the met observer on duty seemed to understand fully why so many locals had been phoning the past several days.

"Hay ready?" he asked.

"It's ready. I'm ready. But we need to hear what you have to say."

"It's an awful responsibility," he laughed. "I'm a prairie boy myself, and I know what a hay crop means. In fact it's stuff like that made the decision for me, and that's why I'm talking to you right now. It's too much work for too little return."

"Yeah," she agreed, laughing softly, "but what about that feeling of independence, what about the self-sufficiency, what about . . . the bullshit?"

"Well, I guess I'm just not the adventurous kind. I might be getting paid pauper's wages here, but . . . so are you."

"Tell you what, son, anytime you get lonely for the old farm ambiance . . . " And he laughed heartily, before she even got the chance to invite him out for the big haying dinner. When he quit laughing she invited him anyway.

Lucy wasn't ready for breakfast. She had a belly full of pills and needed more coffee. She refilled her mug, then filled up the small thermos. She rinsed the coffee maker, put in new grounds and fresh water, and had it all set up for Deb when she wakened. With luck that wouldn't be for at least two or three more hours. By then, Lucy should be just about started.

She padded sock-foot to the mud room with her mug in her hand and the thermos tucked under her arm. She sat on the chair, put the thermos and mug on the lid of the chest freezer, and got her boots. The lace-front ones, because when her leg was acting up she couldn't be sure her foot wouldn't swell up so much she wouldn't be able to get her pull-ons off. Not four months ago, Deb had had to use the miracle shears to cut off a perfectly good boot.

She did the laces tighter on her right foot than her left, pulled on her long-sleeved plaid shirt, tucked the thermos under her left arm, held her mug of coffee in her left hand, and grabbed her cane with her right hand. Step and fetch it, ninety-nine clump.

First she watered the hanging baskets and the iris and lily bed, then she connected the hose to the soaker set-up in the vegetable garden. Then she stumped her way toward the barn and the equipment shed.

The thoroughbred moved toward her, whickering softly. "Hey, there, dead horse." Lucy stroked the soft nose, the long face. "You looking for a treat? I bet you are. Well, give me a minute here, I'll get you one or two of those vitamin things you're so fond of. Yes, I will so. Sure I will. Even a dead horse has to eat, right?"

She got the treats, and made sure the thoroughbred got hers first. "When you gonna stop being so selfish?" she nattered. "That baby is due right here and now, why are you keeping her locked up inside, can you answer me that one? And you, miss Buckskin Wonder, aren't you proud of yourself? Here's yours, don't push and shove or I'll give you such a whack with my cane you'll think the dead horse kicked you. No, no, no, Blue. Calm your-self down, not until the haying is done, I've only got so much energy and you girls are going to have to reach down and pull up your aprons and pitch in here. Lucy needs to do the haying, Lucy has no time for training or trail rides. More's the pity. Oh, don't give me that horse buns. You don't need grain, you don't need hay, you don't need bugger nothing, look at where you're kept, eight and a half acres of grass, for Chrissakes! If that isn't enough for you, well, you're too fat anyway. That's it, hands empty, pockets empty. Go get yourselves a good drink or something. Go on, now, beat it."

She stumped toward the equipment shed and the mares followed her. The dead horse walked so close that her long face was even with Lucy's left shoulder. The others came behind, nudging each other, even pushing at each other, but not one of them came too close or in any way shoved Lucy. They knew. Some days, when she came out without the cane, they pushed against her, nudged her off balance, got demanding. But when she needed the cane, they stayed well back. Deb said it was the cane, that they knew it could hit them, but Deb was not a horse person. Lucy was convinced they knew it was a bad leg day and they were looking after her. Deb said that was romantic nonsense, but she smiled when she said it, and put her arm around Lucy's waist, put her head on Lucy's shoulder. "You're such a softie," she whispered.

It was one of those nice moments that get themselves put away in a special place, from which they can jump up, fresh and new again, at any moment. If you're feeling bummed out and low, you can reach into the memory bank for them and feel cheered, and sometimes, like now, you don't even have to do that. They are just there, adding to the promise of the new day, putting the shine on things. Those moments made up for the other times, the cold, cutting, sniping, arguing, kiss-my-ass-you-bitch times. Days, even weeks of tension and anger could be exorcised by one golden moment like that. For mares, it's strictly physical. They save their emotions for their young, and, if you're really lucky, for you. Lucy figured she was really lucky.

She filled the tank on the tractor, checked and topped the oil, got the grease gun and made the rounds, then started up the tractor and moved it to where the mower was waiting. She'd checked the mower the day before. All the blades were new, it was greased, it was set to go, but she checked it again just to be sure, because the knot was forming in her stomach. Not a bad one, she thought. It was the other one, the feel-good one, nothing at all to do with the fact the leritine was working and so was the codeine, the hammering awful pain was fading, her low back actually felt fine, just fine, as long as she didn't have to bend. She mostly hunkered now, when her leg allowed it. Bending over was painful, and the mobility was pretty well gone. In the good old days she could bend over effortlessly and put the palms of her hands on the floor. After a few falls, after a few tosses, she could bend over and touch her fingertips to the floor. Now she was lucky to get her fingers down to her knees. Her physician told her that was because her back was fusing itself. The disks were frapped, bone was rubbing on bone, and as it repaired itself the vertebrae were growing together, stiffening. Eventually she'd have no bend left in her. Oh my, keep a stiff spine, my dear.

She hooked up the mower, checked the connection, then drove the tractor forward, bringing the mower out from under the lean-to roof. She drove as far as the gate to the first field before she turned off the tractor, got out, and rechecked the connection. Tickety-boo.

"Okay, girls, let's go. Come on. Come with Luce. Yup, gonna close the gate on you today. Oh, don't you bother pouting. Come on over here, I don't care which one, someone get over here to the mounting block. Good girl, dead horse, damn good girl."

Lucy could no longer vault up onto the back of a horse, not even a short one. But she had a glorious mounting block. Jimboh had made it for her. It was like a little set of steps with a platform on top for her to stand on, but the glory of it was the way he'd carved it. She supposed there were people who would pay big money for it if they knew about it. Or send someone to swipe it for them.

Jimboh. Crazier than a shithouse rat, that boy, but good-hearted, loving and talented. So he sometimes walked around talking to himself. Lots of people sat around watching talk shows on TV. Who was stupider?

The thoroughbred moved to the mounting block. She stood still and quiet while Lucy got herself on, then stepped off smoothly. Lucy tucked her cane under her arm, rode bareback, balanced easily. The others followed the lead mare, the buckskin even daring to trot on ahead, her tail up and plumed out behind her.

"Yeah, well, you can get away with it when I'm up on her back, she's not going to kick the shit out of you with me up here, but don't get too cute when I'm gone because you're years and pounds away from being able to displace her, cheeky bugger."

She checked their water in the big old clawfoot bathtub she'd scrounged from the dump. The things people chuck away! There was a company in Vancouver could redo old bathtubs. For $150 she could have this old beauty restored, then sell it to an antique dealer for a thousand, easy. And if she ever needed a thousand, she would. You could get plastic tubs, complete with automatic water level systems, $225 plus tax at Valley Food and Farm. Figure it out for yourself, $225 plus $150 and she'd still have more than $600 profit. But the tub looked good in the field, it fit what Deb's son called the ambiance of the place.

And thank God for small mercies, he was back in Vancouver doing his thing at the stock exchange, whatever that was. What exactly *does* a stockbroker do? And why? As far as Lucy was concerned the only kind of stock that mattered was the kind she had. The other was just paper. Not worth what it had cost before it got all the rah rah printed on it.

The tub was full, the water was clean, there was plenty of grass. The girls would be fine. Lucy had known before she rode over that they would be fine, but checking doesn't hurt. She pulled their gate shut, wrapped the chain around the post and clicked it shut. The dead horse put her head over the gate and made soft sounds with her leathery lips.

"You'll be fine, my dear," Lucy assured her. "You'll be just fine and you know it. You've got the tree island to go to if it gets hot or buggy, you've got all the fresh water a girl could want and you *know* I'll be back for a while this afternoon with carrots. If you want to go ahead and have that baby, you just go ahead and do it, you know how. I'll keep an eye out for you. Promise."

She used her cane to stump herself over to the stile and into the adjoining pasture, where the cows were lying around, or standing, all chewing cud. They said if you saw all the cows lying down at the same time, it was going to rain. Well, they weren't *all* lying down. Not that she believed what They said.

The tub was fine, the salt lick was fine, and for that matter the cows were fine. But it doesn't hurt to check. She went back by way of the stile and limped her way to the barn, to check the calves.

Deb wasn't too happy about the calves. Sometimes Lucy wondered what Deb thought a farm was.

"For crying out loud," Deb had protested. "There's enough work staring you in the face already, and our own calves haven't all arrived. When they do, you'll have even more work. The last thing you need is to go off to a damn auction and come back with a whack of week-olds!"

"They were as good as giving them away, free-gratis. Here, look." She pulled the crumpled envelope from her hip pocket. "I've got it all figured out, see? Even buying milk replacement, and costing in the price of the calves and even the cost of the gas and all to get down there...which really doesn't belong in there because I was going down anyway, to see the bone cruncher. Even so, up to and including my meals, at the lowest beef price we've got in the past ten years, which I don't think we'll be getting next year, see, it makes real good dollars and cents sense."

"Never mind the dollars and cents, it makes no sense alongside the wear and tear on your back and my nerves!"

"It'll be fine, you'll see."

"I love the way you never talk things over with me! Just here it is, adjust yourself!"

"How could I talk it over with you? You weren't there to talk it over with! You and your boy were doing the art gallery thing, remember? I didn't have time to hunt you up, sit you down, discuss it all, and then get back in time to bid on them! It was do it, and do it inside the next five minutes, or do without."

"You've always got an answer, don't you?"

"Oh, are we supposed to have a fight about this? Okay, but can you reschedule it until after supper? I'm kind of busy right now."

"One of these days I'll slap your face," Deb warned.

"You do and I'll help you pack your stuff." Lucy had turned and stumped off, leaning heavily on her cane. "In fact," she had called back without turning, "don't bother with the slap. I'll help you pack anytime at all."

The calves were fine. They blatted and bawled when they heard her coming. She laughed and called to them. "Hey, babies, how are the good ones? Huh? All the good ones, all the nice ones, oh, such good babies..." She went to the feed bin, supposed to be rat proof, and maybe even was, but don't bet the farm on it. The damn things can get into anything, given a bit of time. She scooped a plastic bucket of milk replacement powder from the bag, took it to the first of several tubs with rubber nipples at the bottom and dumped in the powder. Then she turned on the hose and sprayed a hard stream of water onto the powder while she mixed it with her cane. The calves pressed close, too close for comfort, so she stopped stirring and poked a couple of them with the stick. They backed away and the others followed. "That's better. You buggers keep shoving like that and the damn wall's apt to come down. You weigh more every day, you know."

She looked into the second tub, then went for another bucket of milk replacer. By the time all six tubs had been filled, the bottom of her cane was caked with white. She grabbed a handful of hay from a manger and rubbed the wet coating off the aluminum. She had wooden canes, half a dozen of them, all made by Jimboh, each one carved and turned and fashioned into a work of art. But for barning around she used the aluminum one, not just because it was lighter but because she wouldn't feel glum if she dropped it and it got stood on by a ton of something. If she chipped or scratched or gouged one of Jimboh's canes, she'd feel as bad as if she'd run over a kitten.

The first calves had finished and were moving hopefully toward the trough. They were the biggest, the heaviest and the strongest, and they got first go at the nipples because they could push and shove and bull their way more effectively. The joeys, the little ones, the ones who actually needed more, were always the last to get it.

She poured calf starter into the trough. The fat-layered prime ones snuffled in the ground grain, tongues licking, attention focussed hard on the feed. Some of them were so fat they had creases up their shoulders and necks, and their fur was so shiny a person would think they'd been brushed and fussed like show stock. When the troughs were full and the bigger calves were pushing and shoving at the grain, Lucy got another bucket of milk replacement and went back to the first tub. It was almost empty, the joeys sucking desperately. Poor little christless things, not a chance, unless a person paid attention. She mixed them a good strong dose and moved on to the second tub, just to be sure there was more than enough for the runts.

She didn't have to go in the calf-eteria with the animals. She could move along the divider wall filling tubs and troughs, pass all the way to the back door that opened out into the calf field and never have to run the risk of being pushed, shoved, bumped or bull-charged by the increasingly rambunctious steers. Once in the field, she'd be on her own, but she had to check the grass. A whack of calves like that could chew their way through an amazing amount of it.

It was looking chewed down. They only had a couple of days left, at most, in that field. But they'd be fine for today. She'd bring a good load of fresh-cut uncured hay grass and dump it over the fence—that'd keep them busy. Then tonight, when they came into the barn for their feed, she'd close them in, separate the fat ones and move them into the other side of the barn, let them into a new field with knee-high grass. They didn't need the milk replacer the way the little joeys did. They'd do good on grass, beef maker and plenty of water. She could sprinkle milk replacement in with the beef maker and they'd turn it to milk when they drank their water. Keep the joeys where they were, there'd be plenty of green grass from the haying, give them a chance to catch up a bit.

She moved from the field to the barn, then through the barn to the arena, the front yard of the barn. She picked up her thermos and took it with her to the hay wagon, sat down and rolled herself a cigarette. This was one of the best times of any day, the first of the chores done, everything under control and the way it should be, and her with cigarette and coffee.

She lit her smoke, looked around the place contentedly. It would do, it would do just fine. She filled the thermos lid, sipped, and nodded in satisfaction. She had some pink pills in the little watch pocket of her jeans and she took one, washing it down with coffee. Maybe she should take a good look at those fancy little scooters, or whatever they were called. From what she'd seen, you had your choice of three-wheeled or four. Four would probably be better—three might be too tippy on rough ground. She wasn't sure the stock would adapt to it very easily. It wouldn't be any help at all to have calves freaking out. The dumb buggers had to learn respect for fences. They were predisposed to and perfectly capable of just charging through, never mind that they would hurt themselves. They set their sights on something and headed for it, damn the torpedoes, here we go, closer to stupid than anything else she could think of. Farm fencing or barbed wire, it didn't matter—they'd run through it.

"Hey, you." Deb opened the gate and moved toward the hay wagon, a tray in her hands.

"Hey yourself. I didn't even hear you coming."

"You know me, old creep-in-the-night, tippy-toe herself. Could I interest you in some fresh-from-the-oven biscuits? With red currant jelly and cream cheese?"

"Twist my rubber arm."

"Maybe a touch of fruit salad?"

"Oh, just a touch."

Lucy stubbed out her cigarette and sighed deeply. "Ah, this will do."

"How many pills do you have floating around inside you?" Deb asked. "I see the machinery is all lined up and ready to go. And at least two of your pill bottles carry that warning about driving or operating heavy machinery."

"Nag nag nag," Lucy said easily. "I'm fine. It's an easy day. Just basic dosage." It was an out-and-out lie but she would have believed it herself if she'd been on the receiving end. "One of each is all. I've got a spare in my watch pocket in case I need it later on, but it doesn't feel as if I will. Not yet, anyway. Of course, that could change."

"Yeah."

"You don't believe me?"

"I didn't say that. I was just agreeing with you, it could change in a minute."

Lucy let it drop. "You make a fine biscuit, Deb."

"I do," Debbie agreed. "Have some cheddar. Have a hard-boiled egg."

"You've peeled them and everything. I feel really pampered and spoiled."

"You *are* spoiled. Spoiled rotten. You're so spoiled you don't even know all the ways it happens. If you're going to be out roarsy-roarsy on that red bastard machine, then best you have a belly full of protein to counteract the drugs you've taken."

"Hey—"

"Don't bother. You think I can't see the pupils of your eyes?" Deb's own eyes were shiny and wet. "I know what you think. Nag nag nag, for no reason but I'm a nag. You don't have any idea how it feels to me to see you limping, or see you with your face the same colour as your white tee shirt, or see you standing at the sink drinking water as if it's all that's going to save your life, and sweat dripping from your face. Okay, so you manage. Big fucking deal, Lucy! You'd be better off right now if instead of getting ready to fire up a tractor, you were settling yourself into a nice lawn chair, with a big umbrella for shade and a good book."

"All's I'd manage to do that way," Lucy said, calmly doctoring up another biscuit, "is drive myself to the loony bin. I can't live like that."

"How do you know? You've never tried!"

"I know." Lucy ate half a hard-boiled egg, sipped coffee, then finished the egg. "I haven't tried because I can tell what it would do to me. I don't want to fight with you about it. When the time comes that I can't manage, well, I'll learn a new way of living. But right now I can still manage, and if you don't use what you've got, you'll lose it, and I do *not* want to volunteer to be a crip one day sooner than I have to."

"Ah, Lucy..."

"Deb..."

"Right. I've got fresh coffee here."

"Gladly. I've got thermos coffee. It's only about," she checked her watch, "two and a half, three hours old. Mere youngster."

"You ready to tell me the truth about how much drugs you've taken?"

"I told you, Debbie. Maintenance dose only. I have to stay on top of the pain. If I don't keep it tamped down, it gets to the place where the only way I can get rid of it is to dose up until I'm zonked."

"You know, if you could figure out a way to spread that, you wouldn't have to pay good money for chemical fertilizer in the springtime. You could just start up your rationalizing and heifer dusting and the grass would grow like hell."

"Boy, what a trusting person you are."

"Yeah, I am. I'm going to trust in God that you don't manage to drive over yourself or flip the whole riggins or take it through the fence and into the ditch and cut both legs off with the mower."

"I think maybe it's time for me to—"

"Eat your breakfast, I've said all I'm going to say about it."

"For today, or just for right now?'

"Wait and find out. Want that last egg?"

"That'll make three. What about cholesterol and all that scary stuff?"

Lucy took the egg, bit it, then spread a bit of margarine on the bitten-off end. "Amazing how they hold the heat, eh?" She watched the margarine melting. "You'd think they'd be cold by now."

"And you say you're not ripped?" but Deb was laughing.

"No, I mean it. Must have something to do with density or something. I mean the biscuits have cooled."

"Yes, dear."

"I really like hard-boiled yolk with marg or butter on it. And pepper." She sprinkled some on and took another bite. "I think the average egg requires four bites. You can do it with three but that's piggy."

"One of each, huh?"

"Can you kind of keep a half an eye on the dead horse for me? She was due the day before yesterday. I thought about putting her in the small field by herself, but you know how she gets. When she's split off from the others, she just trots back and forth and back and forth along the fence line until she has herself all sweated up. If you notice her going off by herself or chasing the others away, could you maybe hit the pickup horn? I can usually hear that."

"Don't worry about her. She'll be fine. I'll let you know if she lies down and starts to get herself busy. More coffee?"

"No thank you. But thank you." Lucy leaned over, kissed Deb on the cheek. "I really do appreciate what you do."

"I know you do." Deb pushed Lucy's shoulder gently. "Oh, go on with you, I can feel impatience coming off you like waves at the beach."

Lucy didn't need to be told twice. She lowered herself from the hay wagon, moved to the gate, opened it wide, then climbed on the tractor. She had a bracket just the right size to hold her cane and she clicked it in place, then started the engine. She looked over at Deb, grinning and waving. Deb nodded, but didn't smile. She was packing everything back onto the tray. Lucy put the tractor in gear and drove through the gate, into the smaller field.

She lined herself up and lowered the mower. Before she started, she looked at Deb, who was halfway to the house, carrying the tray, but looking over her shoulder, worrying. Lucy waved and Deb nodded.

Jimmy had sat with the mounting block between his knees, his borrowed hat tipped forward to shade his eyes. He'd carve for a while, then turn his attention to the photo albums, looking at pictures of Lucy with this horse, Lucy with that one, Lucy young, Lucy not so young, Lucy middle-aged, Lucy with a foal, with a yearling, with a two-year-old, Lucy getting ready to climb into the saddle for the first time. Lucy grinning widely at the end of the first session, the young animal slick with nervous sweat, but having started no big bucking competition.

Then he would get up, walk around, maybe get himself a cold beer or a Sprite, smoke a cigarette or two, go into the house for a pee and finally settle himself again. Pick up his knife or his chisel, and he'd be back at work, so focussed on what he was doing that you could go over and talk to him and all he'd do is grunt, acknowledging your presence but not hearing what you said. Not listening to anything but what was going on in his head.

And one by one, they reappeared, all those faithful creatures, one after the other. Sometimes they were in groups, sometimes alone, sometimes just the head, other times the entire animal, maybe bucking or rearing. He even had old Dice digging, bent almost to the point he couldn't help but fall, cutting a cow from the herd. And the manes blowing in the wind, the tails floating, one after the other until there was no place except the stair risers that wasn't home to her memory herd. He might well be crazier'n a coot, but if being crazy was what allowed him to turn raw wood into a horse herd of her favourite creatures, she'd opt for crazy any day.

And weren't they all a few bricks short a load? And wasn't she just about twice as nuts as any of them? And what did it matter anyway? What she had ahead of her today was cutting hay. Acres of hay. Damn near miles of it.

Savannah took the last load of wash to the line and pegged it in place. There were three clotheslines leading to the one pole, at least the size of a telephone or hydro pole, and set in concrete. Jimmy had put it up for Gran, and there was no way anyone was going to live long enough to see it go the way the old one had. Full line of wash, nice blowy day, everything promising, and then—not even a crack or a snap, just over it went, dumping the sheets and towels into the garden. All the old biddy could do was sigh. "Oh goodness gracious me," she had said. "Now the chance to do it all over again. Thank you so much, God." It hadn't been much of a clothesline pole, not compared to its replacement. The old biddy's long-dead spouse had put it up, which, she said, was as good as guaranteeing it would come over, most likely at the least convenient time.

She hadn't talked much about him, and Lucy hardly ever mentioned him. But Lucy hardly ever mentioned anything. She was like Kitty that way. Or Kitty was like her, whichever however.

Savannah, now, she enjoyed a good natter, and, thank heaven, so did Seely when she was feeling okay. Right now Seely wasn't feeling well at all. In anyone else, a person might say something like nervous breakdown or grieving crisis, but with Seel, best you just say she wasn't feeling well. If she overheard anything that suggested nervous breakdown she'd really have one, pitching fits, tossing accusations, telling off everyone in a three-day ride.

Terrible thing. All she did was lie in bed and cry. Sure, she had lots to cry about. It had been a rough row, same as everyone else's. But in other ways it hadn't been all that bad. She'd had plenty of time before the incident to wallow in being pampered. She could go over at lunchtime, or after school, and sit in the room in the basement where she had everything she'd ever want or need. Crayons, felts, water paints, oils, you name it and the Graingers made sure it was there for her. Jimboh, now, nobody cut him any breaks. He'd had to scrounge, steal and barter for what he wanted and needed. Nobody painted a room especially for him, nobody provided him with a table and two chairs and a sound system and some tapes, nobody made sure he had the kind of light he needed. No, Jimboh had a wooden chair in the basement and his first worktable had been an old door set on sawhorses. His light hung from an extension cord run like a ruptured gut from the plug near the back door. Was he lying around sobbing and howling?

Okay, so it was awful what happened to Grainger, but nobody else could be blamed for that. And it was awful how Sandra had got so sick, some weird thing, peripheral neuropathy they had called it. What does that tell you? And yes, Seely had taken the brunt of both Sandra's illness and Grainger's dumb-tit move. Well, each and every one of them had had to take the brunt of something.

Mind you, those bloody girls weren't making it any easier. Wah wah wah. We want to go to the French school, we don't want to have to go to the other one, wah wah, we always went to French school, why do we have to change. Well, the goddamn truth of the matter is, dear hearts, the French school only goes to grade six, and after that, everybody has to go to public school. It's a conspiracy to upset you personally. But, whine whine, it shouldn't be like that, why can't we go to the private one?

Money, that's why. Maybe the dentists, doctors and lawyers can afford to send their precious pups to the private French school, but the rest of us just have to make do. You'd think they were the daughters of the ultra-swank the way they naturally assumed that any little craving that flitted over their shallow minds would fall into their greedy little mitts, just because they blinked a tear or two.

But Seely would have to do more than lie in bed and sob if she wanted to change them. Kids don't get that way all by themselves. Seel said that she'd given in time after time just to keep things quiet and peaceful, because Sandra got so upset if the girls started to yowl. They could laugh and holler and shout and bounce on the furniture and make all kinds of noise and it didn't bother Sandra, but let the whining start and she'd as good as flip out. So, Seel said, she'd given them their own way as much as possible just to keep the peace.

Jimmy was working on the woodshed. Just a few days could make one hell of a difference to a place. Or maybe in the back of his unbalanced mind Jimmy'd had a plan from the time he first built the shed. In any event, all his blocks and chunks of wood were moved, the inside of the place had been swept and vacuumed a half dozen times, the pink fibreglass insulation was in place and the walls nearly done, and he had the stuff for the floor stacked under the roof of his outdoor work shed. He said three more days and it would be ready, two bedrooms and a living room. Actually he hadn't said living room, he'd said loafing barn, but she knew what he meant.

She'd told him she'd cough up the TV set for them. She wasn't gaffing them a VCR, though, they could damn well set their sights lower, or else learn to be bearable enough that the others would welcome them to watch videos with them.

Seely was going to stay in the house with Jimboh—she was well set up in what had been Gran's bedroom. But she wasn't the problem. And the rules were laid out plain and clear, written out on paper and signed by all concerned. Rule number one: This is Jimmy's house. Rule number two: Don't piss Jimmy off. Rule number three: No whining, bitching, yowling, grizzling or snivelling. Rule number four: Do the chores or hit the road.

Lizzie seemed to have absorbed the message pretty well. Every now and again you could see her get all set to go on about something, then take a deep breath and swallow it. The other one, though—well, there was something about that kid that made you wonder about axe murderers and how they get started.

Savannah pushed the line as far as it would go, then put a clothespin on the pulley wheel to keep it from sliding back toward the house. God, just look at the amount of it. Oh, well, what else did you have planned to do today? The Governor General's ball isn't scheduled for this week.

Bobby came lurching and stumbling out of the house, dragging his bright purple foam snake behind him.

"We're goin' swimmin'!" he told her. "You wanna come?"

"Swimmin'? Who said you could go swimmin'? Did anybody ask *me* if you could go swimmin'? What if I turn into a great big grouch and say no?"

"You won't." He dropped the foam snake and hugged her leg. "Carol says she's not coming. She says she'd rather have a fit."

"She's never far from one anyway. Okay, I'll catch up to you. I've got some stuff I have to do. You don't go in the water by yourself, you wait until the other kids are there."

"Vic's going to teach me."

"Yeah? Well, there's something else you're going to learn before you head off across the damn field too. Come here and get the floater vest."

"I don' wanna."

"Did I ask you if you wanted? I said come and get it. And if you don't wear it, I'll send you back to the house."

"Why do I have to?"

"Why? Little boy, you have no idea how much work I've put into getting you where you are. You have no idea how much time I've got invested in you. And you will never know how much I love you!" She picked him up, sat him on her hip and took him back into the house. "So if you don't mind, I don't want you drowning on me. Or getting washed down the creek, into the river, and off to the ocean. I want my Bobby-boy here, with us, laughing and smiling and stuffing his face with cantaloupe. Please?"

"Okay."

The rest of the crew came trailing to the back door. The twins had their floater tubes, stupid plastic things that fit around their waists, supposedly as safe as floater vests. Savannah doubted it. She had never allowed her kids to bugger with them. A proper inner tube, sure, but not these things.

"So, you got everything?"

"We're only taking a coupla towels." Elaine held out the string bag. "I'm in charge of towels. Vic has the cooler jug. We've got grape drink in it, with ice cubes. Alan's got the sunblock and the Band-Aids, Bobby's in charge of his own snake, and that's all we'll need."

"You sure? I thought maybe a popsicle would make the trip through the field a lot easier."

"Would so," Caroline grinned.

"Now you take it careful with that silly thing," Savannah scolded. "I mean it, Brandon, you know how I feel about it."

"I'm careful. See? Victor put a Band-Aid over the stopper."

"The Band-Aid will come off as soon as the thing gets wet. You too, Brit, and don't bother giving me that sideways look or I'll box your ears for you."

"I'll be careful," Brittany said agreeably. "They're just toys, anyway. And besides, Vic's teaching us to swim."

"Jesus, Vic, you're busy teaching. The twins, Bobby... what do you have in mind to teach *me?*"

"To mind your business, Momma." He kissed her cheek. "You coming up later? It's always more fun when you're there."

"Flarch flarch flarch. Of course I will, love. I just have to finish in the laundry room and get dinner started and I'll be up there. For the love of God don't let Bobby drown before I get there."

"What, you want to be there? To watch?"

"She loves me," Bobby said placidly, heading out the back door. He stooped, bums-up, to get his purple snake. "She don' wan' me to drownded."

"God, Bob, what you do to the language!" Elaine said. "It's enough to make a person think you flew in from somewhere else with Bindi."

"I don' like Bindi," he replied, heading off dragging his snake.

"You be careful, now," Savannah warned. "Line up, smooch time."

One by one she kissed them, patted their butts and warned them to be careful, and one by one they hugged her, returned the kiss, promised to be careful, then went after Bobby.

She watched them go, smiling and leaning against the door jamb. Vic hollered at Jimboh, who waved but made no move to join the caravan. Lizzie came barrelling out of the house, wearing her bathing suit and a pair of cheap rubber sandals. No sign of a towel or anything to drink, oh no, depend on the others. Darlene appeared at the door but made no move to join the other kids. Well, she'd been in a strange mood ever since she showed up again. Probably feeling kind of stupid, if the truth be known. Off she goes, out the friggin' window, no less, gonna show the whole wide world just how little she needs any part of them, and two days later she's back, looking like she hasn't slept a wink. Nobody asked for an explanation—nobody even mentioned she'd been gone. That must have griped her. She'd made the big move, the ultimate gesture of defiance, and it passed through the world without making a ripple. Well, kiddo, learn now. It's easier than learning later.

Savannah closed the screen door and went back to the laundry room to finish the cleanup. Rinse the machine, rinse the tubs, open the windows to dissipate the damp air, maybe even sweep the floor, then get the roast in the oven. How many cows a year could these kids munch up, anyway?

You had to give the kid credit, though. At least she'd tried to do it her own way. And to be honest, she'd actually done a lot better than Savannah had when she hit the pike. Circumstances had been different—Savannah didn't have a house in town waiting for her, with food in the freezer and all, and she'd been a bit older, what, two years, three? Not much older, though. She'd hoofed it off and wound up in the motel with the three wise men. At least Darlene hadn't jumped into *that* pot of boiling oil!

The things we do when we're full of ourselves. Speaking of which, where, pray tell, was Carol? And what, pray tell, did she do to justify her goddamn existence? Savannah did all the cooking, and all the laundry, and the kids did the dishes. Okay, the dishwashing machine did them, but you still had to load the bugger and the kids did that. They cleaned off the table and counters, they did the vacuuming, they helped fold laundry, what in Christ's name did Carol do around the place? And where in hell *was* she?

"Hey, Carol!" Savannah yelled.

She had the roast seasoned and in the oven and the salad fixings picked from the garden and rinsed before Carol showed up, hair damp from her shower.

"You yelling for me?" she asked, sounding uninterested.

"Wondered where you were. I'm going up to the creek to keep an eye on the kids. You coming?"

"No, I'm going to drive into the city," Carol said casually. "I'm all packed and everything, all's I have to do is get myself dressed and I'm off."

"The city?"

"Yeah. I thought I'd go check the place out." Carol grinned. "You seem content to live up a back road as pure and untouched as the average nun, but it's not my style and I'm not interested in making it my style. I'm going to stay with a friend of mine, from the good old days, as they say, and check out the night life."

"If Larry finds out—"

"Fuck Larry." Now Carol's voice was bored. "Anyway, he won't care. If he'd been going to care he'd have spoken up when I told him I wasn't going to get married. But he didn't say word one, so..."

There were a lot of things Savannah wanted to say but she didn't say any of them. The last thing she wanted to do was tangle with Carol. Still, it picked her that there hadn't been any discussion about it, not even a Hey, would you mind watching my kids for me. Just assume, presume, fail to give a damn. Carol had changed in the past couple of months, and changed a lot. Maybe it was only to be expected. She wouldn't talk about what had happened, about why the one that had been on its way, wasn't. Was it a miscarriage or an abortion? Savannah had asked her and Carol had snapped, "I don't want to talk about it, okay?" And that was the end of that. Anyway, whatever the reason why she'd gotten so proddy, maybe a week or so in the city getting laid as often as possible would put her in a better mood.

Savannah herself didn't care if she never had another woody poking inside her as long as she lived. Sometimes, when she thought of Lucy and Debbie, or Kitty and Christie, she wondered what that was like. But she wasn't interested enough to find out. Maybe it was the Prozac did that to you, turned you into the invisible woman from waist to knee. And she'd been on the stuff for more than a year, now. At first she had gone through a kind of mental puzzling about it, but now, except for the odd time when something forced her to think about it, she didn't even waste energy on the subject.

She went to her room, changed into her bathing suit, grabbed one of the long-sleeved long-tailed men's shirts she'd picked up at the thrift store, and headed for the creek and the swimming hole. If Carol wanted to drive herself to the city, she could damn well go ahead and do it. She didn't need Savannah to wave bye-bye. Besides, if anyone was going to teach Bobby how to swim, it was going to be his mom, not his big brother.

Good God, how had she overlooked it all, the time spinning past, pretty much out of control. Jesus aitch, Savannah, the big brother is *big*. How could it happen? He was her Victor, her winner, her baby—her passion, if the truth be known. You love them all, but there is something special about the first, no two ways about it. She was not yet fifteen when he was born. It had seemed like a good age to be at the time. Now it seemed she'd been a bloody baby herself.

Savannah left the house before Carol had herself ready to head off to the bright lights.

"Hey, Jim." She stood in the doorway of what had been the woodshed and watched him working. "Time for you to take a break, okay? You've been here since four-thirty this morning. Your brains'll dribble out your ears pretty soon. Come up to the creek with us. I've got roast in the oven, you're having supper with us."

"I have half an hour's more work before I can take a break," he said calmly. "But I'm going to take one. I'll show up, I promise. With a half dozen cold beer, and you'd better be prepared to drink a couple of them or I won't swallow a single bite of dead steer."

When she turned to leave, she saw Darlene the pill ducking back from the doorway to the house. "Hey, Dar." Savannah made her voice relaxed and pleasant. "I'm going up to make sure Bobby doesn't drown, or anyone else. It'd be nice if you came up too. You could make sure your fat, grey-haired slob of an aunt doesn't collapse on the trail."

"Fat." Darlene flew out of Jimmy's kitchen like a shot. "Sure, Auntie. I hope I get fat like that."

"We'll all pray for you, Darly," Jimboh called from the woodshed. "Want to take a boo at your domain before you head up?"

The kid hesitated. Savannah could remember how it felt to be convinced that the entire world thought you were an idiot and a low-life to boot. She swung her arm over Dar's shoulder. "Wait'll you see what he's done. I mean, really, this is extreme. It's far too good for a couple of headaches like you two, believe me."

Darlene moved slowly to the doorway and looked inside. The expression on her face didn't change, but she stared, her head moving slowly as she took in the interior of the building that could no longer be called a woodshed.

"Come on in," Jimboh invited her. "Give you the grand tour." He dropped his hammer into the loop on his leather tool belt and held his hand out to her. She took it, and Savannah noticed Darlene had gnawed her nails to the quick and even beyond. Some of them had bled and they all looked sore. "Bedroom at either end, see? Same size, same layout, this one's got a view past Savannah's place up to the bush, the other one's view is down the field to the bush. Big closet in each one. Built-in dresser drawers too.

Built-in bed, with more drawers underneath. I built it kind of backwards, see, the head goes here. That way you can have shelves at the other end, where your feet are. I like shelves by the bed, myself, but Jesus I hate sitting up in a hurry and banging my head on 'em. Besides, this way you can look out the winda, see? I say *you* because whichever you choose it'll be the same."

"Wow," the brat breathed.

"You think so?"

Obviously she did think so. In the movies, Darlene would look up at Jimboh and her eyes would fill with tears. Wordlessly, he would enfold her in a gentle hug, and the music would start. Soft classical guitar music, slow and easy at first, then faster and faster, more intricate, and then the kid would say, Oh, Uncle Jim, I am *so* sorry, and he'd say something wise like, We all have to find our way in life, and all of us make a few detours. Then they'd hug, and life would go on forever and ever with never another clash of wills, never another quarrel. Yeah, right.

Darlene's mood was much improved on the way up to the swimming hole. No wonder, Savannah thought sourly, she's just seen a place the royal friggin' family would envy. Probably lording it over everyone in her head, thinking up nasty things to say to the other kids, nyah nyah, you just got a bedroom, I've got something special. If she does, I'll whack her, so help me God I will.

Bobby was wearing his floater vest, kicking his legs mightily and flailing his arms in his own version of overstroke. The purple snake lay on the bank, ignored and smeared with dirt. The twins were stubbornly trying to master the intricacies of dog paddle, their silly plastic floaty-hoops farther up the bank than the snake, one of them already deflated and looking pathetic. Brit saw Savannah first. She stood up in chest-deep water and waved, then walked out, breathing hard. "I see your plastic thingamy bit the dust." Savannah sat on the grass, suddenly feeling relaxed and lazy. It happened every time. All she had to do was come to the swimming hole and the world became softer.

"That's Brandon's. Mine's still okay. His ripped."

"How'd that happen?"

"He cannonballed it and the seam gave out."

"What's the water like?"

"It's kinda cold at first but then it's nice. You comin' in?"

"In a bit."

She could smell the roses Jimboh had planted, and something else, she wasn't sure what. Something sweetish and heavy, a bit like what she remembered as honeysuckle, but not exactly.

Lizzie was splashing Elaine, and Darlene swam over to get in the fun and went too far right off the bat. She tried to dunk Elaine's head. Elaine hollered and Caroline dunked Darlene. Lizzie splashed Caroline, and the water war was on, but everyone was laughing and grinning, and Savannah could only hope the dunking would draw a line for Darlene, let her know that when you go too far there are sibs on hand to help.

Jason was floating on his back, watching the sky. Funny little fellow, that one. Curly curly hair, with a reddish tint to it—you'd think he was Savannah's little guy, not Carol's. Skin much paler than any of the other kids, and light-coloured greyish eyes sometimes. No, more than sometimes. Savannah had wondered about him, and about Carol, and felt disloyal about doubting that he was from any one of the three wise men. Looked more like something you'd get as a door prize at a St. Patrick's day dance.

She yawned, then got up and walked into the water. Vic waved and grinned. No doubt in anyone's mind about where or how she'd got him! If you let his hair grow, took him back to the old country and put him in different clothes, he'd have fit right in. She cracked jokes about how she hadn't made much of an impression on him, and other jokes like what do you expect, they were all three of them in on it, what chance did any of my chromosomes have, outnumbered three to one?

Jimboh was being the human diving board when Savannah pulled on her over-large shirt and ambled back down to the house. She put on a huge pot of spuds, made a vegetarian rice curry and put the salad together. She took two dozen garlic buns out of the freezer and put them in the oven to thaw and warm, then put the roast on a big platter and began to make gravy in the roasting pan. Her damp swimsuit was itching her backside, so she made the time to grab a quick shower, then change into shorts and a cool cotton top.

The rest of the crowd arrived back in time to tidy up, sit down and start packing away the food. She overlooked the several damp bums on her chairs, and ignored the fact that Bobby's hands were not exactly spotless. He looked as if he'd been making sand castles, except there wasn't any sand at the swimming hole, just dirt.

"Momma," Victor winked, "do you have any idea how *pale* you look?"

"Me? Do I look pail when hit by a bucket?"

"You look like a ghost," Vic teased. "Uncle Jimboh has a tan, so he looks normal, and even Dar and Liz look, well, maybe a bit faded, but not like you."

"Hey, you will never know, being as how you're who you are, but I'll tell you something. When a person is white, a person is completely white. And anyway, I do so have a tan."

"Nope." Vic shook his head and poured more gravy on his second helping of potatoes.

"Look." She stood up, lifted her shirt, put her arm against her belly. "Now *that* is white."

"Oh, she *is*," Elaine gaped. "Look how white her tummy is!"

"See?" Savannah sat down again. "We will hear no more about Momma being as white as a ghost because Momma does so have a tan."

"Uncle Jimmy said we had to ask you if it would be okay for him to tell us what it was like in the olden days, when you guys were kids," Alan blurted.

Savannah looked at Jimboh. He was watching her, and she couldn't tell whether he was hoping she'd say no and save him the memories, or whether he wanted her to say yes so he could off-load some of the burden.

"We asked him—well, I asked him," Alan continued, "what the swimming hole was like when he was a boy, and he said there weren't any roses or benches, and no bridge, and no dive-off place, but that you all had fun, anyway. So I asked what you were like, you know, when you were my age, and that's when he said we had to ask you. He said some people don't like to have their history shared."

"What's history?" Bobby asked.

"History is, well, it's like the time when we were all kids, living in the big old house that isn't here any more because it got burned down."

"How come?"

"It was easier to burn the bugger than to try to clean it up," Jimboh said, and the kids all laughed, thinking he was joking.

"And we had rats in the house." Savannah grinned at Jimmy. "And your Uncle Jim decided he'd had it with rats."

Jimmy started to laugh. He put down his knife and fork, he pushed his chair back from the table, his face creased in a dozen ways and he just let it roll. The kids had never before heard Jimboh climb into his own laughter, and they started laughing too.

"Oh, Jesus," Jim managed. "And Kit-Cat with the damn softball bat."

"She wasn't the only one swinging a bat," Savannah agreed. Her own laughter started to bubble. "And then your mom," and she looked at Lizzie, "who was, at the time, probably the same age Darlene is now, found Patsy-Ratsy and would *not* let Jimboh kill her too."

"Them rats out behind my place are the umpteenth generation of grand-rats from Patsy-Ratsy."

"What you do with those rats is gross," Elaine said calmly. "You think we don't know about the snakes and owls and hawks and stuff?"

"So poison them," Jimboh shrugged. "Next thing you know Seely will be down your neck like a jug of cold water, shrieking about how they're the children of her dear Patsy."

"She will," Lizzie agreed. "She's kind of dippy about that."

"Has anyone ever seen, like, a real ghost?" Darlene said quietly.

Jimboh looked at her, his laughter cut off suddenly. "You mean, like a Casper kind? A bedsheet floating or something?"

"No, I mean . . ." She swallowed several times. "Oh, like maybe a skull thing or a kind of an ugly face thing."

"I'll let you come into my hell hole with me tonight," he said softly, "and you can see some of the masks I've done."

"Have you? Seen a ghost I mean?"

"Yeah, I see 'em all the time." He picked up his fork and turned his attention to his supper. "It's no big deal."

"Do you see them?" Darlene asked Savannah.

"Me? No. Nor hear voices, neither."

"I only see what's here," Alan decided. "What I can go over and touch."

"Yeah, right," Elaine sneered. "I can just see you going over to touch a cloud. Oh, we'll say, there goes Alan again, up to the sky to touch clouds. Oh, don't bother waiting supper for Alan, he's gone up to touch the rainbow. Alan? He can't do the dishes, Mom, he's gone up into mid-air to touch a seagull."

"You know what I mean." Alan pulled his meanest face. "You just like to nag."

"If the nattering doesn't stop I'm going to get into it myself," Savannah warned.

"Oh, *no!*" Vic yelled, jumping up from the table and backing away, hands raised in defence. "No, Mom, please, not that! You guys stop it! Oh, no, not Mom getting into it."

Savannah was off her chair and after him in a flash. "I'll get you, Victor!" she hollered.

Elaine cracked up laughing, Brit started clapping and Jimboh stared, his fork halfway to his mouth, salad dropping back to the plate.

"Jesus Christ," he managed. "I'm sure as hell not taking this bunch to any restaurant for supper."

"Let's get Uncle Jimmy," Bobby suggested. "We could hold him down on the floor and tickle him until he peed."

Jimmy and Savannah sat on the back porch watching the sunset and sipping cold beer while the kids did cleanup in the kitchen.

"You're sure you won't mind if I tell them some of what it was like?"

"I don't mind, Jimboh. We made it through. Might do them good to learn that what they've got is about fifteen rungs up the ladder from what we had. God, sometimes—well, all the time, really, if I remember any of that shit, I can't really believe it. I mean, I *know* it happened, all of it, and probably a lot more that I can't remember, but... it's like watching a movie. Like yeah, it happened, but it must have happened to different people because we're not... you know?"

"Yeah. It's like we all had the flu at the same time, a fever or something." He sounded very sad. "I just wish I wasn't crazy. I'd like to be not crazy."

"No you wouldn't." She slapped his knee gently. "You wouldn't have the first clue how to behave. Neither would I."

Darlene looked at the masks on the shelves, without speaking or glancing at anything else in the room. Her attention was fixed on the faces, the fright faces, the spook faces, the horror faces, the baleful, malevolent and sometimes benign faces. After several long minutes, she nodded. Not a word, just a nod, and she turned to leave.

Jimboh took her by the arm, not a firm grip but a mere suggestion. He walked her to the big old stuffed chair that in earlier days had belonged to Gran. He sat down in it, pulled Darlene into his lap and gave her a gentle nudge so that she lay with her head against his chest, his chin on top of her head. Neither one of them spoke. It took an hour for the stiffness to drain from her body. In that hour her eyes went from one ugly-face mask to another, and several shudders wracked her body. When she finally let go of her fear and her pain, when she sighed and sagged against him, her breathing eased and her fists relaxed, Jimboh nodded, his chin rubbing her head.

"Get easy with them, sweetheart," he said softly. "It took me years and years and more scars than make any sense." He held up his arm so she could see the tracework of fine white lines. "And finally, just after the old biddy died, I stopped fighting them. They can't help how they look. None of us can. I mean, if I'd had a choice, do you think I'd look the way I do?" He was rewarded with a little twitch at the corner of her mouth. "Not me, I'd be tall, and slender, with big broad shoulders and a chest on me like Arnie, and I'd have blond curly hair and big blue eyes, and I wouldn't have a plain old name like Jim. I'd have one of those movie star names."

"Is my momma crazy?" Darlene dared.

"Sweetheart, this entire family, from Savannah and me down to you and Lizzie and even Bobby and Victoria, is crazy as hell. Your mother is actually one of the least crazy of the bunch."

"I don't want to be crazy."

"I don't want to be crazy, either, but I am. The trick to it is to set yourself a goal. When I figured out people would actually pay money for my carvings, I decided I'd be a carver, a wood-turner, the best one I could be. Because then, you see, they aren't allowed to say 'crazy.' They have to say eccentric, or colourful, or enigmatic, or some other big word that sounds nice. And as soon as they quit saying 'crazy' . . . you aren't."

"What?"

"Crazy is like a reflection in a mirror, and other people are the mirror. If the mirror says you're crazy, you are. But as soon as the mirror starts saying you're—oh, spiritually philosophical or something—you aren't crazy any more."

"That's nuts."

"Sure it is. Pretty much everything is nuts."

They stood up and he led the way to the door. He stepped aside to let Darlene walk through to the basement, then turned off the light, closed the door and locked it. Then he followed the kid up the stairs to the kitchen.

Seely was sitting at the table eating a sandwich that looked as if it had been taken away from Dagwood in the funny papers.

"I thought you were supposed to stay out of the cellar," she frowned.

"I was with her," Jimmy said quietly. "We were bonding, like they say in the magazines."

"Bonding?"

"Yeah. Right, kid?"

"Correct, my dear James," Darlene answered.

"How'd we wind up with such a smart ass at such an early age?" he asked, shaking his head in mock puzzlement.

"I don't know," Seely sighed. "She's all of eleven and getting to be more of a smart ass with each passing day."

"Why'd you have me?" Darlene asked.

Seely put down her sandwich, swallowed and took a drink of milk. "I had you because I loved you."

"You didn't even know me!"

"I didn't have to know you. I loved you, anyway."

"Before you even saw me?"

"Before you were even started. Before I was even pregnant. I've loved you since I was old enough to understand where babies came from and how they got there. I've loved you since before I was as old as you are now." She smiled. "I still do, and I will until the day I die, and maybe even after that."

Jimmy left the kitchen and went back out to what had been the woodshed. Seely picked up her sandwich again. Darlene went to the stove, put the kettle on to boil and got the teapot and tea bags.

"There's cake," Seely said. "In the fridge. Chocolate, with chocolate icing."

"You're a mind reader, right?"

"I'm a baker is what I am."

Savannah brought in the washing and dumped it on the sofa. She started folding and sorting things into the correct piles. It was hard, though, because there were so many kids, and so many of them the same size. Was the blue-and-white striped tee shirt Brandon's or Alan's? And whose was the white with blue stripes?

"Gimme a hand here," she muttered.

Brit moved to the piles and started picking through them. "That's Bobby's." She put it in the proper pile. "This is mine, not Elaine's."

"I should get everything the same colour and everything in three sizes: small, medium, large. Then I could just heap it all in the middle of the floor, sit in the big chair and watch while you fight over it."

"I'll take the other end of the sheet," Elaine offered.

"I'll carry some stuff to the bedrooms," Jason decided. "Here, give me Bobby and Brandon's stuff. How come Bobby goes through so many shirts? I bet he's got twice as many as anyone else."

"He's having the same trouble you had when you were his age. He knows what's supposed to go in his mouth, he just can't always get it there without smearing it all over everything else first. You had one tee shirt we kept just for spaghetti suppers. The front of it, my God. You wouldn't believe a kid could spill so much sauce."

"I've still got that shirt," Jason grinned. "It's on my teddy bear."

"What a sook," Caroline teased. "Big lump like you with a teddy bear."

"Yeah, and you with all those damn doll babies."

"Don't swear," Savannah warned. "It sounds like hell and it makes the fuckin' neighbours mad."

three

BY THE LAST EVENING OF THE STAMPEDE, the bounty on Decision had grown to fifteen thousand dollars. Decision stood in his corral, primed for the contest and looking like it. He'd done this often enough, seen the routine often enough he knew the difference between an evening when he was going to compete and an evening when all he had to do was eat, drink and snooze. He knew the difference between the excitement of packing up and moving on, and that of please-the-crowd time.

His coat was sleek, shining in the glare of the lights. He paced and shook his head, so agitated Kitty didn't dare go in to brush him. There was no sign of a limp, no sign of a hitch in his git-along, and hadn't been for the duration of the stampede. Time and again he'd gone out, both afternoon and evening competitions, and each bull rider who drew him walked a bit taller and looked just a bit more determined, not just because they had a chance to win the bounty but because they, by God, could say they had ridden the white-faced black bastard. And all of them had gone into the dust.

Kitty dug in her pocket for some of the treat biscuits the bull liked so much. She moved to his feed trough, trickled in the flat squares. "Hey, guy," she crooned, "here's some fast energy for you. Come see what Kit's got for you, that's a good boy. Here, calm yourself a bit, take it easy. You'll have yourself so worked up you'll be worn out before they move you to the chute. Attaboy. Know who's got you tonight? Well, I'll tell you, old fart, you've got the guy who so far has the highest aggregate score for all-round cowboy, you're up against the cream of the crop. I've got a ten-dollar bet on you. I don't think the guy is good enough. I don't think anybody is good enough. I know I'm sure as hell not. And never was. And wouldn't ever have been, even if I hadn't got racked up. Here, have a few more. Yeah, I'm kissing your shite-encrusted arse, because I have to be out there at the same time you are, and I want you to know that the one with the orange hair and

Aunt Sue's straw hat with the wooden cherries on it is the one who treats you good. If you're going to stomp someone, pick one of the others, okay?"

The JimmySpook lay along Decision's back, his head supported by his bony hand, his elbow resting on the hump of muscle on the bull's front shoulders.

"And I thought you were hurt," she mocked herself. "You've been out more than any other bull, and not a sign of a problem. What was it, you had a charley horse or something? And just lying around worked it out? Here, this is the last of them. Look at you, slobber-and-drool, slobber-and-drool."

Slowly and carefully she reached through the bars of the corral and patted the huge, flat forehead. Decision looked straight at her. He reached out his great raspy tongue and wrapped it around her wrist, then licked his mouth. The tip of his tongue was exactly the same shape as his nostrils, so he could reach up and dislodge grass seed, chaff and dust. He rumbled, farted repeatedly, then burped.

"Easy there," Kitty teased, "They'll mistake you for an airedale. The experts have figured out that cows burping and farting are a big part of the ozone layer problem."

She heard the announcer's voice through the loudspeakers. Sometimes she wished she could wear earplugs. The voice was loud and the words were distorted, but she didn't dare plug her ears because the reaction of the crowd was part of her own warning system.

She moved toward the ring, found a place on the rail fence and checked the laces on her sneakers. She'd paid a hundred and seventy-five dollars, plus tax, for her shoes. She'd have preferred to wear her rider's boots, but nobody could do that. You didn't need to stumble on your own heel, or twist your ankle, or slip. You needed your feet, and you needed to know where they were and what they were doing. You had to be able to dodge and dart, and slide and roll if necessary.

"God *damn!*" Merv leaned on the rail fence beside her. "You can *feel* the crowd tonight." He grinned, tense and eager. "But I have to tell you, I'm not going to sit in the dirt and weep when this is over. It's been just a tad much. Not too much, mind you, but much."

"Stock looks good," she agreed. "The old man really babies them and it pays off. They're in prime shape."

"There's a saddle bronc mare he's taking off the circuit after tonight. She's about seven months pregnant and starting to show, and you know how he is about that."

"Yeah. He say where he was sending her?"

"Not to me he didn't. Well, here we go, darlin'." He stuck out his hand, she took it and they shook hands, smiling and nodding. "You watch my ass, I'll watch yours."

"Deal."

"You know, I didn't like the idea of workin' with a woman," he said, "but you're okay, Kit. You do your job, and you do it well."

"Thanks, Merv. Appreciate it."

Old man Farnsworth paced back and forth, back and forth, chewing on his toothpick and watching the action. His dream was that before he packed it in and retired or died, there would be a night when each and every one of his bulls threw the rider, each and every horse took its victory jog around the ring, the rider limping, slapping the dust from his backside, glaring at the animal that had snatched the prize money from his hands.

But with the calibre of riders these days, he probably wouldn't see that dream come true. They could talk all they wanted of how good this one or that one was, the hard-boned truth was that the good ones today had nothing at all to feel worried about. They could go up against the best of yesterday's champions and not look shabby. Some said it was because the gear was better, but the gear won't keep you up there if you can't ride.

Time and again, bull after bull the clowns went out there, sweat pouring from their faces and smearing their silly makeup. Kitty felt as if she'd done a whole month's worth of work in one night. But it felt good.

And then it was Decision's turn. Last bull of the night. The announcer's voice echoed and vibrated, reminding the crowd of the bounty, reciting the bull's record, bragging about the skill of the rider. The tension and excitement crackled so that you could almost see it, like blue sparks flying from the stands and the chutes, coming off everyone in the place, even old man Farnsworth, chewing on his toothpick.

The JimmySpook sat on Decision's rump, behind the rider. He wore a battered, shapeless old grey hat pushed back on his head, and he was leering and laughing. Kitty checked her shoelaces. She hitched up her pants and wiped her palms on her legs.

The gate swung open and Decision came out bucking and kicking. The longest five seconds of anybody's life dragged on while the crowd leapt to its feet screaming and the old man spat his toothpick to the dirt. It looked as if the bounty was going to get paid out after all, and then Decision went high in the air, twisting his body, rolling his belly, flailing his hind legs, and when he landed, his right front leg crumpled, he hit the dirt, rolled once, and was on his feet immediately, still bucking and kicking.

The gasp from the crowd was like a thunderclap. The rider lay in the dirt, his legs twitching. Decision whirled, head down, and charged. Kitty moved quickly, pulling off her straw hat and slapping it in Decision's face. The bull ignored her and raced forward, his huge forehead slamming into the downed rider. All three clowns were moving and the exit gate was open. Two riders thundered in from the side gates, their ropes swinging. Decision kicked, the bull rope fell, the clang clang clang of the bell stopped. Head up, limping noticeably, Decision made one charge around the ring, then went through the exit gate as if he had always intended to do just that.

The first aid attendants arrived with a stretcher. The JimmySpook sat on the top rail of the fence, watching, chewing a toothpick, no sign of glee. Kitty looked at the blood in the dirt. For one terrifying flash she was again hung up, caught in the hole, and hearing her wrist bones snap as the heavily muscled shoulder came toward her face in slow motion.

When she got to Decision's corral pen he was standing on three legs, favouring his right front. Dried blood, not his own, was dabbed on his white face in a patch about the size of someone's hand. He was still breathing hard and still slobbering in fury. As he shook his head, the slobber flew in long strings. A photographer sidled up to the fence, raised a camera before anyone could stop him, and snapped. The flash went off and Decision whirled awkwardly.

Kitty grabbed the photographer and shoved him back from the fence.

"Hey!" he snarled. "Careful with the camera!"

"Keep back," she said coldly, "or you'll need surgery to get the damn thing out of your face."

"You threatening me?"

"No, mister, I'm saving your life," she said. "That metal fence has an electric charge in it that could drop most any bull on his arse, but this isn't most any. He's mad, and if your flash pisses him off he'll go right for you, through that fence and any other that gets in his way. You want a picture, don't use a flash."

"Careful with the camera," he repeated sullenly.

She shrugged and walked over to old man Farnsworth, who was standing watching the incident with the photographer. He had a fresh toothpick in his mouth but he wasn't chewing it.

"Sometimes you wish you could just..." He sighed. "I wonder if they go to school to learn how to be that stupid?"

"I think they get the idea the media is Everything, and they're part of it, so that makes them Everything too."

The photographer fiddled with his other camera, then moved closer to the bull pen. Decision was sweating heavily, his hide gleaming and damp. He rumbled, opened his mouth and mooed angrily. Kitty couldn't stop the grin.

"He's got the same kind of voice the rapist boxer has," she said. "You expect this great huge beller and out comes a high-pitched squeak."

"Yeah, they say it's because he's got so much muscle that it presses on his voice box," the old man agreed. "Someone told me those weightlifters have the same problem."

"He's still in a total fury."

"He is. Had to turn on the electrical. Turned it right up. He charges it and it'll fry his ass. Just hope it knocks him out too."

"How's the rider?"

"Funeral in four days," the old man sighed. "I like to see my stock win, but what happened tonight makes me sick."

"Can't blame the animal."

"No blame anywhere. Just makes me feel sick anyway."

"He's some racked up, doesn't want to put any weight at all on that leg."

"He took one hell of a fall. Looked to me like it just gave out and down he went. Of course, they're going to say he got it hurt because he deliberately smashed up a cowboy. They'll call him killer and so on."

"Deadly Decision," Kitty guessed. "The Devil's Darling."

"You write that stuff for them?"

"I think I'm glad I'm not driving stock truck tonight," she sighed. "Poor old bugger."

"Oh, I'm not loading him tonight. It'd just make him even angrier than he is. Just leave him in his pen. Give him lots of time to calm down. Wish I knew how to get some butazole into him. Maybe if we could do something about the pain in that shoulder he'd stop being so snuffy."

Kitty and the old man mixed the bute with beefmaker feed and rolled it into little balls, which they dipped in molasses and dropped into Decision's feed trough. He limped over when he saw Kitty putting treats in his dish, mooed his squeaky noise and shook his head, snuffling and snorting, still upset. But he licked up the balls, one at a time, and if he detected the bute it didn't keep him from wanting more grain, more molasses.

"There you go, old guy. Give it about ten minutes, you'll feel way better."

He wanted more. He snuffed in his trough, his big tongue licking the sticky sweet residue. Kitty dropped in half a dozen treat biscuits, then went to change out of her clown costume and help load the stock trucks.

As soon as the late-night news announcer started talking about the stampede, Lucy turned on the video recorder. She was collecting snips and snippets of rodeo footage that showed the clowns at work, and she always knew which of the three fast-moving blurs was her Kit. But tonight, when the news was over, Lucy rewound the tape and played it, again and again, in a state of shock. Kit-Cat must have had the hand of God on her. She had practically climbed right up that animal's face. It could have turned her into mush.

"They did as much as anyone could," Lucy said softly.

"It's barbaric," Debbie snapped. "I can't stand it!"

"What?"

Debbie was glaring, past anger to something else. "I guess now you'll play that thing until the tape is worn through. Every time I come into the living room you'll be watching some poor slob get slaughtered. Unless it's a boxing match and *two* poor slobs are getting slaughtered. Or pounded into senility."

"Must be bedtime," Lucy decided. She got out of her chair stiffly, using her cane. The hours on the tractor had her as stiff as a varnished plank. When she walked, her leg dragged and her toe scuffed along the floor.

"Look at you!" Debbie raged. "Just look at the mess of you! And you can take your rap about use-it-or-lose-it and shove it sideways up your nose because this is something else. If all you wanted to do was use it, you could go to the complex and swim, you could sit in the swirl pool, you could take yoga or tai chi or go to a physio. But oh, no. Not you."

Lucy stumped her way to the kitchen and got her nighttime Trazadone. The pills were small and pink, and they were supposed to inspire the brain to produce more of the body's own natural pain suppressor. Her joke was that she was all in favour of anything that would inspire the brain. Usually she took two but tonight she took three. About ten, maybe fifteen minutes after she took them, she became so sleepy she could have slept through a tidal wave. The downside was that she couldn't remember her dreams. She wasn't even sure she'd had dreams.

"Don't you dare walk away from me when I'm talking to you!" Deb shouted.

Lucy ignored her. She went to her bedroom, sat on the edge of her bed and began to peel off her clothes. As always, the shoes were the hardest part. In the house she wore sneakers, and she kept them laced and tied so that all she had to do was slide in her feet. Most nights all she had to do to get them off was hook the heel of one against the toe of the other and push. On bad nights it wasn't that easy. She couldn't lift the toe of her left foot to push off the right sneaker, and she couldn't angle the left foot so the right foot could do what she wanted it to.

She hooked the ankle of her left leg with her cane, pulled the leg back until the knee bent, then kept pulling until she could reach down and push off the shoe. The sock followed. She'd tried a bootjack, but all it did was bugger her balance so she lurched sideways and came up against the wall. Awkward as this method was, it was easier. Safer too—if she toppled, she'd land on her own bed. The way things were going, she figured she'd soon be sleeping with her shoes on.

"Are you going to discuss this with me?" Deb stood in the doorway, white-faced with fury.

"Discuss," said Lucy. "I didn't know this was a discussion. I thought it was that other thing, where you yell and holler and tell me I'm all kinds of an asshole and then, when you feel sufficiently unloaded, you stomp off to your bedroom and ignore me."

"Ah, I see. Lucy the Snot has arrived. Lucy the human scab, the one who parades her limp, her hitch, her lurch, as if it was something to be proud of, the one who is just oh *so* above it all. I'm trying to make you hear me! I'm trying to make you hear that I cannot stand watching what you're doing to yourself! You got up on that goddamn torture rack before ten this morning and you were up there until eight at night! And no lunch. Oh no, not Lucy, she says it'll just make her sleepy if she eats. Hour after hour and nothing by way of nourishment, just jug after jug after jug of iced tea. And when you do finally come in, your face is the colour of a fresh-picked beet, your fingers are swollen, for God's sake, you've sweated so much you have salt crystals down the back of your shirt, and the first thing you do is head for the drugs. Oh, let's see, what will I have instead of sup-per? How about two of these and one of those, and yes, one of these ones, I think, I'm feeling a bit of a need and God forbid I go into withdrawal and have to admit I'm hooked, like an addict on Skid Row. Yum yum, and when I'm well and truly zonked, perhaps a spoonful of potato salad, a slice of cold roast beef with a tad of horseradish, and perhaps even a tomato.

There, that's better. I've got some food in my stomach and I can feel all the drugs working. Let's just park ourselves in the chair in time for the late news. Goody goody, look, here's some poor son of a bitch being turned into the very dust and dirt on which he's lying! And there, for a brief moment, there's our very own flesh and blood, in drag no less, out there doing her thing for the crowd, walking into the teeth of death itself. No, not walking—running, full-tilt boogie, another in the goddamn suicidal family."

"Excuse me." Lucy pulled off her jeans and tee shirt and dropped them on the floor. She sat in her singlet and underpants, her head buzzing faintly, her mouth thick. She was thirsty enough to drain the river. "Excuse me," she repeated, and limped to the doorway. Deb didn't move. "I need a drink of juice."

"Get into bed you goddamn fool, I'll get the juice!" Deb grabbed Lucy by the arms, spun her around and gave her a slight push. It wasn't much of a push, but right then, off balance, with an unresponsive leg and dosed with pain medication and the pills that inspire the brain, Lucy lost her balance. She pitched forward, and her left leg twisted and gave out so that she slid sideways. On her way to the floor she slammed her forehead against the edge of her own bed.

"Oh, *shit!*" Deb screamed. "*Now* look what you've done."

Deb ran for a towel and Lucy held it against her split forehead, smelling her own blood and not caring. She got herself off the floor and pulled herself one-armed to the bed, holding the towel with her other hand. Somehow she got herself in bed and sat almost upright, propped by her pillows, waiting for the blood to thicken, slow and eventually stop. Deb, white-faced and oozing guilt, rushed in with a big glass of cold soft apple cider.

"Thank you," Lucy said politely. She drank the juice, then leaned back against the pillows, her hand dropping away from the towel and falling to her lap. She closed her eyes, yawned, and the pain in her leg washed away, like grass seed dropped on the surface of a slow-moving stream, drifting away quietly, slowly, until there wasn't any left in sight.

She felt Deb washing the blood from her face, but she didn't care. It didn't matter. She wouldn't die. It was just a split, three inches long at the most. It probably wouldn't even leave a scar, and if it did, it would be just another line on her face. She'd had worse. She'd had worse before she was old enough to go to school.

And now little Lucy was back in her bedroom. It wasn't finished yet, so she must be in—what, grade two? Seven years old. The old fart came back from driving the babysitter home and Lucy heard the sound of the icebox door, then the hissing sound as the cap came off the beer bottle. She heard him talking, heard Momma answer, her voice soft and young, with the sound of laughter trapped in it. Lucy snugged into her pillow and time became an accordion, opening, closing...

And then Momma was sobbing. Jesus, Jesus, what have I done? I've done nothing! Why are you doing this? And the sounds, slapping sounds, punching sounds, sounds of a body slamming into the wall. She could hear her brother yelling. He was older, he was bigger, he'd stop it.

Momma screamed and the window smashed, and then Lucy was out of bed and racing from the room, heading for the door, heading for the safety of the darkness outside, and the old bastard was in her way, drunk past the point of madness. He saw Lucy, his big hand swung, and she didn't even feel it connect.

When she came out of the fog she was in the hospital. Her brother was in the bed next to her. He was asleep and he had bandages everywhere—his hands, his arms, his face. He had a long tube coming out of his arm.

"Momma!" little Lucy called.

"Sssshhh, darling," a voice said. Soft voice, woman voice. But not Momma. "I want my momma."

"She'll be here soon, dear. Until she gets here, you've got me. My name is Jocelyn, and I've got some orange juice for you. There's a girl. I'll lift your head, and you just suck on the straw, that's it."

"My head hurts."

"Sure it does. I'll just push this button...hear the ding down the hall? No? You didn't hear it? Okay, tell you what, you push the button and at the same time as you push, stretch your ear out that door and down the hall, like a big bunny ear...did you hear it?"

"No."

"Tsk tsk, you must have people ears and not bunny ears. Okay, here we go. I'm going to lift you up a bit, get a pillow under you. Ah, see, here comes my very good friend Evelyn. People make jokes about that, Jocelyn and Evelyn, sounds like the start of a nursery rhyme. Jocelyn and Evelyn went to town, one foot up and the other foot down...okay, Evelyn's going to prick you in the arm. It won't hurt, though. It'll just feel like an annoyance, okay? See? Didn't really hurt at all, did it? The pain in your head will be gone before you can count to fifty."

She tried counting, but she kept losing her place and having to start over again. And then she was waking up and a doctor was shining a light in her eyes. Two policemen stood around her brother's bed, talking to him. Momma sat in a chair beside Lucy's bed. Her face was all swollen and bruised, and she had stitches in her eyebrow.

"I want to go home," Lucy said, the tears spurting.

"Hush," Momma said. "Hush now, Lucy. You can't go home yet. Maybe tomorrow. One more sleep."

But it wasn't tomorrow. It was days later, sleeps later before they went home. And even a longer time before the old fart showed up. When he finally walked in the back door, into the kitchen, Momma just gave him a look, then turned and went into the living room. He followed.

That night he slept on the couch in the living room. But he was home. And they all pretended nothing had happened.

"Lucy!" Deb was trying to get Lucy to answer her.

Lucy would have liked to. She would have liked to say, Just leave me alone, for the love of God, but all she could do was open her eyes and focus them. She could see the doorway, like a picture frame, and Deb outlined almost in the middle. Except Deb was right by the bed, not over at the doorway at all. She had adhesive tape in her hands. Lucy could smell rubbing alcohol and it made her feel as if she wanted some of the real stuff, not just a beer but a good stiff shot of something she hadn't tasted in over twenty years.

"Oh, Lucy," Deb mourned. "What are you doing to us?"

"All's I was doing," Lucy said clearly, "was trying to get a drink of juice. You did the rest."

"I just wanted you to go to bed. You were so blasted you could hardly stand up."

"You have to stop beating up on me," Lucy yawned. "Bad enough when you do it with words, but this business of cracking open my skull has got to stop. The neighbours will be talking." She closed her eyes, sighed, yawned and dove into sleep.

When she wakened, the house was quiet. She was still sitting up, her pillows bunched behind her shoulders, but she was no longer comfortable. She sat upright, swung her legs over the side of the bed and waited to see what kind of getting-up it was going to be. Her head felt fine, no fuzziness, no buzzing, although her forehead reminded her it was there, a small dull ache.

She took her weight on her good leg, slid out of bed, reached for her cane and padded to the bathroom. She peed and washed her hands and face, and then she looked in the mirror. She had dried blood in her hair, more of it in her ear. Damn. She ran a basin of water and soaked her head, rinsing her hair and cleaning her ears and the back of her neck, anywhere blood might have trickled or collected. She drained the basin, brushed her teeth for a long time, rinsed her mouth and reached for the hairbrush and comb.

In the kitchen she got the coffee started, then took her morning medication. Her nose felt stuffy. She hoped she hadn't banged it and made it bleed when she went arse-over-appetite. Poor damn nose had already had more than a lifetime of abuse. The crazy old fart had broken it how many times before she was old enough to pack her stuff and leave. And leaving hadn't protected the nose either. She'd gone off more four-legged stock than most ranches would ever see, but by God didn't she have a collection of belt buckles. Grinning sourly, she went back to the bedroom and started the morning fight with the socks.

Lucy was fussy about her socks. As soon as they started to get the least bit worn, the least bit limp, they went into the garbage. More than a few times Deb had tsk-tsked, fished them out, washed them and took them to the thrift store. Lucy didn't care. She liked them thick and soft and snug. No sags or droops, no worn-out heels or holey toes. She'd been particular about socks since she'd managed to get enough babysitting and weekend job money to buy her own. She preferred white, thick-soled sports socks, but for working around the place she'd take grey or blue—never black, she hated black socks. And not ankle-height, either. They had to come well up her leg so that her boot tops wouldn't rub her skin. Wouldn't even touch it.

On mornings like this, getting the damn sock on the buggered leg was tantamount to organizing the invasion of Normandy. She hooked her cane around her foot again, got her brand-new speckledy grey sock on her foot and made sure there were no creases or lumps to rub her foot raw. She wouldn't feel it if it happened, because she had practically no feeling from the knee down, except for the constant sciatic pain.

Then the jeans. Loose-fitting leg ones, not riding jeans. Easier to get on and off, easier and more comfortable for riding the tractor.

She had her first coffee and cigarette sitting on the back porch in the chair Jimboh had made for her. He'd bought a brand-new naugahyde recliner, then fancied it up a bit with a wide wooden tray bolted into the left arm and two little scoop-outs. One round one, just big enough for her mug, and the other squared off, for her ashtray. He'd carved spirals and loops around the holes, and long-tongued dogs and birds with beaks that went on forever. If she ever went broke, she could unbolt the thing and take it to the nearest art gallery and walk out with five hundred bucks in her pocket. He was a nice guy. She sometimes wished she'd known him better when he was younger, but she hadn't, and you couldn't go back and change anything. She didn't even begin to get to know him until Kitty had been living with her for two, maybe three years.

And then he showed up, pale and thin, his fingers stained with nicotine, his eyes dark-rimmed. "Gran said you said it was okay if I spent some of the summer vacation here," he muttered without looking at her. He was standing at the bus stop beside the highway, looking down at the gravel.

"The biddy always tells the truth," Lucy agreed. "Heave your stuff in the back and climb in. We'll go by the school and get Kit-Cat. She's got three or four days of it, yet."

"I'm Jimmy."

"I know. I'm Lucy. Debbie's back at the house. You'll meet her later."

"It's nice of you to let me come." He swung his shabby backpack into the bed of the truck, then climbed in the front seat, sitting as close to the passenger door as he possibly could.

"Kit-Cat's as excited as a terrier who smells rats," she smiled, trying to charm him. "I bet she hardly slept last night. She misses you."

"Yeah," he nodded. "Me too. Miss her, I mean."

It took a month and a half for him to relax enough to smile at a joke. Originally, the old biddy had suggested he stay a couple of weeks, which seemed a bit much to Lucy. But it was her idea to extend the holiday, and the old woman had been relieved.

"He's a good boy." Her voice through the phone sounded more sad than tired. "He's a very good boy. But haunted."

"It figures. Who wouldn't be?"

He hadn't carved anything that summer. Not even his initials in a tree. In fact it was several years before he began to leave his mark on her life. People looked at her salad bowl and their eyes widened.

"Oh, it's too good to use!" one of Chad's girlfriends had blurted.

"Jimboh said to use it," Debbie answered.

Lucy ignored the remark. She could understand Jimboh's point of view but couldn't understand the other one at all, the one that wanted beautiful and useful things to be put on shelves and dusted.

She fixed herself a second cup of coffee and went into the bathroom to remove the damp gauze from her forehead. Her hands weren't shaking now, and the world looked well in focus.

Deb had made what she called butterfly strips, to hold the edges of the gash together. It really wasn't much of a gash—only about as long as Lucy's thumb. And it hadn't gaped. Or if it had, the butterfly strips had pulled it shut. She dabbed at it with rubbing alcohol, hissing at the sting, then put a squarish Band-Aid over it, not because she was afraid it would bleed but because she didn't need any bits of the field getting in there and festering.

The flesh-coloured patch didn't stand out against her tan the way the gauze and adhesive tape did, so the whole thing was much less dramatic than the white one Deb had put on. As soon as the wound scabbed, she'd be able to leave it to the wind and air.

She took her third cup of coffee to the barn with her. The dead horse came to the fence and whickered. "Oh, you just stop that whining and complaining," Lucy crooned. "Look at how badly treated you are. A bathtub full of water, a field full of grass and someone standing here giving you vitamin treats. Jesus, but life is hard, eh?" The buckskin came over, tossing her head. "Don't you get yourself in a twist," Lucy warned. "You're second fiddle here, and that's the way it is. Here, this is for you. Yes, you're a good girl. What you're good for, I don't know, but there you have it. Blue! Hey, Blue, come on over here, you silly thing, you come in on the other side of the dead horse and that cranky cream-coloured bitch won't be able to run you off. Good girl. Yes, she is, she's a good girl, and as soon as we've got all this hay in the barn you're going to find out what a saddle is for, and you're going to take me for a ride. Good one. Here, you bitch, you watch it, I'm warning you, get back where you belong or I'll tell the dead horse to kick in your block head. Don't you forget, three's a crowd, and you'll be the one to go first."

She did the chores, then went back to the house to fix her thermos. There was still no sign of Deb. She had probably sat up most of the night telling herself off or adding to her list of Lucy's sins. They both knew she had in no way intended to cause the accident, but that wouldn't make any difference to Deb. She'd use her own guilt as a whip to beat herself with. Mind you, she'd also choke before she said she was sorry. Lucy could count the number of times she'd heard that from Deb on the fingers of one hand. And still have fingers left over to scratch her head.

She put some oranges and a grapefruit in a plastic bread bag and put her cigarette case and lighter in her pocket. Then she went to the second field, lowered the mower and started cutting the long grass. Some people brought along portable CDs or tape players and cut hay to the sound of music, but Lucy preferred to provide her own. She couldn't carry a tune in a basket, but out here, with the sound of the engine drowning out any song she might massacre, she could warble to her heart's content. She could also crawl into her own head and try to figure out what had really been going on, all those times when she didn't know what was coming down. Times when she ought to have sucked on her tongue and walked off, instead of jumping into the middle of the confusion and defending whatever part of her was threatened, insulted and/or enraged. Times like that all-too-recent time . . .

She had finished the evening chores and was putzing around, pulling some grass out of the lily bed, struggling yet again with the damn curly dock that would *not* give up and die no matter what she did with it. She had dug it out, pulled it out, cut it back, sprayed it with some stuff they gave her at the nursery, stuff they said would kill any vegetation it touched. "Be very careful with it," the woman warned. All it did was make the dock curl up on itself and sulk. It didn't grow any more, but it produced about eight times as many seeds as usual, and it was already one of the seediest weeds on earth. She sprayed it and sprayed it again, and it curled some more and went red, but it didn't die. Finally she cut it off at ground level and squirted the vaunted killer product into the hollow of the stem, hoping to poison the roots. Not a month later the dock was sending up new shoots. They were pale, they were sickly, they were spindly, but there they were. She cut them off and sprayed the stubs again.

So when she noticed that the blackberry bushes were invading an area out behind the old shed, she had gone to get the killer herbicide. There wasn't enough left to kill anything. And the dock was growing again. She had gone out to the barn where Deb was.

"Have you got anything that will kill blackberries?" she asked. "A spray or something?"

"I don't have *time!*" Deb yelled. "I've got too much to do! You know I'm busy!"

Lucy ought to have dropped it right then and there and walked away. But no. "What the fuck is the matter with you? All I asked was if you had anything."

"Why are you talking to me like that?"

"Aren't you the one just bit my fucking head off?"

"You don't have any right to talk to me like that!"

"Oh, but you can talk to me any way at all, right? I asked if you had something to spray blackberries. All I needed was a yes or a no. What's all this other shit about, anyway?"

"Leave me alone! Just *leave me alone!* I've got enough to do already, I don't have the time to go around spraying blackberry vines just because you think I should." Deb's hands trembled. She was almost weeping.

"Did you hear what I asked about, or didn't you? Yes you do or no you don't *have* spray. Did I ask you to *spray* blackberries? Take the goddamn hysterics and vent them on someone else, you fucking cunt!"

"I don't have to listen to that kind of—"

"Oh, fuck you! Just *fuck you!* You are the most tiresome twat!" And Lucy finally walked off, so angry she thought she was going to kill something. Something bigger than blackberry vines. She could hear Deb's voice going on behind her but she couldn't make out the words and wouldn't have listened anyway.

They didn't talk about it later. Both of them carefully avoided any mention of it. That pile of cat shit in the living room? Don't mention it. Don't even make out you noticed it. When nobody else is around, you can scoop it up and flush it down the toilet, then wash the floor and open the windows to air out the place, and if anybody asks, What happened to that pile of cat shit in the living room? Just look blank and utterly innocent, and ask, What pile of cat shit?

What had the fight really been about? Lucy would never know why Deb was upset. But maybe, just maybe, she could find out why *she* had gone instantly from a reasonably cheerful mood to rage, to total fury, to the tiresome twat business. As far as Lucy was concerned, there were far too many times when Deb went up like skyrockets over next to nothing and she, Lucy, just backed off and said something neutral, something like, Whoa, I think I'll just go watch the toilet flush, or, Excuse me, I think there's a TV program I need to watch. The intent was to calm things down, but the effect was to make Deb more livid. And there were other times when she held her tongue, said nothing at all, just found something else to do in some other place, out of sight, out of mind. And then out of the blue, no warning, and up *she* went. The worst of those times was when she tried to use calm, detached logic to verbally whip the person she saw as her tormentor.

Lucy wasn't coming any closer to figuring it out. How many times would she have to take the tractor back and forth, back and forth, back and forth, before she began to get some insight? Was she searching for insight, or just replaying the slights and hurts over and over and over again, building up her own case, justifying her own fury, silently castigating not only the person she was angry at, but everyone else in a five-day search?

Well, for crying in the night. If Lucy was so goddamn hard to live with, why was an intelligent person like Deb hanging around? Why, if she was so goddamn smart, hadn't she figured out how to pack her stuff and get it into her car and drive off and live someplace that didn't have a resident asshole in it? All's it would have taken was a yes or a no. And as soon as Lucy had the goddamn hay done and in the goddamn barn, she would go out with a propane tank and the big flame-thrower attachment, and she'd get the goddamn blackberries, just see if she didn't. Even if she had to set the fucking shed on fire. Too bad a person couldn't take a flame-thrower to everything that caught, scratched, gouged and drew blood.

At one in the afternoon she parked the tractor and went into the house to pee and refill her thermos with coffee.

"Are you going to eat anything?" Deb asked.

"I've had four oranges and a grapefruit." Lucy felt as if she was defending herself in some way. "But I think I'll maybe grab a sandwich."

"How's your head?"

"It's fine." She went into the bathroom, got rid of a bladder full of coffee and maybe a bit of fruit juice. She pulled off her singlet, sluiced her body with warmish water, put on more deodorant, then went to her bedroom for a clean, dry shirt.

"Are you wearing sunblock?"

"Yes," Lucy lied.

"You're sure?"

"Jesus, Deb."

"Oh, right, it's Deb's fault. You get skin cancer and see if that's my fault too."

"I promise, if I get skin cancer I'll blame the sun, not you."

"Your sandwich is ready."

"You didn't have to do that." Lucy made sure she smiled. You know what they say, it goes a long way. "Thank you."

"I know I didn't have to do it. I went to the dairy and got a couple of quarts of fresh milk. Maybe you should drink a glass or two."

"Thanks. I think I will." She went to the cupboard and got her pain pills, washed down two of them with water and, as she turned to the table to eat the sandwich, caught the look Deb hadn't meant her to see.

"What?" She pretended innocence.

"What what?" Deb played too.

"You looked like you had something to say to me."

"Whatever gave you that idea? Here, eat. You look about the same colour as that cottage cheese I put on your plate."

Lucy had just seen her own face in the mirror and knew that if she was any colour at all, it was sweaty red.

The sandwich was good. It was, in fact, downright delicious. The cottage cheese was good too, cold and smooth.

"What do you think?" she asked. "In the Bible, what's-his-name sold his inheritance for a mess of pottage. You figure that was cottage cheese or yogurt?"

"Probably cottage cheese."

"Yeah, with chive chopped in it, like this. Might sell my own inheritance. Or just sign it over to you."

"Oh, right. I really need your inheritance. I can hardly handle my own."

When Lucy headed back out to the tractor she had a thermos of fresh coffee and a plastic container of fruit salad with her. She didn't want the fruit salad, but it was easier to carry it to the tractor and store it in the toolbox than it was to debate the question with Deb. And when she opened the toolbox to put in the container, she saw the sandwich from two days ago. When she was back in the field, she unwrapped it and dropped it on the ground. Thanks to the turkey vultures and ravens that had gathered to feast on cut-up snake and exposed baby mice, the sandwich barely had time to settle before it was being pecked at, ripped apart and devoured.

Lucy had the field finished by four. She could have gone into the house, but it was easier to go into the third field and get started on it. She took a pain pill from her watch pocket, washed it down with the last of the thermos coffee, and kept mowing. At five she had to go back to the barn to refill the tank on the tractor, and while she was there she checked the blades on the mower and changed two of them. She felt a bit dizzy, probably like the sensation a sailor has when she steps from the boat to the shore.

Lucy turned on the hose and let it run on her head. The band of her straw hat was dark with sweat and smelled musty. She looked at the sun. Almost five-thirty now. The worst of the heat was gone, she'd be fine with a ball cap. She ran the hose inside her hat, rubbed at the band, rinsed it again, then hung the hat on a nail in the tractor shed. She took the ball cap, an old cotton one, plain blue with no team name, and soaked it before pulling it on and adjusting the bill to shade her eyes.

She wiped the grease from her hands with the piece of what had once been a pyjama top, hosed her shoulders and back again, and drove the tractor back into the field to get as much mowing done as she could before dark. The pain pill she'd taken at four hadn't had much effect, so she took another one and washed it down with warm fruit salad. Now there's a taste-tempting treat, damn near guaranteed to have you puking.

When the pickup horn started blatting, she pretended she couldn't hear it and just kept mowing. After a while Deb took the hint and stopped hitting the horn. Lucy imagined her going back into the house to revise her list of Lucy's sins, and perhaps add to it.

At eight-fifteen the field was finished. Lucy drove the tractor to its shed, topped up the tank, added oil and did her tour with her grease gun. She checked the mower blades and replaced three more. She still had the small field to do, but it could wait until morning.

She took some grain to the horses, gave them their vitamin treats, then headed for the house. The sky was bright with colour, the last of the sun fading. The first evening breeze seemed chill on her sweaty skin, a welcome change from the breeze of the day, not only hot with sunlight but with the heat coming off the tractor engine. She had to turn back and get the plastic container and the plastic zip-lock bag the old sandwich had been in.

By now she was limping heavily. She could both feel the way her foot was dragging, leaving scuff marks in the dust and gravel, and she could even see it. But it had been worse, and at least it wasn't hurting.

She stripped off her sweaty, dirty clothes, wrapped herself in her blue robe and went to the shower. She didn't try to stand under the spray, she sat on the floor letting lukewarm water run over her head, her shoulders, her face. After a while the pounding of her heart slowed and her breathing relaxed. She could see her tan lines. Her butt was the palest, then her legs, and her chest and belly were tanned from when she'd taken off her singlet and stuffed it in the toolbox. Her shoulders, arms and face were dark brown, her hands looked as if they belonged to someone on the reserve.

She struggled to her feet. Foot. She shampooed her hair, then lathered her body and rinsed. The water was distinctly cold now—the hot water tank must be damn near empty. She turned off the taps and stepped from the stall, pulling her robe around her. In her bedroom she sat on the bed with a towel and made sure her legs were good and dry. She checked her bad foot, her numb ankle. No scratches, no cuts, no bruises, no blisters, thank you lord for another good day.

"Your supper's heated up," Deb called, ice dripping from her voice.

"Thank you." Lucy left the bedroom with a determined smile on her face.

"Did you hear the pickup horn?"

"When?"

"When I blew it. For almost fifteen minutes. At suppertime."

"I must have been singing. Just the small field left to do. Oh wow, Deb, scalloped potatoes, my very favourite."

"Yes. I know. With a barbecued steak. Here, let me take your plate into the living room for you, you concentrate on your cane. And salad, I'll bring it in to you in a bowl. What kind of dressing? Ranch? Caesar? Blue cheese?"

"Blue cheese, please. Boy oh boy, do I feel spoiled." She gimped into the living room and settled herself in her chair. Deb handed her the plate of supper and Lucy pretended to be starving. She must have been hungry for real, though, because she could actually taste the scalloped spuds. All too often the codeine blurred her mouth so much, everything tasted pretty much like everything else.

She could taste garlic on the steak too. The dressing on the salad, however, could have been any kind at all. Still, she ate it, every shred, and even managed a small second helping of potatoes. "God, I love scalloped potatoes," she sighed.

"There's rhubarb and berry cake for dessert."

"I couldn't push it down with a tamp-stick."

"At least drink a glass of milk."

"I'll burst, Deb, really I will."

"Oh for Chrissakes, you will not. Here, drink."

What Lucy wanted to do was take the glass and heave it across the living room and down the hallway. Instead, she drank it obediently, as if it were medicine. Tip the glass and start swallowing.

"See?" Deb nagged. "I knew you could drink it."

By ten-thirty the next morning she was hitching the tedder to the tractor. The last field was mowed, the chores done, she was halfway through her thermos of coffee and on her second dose of pain medication.

She took the tedder into the big hayfield and started turning the hay, flipping it so that the stuff on top, curing in the sun, was turned under, and the next layer down was moved to the top and exposed to the sunlight.

Tedding didn't take as long as mowing. She could drive more quickly and didn't have to be as particular about her rows. Twice she stopped the tractor so that she could walk over to the fence line and pee. When her thermos was empty and her mouth was thick and fuzzy, she drove out of the field, parked the tractor in front of the barn and stumped to the house.

No sign of Deb, no note on the table saying where she'd gone, no coffee in the pot. Lucy measured the grounds, added the water, turned on the machine and went to the bathroom. She brushed her teeth and used mouthwash, but the fuzzy, sticky feeling was still there.

The house was quiet, and much cooler than outside. Lucy stretched, and the sore spot in her back spat warning. She went into her bedroom, sat on the bed and used her cane to haul up her foot and remove the boot and sock.

She stood under the shower for a good fifteen minutes, then stepped out and stood by the basin, naked and dripping, peering at her face in the mirror as though she had never seen it before, never seen the reflection of her natural boar-bristle brush, her plastic comb or her soaking wet hair, which she pulled back and tied. She went back to her bedroom and pulled on a long-sleeved cotton shirt, a pair of cotton underpants and her heavy cotton shorts. She put on fresh socks, struggled to get her boot done up, then took her sweaty, soiled work jeans and singlet to the laundry room.

She filled her thermos, filled her cigarette case and made herself two pita sandwiches. Then she headed back to the tractor. She emptied the cat food can ash tray, topped up the fuel tank and headed back out to the fields. There she tedded steadily, drinking coffee and eating her sandwiches. She tasted very little, because her hands smelled of fuel, the air smelled of engine exhaust and her pain medication was working fine. But she ate the sandwiches eagerly, then ate two apples.

Of all the stages of haying, tedding was her favourite. Back and forth, back and forth, up and down the field, brief pause for a fence-line pee, cup of coffee and cigarette, then again, back and forth, sideways, fluffing, turning, curing. She finished the big field and headed into the next one, singing happily. Release me, darling, let me go, I don't love you any more; to live together is a sin, release me and let me love again. You are my sunshine, my only sunshine. I fell into a burning ring of fire. Early evening and the sky was gorgeous. That old master painter from the faraway hills painted the roses and the daffodils.

She stopped the tractor in front of the barn, turned off the engine, grabbed her cane, and headed to the house with her empty thermos.

"Are you going to eat supper?" Deb's voice was low, her expression guarded.

"If I can get in a couple more hours, I'll have the whole thing turned and tedded and I can start raking tomorrow afternoon."

"That doesn't answer my question."

"I'll eat supper later, thanks. Just came in for some coffee."

"Well, one thing about it, no matter how much of the stuff you pour into yourself, you can always take your inspiration pills and be sure you'll sleep."

Lucy ignored the dig and made coffee. While it was dripping, she went to the bathroom for another round of soaking her head, brushing her teeth and washing her hands, arms, face and neck. Her shirt was dirty, smelling of fuel, lubricant and herself. The fronts of her legs were pink, she'd be two-toned tomorrow. Her hair was bleached—there's a limit to how many hours a person can stand to have a hat on her head, and for most of the afternoon she had left her hat in the toolbox so the breeze would cool her face.

She sat down on her bed, did the cane-and-foot trick, stepped out of her shorts and pulled on fresh jeans. The bugs would feast if she went back out in shorts. The little suckers had alarm clocks built into their bodies, ding ding, it's evening, everyone up and at 'em, time to sting, time to bite, time to suck away and leave huge itchy welts on their thin skin. Rah rah team, here we go.

The next time she headed for the house the light was fading. All the edges and corners were softened. She imagined she could hear small bats flitting, feasting on black flies, mosquitoes, moths. Time and again Lucy had looked for bats' nests, or resting places, or wherever they hid themselves. She had seen pictures of bats hanging upside down from barn rafters but never real ones in her own barn. She'd looked, she'd even climbed up on the stacked hay bales to get a closer view, and not one single time had she ever seen a bat at rest. And yet every night they were there, fluttering and feasting. Maybe they didn't live in the barn at all. Maybe they only did that when there weren't any trees for them to hang themselves in and rest. Or maybe she just had a blind spot.

She sat on the chair in the mud room and got her work boots off with her cane. Then she stripped off her damp socks and hung them over the side of the laundry basket. Barefoot she limped into the kitchen and went to the fridge. She got a can of chilled Sprite and took it to the living room, eased herself into her chair and sighed, contentedly.

"You finished?" Deb asked.

"For tonight," Lucy nodded, sipping the cold pop. "Ah, this is good. How was your day?"

"Busy. You ready to eat?"

"Not yet. I have to catch up to myself."

"There's chicken. I made mashed potatoes but they got cold so I turned them into potato salad. I can warm the chicken in the nuke if you want."

"Not right now, love. In a while. Right now I'm just thirsty."

"Lucy, *Jesus!*"

"Deb...listen. I promise you I'm going to eat. Okay? Just give me a few minutes to catch my breath and unwind a bit."

"You're going to get sick if you—"

"I've had a ton of food today. Really. Cross my heart and hope to die. I had salmon salad pita sandwich, I had lettuce-tomato-cheese-and-cold-ham sandwich. I had fruit. I had a big piece of cake, honest, I did. And yes, I'm tired. I could probably sleep on the sharp end of a pin. But I need a bit of time before I eat. I just want to sit here for a few minutes, drink my pop, and relax. Please."

"I'll get it ready for you." Deb was biting her tongue. "I'll just put the plate on the coffee table by your chair, and when you're ready, it'll be there."

"That'd be lovely. Thank you."

Deb hurried into the kitchen.

Lucy's leg was sore. Her foot looked a bit swollen in the instep and the scars were pinked up, not from sun but from inflammation, like rose-coloured snakes. It was definitely a mess. She could use a pain pill, but no. If she took one, she'd eat, then sag, and she didn't want to mix codeine with her inspiration pills.

She put her foot on the little padded stool, leaned back in her chair and drank some more pop. Deb appeared with her plate.

"Holy moley, Batgirl," Lucy laughed. "There's just me, eh? There's enough here for me, Scully, Mulder and one of the aliens."

"Don't tell me it looks good, Lucy. Don't say anything like yum, smells great."

"Aren't you the mistress of understatement! It looks *great*. You heated the chicken, didn't you? And pickled beet slices. Woman, you spoil me, you really do."

"I know I do. What I ought to do is split your head open, but it probably wouldn't register, anyway. How would a nice cup of tea go right now?"

"Like silk. You have some great ideas, if the truth be known."

She still didn't feel hungry, but she started eating, anyway, and she was about halfway through the mountain of food when her hunger caught up to her. The chicken was warm and tender, and with a bit of salt it got even better. The potato salad was rich with hard-boiled egg, and Deb had put horseradish in with the mayonnaise.

But it was the pickled beet slices that clicked on her appetite. Suddenly, out of left field, the taste hit her hunger button and she was so ravenous that her fingers shook and her fork rattled against the plate as she scooped up the food.

"You okay?" Deb blurted.

"I'm great," Lucy grinned. "All of a sudden I'm so hungry I might wind up chewing holes in the plate. Damn, but this is good!"

"Ah, g'wan, you're just buttering me up so I'll pull some outrageous dessert out of the fridge and spoil you even more."

When Lucy went to bed she was so tired she ached. No sooner had she got herself comfortable than she plummeted into sleep so deep that when she wakened in the morning, the bed was barely rumpled.

Savannah didn't miss Carol at all. If anything, life was easier without her. The twins, experts at manipulation and at playing one adult against another, had nobody they could go to for permission to do something Savannah had nixed, and Caroline and Jason dropped their constant nag and natter as soon as they found out it would only bring them a slap on the ass from Savannah or Victor—who told them both, right out, that he was sick and tired of the way they treated each other.

"If you want to rip each other's throats out," he yelled, "go out in the bush and do it, but stop this yammer yammer, the rest of us don't want to hear it."

"Who do you think *you* are?" Jason tried hard to sound tough.

Victor reached out, grabbed Jason's nose, and twisted. "I'm the one is going to rip this right off your goddamn face and push it up your bum," he said, doing his best Clint Eastwood imitation.

"*Mom!*" Jason yelled.

"Give over, Vic. He's got the hint."

Victoria seldom cried. She didn't have to. She had all the kids to hover and she had Seely to fuss, pamper, and croon.

"Did you do that with us?" Lizzie asked.

"Yes, but you wouldn't remember," Seely teased. "You were awful young and awful small at the time."

"You did? Really?"

"And in the very same rocking chair. It was like having the best of all worlds. I was real young, eh, really not much more than a baby myself, and you were better than a doll baby because you were soft. And you smelled so good, and you'd smile at me, or reach out and grab my finger in your teeny-tiny hand. It wasn't as big as a flower, but boy you could hang on."

"Darlene too?"

"She was just old enough to stand up and toddle a bit. I'd sit in this chair and hold you, and either she'd sit on my knee and play with your foot, or she'd stand by the chair and jiggle it."

"Look at her, she's flirting with me."

"She sure is. Hey, Vikki, how's the girl? How'd you like it if Auntie Seely got up out of the chair and Lizzie sat in it? She'd love to hold you. Yes, she would so. And she'd sing to you. She sings way lots better than I do. She sings better than anyone else in the family."

Lizzie sat in the chair and reached for the baby. Vikki crowed and chortled, reached up and grabbed a fistful of Lizzie's hair.

"Oh, yeah?" Lizzie's voice fell into a gentle singsong, the instinctive crooning of mothers with infants. "Going to snatch me bald, are you? Looking for a fight? You gonna pick on poor Lizzie, beat her up real bad? Ah, come on, gimme a break, Vikki, you know there's no way I can win, you know you'll come out ahead. That's better. Here, one finger at a time, let go of the hair, that's a good ba-boo, yes, you can hang onto Lizzie's hand, yes you can. Oh, you just betcha you can."

Seely brought very little by way of furniture. She brought her freezers, she paid a crew to dismantle her ovens and move them to the spot where Jimmy had put his wood when he turned the woodshed into a separate suite for the girls. When the hammering, sawing, pounding and shouting were finished, they would be installed in the new structure being built near the highway. Jimmy would go insane if there were people coming and going, picking and choosing, getting their wedding cakes and anniversary cakes and birthday cakes and loaves of fresh bread from the back door of the house. Basically, Jimmy hated people.

He'd bent over backwards to make things easy for Seely—so far, she figured, that he'd practically dislocated his spine. Sometimes the strain showed, especially in the evenings. He'd be twitchy, and tight around the eyes, and as soon as supper was over he'd just up and disappear.

Seely was pretty sure that most of the time he went to see Audrey, but she couldn't ask and she worried about where else he might go. She didn't question him and he volunteered nothing, and on those occasions when Audrey showed up at the place, she behaved as if everybody knew everything.

"Oh look, the troop has started up to the swimming hole. Let's join up with them!" She had a raft of sandwiches and several dozen banana muffins already made. "You get your pick. Do you want to carry the baby or the snacks?"

"The baby," Lizzie grinned.

"The snacks." Darlene moved to the fridge. "You just get your skinny old self up there."

"Skinny? Old? Hey, come on, I might be...oh, slender...and I might be in the not-too-immediate vicinity of middle age, but let's not go overboard. Do we need a towel?"

"Nah, we'll dry off in the sun, and if you take a towel you know someone will wind up sitting on it and then it'll get all dirty, and for what? They can sit on the grass, can't they?"

The big kids hooted and hollered and jumped from the bank to the deep end of the swimming hole. The little kids stayed in the shallow end, venturing farther than waist-deep only when one of the older kids was willing to stay with them for a while.

"That's it, Bobby! Kick kick kick," Vic chanted. "Now climb the ladder with your arms, that's it, kick kick, stroke stroke."

"If that kid doesn't learn to paddle pretty soon, my brains are going to drain out my ears and make a mess on my shoulders," Savannah sighed. "I don't know if his ass is too heavy, or what, but—" She looked in the snacks bag and grinned. "Ah, banana muffins. Heh heh heh, I knew I'd get lucky if I bought that heap of too-old and starting-to-go-black bananas on the cheap table. We should build a combination cook house and dining room halfway between the two houses. I'll cook the meals if you'll do the desserts."

"And I'll do the eating," Jimmy offered.

"You're going to wind up built like the Michelin tire man," Audrey warned. She was lying on the grass, her oiled skin gleaming. "We'll have to roll you out of bed and bounce you down the steps to your workroom."

"Yeah yeah yeah," he yawned. "Old tub, himself." He sat up sudddenly. "Jason," he yelled. "If I see you doing that again I'm going to reach up your nose and pull your brains out of your head. Can't you have fun without kicking off a fight?"

"What's he doing?"

"Ducking Alan's head under the water."

"Jason!" Savannah called. "You come sit here for a while, see if you can figure out why."

"I was just foolin'," Jason protested.

"Find a game everyone can enjoy. You know Alan can't stand to have his face under the water. Alan, quit crying, okay? Chrissakes, it doesn't bother you to stand in the shower with water running over your face. Get a grip, will you?"

"Why don't we have a dozen of them?" Jimmy asked Audrey. "I mean there's hardly enough of the little scumbags around the place, we could add to the crowd. Maybe get some that like to—oh, I don't know, chew holes in people's legs or something. Fuck, I hate kids."

"If you hate them, why do you want to have a dozen?" Audrey laughed.

"So's I can beat them. I can't beat Savannah's, she'll get jealous. She's greedy, she likes to do all the beating up herself."

"Feel free, Jimboh, do. Beat the crap out of them if you want. It's too hot and I'm too lazy right now."

"What are we going to make for supper?" Seely yawned.

"I thought I'd do a big chicken curry and a pot of rice. The kids love it and it's quick and easy. Well, I mean, the chook has to cook, but you know what I mean."

"Weird food," Jimmy mourned. "Can't we just have some boiled spuds, boiled cabbage and—oh, pork chops or something?"

"You going to peel the spuds? It's hot out. As far as I'm concerned it's either pasta or rice. Unless it's potato salad, or new spuds. All's they need is washed. I'm not standing at a damn sink, peel peel peeling last year's spuds."

"I'll peel the damn spuds," Jimmy said. "And I'll get the cabbage ready too. But I can't make gravy, it always comes out lumpy and it never tastes right. Will you?"

"Yeah, I'll make gravy. Hell, there's nothing easier than making gravy, Jimboh. Why don't you take a lesson?"

"Because then you'd expect me to make it myself. This way you make it for me."

"I'll help with the spuds," Audrey offered. "Are the pork chops thawed?"

"No." Savannah yawned again. "But they're in packages of a dozen per, we can pretend they're a roast and bake 'em in the oven. Unless, of course, Jimboh wants to stroll down there now and put them out to thaw."

"I'm gone." He stood up, dusted off his rump and winked at Audrey "Want to help me thaw some pork chops?" he invited.

"Thought you'd never ask."

Savannah and Seely watched Jimmy and Audrey walk toward the new house. Halfway down the slope, Jimmy reached over and took Audrey's hand.

"Damn, it's nice to see," Seely said softly.

"You know she's a hooker, huh?" Savannah whispered.

"So?"

"Right."

"I was worried for a while," Seely whispered back. "I was sure your friend Carol had her eye on him."

"Yeah. I was worried too."

"When's she coming back?"

"Damn if I know. Haven't heard word one from her since she left."

"She hasn't even phoned her kids?"

"Nope. She's like two people in one skin. When I was packing up to come here she was all sad and bummed out and worried because she wouldn't see the kids very often and rah rah rah. And now?"

"I'm not too fond of her, myself."

"Hell, Seel, you're not too fond of anyone. By you, if it's not family it's a pain in the arse. Amazes me you managed to run your cake business."

"I don't mind people, it's having them around all the time ticks me off. I mean, a customer, eh, they come in, they say what they want, they get it, they leave. It's that other thing—there they are, morning, noon and night."

"You had any offers on the house?"

"Two. It's kind of like a bidding war right now. Well, it's a good buy. House, yard, and look at all the stuff!"

"You shoulda brought more of it here with you."

"Why? You need any of it? I sure as hell don't! We've got Gran's stuff, and Jimmy's got stuff, and—what are you whining and grizzling about?"

"I'm *sorry!*" Jason yelled. "Okay! I'm sorry! Now can I go back in swimming?"

"Watch your mouth, boy," Savannah said softly. "You're pushing the limits."

"Can I? Go back in?"

"Do you think you can go back in and act nicely? I'm sorry, Jace, but I've really had it to the back teeth with all this head-dunking and splashing and stuff. Just watch the other kids and see how they get along and try to copy it, okay? In you go, but you behave, because the next time, it's back to the house."

He nodded. "Yes, Mom."

Three seconds later he was cannonballing into the swimming hole, hitting the water not two feet from Elaine.

Savannah sighed again and shook her head. "The longer she's gone the rattier he gets."

The hay was baled and in the barn, Lucy was caught up on her sleep and Deb had quit worrying about her. And then the weather broke. The sky filled with heavy clouds and rain began to fall, softly at first, then more and more heavily. An hour later Lucy was back out in the fields with the tractor, the fertilizer spreader sending a spray of 18-18-18 pellets evenly across the field. The hardest part of the job was filling the spreader. Every time she had to fertilize the fields, she thought how nice it would be to have two tractors. Then she could get her triple-18 in big bulk packs and use the bucket to load the sprayer canister. Instead she stood there emptying sacks, and it was one of the mysteries of the universe why a fifty-pound sack of grain didn't seem to weigh half as much as a fifty-pound sack of fertilizer. By god, at the end of the day, when the fields were done and the rain was soaking the nourishment into the ground, you knew you'd lifted and poured ten tons—even if you had actually only lifted and poured five tons.

Deb was furious. So furious that she refused to come out and help. "That'll just encourage you," she shouted. "What's the matter with you? Are you so Scotch you can't phone up some big bulky teenagers to do the damn job?"

"They'll all be busy at home. Everybody's out doing the same thing."

"The TV weather said this is going to last three days, maybe five. Do you have to do it all today? You couldn't, for example, wait until tomorrow?"

"It'll be done tomorrow."

Lucy climbed back on the tractor, stored her cane and headed back to the field. Debbie went to the house, yelling something over her shoulder that Lucy didn't catch.

No supper was ready and waiting for her that night. Deb climbed into her car and drove off just as Lucy was parking the tractor. Lucy looked in the oven, looked in the nuke, then went to the freezer and checked. There was a frozen lasagna, but it would take three-quarters of an hour to warm, and there were pizza pops but she detested them. She went to the phone and called the Black Cat café and told them what she wanted. Then she grabbed a quick shower, changed her clothes and drove the five miles to pick up her two works-burgers and her order of jo-jo's. She liked the potato wedges a lot more than she liked the fries at the Black Cat. The wedges were made from real potatoes, whereas the fries started out frozen and ended up tasting like greasy paper towel.

"Anything else?"

"Chocolate bars. Oh Henry and Mr. Big, half a dozen each, please."

She parked the pickup and slogged through the deluge, kicked off her sneakers at the back door and padded sock-foot to the living room. She was back in time for the TV evening news and sat eating her supper, watching the news, feeling herself relax. When she had finished every scrap of supper and washed it down with two big glasses of milk, she showered, took her pain pills and settled back down again to watch some programs.

She was more asleep than awake in her chair when headlights swept across the windows. A horn began honking, then another. Puzzled, she got up, went to the mud room, got a jacket, pushed her feet into her gumboots and headed outside.

"Hey!" Kitty called, waving out the open window of a brand-new pick-up. "You got a spare stall in your barn?"

"Well, Jesus, if I'd known it was you I'd'a come out here with my rifle!" Lucy yelled back. "Yeah, hang on, I'll get the gate."

God knows where, when and how Kitty had got the pickup. Hitched to it was a stock trailer. Christie was driving the old pickup, which was hauling the dipshit trailer they pretended was their home away from home. Christie parked where she was. Plenty of time tomorrow or the next day to get more organized. Kit-Cat backed the stock trailer carefully at the front of the barn, managed to line everything up, then turned off the engine and climbed from the truck.

"Gimme hugs!" she said softly, grabbing Lucy and hanging onto her. "You're lookin' kinda skinny."

"Shut up, you sound like Deb."

"Come see." Kitty's horses looked sleek and well muscled, and the bucking string mare was as quiet and obedient as the riding stock. "She's about seven months," Kitty said, "and the old man won't work them past that."

"What's he expecting as a foal?"

"He doesn't care. He says this is his last year."

"Yeah, we heard."

"That's him in the front compartment."

"That's the killer?"

"Yeah. What have you got for a bull?"

"Don't have a bull right now. Leased one in the springtime, had him with the herd for two months, maybe two and a half. That was enough for me. I've got better things to do with my life than go around fixing goddamn fences."

"Decision won't bother your fences. He grew up surrounded by electricity, he thinks all fences bite you on the ass and the nose. Is it okay to turn him in with the cows or should I keep him locked in a stall for a few days?"

"Move the horses into the right side of the barn, and while you're doing that I'll close the gates on the left side. The cows are all down by the barn anyway, because of the rain. I'll put them in a small pasture space. That'll keep him from wandering around feeling lost in a new place. And give him lots of company of a kind I'm sure he'll welcome . . . that leased bull missed the boat with a good half dozen or so of my Pinzgauers."

"Hi, Aunt Lucy," Noel called from the pickup. "Can I help you?"

"You can help me, but don't bring the dog, okay? She can guard the truck while we're getting things ready."

The kid was out of the pickup in a flash. He ran toward her, his hand stretched out to take hers.

"Look at you," she nagged. "You should have put on gumboots. Your sneakers are soaked already."

"Doesn't matter." He grabbed her hand. "Can we visit with you for days and days? Can we? Kitty says you've got a real farm, with chickens and everything. Do you? Do you got a bunny?"

"No bunnies. Now look, you're wet to the knees."

Within an hour they were drinking tea and starting to sag. Noel was on Kit's knee, more asleep than awake but refusing to be put to bed. Kit didn't push it. How could a guy relax and just bop off to sleep in a bed he'd never seen before, in a room that was totally strange to him, in a house he couldn't see because it was dark outside? He was surrounded by things he didn't know, and he wasn't letting go of Kit. He knew her, the touch of her, the feel and smell and sound of her, and he wasn't about to release his hold on any of it.

"I'll make up the beds in your room and—"

"Maybe tomorrow night," Kitty said. "Tonight I think this toad will sleep better in the trailer, where he's used to things."

"You sure?"

"I'm sure. Plenty of time tomorrow."

"I'll make up a bed for myself," Christie said. "You two can camp out if you want, but the thought of a real live bed—hey, I'm fickle. I can be tempted away with no trouble at all."

"Faithless bitch, eh? Okay fine, I've still got good old faithful Dog."

"Yeah, she's one of the reasons I'm opting for a bed. I can hardly wait to sleep in a bed, in a room with no dog smell."

"You told me that damn flea bag slept in the back of the pickup," Lucy snapped. "Now I hear she's right in the trailer with you? She's a *dog!* They *stink!*"

"Dog doesn't stink. Besides, she keeps the kid's nightmares away."

"Then put *him* out in the pickup too!"

Deb came in the house, already excited. She recognized the trucks, the trailer, knew who she would find when she got to the living room.

"Oh wow!" she smiled widely. "Look who's here! My favourite people. Christie, how are you? You look worn to a nub, you've been driving all day I suppose. Hi, Kit-Cat, you're another looks like what you need is a good bath and a soft bed. I'll go up and make—"

"It's okay, Deb," Christie stopped her. "Two of us are sleeping in the trailer. Noel's feeling a bit out of place right now."

"Oh, poor buh. So have you got a hug for me or are you too tired? It doesn't matter, I'll grab you in the morning, you just see if I don't. I'll have hold of you so fast . . . you won't believe how fast I grab you. How would Auntie Deb's boy like a glass of apple juice and maybe a little bit of muffin?"

"I don't want any muffin, thank you," he said clearly. "I'm not hungry. But I would like some apple juice."

"You be sure to pee afterward." Kitty said softly. "What goes in must come out, right?"

"What goes up must come down," he agreed, grinning. "Inky dinky parlay voo."

He drank his apple juice slowly, then went to the bathroom and managed to pee before falling asleep.

Kitty went in and picked him up, hauled his shorts up over his bum, then pulled off his jeans. "Come on, champ," she crooned. "Head on my shoulder, sit on my hip, here we go, off to bed. Bee eee dee spells bed."

Christie and Deb made up the bed together, and while they were upstairs, Lucy took her trazadone, the inspiration medicine, and got herself into bed.

"How do you feel about a nice hot bath?" Deb asked.

"I might be willing to commit a minor obscenity for the chance," Christie said.

Lucy heard the water running in the tub but it didn't matter. She was sliding down, down into that place where nobody and nothing could tip her over the edge.

At four in the morning she was awake. Her back hurt so badly she felt like putting her head under her pillow and bawling like a three-year-old. She got herself out of bed, got her cane from its place hanging on the doorknob and went into the kitchen to take her pink pills, the ones with codeine.

She could hear the rain slamming and banging on the roof, hitting the aluminum plate where the over-the-stove fan vented. There was a new noise too. Something, she didn't know what, was clittering clittering clattering in the wind. It sounded metallic, but where was it coming from and how big was it? Then she remembered Kitty's trailer, parked in the driveway. Of course, she lectured herself crabbily, *of course*, you idiot. What's wrong with you, anyway, getting the wind up over a sound? You're worse than a damn kid.

No wonder people made those jokes. Must be rain coming, my lumbago is acting up. Oh, it's going to be a three- or four-day storm, my sciatica is raising hell. No, this won't last long, why I've hardly got any trouble with my arthritis at all. No wonder those who had the lumbago or the sciatica or the arthritis were the first to make the jokes. If you didn't laugh, you might start screaming. If Lucy's back was telling the truth right now, this rain would be with them for several days.

Well, it would wash in the fertilizer, best thing that could happen to the field. A person hated to count their chickens before they were hatched, or put hay crop money in the bank before she holds it in her hand. Everything seemed all right now. The first cut would be more than enough for her own stock and the barn was stuffed from front to back, piled ten high along the walls and twelve toward the peak of the roof. And every strand and frond of it dry as a bone and cured to an incredible blue-green colour.

It could change any time, but Lucy wasn't going to bother the goddess with prayers for good luck. Instead she hoped that she wouldn't get served up some bad luck. It went without saying that the second cut was never as big as the first. The grass was finer, less bulky, and hadn't had a long, slow spring to get it started growing. Some years the second yield was a third less than the first. But she had everything she was going to need, and the entire crop—if there was one—could be sold. So, sore back or not, let it rain, St. David, let it pour.

She put on the kettle, stood leaning on her cane until the water boiled, then made herself a pot of tea. There wouldn't be any chance of sleep until the pills kicked in. No sense going back to bed just to lie there in pain.

She took a cup of tea into the living room and arranged herself in her favourite chair. Just like the tin woodman—a drop of rain and you're rusted stiff. The book she was reading lay on the side table with her ashtray and her cigarette makings. She put the box of tubes on her lap, reached for a package of cigarette sticks and started stuffing them, one at a time, into the tubes. The cigarettes went into her Sucrets tins and into her antique silver cigarette case. The Sucrets tins worked better than the cigarette case. Ah, but any old body could have Sucrets tins. How many people had a silver cigarette case, deeply engraved and carved with curlicues, leaves and flowers, and right in the middle a plain circle on which was engraved an intertwined set of letters, so fancy they were almost indecipherable, which meant the case had been a prize at the Silverdale rodeo? Her first real big win. Five hundred dollars and a cigarette case. It was battered now, and the back of it, curved to fit comfortably in a pocket, had a bad dent in it, but it was hers and she loved it.

When both tins and the cigarette case were full, she lit a cigarette, sipped her tea and picked up her book. Two pages later she put it back down again. She got out of her chair, went to the stack of library books on the shelf, looked through them and chose a different story. Sometimes even her favourite authors couldn't hold her attention.

She helped herself to a second cup of tea, trying to get into the book. The codeine had kicked in and the back pain had retreated, enough that she could almost ignore it. Maybe she should write a letter to the pharmaceutical manufacturers' association, if there was one, and tell them that so far nothing they had come up with actually stopped the bloody pain. The best they could do was separate the mind from the body, so that instead of standing with your head in the lion's mouth, you could sit in the stands and watch the lion open its empty mouth. The lion was there, the mouth was there, the threat was there, but at least you were sitting on a bench with a bag of popcorn. Stoned.

It didn't happen often. Hardly ever, in fact. The pain pills usually made her mouth fuzzy, but she remained clear-headed, focussed on what she was doing and not distracted by the goings-on up and down her spine and leg. But every once in a while, and tonight was one of them, she wound up stoned. The trazadone-codeine combination, perhaps. The nice part of it was the stone was the kind where all she wanted to do was relax in her chair, sip tea and enjoy having the beast at bay.

The physician said the depression was an inevitable result of chronic pain. Well, they had pills for that too. Considering the amount of Prozac sold each month, a person could be forgiven for thinking the majority of North Americans were in deep agony.

Lucy had her own theory about it. Might be the basis of a second letter to the druggies. What was the population of North America if not a collection of people who were the children of people who had been totally discontent with Britain and Europe? Boatloads of people had been transported, many of them against their will, people who had been piss-cutters and hell-raisers and general pains in the ass, guilty—or deemed guilty, which was just as damning—of all manner of sin, from stealing a loaf of bread to being promiscuous. Which you were said to be even if you just fucked and got found out. People had some pretty outrageous, narrow-minded ideas in those days. And they still did.

So all these crabby people get dropped off here, and other crabby and cranky people line up for their turn at the boats, and still others trek across several countries to beg for the chance to be taken to the edge of who knows where, generation after generation of the discontented. Once here, they meet up with others and form alliances and have kids, and while they're at it they spread out, always just a bit pissed off, a bit discontent, always just a bit less willing than others to abide by rules. The most discontent and fed up moved west, trapping beaver or hunting buffalo. Some built hoochies or soddies or cabins or even houses and began to raise beef or sheep or some other critters they could boss around and then eat.

There were challenges, and the crabby, cranky, discontent and possibly genetically marked were experts at meeting challenges. Just give them an emergency and watch them excel, shining examples of rah rah rah. The day-to-day drove them insane. The ordinary brought out the worst of their crabbiness and discontent. Open prairie became ranchland, with towns, railroads and cities, and as it happened, the ones who could not abide the easy life moved on, ever onward, until holy-ole-baldy-shit-la-merde, the country was full. Too full for some.

There weren't any new lands to colonize, there weren't any recently discovered continents to appropriate and, quote unquote, develop. And the discontent was still there. With no way to work it off, with no mountains to cross, no frontiers to open, no endless hours of challenging work to do, the discontent had nowhere to go but down, dug its roots in deeper, turned into clinical depression—and the drug vendors came up with a pill.

The ones taking the pills—were they the same ones who as kids were called hyperactive, or difficult, or going concerns? The ones who everyone thought of as rambunctious, as problem children?

Lucy had not been a problem child. As a child she had been too goddamn scared to be bad. Mischief was something for other kids. Lucy toed the line, and so did her brother. If you didn't toe the line, the old man would fix it so you couldn't even walk, never mind run wild.

Robert hadn't started to run wild until he was big enough and strong enough that the old man knew better than to get proddy. And it all happened so fast. One minute they were heading off together to start another school year, the next minute—blink your eye and you'll miss it—Rob was huge. By Easter of that year he was the size of an adult man. By summer holidays the muscles had begun to show and his hands were big and square. And when they headed back into school in the fall, he had to shave twice, sometimes three times a week.

"Gee, Rob," Lucy had teased, "I thought it was the house creaking but I was wrong, it's the sound of you, growing in the night."

"I could have told you that if you'd asked, Shrimp," he laughed. His attitude toward her had changed as much as his body had. He no longer nagged or bossed or power-tripped her, and all the shoving, pushing, slapping and hitting had stopped. Once in a while he even took to reaching out one solid arm, hooking her shoulders, and pulling her against him in a brief but heartfelt hug.

He ought to have finished school. He ought to have done grade twelve and got a scholarship, to trade school if not university. But ought doesn't count. Halfway through grade eleven, with a B+ average, on the school basketball team, the school soccer team and the town baseball team, and the old man came lurching in at two in the morning with a significant portion of his paycheque sloshing in his guts and blood in his eye. It was a replay of too many other times, waking up to the sound of the slap slap bang, the sound of a chair crashing to the floor in the kitchen, the sudden harsh gasp of the one she still called Mom and not The Biddy. Lucy wanted to crawl under her bed and hide, her brain protested no no nonononono, but her feet swung to the floor and her body hurtled from the bedroom, down the hallway, to the kitchen where Mom was trying to back away while the asshole hit hit hit—with his open hand, thank God for small mercies—hit hit and grinning, knowing he could hit hit hit as long as he felt like and all Mom could do was sob and bleed.

"Leave her alone!" Lucy yelled.

"Go back to bed where you belong." The old man swung at her, caught her flat-handed on the side of the face.

"Sit down," she hollered. "Just sit down and I'll make you something to eat."

"If I want something to eat, I don't have to come to this hell-hole for it, I can get myself a steak. Fuck off. Just fuck off," and he swung again.

Her brain was yelling go to bed, her brain was screaming Jesus get yourself out of here, you fool, and her body ducked the heavy blow, her legs pushed, her shoulder got him where the wishbone would be in a chicken. He stumbled backward, roaring threats, telling her she'd be sorry, little bitch that she was, she was just about going to learn her place. And Mom sobbing oh, Lucy, baby, run, please, run as fast as you can, he'll kill you. The old bastard bounced off the wall, then came at her, and his fist was closed, both his fists were closed. She was about to collect the walloping of her life.

Except Rob arrived. He'd taken the time to pull on socks and sneakers, and he had his jeans on, but his belt was wrapped around the knuckles of his right hand, the tail hanging. He stepped in front of Lucy, intercepted the old shit, and for the next thousand-years-of-time all Lucy could see was Rob's back and shoulders. She heard thud thud thud, then swat swat swat

swat, and it was Rob swinging the belt, it was Rob giving the thrashing, it was Rob hitting the old man on the back, the chest, the face, strapping him with the belt the way he and Lucy had been strapped so many times.

"No, Robbie, please!" Mom sat a chair by the kitchen table, blood splattered on the front of her nightgown and a huge bruise forming on one shoulder, sobbing and begging.

"Stop it," Rob said over and over. "Stop it, stop it, stop it. No more of this *ever*."

Lucy stepped between Rob and the old son of a bitch. "Stop now, Robbie," she said, as calmly as if they were all sitting on the bank of the creek knitting socks. "Please, you're scaring Mom."

"I'll kill the bastard," Rob answered.

"Not tonight. Come on, please? Robbie? Do you know who's talking to you?"

"Of course I know, Lucy. Jesus."

"I'll get the cops," the old man blurted.

"Shut up," Lucy snapped. "And get out of here. They won't get here in time to save your worthless skin if you don't shut your mouth. So bugger off. Go back to where you've been and buy that steak you were talking about. *Get out*."

He drew himself up, ready to let fly, and Rob moved toward him and the old man ran for the door.

That was pretty much the end of the bullshit from him. Their very own delegate from the loony bin had learned to button his lip, keep his fists to himself.

Rob started staying out late at night, his homework undone, going off in the family car without saying where he was going. Suddenly he had money, more than his allowance. In fact, he stopped taking the allowance from Mom. The police came to the house and took him off and put him in a lineup. He laughed in their faces when he walked out of the station.

A week after the lineup, he had a job with a gyppo logging outfit. They were still using whistle punks in those days, but Rob didn't stay at that job long. As soon as he figured out which end was up and what was expected, he was setting chokers, and turning himself into a full-fledged West Coast rangytang.

The puzzling part was the old man. She would have been able to understand it if Rob had stayed in the house, living at home, right there to swing a punch or fire a kick when the old man went nuts. But Rob wasn't there. He never wrote, he phoned maybe once a month, visited only for high days and holidays—turkey days, the biddy called them—and the old man could easily have continued to brutalize the two women. But it stopped. It just stopped. Even two hundred miles up a logging road, or in a hell-and-gone float camp they had to fly him to, Rob was there, like brakes on a truck. Just the threat of him, the thought of him was enough to pull the silly old fuck into line. It may have been the first time in his life he'd had to behave.

The beating stopped, the terrifying shouts and fists pounding on the table stopped. And Mom turned into the biddy, the nag, the do-it-my-way-or-else, complete with little lectures guaranteed to have you horking.

"You haven't been out in the world at all, Lucinda, and you just don't know. Don't make the same mistakes your brother is making. Dress conservatively, be very polite and don't argue or debate. Just be nice, Lucinda, it doesn't cost anything."

Worse, she decided it was time for Lucy to begin socializing. "Nice boys want nice girls for girlfriends," she decided. "For heaven's sake don't let them know you're smarter than they are. Ask questions, even if you already know the answer. Let him explain it to you." "Don't you tell him why his engine is skipping, let him tell you what he thinks it might be." "What do you mean, you said no thank you? Lucy, for goodness sake, he's one of the *nice* boys. Of course you want to go on a date with him! Any girl in her right mind would."

But Lucy didn't date and didn't want to. And she paid no attention to anything the old witch tried to teach her. There she was, the self-appointed expert on interpersonal relationships, the answer lady to the rescue for all your puzzlements regarding the opposite gender, a fountain of wit, wisdom and expertise. And who had she chosen, and what kind of life had she had? Is that what a person gets for pretending to be Suzie Crumpet? No, thanks. I'll pass.

Lucy finished grade twelve. She didn't do any of the other things she had planned. She didn't go to nursing school or university or to the veterinarian's college. But she finished grade twelve, by God, if only because Robbie hadn't. Maybe the world hadn't been her oyster, with hubby-baby-picket-fence as the pearl, but she had no regrets. Her body had a few complaints, no getting around that, but all in all, stoned or not, sitting in a chair at five-fifteen in the morning, smoking a cigarette and staring at the same page she hadn't been reading for a quarter of an hour, she had no regrets.

The old bastard hadn't lasted long after she left. Once he had nobody left to dump his bile on, to vent what the biddy called noxi-ocity, it was as if the bad stuff bubbled up in him and eventually ate his guts. Noxious—good word for him. Noxious, and toxic—and very contagious.

All that crabbiness and crankiness from generations of crabby and cranky people, a genetic pool more like a septic tank, and no frontier to challenge, just your so-called nearest and dearest to terrorize and brutalize and turn into duplicates of yourself.

And Robbie. How many kids did he spawn, anyway? They would never know for sure. Not Seely—one look and a blind person could see that she wasn't Rob's. The dumb shit insisted up and down that Kitty wasn't his, either, but that was cow cack. Look at the hair on her, that didn't come from her idiot mother. And the body shape. Not the least bit like Savannah's, but few on this earth are so blessed. My God, Savannah! But that was a horse of a whole other garage. Kitty was built like Lucy, who had been put together on a frame originally designed by the biddy's own mother. Lucy wished she'd had a chance to know her grandmother, but the horror story of that was just too final.

Seely wasn't built that way. How could she be, why would she be? There wasn't a drop of that bloodline in her veins. Nor was Seely built like her mother. Someone in her unknown father's background had provided that blueprint. Same height from waist to head as from waist to feet. Generously rounded hips, grapefruit-sized breasts, small alongside Savannah and even Kitty. Or Lucy herself, for that matter. She'd had to find a way to restrain hers so that she could ride without too much discomfort. Pull on a singlet so the adhesive tape doesn't stick to your skin and hurt, then tape from belly button up almost to the armpits. Keep it under control, otherwise it will jiggle and jounce and hurt like bloody thunder. She supposed Kit-Cat had to do the same thing.

Lucy had the sudden feeling that someone else was in the living room. She stubbed out her cigarette and looked around, groggy and detached. No. Nobody else in the living room. It had felt like someone, though. But that's what happens when you're half-stoned.

She reached for her cane, heaved herself out of her chair, got herself balanced and carefully, carefully made her way to the kitchen, taking the cup with her. She put it on the counter, went back down the hall to go to the bathroom, then back to the kitchen. She peered at the clock on the stove. Hmmm. Okay, let's just deep-six the idea of going back to sleep.

She turned on the coffee maker and went to the bathroom to whip her wig into place and scour her fangs. The coffee was ready before she was. She fixed a mug of it, took it to the living room and sat inhaling the scent of that first, wonderful, magnificent coffee. Nothing like it. Even on top of the better part of a pot of tea, nothing at all like it.

Now it felt as if whoever wasn't in the living room was standing right behind her chair, sniffing at the coffee. All right then, go for it. Sniff away, ghost person. Lucy lit a cigarette and inhaled, and it felt like the first one of the day instead of the sixth. A sip of coffee with it. Yes. Oh, yes. And you, whoever-whatever-whichever-if-ever standing behind the chair, you're more than welcome to join in. Another day, another penny in debt. Lucy smiled. Debt? She didn't have any. Not a one. There was satisfaction in that. If she couldn't pay cash for something, she did without and that was that. All these goddamn plastic cards coming in the mail, from the credit union, the phone company, the gas company—if she'd saved them she could insulate the barn. But Lucy paid cash. She would have nothing to do with this friendly credit company or that friendly bank. Friendly would be to give you the money. Friendly wasn't standing with its hand out and thirty percent interest piling up every month.

The real estate agent sold Seely's house and pocketed the commission with a wide grin. Seely used some of the money to finish her bake shop. The gas-fitters came and installed her ovens, the electricians came and wired up the place for all the mixers, beaters, whippers, kneading wands and ovens, and their friend Gem Bailey phoned to find out when Seely would be back at work.

"I'm not scheduling the wedding until you're ready," she laughed. "I don't care if the kid is up on her feet and walking before you're set up, I'm waiting."

"God, Germ," Seely teased. "What will the neighbours say?"

"Give me a hint. What do I have to do to get you to say Gem instead of Germ?"

"Oh, I don't know, climb a mountain? Tell you what, the place isn't ready, Jimboh is still working down there. But I'll do your cake anyway, there's an oven in the kitchen here." She giggled. "It might be fun, you know, doing it the old way. My arm might fall off from all the beating with a wooden spoon, but hey, you're worth it."

"Next month?"

"Two weeks will be enough. Do I get an invite?"

"Yeah, Jimboh, and Savannah too. How many kids?"

"Figure a dozen," Seely laughed. "We'll bring tater salad and a turkey."

"I'll let you know when, for sure," Gem said. "That way we'll be sure to get the cake on time."

"Yeah, but you know, there'll be more for you if you just hang a photo of it where people can see it, then pick up the actual cake two days after you get back from your honeymoon."

"Honeymoon!" Gem laughed. "Yeah, right, a fast drive around town, then back to the house we'll be sharing with his mom. Fuck, every girl's dream, right?"

"It'll work out. Sharon's reasonable. And you didn't really want to cook supper twenty-four-seven, did you?"

"You think it will work out?"

"Up to you. Sandra and I managed real well, two women in one house. Even before she was confined to her chair all the time, it was fine. You find out who doesn't mind doing what. I'll give you a hint—Sharon will *not* iron clothes. No way. She doesn't mind putting the stuff in the washing machine, but the rest of it ticks her off. You take over the laundry and let her handle the meat. She cooks a killer roast."

"You know me, Seely, if it was up to me we'd live on pizza and bloody sandwiches."

"There, see, it's damn near worked out already. Oh, before I forget . . . keep your mitts off the flower beds! She'll have your head on a plate!"

"Thanks," Gem sighed. "I'm getting cold feet. I don't even remember why it was I said yes. I mean, you've got your girls, and you never did bother getting married."

"Yeah. But don't think it was easy. And it makes a difference to the kid, okay? Even if they don't ask, you can see the look on their faces sometimes. They wonder, they miss . . . Even if the parents are split, there's still some kind of dad in the outback. They might only see him on weekends, or maybe less, but he's there. I thought it was just me, eh, because everyone in town knows I don't have the same dad the others have, and I thought I was the only one wondered. I figured it was just me being a dork again. But I see it with my girls. Go for it. There's nothing in it for you, but . . . the pumpkin, eh?"

"Hell, I don't know why I agreed to that."

"Well, you did. There's still time for the other, though."

"Nah. I'd disappoint them all. My mom, his mom, him, my sisters are nuts about the idea of being aunties, my aunties are nuts...about everything." She laughed shortly. "Some of 'em are more nuts than others. Anyway, I told him it was a secret and he told his mom. She got all excited and phoned my mom. Some of 'em would never forgive me. They're making a list of favourite names."

"Do you have a name in mind?"

"Decklin for a boy, Emma for a girl."

"If you want," said Seely, doing something she had never done before, "you can come out and help put your cake together. Take your turn with the beating. The damn thing needs a dozen eggs per layer, and you have to break in the egg, then mix it in with the fruit and batter, then another egg and more mixing. It gets hard on the elbow after a while, but it's fun! Seeing the texture change, watching the thing grow."

"Yeah? You wouldn't mind?"

"Of course I'd mind, Germ! I've never let anyone else anywhere near the bowl before. But it's you, not anyone else. Besides, I could show you how to make bread. That's something Sharon doesn't do."

Savannah ran an ad for a tutor and got forty applications. She interviewed seven of them and chose Noreen Marinchuk, a retired teacher with short steel-blue hair and an extra forty pounds. Noreen had been married for years to Boris Marinchuk, a huge man with an accent so thick you couldn't chip it with a pickaxe. For years the kids in town had been convinced Boris was a contract killer. How the rumour began, and why it became childhood mythology, was long forgotten. Boris would be at home for weeks, even months, and then be gone for a week, maybe two. Then he'd come back, and if he was asked, he would say, "off working."

They had money, obviously, and lots of it, but nobody had any idea what Boris did to get it. His hobby was teaching karate, kung fu and judo at the boys'n'girls club. He also served as an instructor for the firearms course, which you had to pass in order to get your hunting licence. The combination of guns and hand-to-hand combat fed the contract killer myth and the kids were invariably polite and well behaved, not only around Boris but in Noreen's class.

"Ah, Mom," Alan whined. "Why? It's *summer*."

"That's right, it is. I've been watching. You guys don't head off to the swimming hole until after lunchtime. See, I've got it marked down, right here, on the calendar. And in case you think I've forgotten, which I haven't and won't, you guys got out of school early because we were moving. It wasn't any accident I didn't enroll you for the last couple of weeks. So you've been lying around getting fat and stupid and you're *not* going into a new school that way."

"My marks are okay," Caroline protested.

"Let's get real, sweetheart. I'm not doing this because I'm a mean old shit. Or because I want to ruin your life. You kids are about to head into a school that is so white you won't believe it! You're going to get all kinds of shit thrown at you. Paki. Rug rider. Hindi-rice-ball."

"We'll pound the snot out of them," Victor declared.

"You'll have to. But there's more than one way to hammer them. And the two hours' tutoring you're going to get every morning is going to help you whip their asses in class."

"Can I?" Bobby asked.

"Oh, my darling, of course. Here, up on my knee, cuddle time, quick before I faint... ah, that's my good fellow, what would I do without you? You save my life with your smooches."

"Spoiled baby," Victor hissed, pretending jealousy.

"Yeah," Elaine agreed. "He gets to sit on her knee. I want some of that too." And she sat down on Bobby's lap.

"Me too." Victor sat on Elaine.

"You guys are going to smash the chair!" Savannah laughed. "Come on, give us a break before you squash the Rob."

Bobby met Noreen at the front door, with a pencil in one hand and a small scribbler in the other. "I'm going to school," he announced.

"And I'm your teacher," Noreen smiled. "I'm Noreen."

"I'm Bobby."

"Hi, Bobby. Have you been to school before?"

"No." he shook his head, his curly black hair bouncing. "But my mom said I can go when it starts. She says she'll drive me in and then come and get me."

"Wonderful! And are you going to work really hard?"

"Bictor says don't chew the pencil and stay in the lines."

"It sounds to me like Victor might grow up to be a teacher himself."

Savannah tapped him on the shoulder. "Bobby, you're hogging her."

"Okay." He turned and started toward the kitchen.

"Savannah." Noreen patted Savannah's shoulder. "You look wonderful. As always."

"Some of the kids aren't too keen on this," Savannah warned. "Jason is the one you have to watch out for. He can get carried away with himself."

"I understand these aren't all yours."

"Well, not really. They're mine in all kinds of good ways, but five of 'em's got different birth mothers. It's kind of complicated," she admitted.

Noreen laughed. "The whole town has plenty to say about it."

Noreen set herself up at the kitchen table with the kids. She unfolded the previous evening's newspaper.

"So, let's get to work," she said softly. "Can someone tell me where Bosnia is, and what's going on there?"

Savannah left the kitchen and went out the back door and down the slope to Jimboh's place. He was nowhere in sight, but Audrey was busy at the sink, doing dishes.

"You got coffee?" Savannah sat down in a chair and reached for her cigarettes.

"Fresh brewed," Audrey said. "You take cream?"

"Yes, ma'am, I take whatever's going around. Including a break. Seel's got Victoria, I think she took her into town. The rest of the little buggers are lined up pretending to be well behaved. I hired them a tutor."

"I heard. Your brother is about ready to report you to the welfare for child abuse."

"What a nut," Savannah said fondly. "Leave it up to him they'd never go to school."

"Any of them have trouble? In school, I mean."

"No. Well, Jason, but it's his attitude, not the work. Sometimes I think that kid's brain is put together differently than the others. There's stuff he just does *not* seem to get. God knows he's smart enough—except for Vic, he might be the smartest of the bunch. But he's eleven years old, eh, and if you're around him very long you'd think he was seven, maybe eight." She accepted a cup of coffee, sipped and smiled. "You make a good brew, woman."

"Yeah, I do. I make it the way I like it. Can't see why a person would bother swallowing some of this warm brown blah some people make. So, about Jace—"

"Yeah. It's not that he sits down and plans stuff, or that he's trying for attention, it's ... it's the stuff you don't think about before you do it, you know? Like waiting that extra second so the other person can go through the doorway ahead of you. Not him, he shoves ahead. Little kids do that because they haven't learned politeness, and because they're little kids and they have tunnel vision. And the other kids, well, if Jace is around they sort of step to one side and let him bull on. If he was to think about it, he'd do fine, he'd be polite. There's times he's the most considerate kid you could find. But he has to think about it. Like when Vic was five, you could give him three or four things to do and he'd do them, he'd remember them. Actually, when Vic was five he could probably have kept track of two dozen things. Jace? He can't remember three things. You tell him to tidy his room, say. Strip the bed, get clean sheets, make his bed. You go in and he's done a lousy job of tidying and his sheets are in a tumble on the floor. He's apt to be sitting in the living room watching a spider walk on a wall. He's not absent-minded, it's something else. And his temper is like nitroglycerine. No, I mean it. Someone will say something and *pow*, there goes Jace, all insulted and angry and ready for a fight. But the thing that insulted him is nothing. I mean *nuh-thing!*" Savannah sipped her coffee. "I'm tired of slapping his arse," she confessed.

"So stop slapping his arse. If it doesn't work, find something else! He's yours?"

"Carol's."

"He calls you Mom."

"All the kids called all of us Mom. It was easier."

"So where is she?"

"Not in my pocket," Savannah shrugged. "Or hanging behind the door in the hallway."

"You aren't worried?"

"Yeah, I'm worried! She's kind of... well, she's like Quebec, pas comme les autres, you know? But this is kind of extreme, even for her."

"Maybe you should report her missing."

"No. I phoned the guys, they haven't seen her or heard from her. Larry's out looking. Moe's out looking. Shemp, well, he probably won't look himself, but he'll get other people out trolling for her. What can the cops do? Contact the welfare and get them involved? Hell, we've already got Brandon and Brittany floating around, no sign of their mom for years. Not a phone call, not a birthday card, nothing. I mean, it's creepy, okay?"

"Well, was I you, I'd get someone—like me, maybe?—to sit down and write a letter. You know, being of sound mind and body, care and custody of Savannah, just in case."

"Yeah?"

"Yeah. Then I'd get someone else . . . not sure who but we can find some-one . . . Deb, maybe, or Christie . . . to write another one for the others. And then, just in case, be a shame to break up the troop."

"Yeah. Well, I'd better get back up to the house," she grinned. "I have to start looking for that damn piece of paper. Can't remember where I put it."

"If I see it around here, I'll bring it over." Audrey patted Savannah on the arm.

"Everyone's patting me today," Savannah said. "I must look like a poodle or something."

Noel didn't mind the rain, not when he was on the farm. Kitty hauled on his muddy-buddies and he stuffed his feet into his gumboots and the rest of him into a raincoat with snaps down the front and a hat that looked like a fisherman's hat. Then he could head outside and splash in puddles, or he could dig rivers and lakes in the driveway, make the runoff go where he wanted it to go. He spent hours damming puddles, then breaking his own dams so that the muddy water would flood into his scraped-out river and down, down to the next puddle, the next dam.

He put Lego houses near the puddles, and when the dam broke, the houses washed away. Then he could scoot his fire truck through the water, racing from one otherwise doomed family to another, picking up the little plastic houses and plunking them, invisible families and all, onto the truck to ferry them off to safety.

Dog lay on the porch watching him, her tail wagging. There was no place in this game for her, but the boy was there, and she could see him, and he was fine. She waddled up and down the steps, but other than making fast trips to squat, she was as fussy as a cat about getting her feet wet.

"What's her name?" Debbie asked, putting down a bowl of warm milk. The pup slobbered and slurped at it.

"Pup." Christie rolled her eyes. "I wanted to call her something like Muffin or Angie or . . . but before I'd decided on a nice name, Kitty was call-ing her Pup, and the puppy was coming when she was called. So now we've got a dog named Dog and a puppy named Pup. It's a good job Noel had a name when we got him or he'd be Boy."

Maybe the most fun for Noel was helping with the animals. He was allowed to shovel up horse buns in the loafing barn, but he couldn't make the wheelbarrow do anything except tip over and dump its load, so either Kitty or Lucy did that part. He helped put hay in the mangers, he was allowed to brush those parts of the horses he could reach, and he got to put the grain in the troughs for the calves. One or two of them were used to him now, and would head for the trough even if he was still standing there. The others still didn't trust him. They stood in a cluster and made noise to try to get him to leave. After a bit, he did, and watched through the slat wall as they rushed to shove their noses in and get their share.

He could feed Decision too, but only through the wall. The boards in the wall were thick, real thick, but spaced far enough apart that a guy could poke his head through, although Kitty told him that was a good way to get a black eye—if not from the bull, then from her. The trough fit in the bottom board so it could be filled from one side and Decision could eat on the other side. Noel could sit and watch as the big tongue appeared, then licked up grain. Decision knew he was there, and didn't care. He watched Noel all the time, and at first Noel felt scaredy and fraidy, but after a while he knew the huge black bull was puzzled about him too. Why would a big black animal have a white face? And little curls on his forehead, like little twists, or that old doll he wished was his, the one Lucy called Punkinhead? No matter how much he wanted that doll, Lucy said no, it was hers.

"I'll leave it to you in my will," she said.

"What's that?"

So she told him, and he got so upset by the idea of Lucy dying that he started to cry. He didn't want to, but he couldn't help it. He knew about die. He'd seen die. He saw it when he was sitting on Kitty's hip, with her arms tight around him and nothing on but that stupid jacket from that stupid guy whose name Noel wasn't even going to think, let alone say! Horrible horrible horrible him.

Everything was on fire, and a guy was puking, and they were still in the car, Mom and that horrible horrible and he wanted to cry and scream and all he could do was hang on to Kitty, Thingy was there, jumping and doing somersaults on the burning car, except when he sat crosslegged on top of the cop's hat.

He didn't want Lucy in a burning car, all blacked up. He had needed to know, and Kitty had the barbecue on, and they were parked on the rodeo parking lot. Not at the place where the guy got killed, another place. He didn't remember the name. They were all the same anyway. Kitty had steaks to cook but there were some wieners in the cooler and he swiped one and put it on the grill. There was just him and Thingy there when he put it on. Then Kitty came back and the wiener was just this old charred black thing, not even any meat left, and when she tried to take it off the grill it fell into chunks and the chunks were black all the way through, even to the middle, so she just flipped it on the ground.

"Noel?" she asked, but he couldn't answer, he could only stare at it.

And Thingy was whirling and spinning and all upset and angry, and all Noel could think of was that they were both like that, now, Mom and the horrible horrible. He was glad horrible was like that, but Mom had been nice sometimes, when she wasn't sick. Lots of times she cuddled him and sometimes there was bubble gum, and it hadn't always wound up bad. There had been trips to the park and rides on the swing, and it wasn't until the horrible horrible horrible had started taking over, and why did she even let him? She was the boss, she had always been the boss. Noel did what she asked him to do. But *he* never did.

And now they were just like that wiener. *She* was like that wiener.

Kitty picked him up, right there by the barbecue, and held him against the front of her. He could feel her boobies against him, feel her belly against his legs, and when he put down his face it fit right into her neck. She didn't say anything for a long time, and he cried.

Finally she said, "Tell me, little man. You have to tell me."

So he did, he told about stealing the wiener and then wasting it. And he told her about how Mom got burned up the same way.

"Oh, my dear." She sounded like she was crying too. "Oh, my dear dear little darling."

She sat on the silly steps up into the trailer and moved him around so that he was sort of sitting on her knee, and she held him, her body swaying almost like she was dancing, and she talked about life and being alive, and how someday the you that lived inside your body just got tired of being here, and it left. Kitty said it left out your mouth, just eased out, soft and slow, and drifted off to a better place, where it could rest until it was time to come back again if it wanted. In a little brand-new baby. To try again, she said, and maybe next time things would be way lots better.

"She wasn't even there when the burning started," Kitty told him. "It was just the body, just the meat and the bones. *She* had already started drifting off to the resting place."

He hoped so. He really hoped so. They didn't have supper until real late that night, and he ate his steak but nothing else, not salad or anything. Then

Kitty had to go put on her clown suit. Usually Noel watched because Kitty was so funny sometimes, but not that night. And Christie held him. She washed his hands and face and got him into pyjamas, then put him in bed and lay down beside him. He was under the covers and she was on top of the covers and Dog was lying near his feet, on top of the covers, and Thingy was sitting on the pillow right next to Noel's head.

Christie said some people were so tired by the time they died that all they wanted to do was live quietly for a long time, so they came back to nature and lived in a tree. Other people might feel even more tired and go into a rock. But most people came back as new babies. That's why for someone new to be born, someone else had to die, so there'd be a soul for the new baby. You'd think they'd have extras.

"Will you die?" he asked.

"Oh yes, and in my next life I think I want to be a whale."

"Will Kitty die?"

"Yes, dear, she will."

"What will she come back as?"

"I don't know. But I don't think it will be anything quiet, like a tree or a rock, do you?"

"What about me?"

"Well, sweetheart, think about it. No pee gan um, that's how we say *think* in my language. No pee gan um."

"What? What do I think about?"

"You aren't going to die for a long long long *long* time. And guess why?" She waited, stroking stroking stroking his face. It made him so sleepy he couldn't think about anything except the stroking. "You had your chance to die," Christie told him. "You could have died when your momma did. There you were, on your way to die, smash-on-the-ground, and instead, you saw Kitty and when she reached up to catch you, you reached down to catch her. And you might have had the wind knocked out of you but you didn't die, your chance was gone. And so now you have to wait until your next chance, and they don't come all that often."

That was nice. He'd had his chance, and he'd grabbed Kitty. He remembered her grabbing him, and maybe he grabbed her, but he couldn't remember. He hadn't even seen her—all he could see was Thingy, flying and falling with him. And then...*something* had him, and Thingy was laughing and spinning and zapping from his stick, zap zap at the horrible horrible, who was screaming and trying to get out of the car, zap zap went

Thingy and horrible screamed and screeched. Noel could see it. Not with his eyes, but he knew, from the movie Thingy made happen in his head.

And Thingy on the pillow was making another movie happen. In this movie they were driving away from the cop cars, just like before, and Mom was crying. She was so sad, so scared, and she was crying, and horrible horrible was swearing very bad swears, and Noel was hurting so bad, in his bum, in his belly, and then there was the truck on the bridge and Noel went flying out the broken door. But in the movie Thingy made happen, Mom yawned and stopped sobbing, and she just shook her head and said, "Shit," and put her head on the back of the seat and she went to sleep. All that noise and sound and things bumping other things and Mom asleep, and not because of her medicine. She looked so pretty. He didn't see anything come out of her mouth, or her nose either, and so maybe her soul was invisible. But even as the fire started to burn her clothes she was smiling. Not a big smile, just this little one, like leave me alone I have to sleep, even when the gas tank blew up and the whole inside of the car was fire, she had that little smile on her face. Except it wasn't *her* face any more. It was just a face. *She* wasn't in the car, she wasn't anywhere near the bridge.

"Could I plant a tree?" he blurted.

"A tree?"

"For my mom."

"Oh, you just bet you can."

And they were getting ready to do it too. As soon as they called, he had to go in the house and have a quick bath. Then he'd get clean clothes on and they were going to go to the place where you could buy trees, all kinds of trees.

They looked through a book last night, him and Kitty and Christie and Lucy and Debbie. All kinds of plants and flowers and trees in it, and they made a list of the kinds of trees they liked the best. No one picked the same kind as anyone else, and Debbie said of *course* everyone would pick a different tree, and Christie said of *course* they would, and the two of them laughed and laughed and laughed.

Then they talked about it. All of them. They even listened when Noel talked.

"Hey, baboo," Kitty called. "Tub time."

He picked up his Lego houses and his fire truck. Kitty came over to help him with the tools he'd taken from the shed. "You've got the whole Fraser River delta in the driveway," she laughed, but Noel didn't know what was funny. It was like that lots of the time. Big people said things that didn't make any sense at all.

Lucy and Debbie went in their pickup truck and Kitty drove the new truck they'd taken from the underground parking lot the day after horrible horrible wound up looking like a burned-up wiener. They had the canopy on and Dog rode in the back, with Pup sitting on Noel's knee.

Noel was wearing his black jeans and a white tee shirt with team Canada printed on it in red. He had on a pair of brand new socks, nice flecky-grey ones, and his good sneakers, black high tops with RAD written on the side. The best thing about them was the lacers Christie had gotten for him. You didn't have to tie them or anything, you just pulled until the shoe felt good. The lacers were all stiff and twisty and they didn't come loose. Noel loved them. He wanted lacers like that in all his shoes from now on. That was better than the little bunny ears, which he couldn't learn how to do.

And his jacket. It was probably the best jacket he had ever had in his whole life. Kitty bought it for him, a bit big so he'd grow into it and it would last a long time. She wore jackets like this all the time—jean jackets, she said they were. They took his home from the store and she washed it and washed it and washed it and got all the stiff store-stuff out of it, and then she took it to the laundromat and put it in the dryer and when it came out it was dry and it looked as if it was his jacket already, not brand new.

He wore it all day, and when he went to bed the jacket was on the pillow. It was still there in the morning, but Christie had taken it away in the night and done beading on it. She had put something on it, like a dream-catcher only different. She said it was the medicine wheel. She'd had it in with the stuff she sold from her stand but she'd never put it out for sale. Red and yellow and black and white, and she'd stitched it to the front of his jacket—right above his heart, she said, so the magic would work right away. She did beading on the back too. Other things from her stand, sewn right onto his jacket.

"Never be able to toss it in the washing machine again," Kitty said.

"Never have to," Christie answered. "You watch. There's so much magic on this jacket, all you'll have to do is just . . . like this, with your fingers, and the dirt will fall off, no problem."

One time they were walking toward the stands, and this man with white hair stopped them and asked if he could buy Noel's jacket. Christie said no, but she would make one for him if he wanted. He did want it, and she did it. "My agent," she teased Noel. He didn't know what that was, but Christie gave him five whole dollars all for himself, because if he hadn't been wearing the jacket and looking good in it, the guy wouldn't have paid all that money to get one for his grandson. The guy was real happy, but Noel knew the other kid's jacket wasn't anywhere near as good as his. Nowhere near.

Christie wasn't the least bit sure how she felt about all of this, but if it made Noel feel better, she'd do it. To look at him, sitting there with Pup and watching everything through the window, you'd never guess he'd already been through more horror than most people had in forty or fifty years. He looked totally gorgeous, even if you discounted the jacket he was so proud of. Okay, she was proud of it too. Very proud. Anybody in the world would look at him wearing it and know right away that somebody loved him. Maybe more than one somebody. This was a cherished child.

The nursery parking lot was as good as empty in the rain. The nurseryman came over to greet them and shake hands.

"Not the best time of year to plant a tree," he warned.

"I've got a soaker hose set up. I'm just going to let it drizzle from now until the first frost."

"Why not wait until autumn, when they've gone dormant and—"

"It's a memorial for the young man's momma," Lucy said. "He wants to do it now. If the trees don't make it, we'll do it again later."

"What kind of tree, sir?" the nurseryman asked Noel.

"This kind." Noel held out the note on which Lucy had printed the tree Noel had chosen.

"Ah," the nurseryman nodded. "Next spring you'll have the most beautiful flowers. They look almost like bunches of grapes, if you can imagine flowers like that. White ones with coloured centres. Come with me, young sir, the trees in question are over here."

The catalpas came in two sizes, and predictably, Kitty chose one of the larger ones. It was in a huge peat pot that was set inside a plastic pot.

"All you have to do," the man told them, "is get the planting hole ready, lift it out of the plastic pot and put it in the hole, peat pot and all."

Noel chose catalpa, Kitty chose Japanese flowering plum, Lucy went for weeping cherry, Debbie chose golden plum, Christie wanted a cedar tree but settled for a black pine.

When the holes were ready, the heavy rain stopped while they planted the trees. Noel didn't look like someone who was grieving or planting a memorial tree. He looked like someone who was deeply satisfied, doing something he had wanted to do for a long time.

They set the soaker hose at the roots of the trees and connected it to a bright yellow hose. Noel turned on the hose, even though the sky was refilling itself with rain clouds.

"Looks good," he announced, nodding his head repeatedly. "Looks fine. If she needs to take a rest, she's got a place to do it. She was awful sick," he explained to Debbie, "and awful *awful* tired a lot of the time."

"Take all the time you want," Lucy said. "You let me know when you're ready, and we'll go back into town and go to the Golden Dragon for a family meal. This is a real special occasion and we're going to do it up right."

"I'm ready," he said agreeably. "I just have to change back into my sneaks. I don't want to go to the Golden Dragon in my gumboots."

"No." Christie stroked his head. "I think we all have to change into our sneaks."

They were halfway through dinner when Kitty realized that the JimmySpook was nowhere to be seen. He had been there, glommed onto her or to Noel, for what seemed like forever, but now he was gone. Now that she thought about it, he hadn't come along when they went to buy the trees, either. To her surprise, Kitty felt almost abandoned. She'd been getting used to him.

But he was right there when they got back to Lucy's place, hunkered down by one of the puddles, watching the water overflow the dam and spread out, moving on to the next one, following Noel's scraped-out river. The spook looked up when Kitty stepped out of the pickup. He wore no expression on his face. He just watched, as if waiting.

"I'm gonna put on my raincoat and boots," Noel announced.

"And your muddy-buddies," Kitty said.

"That was sure good supper." Noel brought a spring roll out of his pocket. He unwrapped it from the napkin carefully, and then, staring at the JimmySpook, he lifted it to his mouth. Kitty watched. Anyone who didn't know, anyone who couldn't see, would have thought that a kid was standing in the rain, enjoying a treat. In fact it was Noel who lifted the spring roll, but JimmySpook who ate it. He wasn't squatting by the puddle. He was with Noel, one bone arm around the kid's shoulders, and he wasn't expressionless, not in the slightest. He was grinning, chewing, relishing his meal. "I've got some other stuff too," Noel said. "I'll eat it after I change."

Jimmy came out of the hell hole looking like someone with a bad case of flu. He went to the kitchen sink, turned on the tap and let the cold water run and run and run. Finally, as if he had just remembered something, he got a glass and filled it, then drank it non-stop. He drank two more glasses, then wandered to the bathroom and began to fill the tub.

The water seemed to waken him. There was no standing blank-eyed, rubbing his trembling hands on the legs of his jeans. He went into his room, came out with clean clothes and made a sound—not a word, just a sound— then went to turn off the kitchen tap, which was still running. He stared at the drain hole briefly, then went into the bathroom and closed and locked the door.

The locking of the door was like a small sliver of bone caught in his throat. He had enjoyed life more when all he had to do to take a bath was take it, and not worry about this one, that one or the next one walking in on him. He'd been so fortunate for so long, and now he finally knew it.

When he pulled his tee shirt over his head he smelled himself. No wonder the word *pong* worked better than the word *smell*, or even *reek*. He tossed his clothes into the corner and tested the water, one of those safety habits left over from being a little guy and having Gran remind him, time after time. "Test it for your ain self," she would say. "No way your old Gran can tell if it's right for you. I only know when it's right for me." He'd felt grown-up, and responsible, and very, very protected.

The water was hot, but not too hot, and Jimmy lay back in the big old tub, hoping the tension would leave his shoulders. His neck was so stiff he felt as if another headache was coming on. Please, Gran, get some of your angel friends to help. Please, I can't deal with a headache right now. Just get that buzzing sound out of my ears and let the water do its thing.

Here now, she'd say, here now, my ain wee one, give me that finger of yours and I'll care for it. Och, Jimmy boy, look what ye've done, cut it so bad, so verra bad. How many times has Gran told you, you're too wee for that knife. Use the small one I gave you.

And there'd be the whole taradiddle, the towel folded thick and placed on the table top, the grubby hand put on it, the basin of water, the soap and cloth, the fuss, the wonderful fuss. Now, here's a wee bit of candy for you to bite on while I put on the peroxide. It might sting a wee bit. Oh, look at it bubble! It's bubbling the germs and the poisons right out of your finger, see how it works? And when it's finished, we'll put on some antiseptic powder and a Band-Aid. And then I'll warm your arse for using the wrong knife!

Except she didn't warm his arse. Not then, not those times. Oh, she had no compunction at all about giving him a swat if she figured he deserved it. Working overtime, are we, she'd say, working like a fiend because our bum is itchy and we need it flattened a bit. Well, take it like a brave heart, my lad, because you're getting it whether you screech or not.

Three of them. Always three. Now, then, you damn wee scamp, remember that the next time you think it will be fun to chase the hens.

The cut on the finger might be only a scratch, but the go-round was the same each time, the ritual unchanging. The one time he really *did* gash himself she took one look, gasped, Oh dear, sweet suffering Jesus, wrapped the towel around his hand and had him in the car so fast he wasn't sure what was happening. No peroxide that time. To the Emergency, and they put in the stitches, right across his palm from thumb to the base of his baby finger. The bandage they put on it was the size of a loaf of bread.

"Leave it on," the doctor told her, "and bring him back in five days to have it checked. And you." He glared at Jimmy. "Don't even try to wiggle your fingers inside that. Don't get it wet, don't bump it, and *don't* take it off. If you do, you could lose your hand."

Scared? Dear God, he nearly burst out crying. Lose his hand? Lose his good left hand? But Gran had put her arm around him, one of the few times she showed any affection in public. No need to scare the shite out of him, she'd said, in a pleasant voice with steel at the core. He's a good boy, this one, and he'll do as he's bid. Level-headed is our Jim.

Level-headed. As if she knew he hadn't done it himself. As if she knew it was that silly bugger Glen trying to scare Savannah. That's all Glen intended, they all knew that. And that's why Savannah pretended not to be worried. But Glen drew closer and closer, swinging the knife, cut off your tits, cut off your nose, cut off your chin, slash up your face, it was like a song, a stupid stupid stupid song, and then Jimmy couldn't handle it any more and he jumped in front of Savannah and yelled, smarten up you stupid fucker, and that's when the knife hit his hand and the blood spurted, a spray of it across the front of Glen's tee shirt. Savannah screaming, Kitty swearing and yelling, Seely, just a toddler, sitting on her chair and bawling her head off, understanding nothing.

Savannah wanted to fix Jimmy's hand, but he ran. He had to get to Gran. She'd fix it. She'd make it better. She always did.

Poor bugger Glen, he never had quite managed to get it. That kid at Savannah's was like that too, that Jason kid. Just a half a beat off the music.

Laughed that little bit longer than the other kids, talked on just a sentence or two too far. The kids at school were going to have hell's own good time razzing him. He'd be lucky if the worst they called him was nerd.

The water was cooling off. Jimmy got out of the tub, let half the water out and turned on the hot tap. While it was running, he used the electric toothbrush on his teeth. How many cigarettes had he burned up this time? Enough that the nicotine stains were back on his right hand. Well, he could fix that. A bit of hand cleaner, little sand grains smoothing the ridges of the callous where his tool handles fit, and some peroxide, Gran's cure-all. Good bleaching agent too. Maybe he'd use it on his hair and scare the bejesus out of everyone.

He got back in the tub, turned off the tap and leaned back against the sloped tub. It was almost but not quite too hot. Sweat popped out on his forehead and his upper lip, he just stretched out, his dork floating, swaying, looking so ridiculous, so pathetic and silly. Savannah had told that joke once, when she was—fourteen, it must have been, just before she left home for good. And Kit was what, thirteen? Twelve and a half? Savannah was washing dishes and Kit was drying them. Glen wasn't doing much of anything except glaring and being jealous. Savannah told Kitty about this guy who wanted to play doctor with his sister, and she was younger than him, eh, and he talked her into it and they stripped off their clothes and he started reaching out to touch her, you know, and she looked at him and backed away and said Oh no you don't, you're not going to play with mine! You've been playing with yours and look, you broke it! And the two of them laughing laughing laughing. Then Kitty told the one about these two girls who were walking down the street at night and this guy jumped out of a doorway, and he had his zinger hanging out, and both girls stopped. The guy waved it at them and said dirty things and then one girl looked at the other and said, have you ever seen anything like that before? And that one bent forward and took a good look and said, I'm not sure. My baby cousin has one something like that but his is a *lot* bigger. And they were off again, cackling and giggling. Yeah, a *lot* bigger.

Jimmy would have fallen asleep, but the back of the tub was just a tad too hard. He grabbed the soap and lathered himself, washing away the sweat, the staleness of days of working almost non-stop, and when he had washed himself two or three times, he pulled the plug, stepped out, grabbed the bottle of shampoo and got into the shower. There was nothing like a bath to relax in, and nothing like a shower to get your hair clean.

When he came out of the shower he was clean. Squeaky clean, like that old window cleaner commercial on TV. He let the water drip onto the red rug on the floor in front of the basin and used the Water Pik. He had absolutely no faith in the thing, it seemed like just another of those silly things people invent, like that riggins for taking the tops off of strawberries. Stuff. Stuff on its way to being junk. But Seely had given it to him, no Christmas or birthday or anything, just because he had such nice teeth. Best in the family, she said.

Well, that was Gran too. They'd all of them have been sporting china clippers if not for the old woman. How in hell did she ever come up with the money for that? Mom, dumb bitch, all she had to do was show the welfare card, but she never even thought about it. So Gran marched them off every six months, starting with Seely so she wouldn't get cranky from waiting. Everyone knew Seely wasn't any part of Gran, but Gran would stand right next to the chair and hold Seel's hand and say, Now, Celia Mary, you grip on to me, and don't let go. I know you're scared, but there is nothing bad going to happen. You can cry if you want, but don't get to sobbing or the man won't be able to do his trade.

Seely didn't know at the time that Gran wasn't really her Gran. She found out later, the hard way, from the kids at school. God, how she'd cried. And cried and cried, until she was throwing up. No sign of Mom, of course, so Savannah ran for Gran. Told her about the teasing, told her what they'd been yelling at the Seel. Gran came up the slope from her house to the house where they all lived, and she ran into the place and lifted Seely from where she was kneeling at the toilet. She wiped Seely's face and held her, rocked her, crooned to her in Gaelic, all those soft sounds. And Seely sobbed and sobbed and Gran never once said stop it. She waited.

When the crying stopped and Seely herself told Gran what had been said, Gran shook her head and said, Och, my wee Seel. My own swim-in-the-water seal. Of course I'm your Gran! Them others, the ones at school, their Grans got stuck with them. Like them or hate them, they're stuck with them because they're related. I was never stuck with you, never once. I'm your Gran because I *want* to be your Gran. Because I want you to be my own dear seal, my Seely, my Celia Mary, my sweet darling. You can ask any of these others here right now. You know there's not a one going to lie to you or tease you. She gave Glen a look that could have fried eggs and he nodded, knowing to keep his mouth shut this time or else. Now, am I or am I not this little girl's Gran? Jimmy? Am I? Yes, Gran, you are. Because she's my sister and you're my Gran. Savannah? Of course, Gran, you're all our Gran. Glen? She fixed him with that look. Yes, Gran, you're Seely's Gran too. She loves you just as much as we do. Kitty? Oh, yes, Gran, those kids at school are just jealous, is all.

Gran stayed holding Seely until she fell asleep.

"I'll whip their asses, Gran," Jim promised.

"No, son, don't do that. It's what they want. They want all of you in trouble with the school. What you *will* do, though, is going to be harder. Ignore the skites, and concentrate on being nice to Seely. Glen, I want to put you in charge of this, son. If they start in on her again, I want you to go over to the little kids' side and pick her up. That's all. Just pick her up, and hold her against yourself and whisper to her. You can whisper the times tables if that's all you can think of."

He gaped at Gran. "Why me?"

"Because, my boy, everybody would expect it to be Jimboh or one of the girls. They don't expect it to be you. Bloody little bastard skites."

It happened again and again. One time Seely went racing down the hill to Gran, screaming with frustration and fear and who knew what-all. Gran closed the door and wouldn't let the other kids in, even when Glen pounded and yelled. They didn't know what went on inside, but when it was over, Seely was bombproof. Just goes to show, she'd say coolly, goes to show how much *you* don't know.

Jimmy pulled on his clean clothes and carried the bundle of dirty ones to the laundry basket, which was damn near full. Time to return to the real world, James my boy.

He put on a pot of coffee and started separating the laundry into piles. Jeans and work socks here, shirts and towels and such here, whites right into the washer. Well, for Chrissakes, no wonder the basket was so full, bloody brassieres and silky underwear and what in the name of God is this thing for, anyway? Maybe he should get another basket, for just his stuff. He wasn't sure he wanted to be sorting bras and bikini panties and all that. Oh well. Put them through anyway.

He added detergent and washing soda, then turned on the machine and left it to its work. He fixed a mug of coffee and put a half dozen cabbage rolls in the nuke. At about the time his belly was full the washing machine was done. He took his second mug of coffee into the bathroom and set it on the basin while he moved everything from washer to dryer, then stuffed in a new load and turned on the washer and dryer. Christ almighty, all that electricity and water just to clean some clothes that they probably didn't need anyway.

Even with two mugs of coffee in him he was feeling dozy. But hell, if he went to bed now he'd be wide awake by midnight. And then what? Read a book? Watch television with the sound off so Seely could sleep?

He went to the kitchen for his third cup of coffee, took it to the back steps and sat staring out at nothing, at everything, at Savannah's huge new house, at the new bake shop where Seely was giving some kind of lessons to some woman Jimmy almost recognized. He yawned and moved his shoulders around. The stiffness was gone from his neck. Thank you, Gran, and thank your angel friends too.

The first load was dry, the shirts and stuff were hanging on the line and the jeans were washing when Audrey arrived. She parked her car, walked to the steps, sat beside him, and patted his knee.

"How'd you know I was finished?"

"I know everything about you," she teased.

"No, really, how'd you know?'

"Just knew, is all. Just . . . knew."

"Want a coffee?"

"I'll get it."

"No, you won't. Guests don't, remember? I'll get it." He emptied his mug onto the grass. "I must have been daydreaming or something, it's gone cold."

"Falling asleep, more like. You look drained."

"I feel drained. Wrung out. I feel like a string mop after it's been used too much and gone all grey."

When he came back with their coffee, she was sitting almost sideways on the second step, smiling up at him. He had poured her coffee in the mug she liked, the one with the outline drawing of two women sitting side by each. He'd got it at the table in the mall where the Transition House had its information booth and tee shirts, cookbooks, and such for sale. He'd given them fifty dollars and when they insisted, he took the mug. Damn if he was going to wear a tee shirt that said You Can't Beat the Women at Grace House. The same message was printed on the mug. Maybe he should give the mug to Audrey, she liked it so much. Maybe he'd get her another.

"So you just knew, huh?"

"Yeah."

"That's nice. It's like sometimes you an' me'll just be sitting around, and all of a sudden both of us speak up at the same time and say the same thing. I like that."

"Great minds think alike, eh?"

"So anyway, a while ago . . . month or two, I guess, I made something. Then I chickened out, and had to think think think, you know, chewing on it and scaring myself out of it and back into it and . . . you know how I am." He brought it from his pocket. "Anyway, what do you think? Would you?"

She looked at the ring and her eyes sparkled with unshed tears. "You made it?"

"Yeah. It's the first one I didn't get mad and melt it down. It'll fit, I made sure of that. The thing is . . . will you wear it?"

"What does it mean, Jim? I mean . . . yeah, what does it mean?"

"Well, that's up to you. I can't say this is how it'll be or that's how it ought to be."

"What do *you* want?"

"Oh, you know."

"No." She still hadn't taken the ring. "I need to know some stuff, Jimboh. If you were writing the script for a movie, how would it go from here?"

"If it was up to me and I got my own way, without any compromising or anything, just what I want . . . you'd slide your finger into this ring, third finger, left hand, and I'd kiss you, real soft, and then we'd get in my pick-up truck and we'd drive to your place and we'd pack your stuff and put it in the pickup and bring it here and you'd move in with me and live with me, and I'd live with you. And we'd be, like, together."

"How long together?"

"Resta my life."

"Want a prenuptial agreement?"

"What's that?"

"So's I can't take you to the cleaners."

"Yeah, right! Like I've got zillions packed away for you to clean out."

"We could get a lawyer to draw up a good one."

"I don't need it."

"I do."

"Fine, then," he shrugged. "You want the whole nine yards?"

"You just bet your damn socks I want the whole nine yards," she laughed, but the tears were falling too. "I want the whole shiterooni,

Jimboh. I want the trip to the courthouse, I want the justice of the peace, I want the photographer and I want a banquet."

"How many people?"

"Us. Your family. Kids and all."

"Yeah? Who else?"

"Nobody. You?"

"Nobody else. Just us."

They drank their coffee slowly, and halfway through it she reached over and slid her finger in the ring. "This is gorgeous," she said softly.

"It's the spiral, eh?" He felt shy, like when he gave the stool to Gran and she took it and held it and rubbed her hand on it as if it was a little soft-skinned baby, or a treasure she'd been looking for all her life. "The Celtic spiral of eternity. And see here, this is the knot, it was, like, the sign for being married. It might not be on a ring, it might be a bracelet or even, like, your belt? And this, this is the raven, stretched out, see, and she's the sign of a poet, or a tale spinner or... and this is the salmon, she's another sign for poets and fortune tellers and for navigators and explorers... and, well, that's what you are, for me. I mean, a kind of navigator." He could feel himself blushing. "I'm not very good at this, this talking stuff."

"Do you love me, Jim?"

He didn't want to answer, he didn't want to put his pecker in a leghold trap, but it was a fair question and he did want her to know. He had hoped the ring would tell her, but if she needed it in words, well, it wasn't going to cost him his life, it just felt that way.

"I love you, Audrey," he managed. "Other than my Gran and my sisters, I never loved anybody before, and I'm prob'ly not very good at it."

She held her ring up and smiled. "You'll do, Jimboh. You'll do." And then the teasing was gone, and the smile was gone and she was looking at him so hard he thought she might make holes in his face. "I love you," she said. "I want you to believe that, every day and every night. I don't expect anything at all from you except the chance to just keep on loving you and to have that love trusted and accepted and believed. I don't want to love you and love you and love you and know you don't believe me or trust me."

"I trust you." He held her hand, kissed the palm. "That's why I love you so much, I can trust you."

"If we do this... I want it understood, nobody else in my life, nobody else in yours. You dick around on me and so help me God I'll cut it off and hang it out for the birds."

"Ah, I wouldn't do that," he grinned. "I would never do that. Why would I want to? I mean, look at you!"

"Okay, let's go get my shit. If you really mean it."

When Savannah saw them unpacking the first load, she was down the slope in a flash.

"What the hell is going on?"

"Audrey's moving in with me." Jimmy felt so defiant and defensive and scared.

Savannah stared. "You're kidding."

He shook his head.

"Audrey, is this true?"

"Yes." Audrey sounded defiant and shy too.

"Well, I'll be go to hell." Savannah was suddenly hugging him, squeezing him so hard it was almost funny. "I'm making us a *huge* supper," she decided.

"Don't you cook any of that stinking curry stuff," he warned. "I hate that shit."

Audrey didn't have much stuff, and most of what she did have was fourth- or fifth-hand. They brought the things she wanted, like an old phone from the days when they were big wooden boxes with black bells on top, and a sort of record player that played little tube things. She had a little cedarwood box with a dragon carved on it, and she had a lamp that looked as if it had originally been a real lantern and someone had converted it to electricity. She had some old dishes and bowls she said were Depression glass, and a mug with a picture of Queen Victoria on it.

"The rest can go, by me," she said.

"You sure?"

"Yeah. Except for the dressers. I need them for clothes and stuff."

"Can I have this rug?" he asked.

"Sure, if you want it."

"For the hell hole. The floor gets cold." But that wasn't the real reason. Each and every time he'd been with her, here, in her bed, he'd felt safe, and when he got up to pee or get dressed or get a beer from the fridge, he stepped barefoot on this rug. And he didn't want anybody else stepping on it. He knew damn well that lots had already, but from here on in, nobody but him was going to get the chance.

The move didn't take long. Two loads to the house, the main load to the Sally Ann, and the place was empty. They could probably have made one trip home, but that would have required some planning and some careful packing, and neither of them was much good at either.

Nothing much got put away when they got back to the place. Seely was busy in the kitchen. She had the music turned up way loud and she was singing along, smiling and almost dancing. She hugged Audrey, then Jimmy, and both the girls got huggy and excited. Jimmy wished he were someplace else. But Audrey looked so happy that he made himself stay where he was, not take off into the bush the way he wanted.

Supper was incredible. They had to carry Jimmy's kitchen table up the slope to Savannah's house to make room for everything and everyone. All the kids had been scrubbed shiny and even Bobby's hair was slicked down and temporarily under control. They were wearing clean clothes and their good shoes, and Victor had even put on a tie.

"Congratulations, Uncle Jim," he said formally.

"Thank you, Vic." Jimmy knew that Vic wanted to shake hands, like two guys on equal footing. He stuck out his hand and the kid took it, and beamed. "I'm going to need a best man. Would you?"

"Doesn't a guy have to be nineteen or something? You know, an adult?"

"Fuck 'em. I want you."

"What about me?" Jason demanded.

"You I need, too. In fact I need Alan and Bobby and Brandon, as well. Groomsmen, they call them. I think in the old days they were supposed to make sure the guy didn't get cold feet and run away." He grinned. "Be much obliged."

"Will we get to be in the picture?" Brandon asked.

"You betcha. There you'll be, all slicked up, white shirt, tie, carnation in your buttonhole, she wants the whole thing."

"You guys going to stand around talking guy talk all night, or can we sit down and eat?" Elaine called. She was tucking a bib around Victoria's neck.

Supper went on and on. Every now and again Darlene or Lizzie would hop up, clear some plates and take them to the dishwasher. By the time the meal was actually finished, dessert and everything, the dishwasher was nearly full. Clearing the table took no time at all, and then the kids swung into their clean-up routine and the adults headed for the living room with mugs of coffee.

"How many people?" Seely asked.

"Us." Jim sipped the coffee "You put cinnamon in it."

"Yes. Don't you?"

"Never had it like this before. It's good."

"Just us? You don't have, like, maybe your agent or—"

"Fuck him, he's just another kind of pimp."

"Well, we have to phone Aunt Lucy."

"Yeah, that's good." He sighed deeply. "And I was wondering about ... well ... the old man."

"Who?" Savannah said, slow and lazy.

"Gran's absent son," Jim grinned. "You know, him as what's not here."

"Why?"

"I don't know. I'm asking as much as saying, eh."

"Makes no never-mind to me," Seely said. "He's nothing at all to me."

"He's nothing to me, either," Savannah agreed. "But he must be something to Jimboh, or else where did the idea come from?"

"I just thought ... well, it's an excuse. I mean, we hardly even saw him at Gran's funeral, he was in and out again. He and Lucy had a couple of talks, but ... well, might be nice for the kids. He *is* their grandpa."

Savannah sighed. "Do you suppose if I hit him on the head with a brick, it'll make his brain work again?"

"Doubt it," Audrey yawned. "Well, much and all as I'm enjoying this, it's my day off. I'm just about asleep here."

"We'll bring the table down," Seely said.

She didn't, though. When they got up the next morning there was no table in the kitchen. They took their coffee to the back steps and drank it, leaning against each other, smiling often. And after the second cup, there came Seely, still without the table, down the slope with Victoria sitting on her hip.

"I'm damned," Audrey whispered. "She spent the night there, to give us some privacy."

"If I'd a known that," he answered, "you wouldn't have got any sleep at all."

"Brag brag brag."

Jim went up the slope and got the table, carried it down and set it back where it belonged. He looked at Audrey and winked, and she understood immediately. She got up and headed for his pickup truck.

"See you later," Jim said casually. "We've gotta go pick up the marriage licence, make some arrangements, stuff like that."

"Did you phone the old man?"

"Nah, not yet."

"Aunt Lucy?"

"Not yet."

Seely shook her head, but didn't say anything. She waited until Jimmy and Audrey drove off, then she went and got the phone book. There, in the pages at the back, the frequently called numbers pages, she found what she needed. Possibly the least frequently called number in the world.

"This is Celia," she said stiffly. "Jimmy is getting married. He'd like it if you'd come. I don't know the exact date yet, but it will be as soon as possible, in the next week, probably. Think about it and phone back tonight, after supper." She hung up before he could ask any questions at all. Such as, Celia who?

Maybe Audrey was knocked up and that was why the hustle and hurry. And if she was, who knew whether it was Jimboh's kid or not? It was no secret she'd got slave wages at the two-four and augmented them on a fairly regular basis. You'd think she'd have better sense than to get up the stump, and if she didn't, she'd have a dozen or more of them hanging on to her. And if it wasn't Jimboh's, who would know, and how? And if he did know, would it make any difference to him? Seely hoped not. She happened to know that it wasn't fair to the kid who got chucked aside. Oops, sorry, this one doesn't fit. Toss it over there, and another kid in the new'n'used shop. Still, it was nice to think he'd finally found contentment. Happy? Well, we don't dare ask for happy, but a bit of contentment from time to time is most welcome. Happily ever after was too much to ask for.

She liked Audrey. The hooker part of it didn't bother Seely at all, and anyway she'd never figured out what all the damn fuss about such things was about. Sex had been blown out of proportion, such a fuss over a few minutes of wriggling and squirming.

Anyway, she had to get a cake made. It wouldn't have time to cure and be the best cake she ever made, but damn it, she'd made cakes for people she hardly even knew. She wasn't going to miss out on making one for her own brother.

The highest she'd ever gone was four tiers. Well, never mind that. This was going to be the cake to end all cakes. She knew what she wanted. She wanted a cake that looked like a triumph. If she put two eight-inch square ones side by each for the bottom layer, then a big round one sitting on top, and a slightly smaller and slightly smaller and so on, up to the one she made in a plant pot, it wound up tapered bigger on one end than the other, and that was fine, that was just fine. No little bride doll and little groom doll, though, not this time. And no hidden hand grenades or machine guns, either. She knew exactly what she was going to do for the top. She was going to make roses, really nice roses, pink ones and white ones, and she had to have at least a dozen because each of the kids would want one. Never mind the little silver paper leaves, either. She could make her own. She had been practising since she was eleven years old and she could make a hell of a leaf. And lilies, she could make lilies. And what a person could do, she could make a dozen or more roses around the outside, like a wall or a rim of roses, and then put real rose petals inside it. That would be nice. She could gather the petals from rose bushes she'd planted down near the bake shop, the lilac-coloured ones would look good. She liked the greeny ones too, but they wouldn't go with the pink candy roses. They'd look as if she'd tried to dye them and hadn't managed to get the colour right.

Eggs, she needed eggs. She checked the fridge. Jesus Christ, wouldn't you know it, only two dozen left. And no way was she going to use those white things from the store. She'd need cream too, the thicker the better, so instead of standing around here worrying about what she didn't have, why didn't she just wiggle her jiggle over to the farm down the highway and get plenty of what she needed. Some of that feta the woman made herself too. It was a bit too mild to use in something like a Greek salad—not enough brine or salt—but it was a nice cheese and it would make a fabulous lasagna. And pick up a few litres of that kefir drink, Savannah's kids loved it. Maybe she'd take Victoria over with her, show her the baby goats. She could probably put up with Bobby too. That's where she drew the line, though. Well, Vic was a great kid, and Elaine, no flies on her. But Alan, there was something sneaky about that kid, and those twins were only too obviously related to her own two—if you went back a ways. Everybody on the face of the earth had two parents and four grandparents, whether they knew who they were or not. Just keep multiplying, figure it all out, and inside of twenty-five or thirty generations, you were linked to everyone else on the planet.

Savannah waved good-bye until Seely's car was on the highway, then she headed to the fridge for the milk, and filled the bowl on the clothesline stand for the cat. Years and years earlier, Jimboh had swiped a cat. He didn't seem to want it, but he swiped it anyway because there it was, winding around his ankles, rubbing on him at the school bus stop. So he picked it up and put it under his shirt, against his skin, and got on the school bus so smoothly that none of the other kids even knew he'd taken it.

Siamese, and it must have been a good one because it had a number tattooed in one ear. No sooner did Jimboh have the cat home and settled in a box of old sweaters and rags, than she popped out a litter of kittens. He sold one of the kittens to the very people who had originally owned the mother cat. Oh, they had such a sad story about how their darling registered wotzit had got out of the house and must have been killed by a dog or a car or something, because it never did come home again, and they missed it *so* much...

He sold the other ones too, and the subsequent litters, even though by that time it was obvious they weren't pure Siamese. The cat hanging around now was from that stolen cat, and every other tom that came anywhere near the place. But it was gorgeous. All the crossing and recrossing, inbreeding and outbreeding, and the cat was as cream-coloured as a pedigreed Siamese, with orange tabby markings. And tame? One day she walked out of the bush and sat on the clothesline stand. Stared at Savannah as if trying to figure out what in hell *that* was. So Savannah put out a bowl of cream and a saucer of scraps.

You'd have thought the cat had known it would be there. She went right to the dish of scraps and started eating, daintily reaching out with her paw, hooking a shred of meat and lifting it to her mouth as if she were a person in disguise.

Pretty thing. Friendly, too, but she scooted if one of the kids tried to pick her up. So Savannah made sure they all understood it: keep away, she's mine. Not even Bobby could get near her.

It was nice, real nice, having a living thing pick her out, from everyone in the world. She didn't feel that it was her cat so much as that she was the cat's person. And not just for the food, either.

It was a female and it was pregnant, and Savannah knew that if she had her kittens anywhere near the house, they'd wind up permanent pets. The kids would get their revenge one way or the other. They'd all wind up sterilized too, each and every one of them, tabby and tom. Probably wind up costing five hundred bucks. God, an arm and a leg everywhere you turn. Things were easier back when Jimboh's swiped cat wandered in and out and turned out litter after litter of kittens. A lifetime of being kept inside, often in a cage, taken out only to go to cat shows, and that creature Jimboh called Nice didn't even have enough instinct left in her to hunt. She would even lie down and snuggle with Patsy-Ratsy. The only time there was any trouble was if Patsy tried to eat the cat's food.

The cat made up for lost time in the wandering-outside department, though. The minute Jimboh left for school, the cat hit the bush. Smart cat. If she had hung around, Mom or one of her stalwarts could have taken her to town and sold her for booze, or tripped over her and landed on top of her, squashing her flat. That cat had no use at all for Mom or her many studdlies. Didn't yowl or hiss or scratch, just took a hike. They'd get off the school bus at the foot of the driveway and the cat would be there, waiting for Jimmy to pick her up and put her on his shoulder so she could lick at his ear and as good as talk to him. You'd have thought she was telling him everything that had gone on that day. When the other kids complained about the constant yowling, Jimmy didn't even argue, he just took the cat with him and went down to the basement.

"You a good cat?" she crooned, hunkering to watch the cat fishing scraps from her dish. "Are you? You're sure pretty. I don't know I've ever seen such a pretty kitty as you. I've got a sister named Kitty. Wait until you meet *her*. She's got a dog she calls Dog and somewhere they picked up a puppy they call Pup. She'll probably call you Cat."

The cat looked at her and did everything for a meow except the sound. Savannah laughed softly and sat on the step leading up to the clothesline platform.

"What is that supposed to be? Is that the ultimate manipulation or what? You want to know something? It works. Want to know something else? You don't have a Siamese-y face. They have sharp faces. That cat of Jimboh's looked as if her face was made out of straight lines and sharp angles. You're way prettier, you've got a lovely nice round face. You look like a cat should look."

The cat finished the scraps and turned her attention to the bowl of milk.

Savannah could hear the sound of laughter and hollering from up at the swimming hole. All of them except the two youngest, and they were with Seely. If she had any sense at all she'd go to bed and catch a power nap. She had a whack of stuff to do and she ought to be up and doing it right now, but it was nicer to sit here and space out for a while. She lit a cigarette and thought of making a cup of coffee to go with it, but the idea of getting up and going into the house and doing it was too much to pull together right now.

The tutoring was working. The kids were practically jumping through hoops, even Jason. Who'd have thought that would happen!

"Nobody really knows how children learn," Noreen had said, sipping her tea. When Savannah lit a cigarette Noreen grinned and reached into her bag for her own. Savannah gaped. "Oh, I know," Noreen teased, "you kids thought that once school was finished, the teachers went home and hung upside down in the closet, like bats."

"I guess maybe we did," Savannah admitted.

"So, anyway, what we do know is that it's a miracle kids retain anything in the usual school situation. The more we find out, the more amazing it seems. Just learning to read—none of us had any idea how much of the brain was involved in that, how many processes had to come together for it to happen. To me the mystery isn't that some children have trouble learning to read, it's that any of them ever do learn!"

"Jace is . . . difficult," Savannah said. "There are times I could just—"

"Yes, but he's just about mastered reading. And once he's got that aced, he'll do well and he'll be *much* easier to get along with."

"He couldn't *read?*"

"Not well. Looks like he did an incredibly good job of hiding it, though. Think how much brains and wit *that* takes. His other annoying habits, well, some of them are never going to go away. My advice is we stop worrying about it. He'll always blurt things out. Instead of getting upset, make a joke of it. When he blurts like that, he's telling the absolute truth as he sees it."

"So what's wrong with him?"

"Nothing. His brain is working overtime. He's probably getting two or three times the sensory stimulation most people get, and for reasons we don't understand, it all has the same importance to him. Jason cannot and never will be able to automatically sort out what is and isn't important. To him it's all the same. The rest of us know instantly that a spider on the wall is not as important as the baby reaching for a loaded mousetrap. But Jason would dither. He wouldn't know whether to tell you about the spider, or tell you about the baby, or grab the baby or kick the mousetrap aside. So he'd do nothing. And when the baby started to yowl, we'd all holler Jason. Why didn't you do something, you were right there!"

"He tells lies."

"He tells you what he thinks you want to hear. But since he can't sort things out in an ordinary way, he's a bad liar."

Amazing the difference it made to have just that little bit of information. Savannah's worry and resentment gave way to compassion. If you can't help it, you can't help it, and if it gets you in shit all the time, you're as disabled as if you'd been born with an extra leg. She and Noreen talked about it over three cups of coffee, and the next day Noreen explained to the kids why their brother was such a goof. Jason listened, as interested as any of them. Savannah expected him to show some sign of relief at being understood at last. But he behaved as though Noreen was talking about someone else. There was no relief, no sudden change in his behaviour or personality. His reaction to this was as weird as so many of his other reactions. But the older kids changed. Instead of stepping aside to let Jason blunder through the door, Victor would reach out, take Jace by the shoulders, and tell him, "Be polite, Jason." Savannah didn't think it would work, but Victor was convinced that one day Jason would catch on, that the endlessly repeated correction would find a place to slip into and the pushing and shoving would stop.

The cat slipped onto Savannah's lap and settled herself, licking her front feet and purring. "Aren't you something special," Savannah breathed. "Good, good girl, nice girl, pretty girl. Yes, you are. Pretty girl. I guess we should start looking for a good name for you. You want one like Jewel, or—no, can't call you Gem because then we'd think you were Germ. Or do you want to be named after a flower? Like orchid, or rose, or—or a person-type name like Kate or Mary or Bridget?"

The cat gave her silent meow and began kneading Savannah's lap with her front feet. "Good Puss," Savannah crooned. The cat meowed. "Is that the name? Puss? Such a good puss-cat, yes, she's a fine, fine puss-cat."

When Savannah went into the house to answer the phone, Puss followed her. And when the call was finished, Puss was in the living room, lying on a big chair, curled in a ball, snoozing.

Savannah stroked the cat, then went into the kitchen. So much to do! And that long-absent old man was coming. Said he was bringing his wife and two of the kids. Jeezly, she should have asked how old the kids were! Well, there was no room for them at her place. They would have to bunk in down at Jimboh's place or stay in the Lazy Daze down the highway. Jimboh had said he'd pick up the motel tab. All this for some asshole who had taken a hike and left the whole pack of them at the mercy of the craziest bitch in Christendom.

Lucy arranged for Conway's part-time hired hand to stay at the place and look after things while they were gone. "Don't go near the bull," she warned. "You can grain him through the slot in the wall. He's got water, he's got his girls, he's fine. If you go near him he'll kill you."

"Yeah, I saw it on TV."

The guy looked like an old worn-out hillbilly, but he was probably no older than Kitty. Just goes to show what a lifetime of dedicated rangytang can get you. He had bad teeth, too. Jesus, he ate with those?

They piled into the rented car, Kitty driving. Lucy sat in the front so she could stretch out her leg. Christie and Deb were in the back and the damn kid was anywhere he wanted to be. Dog was on the chain, yowling and howling and wailing. She'd keep that up until they were out of sight, then she'd resign herself and settle in to be the guard dog–watchdog–farm dog of all time. The puppy was sitting in the hired hand's pocket, her head poking out, no bigger than a small Christmas orange. She ate and she ate and she ate, but she didn't grow much. This made it easy to tuck her out of the way.

"Everybody comfortable?" Debbie asked.

"I'm fine," Christie answered. "Of course I'm convinced we've forgotten something vital. Every time we pull out I get this clutch in my stomach and start trying to think of what it is I forgot to do."

"Me too," Deb nodded. "And that total conviction that when you come back there won't be a house, just a blackened shell?"

"All the animals dead of some previously unidentified plague?"

"And a blight in the fields, killing off all the grass."

"Such a cheery bunch in the back seat," Kitty laughed. "They'll have us all dead in a car accident before we even reach the highway."

"You got your activity books, boy?"

"I've got my books, and my crayons and my Game Boy and my bear. And my good clothes, and my new shoes and—"

"What Game Boy is it?"

"It's like a road race thing. You can pick which car you're going to be. There are four of them. See? What do you want to be?"

"I want to be the red one."

"I'll be blue," Debbie volunteered.

"Okay, and I'm the old old one. See, you've got a real old car, like in the cartoons, and you've got a freight truck, see, and a race car, and a funny car. And there's no red and no blue."

"Well, then, I'll be the funny car."

"And I'll be the eighteen-wheeler."

"Auntie Lucy can be the race car."

"I'm driving *this* car," Kitty laughed. "You other guys play."

"You can't play anyway, there aren't enough cars."

"Now, see, I get to steer and everything because I've got the box. You guys can't because we don't gots the other ones. You can get plug-in things, with the control buttons on them and everyone can play, but we don't gots 'em so the Game Boy will have to play it for you."

Debbie stifled a yawn. "Is that fair?"

"I don't know," Noel said seriously. "But it's what we got."

Noel's old car came in second. The race car won.

"See?" Lucy teased. "Even from the front seat I'm the champion."

"You cheated," Debbie said calmly.

"I did not!"

"You always cheat."

"I never do."

They nattered and teased and Noel laughed happily. He reset the Game Boy and bent over it, intent, concentrating on his play-by-play description of what was happening on the little screen.

"This kid needs glasses." Debbie said. "See how he has to peer at it?"

"The screen is so damn small anybody would have to peer," Lucy countered. "Those things were probably designed by the guys who make glasses. Hundreds of kids squinting and frowning and ruining their eyes and those guys just raking in the dough."

"Seriously," Deb said. "Let's get his eyes checked first thing we get back."

Kitty felt as if she was driving an emperor-sized mattress down the road. But it only made sense. They couldn't all cram into one pickup and it was silly to take two of them, although it would have meant Dog could come with them. She missed Dog already. But you can't cram a dog into a huge rented boat like this and expect anyone else to stay in a good mood. Dog shed, no denying that, and Dog had an odour. All dogs had it. Even if she bathed Dog and made sure she didn't get a chance to roll in something stinky, the dog smell would be back within hours. And you don't need puppy pee on thick carpeting. Silly idea, that, just more work yelling to be done. Or maybe the ritzy folks who drive these things all the time never get their feet dirty.

Noel kicked off his shoes and sprawled out with his Game Boy. It was good that there was enough room in the thing for him to be sort of comfortable. In the crew seat he had his stuff where he could get it easily, and he had Dog for company. She wasn't sure how it was going to work out without Dog, and with other people in the back seat with him. When it was someone else's turn to drive, he could sit on Kitty's knee. He'd like that, and so would she.

JimmySpook lay on his back on the hood of the rented Caddy. He had his power stick with him and what looked like a pile of spring rolls. He rolled onto his belly and stuck out his tongue. In the back seat Noel giggled. JimmySpook pulled more faces, then did a handstand. He balanced on both hands then slowly withdrew the left one. Now that was a trick—a one-handed handstand. One by one he lifted the fingers of the supporting hand and folded them in, until he was balanced on his index finger. In the rear-view mirror Kitty could see Noel, Game Boy forgotten, leaning forward with his chin on the back of the front seat, watching intently. Slowly JimmySpook started to spin on that one finger.

"I wish I could do that," Noel said softly.

"One day you will, dear," Debbie answered. "You'll be tall enough for your feet to reach the pedals, and to see over the dash, and then you'll learn to drive too."

Kitty coughed and JimmySpook moved from the hood to Noel's shoulder, his white-trimmed mouth against the kid's ear. He never spoke to Kitty, never gave her messages she could understand. But she could see what was going on. Noel had been about to tell Debbie he wasn't talking about learning to drive, and now JimmySpook was warning the kid not to tell Deb about him.

The traffic was heavy and the damn rain was still pelting down. The second crop of hay was going to benefit, and if it didn't stop raining soon, they could plant rice. They'd had enough sunny days to encourage the grass to start growing tall, then several more days of rain, then a week of sunshine, and now it was raining. Savannah had said they'd hardly had any rain, that the grass was starting to go yellow and she didn't have to mow the lawn because it wasn't growing. Kitty hoped they didn't take the rain there with them. She wanted to take Noel swimming. She wondered if all parents, natural or adopted or what-have-you, felt the need to share with their kids the best of what they'd done when they were short and broke and had to obey everybody taller than themselves.

It was the memory of Victor at the swimming hole, the memory of her deep satisfaction in introducing him to the water. He'd been so worried about putting his face in it. And by the end of that first visit to the swimming hole, he was happy to go under completely. On the next visit he cannonballed off the bank. Those two days were like headlights—everything had come together. If there was such a thing as a perfect day, she'd had two of them. And Savannah, hadn't she been different? It was like magic, no sign of the resentment, the simmering fury, the frustration, and no sign of the toughness. She'd been quiet, sitting in the shallow water with Elaine bouncing on her knee or splashing happily. The baby had found the mud and was picking up handfuls of it, watching and laughing as the blackish mess dribbled between her fingers. It was a great old game—grab a handful, smear Mom, rub it on your arm, then swish your arm and the black stuff is gone.

They didn't see the three wise men at all in those days. She'd never asked, so she didn't know if it was because Savannah felt shy about it or the guys did. Why not, considering how pissed off Jimboh was? He'd come around after a while, but it was a long while. It just didn't sit well with him that Savannah was shacked up with three rug riders. The three part of it didn't seem to bother him—it was that other. To be honest, they'd all kind of resented that.

"Here, now!" Gran had given it to them, her face hard, her eyes narrowed. "What difference does it make to you if they're black or green? I won't have that, you hear?"

"They don't even wear *socks!*" Jimboh blurted. "You see them all duded up, brand new suit, white shirt, tie, the whole thing, and no socks."

"Oh, and I suppose we'll hang them from trees or crucify them on the phone poles because they don't wear socks. Why do you wear socks? Because everybody else does? Half the time you've got holes in your socks, anyway."

"Their food stinks!"

"What do you care? You don't have to eat it. There's lots in town have too much to say about you, my lad. About all of us. And you don't like that. Not one bit. Well, what you're doing is the same thing."

"It is not!"

"Big fleas have little fleas upon their backs, to bite them. And little fleas have lesser fleas, and so ad infinitum."

"What does that mean?"

"Think on it, James."

Kitty wondered if the threesome would show up for the wedding. Probably. They were good about meeting people halfway, and good about their kids too.

Audrey started at one end of the house and scrubbed her way to the other. She knew that it was nerves, it was just a way to work off her terror. Seely kept the place clean and tidy, and Jimboh was no slob. But she had to have something to do or she'd start screaming. What if, what if, what if . . . how much rotten luck would it take to ruin this? Of all the things she'd done in her life, she'd never once been married. She'd had some more-or-less long-term shackups, but had never once considered or wanted marriage. And suddenly, when Jimmy showed her the ring, she wanted the whole magilla. Even knowing what she knew, she wanted it. Dumb dumb dumb, so very dumb.

And the look on the face of the asshole in charge when she'd handed him the letter of resignation. Why did they think people were dying for the chance to stand behind a counter and be insulted by any creep who felt like venting spleen? Probably because they were. So many people were so desperate for work, they'd smile from ear to ear for a job where they could risk being shot or stabbed by a junkie in the middle of the night.

"Oh, hell," Seely had snapped. "If you can't live without a job, Audrey, you can come work the counter in the bake shop. I hate working the counter."

"It's just that—"

"You don't have to explain anything to me. I wouldn't work in that damn two-four, either. Or anywhere else where that creep was going to be my boss. You shoulda quit a long time ago. Except for the small matter of rent and food and the occasional birth control pill, right?"

"Jimmy hasn't really said anything, but . . . when I told him I was thinking of it he just nodded and then . . . he hugged me."

"Course he did. He's not stupid. So when's your last day?"

"Oh, it's gone. I gave him the note, he read it, looked as if he was going to drop his false teeth on the floor, then he just went to the phone and . . . "

What he'd done was glare at her after he hung up the phone. "You don't need to bother with notice," he said, as if she were a misbehaving child and he had decided not to punish her. "I've got someone else coming in tonight."

He must have thought she'd protest, tell him she needed the last two weeks' work, the extra pay. And so she smiled, with her total wattage. "You're a doll," she told him. "That's really nice of you, it's more than I'd hoped for." You couldn't lay it on too thick for some people.

But she didn't want Jimmy to feel that she was mooching off him. She'd always paid her own way, from the time she was old enough to cut lawns and clean garages. You'd think she'd have caught on that day jobs and manual labor paid zilch, you'd think she'd have hung in and got herself some kind of training, but no, not her. Quit school in grade ten, go slinging hash in the Modern, which everyone called the Mod Run, and minimum wage from then on. Except for the times she'd gone cooking in camp, but that wore thin. Too many guys putting the tap on her. A person couldn't even go to bed and go to sleep without having to lock the door and windows, and even then there was the banging, the sly hints and comments, the lies. You get sick of it.

Jimmy said it wasn't too late, that there were lots of courses at the community college. She'd looked at the catalogue and found he was right—there was just about anything that might hold a person's interest. Or not hold it. Most of it she discounted completely, but there were two of them she couldn't get out of her mind. One called Journal Writing, the other Creative Writing. She had no idea what either of them might entail but the words echoed in her head like a snatch of half-forgotten song. There was that one year, waitressing in the city, when it seemed like everyone who put money in the jukebox chose the same goddamn wailing horror. You picked a fine time to leave me, Lucille. As if there was a good time to do it. The guy seemed more upset about having to get a babysitter so he could harvest that crop in the field than he did about his wife taking off on him. And one year it was that other one, Delta Dawn, what's that flower you've got on. She'd nearly gone around the bend with that one. And now it was Journal Writing, Creative Writing, as if some imp from hell was sitting on her shoulder whispering in her ear.

One thing about it, she had wads of stuff to write about. Years of people, years of fumbling, years of keeping some part of herself detached from what was going on, years of watching the soap operas that were other people's lives, years of being part of the soap opera. As the stomach churns. All my arseholes. Like the time that little tiny woman, plump as a plum, with her hair done just so and her makeup in place, walked into the bar as if she owned it and over to the table where Audrey was sitting with several friends and some guy she'd been boffing on and off for a couple of weeks. "Oh, no, you don't!" the little bit of a thing said, and she swung. Why she'd chosen Audrey to knock arse-over-the-moon instead of loverboy was a puzzle. But then she got him too. He started to get up, either to argue with her or to help Audrey, she was never sure which, and *slam*, he landed back in the chair. And the plump little plum dumped a whole jug of suds on his head. "Get yourself home where you belong!" she yelled. And by damn, he did. Nobody laughed. Dead silence in the pub. Audrey got herself up off the floor and into a chair, too surprised to plan any vengeance.

Once the walls were scrubbed and the carpets shampooed, once the windows were spotless and the steps and porch had been swept and scrubbed, there was nothing for Audrey to do except sell buns and lemon squares and matrimonial cake and watch as parents arrived to pick up wedding cakes. She knew Seely was building one for her and Jimmy, but she had no clue what it would look like. Trying to find something out when Seely had made up her mind to keep it a secret was like trying to find pope shit. Everyone knows he must do it, but of all the holy relics, finger bones and nail clippings, and maybe you could even buy one of the rocks that killed St. Stephen, no sign of pope shit. She should write him a letter—they were missing out on a fortune. Every faithful pilgrim could have a holy turd. They could dry them, varathane them, mount them on small varnished plaques, stand them on the mantel along with the graduation pictures and the dried first-communion bouquets.

When the long-absent one arrived with his wife and two teenaged boys, Jimboh wasn't home. Wouldn't you know it! This guy walked into the bake shop and it took Seely a minute to realize who he was. She'd only seen him briefly at Gran's funeral and he hadn't shown up for Glen's. But he probably hadn't been told about it until weeks later. She hadn't phoned and she was pretty sure Savannah hadn't, and if you counted on Jimmy to do things like that, you'd wind up waiting a long time.

"May I help you?" Audrey asked, all professional and polite.

"I'm looking for Jim," he answered. He tried to smile, but it was a kind of weak and wobbly thing.

"Jimmy's out right now. Seely sent him off to pick up a ton of stuff."

The dime dropped. "Oh for crying out loud." Seely moved quickly from the work area to the counter.

"Celia?" he smiled. She wanted to ram something sideways into his ear.

"Yes, sir. Audrey, this is Jimboh's dad. And this," she said, without trying to name the creature, "is the bride to be, so to speak."

Audrey blushed beet red and so did Jimboh's dad. They shook hands awkwardly, then stood there without knowing what to do next.

"Did you get yourself checked into the motel?" Why did everyone assume that Seely was in charge of conversational traffic?

"Yes, we did. And it's, uh, very comfortable. Both rooms. Will Jim be long?"

"Should be back real soon. Tell you what. Audrey, you take your soon-to-be father-in-law up to Savannah's place. At least there's someone there to make a cuppa. I'll finish up here. We've got two cakes due to be picked up this afternoon, and then I can close the door and put up the Outta Luck Try Again sign."

"Okay." Audrey was flustered, anyone could see that. She took off her apron and stood holding it uncertainly. Seely snatched it away, shook her head and gave Audrey a gentle shove in the general direction of the doorway. "She's been like this for the past couple of days," she said conversationally. "I thought she was a real together person until all of a sudden she turned into a total basket case. Just get in the man's car, Audrey, and ride up the hill to Savannah's place. Here, take these with you. And a dozen of these, as well. Hell, make it two dozen." She handed over a tray of raisin scones and two boxes of lemon squares. Audrey took them and stood looking as if she didn't know what to do next.

"Come on." Jimmy's dad took Audrey by the arm and smiled at her as if they were old friends. "Come with Poppa."

"What do I call you for real?" Audrey blurted.

"Rob. Those kids out there, well, the oldest one is called Rob too, and the younger one, he's Les. My wife's name is Myrna. Did you know Jim's name is James Robert? And Glen's name was Robert Glen. But it didn't stick with either of them, had to wait until I met Myrna. I tease her the only reason I got tangled up with her was that she already had a boy named Rob. Even if his name is Robin instead of Robert. You know that they aren't actually mine, but they call me Dad and I call them my kids, so ... here, careful getting in, don't bump your head. Rob, Les, move over. Myrna, this here is your daughter-in-law Audrey."

Jesus, what a motor mouth. Seely wondered if he was like that all the time. Or was he just trying to cover up the fact that he was every bit as nervous as Audrey, maybe more so? Well, give the devil his due, the child maintenance cheques had always arrived on time, and if he sent them to Gran instead of to Crazy Mary, that just showed he knew which end was marked Up and which was a vortex that would drink it up and forget all about groceries.

Savannah wouldn't have known what to do, shit or steal third base, but by the time Audrey got to the house she was over her paralysis. "We came for tea," she laughed, putting Seely's baking on the counter. "I guess you know who this is. And this is your step-mom Myrna, and these are Robin and Les. Who would probably love the chance to grab some lemon squares and then head up the hill in the direction of the noise. That's the swimming hole," she told them. They grinned. "Extra bathing suits around here, somewhere, I bet."

"Savannah. How are you?"

"I'm fine. And yourself?"

"I'm okay. You look gorgeous."

"Thank you. I'll get trunks for those guys. Vic has plenty and they'll fit."

Myrna sat down at the table, sighing gratefully. "Honest to Pete," she said, totally at ease, "I don't know how a person gets so tired sitting in a car. Mmm, maybe I'll just snatch me one of those scones, they look delicious."

"I'll put out plates and get the butter and stuff." Audrey filled the kettle and put it on the stove to heat. "And you have got to try the lemon squares. Savannah makes good ones but Seely, she makes them so lemony you can't believe it, and they're not sour or too sweet, either, just lemony."

The boys headed off wearing Vic's trunks and the adults settled at the table with tea and baking. Savannah sat stiffly, with a defiant tilt to her head. No reason for that. She was in her own house, on her own turf. If anyone should be off balance it was Rob.

"I guess you're still mad at me, huh?" he asked.

"Don't know that I was ever mad. Mixed up. Scared as hell. Resentful, because what did I do to get dumped? I can understand off-loading her but...I never did understand."

"The only way to be rid of her was to be rid of her." He wasn't apologizing, not a bit of it. He took a scone, buttered it, put on a dab of green plum jelly. "I kept in touch with Mom."

"You coulda tried keeping in touch with us."

"I should have, for sure. I was younger at the time than you are now. Hope you're smarter than I was."

"I'd kill before I'd let anyone—*anyone*—get between me and my kids."

"See? You *are* smarter than I was. I'm sorry. I'm very sorry. It was a jerky thing to do."

"Shut up," Savannah said easily. "Eat the goddamn scone before it falls apart in your hand. Spilled milk under the bridge and all that. Just don't expect anything, Rob, because it won't happen."

"I don't expect," he agreed. "Nor you, neither."

"I don't expect a fuckin' thing." She smiled pleasantly. "Try the lemon square," she said to Myrna. "I taught her how to make them and then she turned around and got better at it than I'll ever be."

"I hear Jimboh's truck." Audrey felt a surge of relief.

"Great," Savannah laughed. "We can all stop walking on eggshells if Jimmy's here. Helluva thing, eh?"

"Helluva thing," Myrna agreed. "Maybe you can teach me how to make these. They're the best thing I've ever tasted. Except for something we had at your mother's funeral." She looked at Rob. "Those little shortbread things that looked like stars."

"I can teach you how to make that," Savannah said. "I made them for Gran's funeral. Was up all night making them, one tray after another. They were her favourite."

Jimboh backed the pickup to the side door, parked, then went around to lower the tailgate. It was a trick tailgate, he always said, a trick tailgate to thwart thieves. Really it was old and worn and rusted, and in its last incarnation. To get it open you had to do the trick with the lock in the middle, then lift, but you had to lift one side a tad more than the other or you'd get hung up, half open and stuck. When that happened there was no telling how long it would take to struggle the thing either open or shut so you could try again.

"Why don't you get a new truck?" Seely nagged him. "God knows you've got more damn money socked away than you'll ever use in one lifetime. You think I didn't see that write-up in the paper about them selling that pendant you made? I love you, Jimmy, but I have to tell you, the day I spend a hundred and fifty thousand for something to hang around my neck is the day before they take me off to the rubber room."

"The gallery gets half right off the top." He handed down a bag of sugar and she set it down. "Then there's the agent, he gets twenty percent. It used to be ten, and there was no negotiation to raise it but all of a quick it was fifteen, and in no time flat it was twenty."

"So you get less than half? You should build another place, just like this one, and sell your stuff yourself."

"And then when would I get any work done?"

"Audrey could run it. Put it on the other side of the bake shop. Easy. Give the gallery's half to her. Give the damn agent's twenty percent to her. You don't need an agent. All's you need now is someone to keep track of the list. The customers are lined up."

"Where'd you get your ideas? You'll have us all so organized up, we won't even know who we are."

"Your dad's here. That's his car parked up at Savannah's place."

"At Savannah's? Christ, they'll prob'ly kill each other!"

"So, you hoping there's gonna be like a big reunion thing? People having sudden insights and falling into each other's arms?"

"No. I'm not expecting anything. But I really wanted him here."

"Well, he's coming, darling, left foot right foot down the driveway. You'n'him can unload this stuff while you have your dad'n'son talk. Me, I've got a carload of customers turning in off the highway, gotta go."

She left the bag of sugar on the step.

"Jim." Rob moved to the truck, held out his hand.

"Hi, Dad."

"Give you a hand?"

"Appreciate it."

"You get to be the gopher, is that it?"

"Yeah. Sometimes I feel like all these women got me on a string. Jimboh, I need some wood cut for the fireplace, Jimboh, could you fix something for me, Jimboh, can you take your truck and go get... I'll be glad when some of Savannah's kids are old enough to drive."

Seely watched the faces of the two dads when they first saw the wedding cake. That was always the best part of the whole thing, even better than putting their money in the till. When she built the cake she didn't close up the box it would travel in. She left the sides down, the whole thing sitting on the carry tray with handles that Jimmy had made for her. That way everyone got a chance to get a real good look at it. There was always a moment of silence. The mothers always moved closer, their faces gone soft. Some of them cried, some just stared. The dads always looked suddenly shy. There was something about the cake that hit them in a very personal and private place. Something like confirmation, especially to the dads, that their kids were fucking, and more than that, that there were emotional ties. The cake meant lie-down-and-die-for-you. Brides' dads, grooms' dads, they all became shy.

Today the mother of the bride was looking a bit grim. But being Germ's mom could do that to a person. Mary Bailey had expected big things for her daughter.

For a while Gem had dutifully walked the path chosen for her before she was born. No bigger than a minute and she was in her majorette outfit, too little to walk down Main Street in the parade, so she rode on a float. She could prance, she could twirl her baton and she could kick like a Rockette. And cute as a bug's ear. However cute the ear was on your average bug.

She had no choice but to practise, and then there were the lessons in deportment, and the trips across the border to baby beauty pageants, and the growing collection of ribbons and trophies. Mary had her eyes set firmly on Gem winning the May Queen prize too. Mary had been May Queen, and she was convinced that she could have gone on to greater things if only her parents, who set no store at all in such things, hadn't made her sit and practise the piano and do school homework instead.

But now, everything was going along just tickety-ickety-boo. Gem kept doing what her momma wanted her to do, moving on to ballet and jazz dancing. When the kid found time to brush her teeth or pee, no one knew. If she wasn't in school or working with a tutor, she was at some lesson or practising up for the next one.

The brothers ahead of her didn't envy her in the slightest. Let the family baby get all the attention, all the oohs and ahs. They shone in their own ways, in soccer and lacrosse and baseball, and they had some measure of freedom because their mom was so fixated on Gem.

And then Gem said no. She just up and said no. To those not in the know, Mary Bailey presented a calm enough front. Talked of how a growing girl needed time to learn who she really was, said things like, It was only ever for the fun of it. Privately, however, a war was in progress. Suddenly, free of all the lessons, the practice sessions, the trips off to competitions of one kind or another, Gem had plenty of time on her hands. And a town full of teenaged boys more than eager to help her fill that time.

Mary Bailey went so far as to consider a convent, but Dick Bailey put his foot down. Finally. Instead of heading off to the sisters of charity and piety, Gem quit school and went to work for the local vet. At first she answered phones and made appointments, and after a while she started doing more. The vet picked up the tab for a couple of courses, and at about the time she should have been graduating, Gem was the one cleaning the teeth of the cairn terriers. The vet put them under and Gem did the rest.

Scraped the teeth, pulled hair and wax out of the ears, drained and rinsed the anal gland, clipped the toenails, all the stuff the dog won't put up with when it's awake.

Within a few months of learning how to do that, Gem was going on farm calls with the vet, helping deliver problem calves, helping castrate llamas, helping repair goats whose feet had given out because of thrush and neglect.

Mary Bailey hated every minute of it, and she hated it worse when Gem got sick and tired of hearing about how she was wasting her life, how she could have been a model by now or a TV star. Gem moved out. No warning, no discussion, no nothing, and she moved into a basement suite. Mary Bailey just about exploded. She hadn't driven all those thousands of miles and paid out all that money just so her only daughter could live in someone else's basement.

To add insult to injury, Gem was pregnant. And to add horrible to awful, she and the lout were moving in with his mother, Sharon. They had to. He couldn't be counted on to feed himself, let alone support a wife and child! Useless, just plain useless. Bone lazy for a start, spoiled rotten on top.

"I have no idea where we're going to keep this," Mary Bailey fretted, looking as if she were ready to gnaw holes in planks and spit the sawdust in the eyes of the world. "I wasn't expecting anything so ... big."

"It doesn't need to be kept anywhere, not in a fridge or such. Just keep this cheesecloth over it, because you don't want the flies leaving little black dots on the icing." Seely waited a polite moment, then said, "See you tomorrow." She felt as if she was going to have to shove them out the door. There they stood, gazing at the cake, Mary looking as if she'd really rather puke on it.

Seely closed up the box and taped it shut, then stood aside while the men took it by the handles and walked carefully to the station wagon. Mary Bailey pulled out her chequebook.

"You don't owe me anything," Seely said, making herself smile. "Gem and I have our own understanding about it." Damn if she'd tell this crabby old scut the cake was a present. Damn if she'd put herself in the position of hearing thank-you spoken like fuck-you. If Gem hadn't told her mother, Seely wasn't going to.

"It's gorgeous." Sharon gave Seely a quick hug and a little kiss on the ear. "The photographer is going to take some special shots of it, I'll be sure you get one. Pity they don't have competitions, you'd win."

"Oh, they have them. In the city. Several cities. I just can't be bothered."

When they finally left, Seely was tempted to open all the doors and windows and air the stench of disapproval out of the place, but another family was due to collect their cake in ten minutes, and she still had to put away the stuff Jimboh and his dad had carried in for her.

Her legs were starting to ache. Good thing she'd be off her feet soon. Savannah and Audrey had said they'd make supper, all Seely would have to do was sit down and eat. Then she could put her feet up for a while, watch the evening news, have a quiet cup of coffee or two. Then Victor, Elaine, Darlene, Lizzie and Brittany had volunteered to come down and help her with the rest of the baking. Actually what they'd said was that she could sit in a comfy chair, which they would carry down for her, and she could tell them what to do. Yeah, right.

What in hell stunt had Germ pulled to put Mary in such a mood? Or was it just a buildup of frustration? Patrick and Germ had moved into Sharon's place, and maybe Mary couldn't stand it that Germ would so willingly move in with Pat's mother after having fled from her own.

four

GEM'S WEDDING WENT OFF WITHOUT A HITCH. To Seely's surprise, there were no arguments, no tense moments, no smiles that looked more like grimaces.

They didn't see the ceremony itself, because there wasn't enough space in the little room in the courthouse. The newlyweds met everyone at the rented hall in the basement of the Legion, for the reception.

Gem had won that one too. Mary would have invited the entire town. Gem would have invited nobody. The compromise filled the hall, but then once you got Savannah and her kids in a room, it seemed full even if nobody else showed up. But others were there, and plenty of them. Gem's brothers and their girlfriends and kids, Patrick's mother and his aunts, none of whom brought their kids, and his father and several friends, which guaranteed plenty of dance partners for women whose drones preferred to stand outside drinking beer and smoking cigarettes. And Mary's brothers and their wives and kids. The count grew, the trays of sandwiches vanished, the bowls of potato salad, Greek salad, green salad, bean salad, and the cold sliced roast beef, the platters of Jamaican chicken, pastrami, and other cold cuts from the deli, all dwindled. Twice they had to bring out more paper plates and stack them on the buffet table.

There was no need for Seely to do anything. She was a guest, invited by the bride herself, so she could have sat on her duff and done nothing but smile and fan herself. However, she was Seely, and she couldn't ignore things that obviously needed done. The truly great part of it was that the kids seemed to agree with her. Vic was moving around like a trained maître d' and Elaine could have given lessons in how to be helpful and charming. Even Darlene, never an easy kid, was in there doing her bit, refilling sandwich trays, checking bowls of salad, going for more when needed. Brit, who was usually so quiet you didn't even know she had a tongue, was in the kitchen, at the sink, washing up the plastic knives, forks and spoons the littler kids brought in.

"Hey, Seely," the caterer grinned. "If you ever decide to go into business, let me know and I'll apply for a job, because there's no way I could compete against this team of yours."

"Aren't they great kids?" Seely agreed. "See that mountain of macaroons? Those kids made them. Last night. Didn't mean to pee on your leg and try to tell you it was raining, I mean I knew you were catering it, but they wanted to help out, and... don't worry about them, we'll take the leftover ones home for Jimboh's big do, day after tomorrow."

"You having it here?"

"No. Out at the place. Just family. About the time the last dog is hung I'm going to lie down and pass out cold for probably a week."

"G'wan, you love every minute of it."

"And you don't? Listen, if these kids get in your way—"

"I don't mind. Hell, I actually get to see something, for a change. I've even had a cup of tea, that's never happened before. Maybe I should hire them on."

"I think they're practising up for the big do. They're so excited about it you can feel the heat coming off them."

Gem and Patrick looked like models on the covers of high-priced magazines. They also looked happy. Sharon and her ex, Patrick's father, stood talking together, so civilly that anyone who didn't know would have thought them a long and happily married pair. Mary looked as if she had a toothache but was determined to have a good time in spite of it, and Dick, outside with the smokers and beer drinkers, was hardly seen.

Jimboh's dad went from this one to that one, shaking hands, talking about those long-dead good old days when they'd all been in school. He was one of the very few of his generation who didn't have a huge beer gut and gleaming dome. He was heavy, yes, and thick around the waist, but he owned it, rather than the other way around. Myrna and her kids looked completely at ease, even though they knew none of the main characters in the soap opera.

But it was nice to leave early. Seely thought she might get at least one of her kids to go with her, but no sooner had she whispered to Savannah that she was packing it in, than the exodus was on. How did Savannah do it? No fuss, no confusion, she just cuddled Bobby and whispered to him, and he trotted over to Brandon, then to Victor, and the kids collected themselves and slipped unobtrusively out of the Legion.

Nice to get home. Nice to lie in the hammock and sip lemonade. For all their busyness and involvement, the kids were more than happy to take off their second-best clothes and head for the swimming hole.

Jimmy and Rob had gone off somewhere by themselves, Myrna was up at the swimming hole with Savannah, the sky was painting itself in pink and peach, and Seely was just starting to feel like she could go to sleep, when a Caddy half a mile long pulled into the driveway. Seely was all set to blow up and ask why in hell people thought they could drop in any old hour of the night or day to get a donut, and then she realized who was getting out of the car.

"Fooled you, didn't we?" Lucy laughed. "Didn't think for one minute it was anybody you knew in that chrome-mobile, right?"

Seely got right to the point. Kitty would need plenty of time to get herself ready for it. "Rob's here. He and Jimboh took off, probably to the pub to get stinky drunk."

"With our luck they'll be checked into the same motel."

"Lazy Daze?"

"Good God. How do we manage it each and every time? Oh well, hell with it." Kitty shrugged.

"Hey," Lucy said. "Get yourself under control. Rob's okay, I keep telling you that."

"Yeah. Right. An absolute prince of a man."

"You got anything to eat?" Noel asked, going over to Seely for the cuddle she was offering him. He stepped into her arms and wrapped his own around her, his face pressed to her belly. "I'm hungry, Auntie Seely."

"There's so much stuff waiting for you that you'll have to stay here six years just to taste each thing." She kissed the top of his head. "You go check out the fridge, guy. Anything you see you can have."

He moved toward the door, as tired as he was hungry.

"He's put on weight," she remarked. "Good to see."

"Yeah, he was a bone rack. I don't know why he's so hungry, he's been eating all day."

"Everyone's up at the swimming hole. There's beer in the fridge, and some white wine. I can make coffee, tea, whatever you want. Lots of food. If you're waiting for me to get something for you, you'll have one helluva long wait. Make yourselves at home, get your own." She sat down in a chair. "See how nice I am, I'm leaving the hammock for the company."

"No," Lucy said, "you're leaving the damn thing for me!"

"Way to go, Lucy," Debbie muttered. "Just move to the head of the line."

"You want it? Okay."

"No, I don't want it. You want something to drink? Tea?"

"No thanks. Maybe a beer later on, but right now I'm fine."

Jim and Rob tumbled back in with two cases of beer each and quite a number of others tucked behind their belt buckles. Rob and Lucy stood hugging each other, not saying anything, just cuddling.

Kitty shook hands with Rob and smiled welcome at Myrna. Robin and Les did the teenaged thing, shuffling from one foot to the other, but managed to shake hands and say the proper things. Then Victor arrived for his hugs and kisses from Kitty, one of his all-time favourite people. When Vic left, he took the other two with him, to their obvious relief.

Somehow they wound up doing their visiting on the back porch of Jimboh's place, in the growing dusk. Noel was so tired he went to sleep on the sofa in the living room, and Kitty just left him there. Seely put a thin sheet over him, not so much to keep him warm as to keep the mosquitoes away from his baby legs, and she wiped his face with a cool cloth. He didn't waken, not even when she lifted his head and washed his neck to cool him off.

She watched him sleeping for a few minutes, then went to her own room to take a quick, cool shower. Out on the porch they were telling jokes and laughing softly, and she knew she would be as welcome as the flowers in spring if she joined them but she was too tired. She closed the door carefully and went to bed.

No sooner was she snugged in than Noel arrived.

"I thought you were asleep."

"I was. I had to pee."

"And did you?"

"Tons." Without even asking, he crawled up on her bed.

"Shuck off a few clothes," she suggested, "or we'll both sweat ourselves to death."

"You promise you won't, you know."

"You can bet on it, boy. From now until the day we both die, I promise, the only touches you'll get from me will be feel-good ones. No icky ones, I pinky swear."

He hauled off his outer layer but kept on his undershorts, and crawled under the sheet.

"Nice ginch," she yawned. "Kitty get them for you?"

"Yeah. They're boxers. They're the best. See, they've got writing on the elastic part."

"Yeah, and pigs. I never saw boxers with pigs on them before."

"That's *Babe*. Not just pigs, *Babe!*" He lay back, then lifted his head, rumpled the pillow and rolled on his side, facing her, his head on his mess of a pillow. "You remember, you promised."

"I remember. I promised. You have to promise too."

"Me?" He gaped.

"Sure, you. Fair's fair. Equal equal."

"Okay. I promise."

"And no tickling. I hate it when you go to bed with a guy and he starts tickling."

"I won't tickle."

He yawned, and it was contagious. Seely yawned. Noel yawned again, and so did she, and then they drifted into sleep.

Hours later, when Kitty was ready to head back to the motel, she looked for Noel in the living room, then started checking the other rooms. When she finally found him, sprawled on top of the sheets in Seely's bed, she smiled and closed the door again. "We'll pick him up in the morning."

By the time they arrived to collect him, Noel was up and eating his way through a pile of pancakes.

"Blackberry syrup," he laughed. "Auntie Seely made it last summertime. And whipped cream too."

"What a spoiled brat you are," Kitty pretended to sulk. "Everybody in the family fusses over you. They all spoil you. Nobody spoils me!"

"I'm nicer." Noel could play the game as well as Victor could. "And I'm a lot better looking."

"Are not!"

"Am so. I've got eyelashes. You don't."

"I do so have eyelashes, look!"

"Yeah. Little stubby ones. Look at mine...see?" He batted his eyes at her and she burst out laughing, called him a flirt and a heartbreaker. "We made a pack." He swallowed and licked his lips. "Auntie Seely said it was a pack. I won't icky-touch her and she won't icky-touch me."

"Good pact. Really good one. The word is pact, okay? A pack is a whole bunch of things, like a pack of dogs or a pack of children. A pact is a promise. Stronger than a pinky-swear. Stronger than cross my heart and hope to die. The strongest."

"You want some pancakes?" Seely asked hopefully.

"Love some. Maybe six dozen of them."

"Right. Auntie Lucy?"

"I've got my napkin tucked under my chin already."

"Good. I'll put on fresh coffee. Jimboh, you okay with pancakes or do you want some bacon and eggs with it?"

"Pancakes suit me just fine. Aud?"

"Bet I can eat more than you can."

"Nobody," Seely said firmly, "can eat more pancakes than Jimboh can."

"I can," Noel said quietly.

"Can not," Jimmy challenged.

"Can so. I already have!" and the boy laughed so freely, a person would believe nothing the least bit tacky or trashy had ever come down anywhere near him. "I've eaten four already. I win!"

"Hey, I haven't even had a chance."

"It's over. Contest's over and I win."

"Kitty, I do believe you're raising a cheater."

"No, we're raising a winner, right Noel?"

"Can I take one outside with me?" Noel asked Seely. "Please?'

"Sure. Here, I'll make you a sort of sandwich, see, we'll roll it up and you can hold it like a lollipop."

"And that's five," Noel said to Jimmy.

"Yeah, but that one won't count because you aren't going to eat it. You're going to give it to your invisible friend."

"So what?" And the kid was hurrying to the door. "I win. I win."

By bedtime that night everything was set up and ready, except for the items that had to stay in the fridge, like the cold meats and the potato salad. They all went to bed early. Seely was half hoping Noel would crawl in with her again, but he was velcroed to Kitty, as if he were worried she'd leave him by the side of the road.

They all slept late, even Bobby, who could usually be counted on to serve as everyone else's alarm clock. By the time they were up and fed and the dishes were done, they'd cut it so fine that Savannah started to worry-wart them about being late.

They made it on time, no problem at all. They had warned the justice of the peace and he'd scheduled the ceremony, brief as it was, in the biggest empty room he could find, a courtroom. They sat one beside the other, like cormorants on a log, watching as Jimmy became Audrey's husband, instead of being sent off for eighteen months for punching out the bartender.

Vic looked so adult, so gorgeous, and he didn't miss a beat, and Elaine was so beautiful it made Savannah feel shy. The words were spoken, the paper signed, the rings exchanged and it was over, shockingly quickly.

Rob looked to be on the brink of crying. He clutched Myrna's hand and blinked rapidly, his eyes glued to Jimmy's face.

Savannah hoped his heart was breaking into seventy zillion jagged-edged pieces. All that emotion, all that so-glad-we-finally-know-each-other bull-shit. Yeah, jagged-edged, so that each and every one of them pricked him, tore at him and hurt. He could have had so much, and now he knew it, but however much he knew it, he knew nothing compared to what the ones he'd walked away from had been forced to learn.

Just before they entered the room, Audrey took her ring off and gave it to Vic, who, when it was time, handed it to Jim to put back on her finger. Then Elaine handed something to Audrey and she reached for Jimboh's hand. The ring she slipped on his finger was wide, and absolutely plain. He looked at it as if he had been given the moon.

And then they were on their way out again. None of the kids made any noise at all until they were out on the sidewalk, and then the little buggers cut loose in what was obviously a rehearsed plan. "Three cheers for Jimmy and Audrey!" they screamed.

Audrey jumped, Jimmy laughed and blushed beet red, and passers-by jerked around, surprised. A dozen kids' voices can carry an incredible dis-tance. "Hip hip, *hooray!*" they all yelled, even Victoria, who had no idea what was going on but had been coached.

The party was most properly defined as a wingding. Even though they had all agreed it would be family only, others showed up. Noreen and Boris, and Jimmy had made sure Grisham was invited. And Fred the friend-ly faggot who had stuck with Glen right to the end, and was now untan-gling his own ties to this earth and getting ready to die. He came with his current boyfriend, an older man with grey hair and calloused hands. Fred introduced the guy as Joe, and after some uneasiness, Rob discovered Joe was a logger. With some difficulty Rob pushed past his knee-jerk recoil against gearboxes and started a conversation.

Noreen amazed the kids by drinking beer mixed with tomato juice. "What?" she teased. "You thought teachers didn't eat or drink or pee or anything?"

Gem and Pat dropped by, saying they couldn't stay long, then stayed for the whole mad show.

And then, at a nod from Seely, the kids faded quietly, and a moment later, Seely pulled her own disappearing act. In a giggling bunch they ran for the bake shop. It was so much fun when she could see it through, when her cakes didn't get carried out of the shop and left to the dubious mercies of people she hardly knew and sometimes could barely tolerate.

Jimboh's cake was too big to carry, but that was fine, thank you, they had come prepared. Victor backed the pickup to the side door. Instead of fighting with the trick tailgate they took the bugger off entirely and propped it against the side of the building. Elaine got the ramp that Seely had coaxed Jimboh to make, "in case you're busy working or something and I have to get a load of stuff. I won't be able to lift it out, see?" Because Jimboh had made it, the thing fit perfectly.

Victor was going to be every bit as handy as Jimboh was. No sooner had Seely told him what she wanted than he set about getting it together. In the second-hand store they'd found an old-fashioned English pram, with the big easy-rolling wheels. An hour or two of intense work and Vic had the buggy hood off and a brand new piece of plywood in place. The plywood was freshly painted, white, and it didn't take any more than ten minutes to get the splatters and mess off the kids' skin, although they did have to hide Bobby's blue denim shorts until after the wedding, in order to keep the secret. Even Bobby managed not to spill the beans. Once he almost told Noel about it, but didn't. Victor gave him an entire chocolate bar, all to himself, for holding his tongue.

When the plywood was in place, and secured with straps that went under the buggy frame, Seely built the cake. Exactly as she had envisioned it, layer by layer, two square ones side by each for the bottom, then the magical tower.

The kids helped. Seely wanted to yell at them to go away, fuck off, get lost, go play on the yellow line on the highway. Really she wanted to do it all herself. Whose brother was Jimmy? And hadn't she been practising all those years, making cakes for other people, finding out what worked better, what worked best? And who were all these damn kids? Why should she have to include them?

Well, to shut them up. And to get them on her side. She couldn't work on the cake during the day, not with Audrey down there, she had to make it in the evenings, and the only way she could do that was with their help.

She coached them so that whenever someone asked, "Where's Seel?" a kid would answer lazily, "She said she was going to bed early, her back is sore," or, "I think she went up to the swimming hole." If the bunch of them were at the swimming hole, it was, "She went back to the house for something."

What they had actually done was 'fess up immediately, every time. Seely thought they were making excuses, but in fact they replied, offhandedly, "Prob'ly working on Uncle Jimboh's cake."

The baby buggy, with its increasingly heavy treasure, was covered with a clean white sheet and kept in the walk-in cooler during the day. Once the rest of the family had carefully explained to Audrey what Seely was like when she thought she'd been thwarted, Audrey made sure she didn't go near the cooler. "We're going to need more raisin buns out here, Seely."

"I'll get 'em!"

"Some woman named Sarah just phoned and asked if you could put aside three lemon squares for her. She'll be out in fifteen minutes."

"I'll get 'em!"

No matter what she'd been doing, Seely had put it aside and dashed into the cooler.

Now they brought the pram out of the cooler room and removed the sheet. Brittany, Darlene, Lizzie, Elaine and Caroline had gathered fresh roses and picked off the petals one by one. At first Seely was ticked off because they hadn't restricted themselves to the ones she wanted. But even the Navajo deliberately weave a mistake into each blanket, because nothing is perfect, nothing is supposed to be perfect, and it would tempt creation to dare defy the supernaturals, each of which has some little or big thing wrong with them.

Anyway, even if it wasn't exactly what Seely had had in mind, it worked. In fact, she hated to admit it, but the cake actually worked better than if the petals had all been the same colour. Every layer had petals sitting on the part that stuck out from the layer above it. And on top, where she'd made the little wall, it was as close to perfect as you could get without tempting creation.

"Okay, line yourselves up, Aunt Seely in the middle. Leave a space for me." Elaine fussed and fiddled with the camera, then hurried to get into the photo. The flash went off sooner than they expected, so of course they had to do it over again. Then they did it over five more times, just to be on the safe side.

Then the clean sheet went back on, to protect the cake and to hold the rose petals in place, and with everyone pushing gently, they got Seely's masterpiece into the back of Jimboh's rickety old fart of a truck. Vic drove, because Seely was on the verge of fainting from worry about the cake and didn't dare leave it for one minute.

They didn't even try to go up the slope to Savannah's place, although that's where the wingding was supposed to happen. Hell with it. No way they were taking the risk of anything slipping or sliding. Victor hit the horn. The kids yelled, shouted and waved. Elaine had to hang onto Bobby or he'd have been over the side, he was so excited. Noel had been included so he wouldn't feel left out, and Robin and Les were sitting in the truck with Vic.

When the others saw the truck and heard the noise, they ran down the slope to Jimboh's house. Seely waited until they were all there. "Jimmy," she said, almost in tears. "Jimmy and Audrey...I made you guys a cake."

Caroline supervised, and the kids lifted off the sheet quickly. One or two petals drifted as the kids stepped back. Jimboh stared. Everyone stared. Not a word was spoken.

And then Jimboh started to cry. Audrey put her arms around him and he cried on her shoulder. His dad went over and put his arms around the both of them, but he didn't quite fit into the picture and nobody knew it better than he did.

"Well done," Lucy said. "Congratulations, Seely!"

Then Seely started to bawl, which kicked off Savannah, and once the first tear slid down her face, all three wise men had to rush over, snow-white hankies in hand, dabbing gently and talking softly to her. Seely knew she would never in her life make a lovelier cake.

Elaine set up her camera and Victor brought out the knife, specially sharpened. Seely showed Jimboh and Audrey how to cut through the icing.

"There's a trick," she said. "The damn stuff is as hard as plaster, but...see...if you use the electric carving knife...and blow gently so the powdery stuff doesn't blur up the roses?"

Pictures pictures pictures, new roll of film, more pictures. Savannah had her goddamn video camera going. What a pain in the face those things are! Every time you turn around, there's one of them practically shoved up your nose. What, everyone in the world thinks they're going to be Oliver Stone? "Three cheers for Aunt Seely!" young Rob hollered. The noise was incredible. And then it was three cheers for the cake.

Seely climbed down off the back of the box of the pickup and Jimboh hugged her. "Thank you, smooth little seal," he whispered. "That's one hell of a cake!"

They ate, then ate more. They drank, then drank some more, then ate again. They danced with each other or by themselves. They trooped up to the swimming hole to drink a toast to Gran and to Glen, and trooped back down to the house for refills. Rob disappeared for a half hour and came back with a small travel cage in his hands.

"Understand you used to swipe 'em, so thought I'd get you one of your own," he teased. Jimmy looked inside the cage, and his look of surprise was so comical that everyone else laughed before they even got to see the joke.

"What's *that?*"

"That, my boy, is an English moor cat. She's a year and a half old and she's pregnant."

"Is she part elephant?"

"Nope. What I understand is, they probably started out as ordinary cats, and then, over the years, centuries maybe, they developed into what you see. They come in any colour of any other cat, but they're all big."

"How much does she weigh?"

"Thirty-five pounds." Rob set the cage on the ground. "I guess what happened was all the small ones got picked off by hawks or something. Only the big ones could survive. So they just kept breeding big to big until they had bigger."

"I'll tell you right now," Savannah said firmly, "if that goddamn monster of yours eats my cat, there'll be a barbecue in the back yard."

"Oh, she's a sweetie, aren't you, Mabel."

"Mabel? Who called a cat Mabel?"

"I did," Rob laughed. "When she came, her papers read Benderly's Moor Maiden Sylph. But I call her Mabel. You know, get off the table, Mabel, the money's for the beer."

"I'll be damned."

"I'd keep her in her cage for a few days, let her get used to the place."

"I'd keep her in her cage for the rest of her life," Savannah countered. "At least until the little kids are a bit bigger, so they can fight her off if she gets hungry."

Noel let her out of the cage within minutes. Mabel made no attempt to flee. After all, Noel had a plate of sliced turkey and several pieces of cold cuts. Mabel meowed and Noel sat still, holding out a piece of meat. Mabel reached out with a paw as big as a marshmallow, hooked the meat gently and took it to her mouth. "Poor you," Noel crooned, "you're real hungry. Poor girl. Poor poor girl." He gave her a slice of turkey, which she took with her paw and laid on the floor to be eaten. "Nice Mabel." Noel stroked her, and she purred briefly through the chewing.

Noel liked the cat. He wished she were his. But it wouldn't be a good idea, not with Dog and Pup waiting. Mabel wouldn't be happy if Pup chased her, and Pup wouldn't be happy if she caught Mabel.

Anyway, Thingy always knew best and Thingy said to wait. Thingy said to get off the floor and get Mabel a bowl of water to drink. Thingy sat next to Mabel and stroked and stroked and stroked, and Mabel paid him no attention at all.

"Noel, did you let the cat out of the cage?" Aunt Audrey asked.

"She's hungry," Noel answered calmly. "And that cage is too small for her."

"She doesn't even know this place."

"She don't care." He lowered the bowl carefully, but slopped a little anyway. "Hey, Mabel, look."

"If that cat runs away, young man, you'll be in real trouble."

"She won't."

"You have to learn to leave things alone when they don't belong to you."

Sometimes Aunt Audrey could be a real nag. How would she like to be inside a too-small cage while everyone else was having a good time and eating as much as they wanted and drinking and laughing? Of course Mabel wanted out. Cats love parties!

When Audrey reached down to put the cat back in the cage, Mabel hissed.

"She don't want to go in that thing." Noel didn't want to be cheeky, but sometimes you have to almost yell at big people.

"Don't get sassy."

"No, but look." He stroked the cat. "If you stroke her, she won't swear like that. If you try to put her in that cage, she might bite or something."

"Dear sweet God in heaven, tell me I haven't arrived at the place in my life where I take orders from a smart-mouth brat and a jumbo-sized alley cat."

"I'm not a brat!" he flared.

Audrey shook her head and went to get some more ice. Kitty must not have any idea what a little fart her precious Noel was. Treated him as if he were made out of fine-spun glass. Well, she was just making a stick to beat her own back with. He'd be a handful or worse by the time he was ten. Jimmy talked of having kids, but Audrey wasn't convinced. What did she know of raising them? What did anybody know? When she'd said as much, Jimmy had laughed, "Hey, we can always take it up and dump it in with Savannah's crowd, she'd probably never notice one or two extras."

"She could tell by the colour," Audrey snapped, and Jimboh thought she was joking one hundred percent.

Audrey was scared of the whole damn idea. She'd heard that after age thirty, a woman's eggs started to age. What did you get with old eggs? Pray God she wouldn't find out. She could keep on taking the pill. She could even hide it from Jim that she was taking it. Would that be fair? Or she could just claim that she was terrified to have a baby because the cat might eat it.

What kind of dip-shit present was a thirty-five-pound cat?

She went back out with the bowl of ice and right away everyone was talking to her and laughing and asking questions, and the next time she saw the cat it was following Victoria around.

Audrey couldn't help it, she gasped. "Watch out," she blurted, "Mabel might bite Victoria."

"Don't worry," Savannah laughed. "More chance of Vic biting the cat."

"How'd the cat get out of her cage?" Rob asked.

"Noel let him out," Audrey answered, just about ready to utter a few truths about dear darling spoiled rotten Noel.

"Little bugger needs his arse warmed," Rob flared.

"The cat was hungry." Audrey was suddenly on Noel's side.

"He was *told*," Rob insisted.

Young Robin turned away, looking for Les. They looked at each other, then moved toward Noel.

"Ah hell," Jimboh laughed. "Hey, Mabel, don't claw up any of the kids, okay? I know they're all pains in the toosh, but their parents are kind of fond of them."

"I'll put her back in the cage." Rob made as if to go get the cat.

"Leave her, Rob." Jimboh's voice lost its soft tone. The smile was gone.

Rob looked at him. Something passed between them and then Rob was shrugging, laughing.

"She's not going to run off," Jimmy said confidently. "If she'd been going to run off Noel wouldn't have let her out, would you guy?"

Noel's face was flooded with relief. Audrey watched him with Jim, watched as Jim took a fork and a paper plate, loaded it with ham and gave it to Noel.

"Would you feed my cat for me, please?" he winked.

Bobby was right there. "Can I help?"

Victoria sat down beside Mabel and the baby had a slice of ham too. The rest of the kids hunkered or squatted or sat or stood watching and Mabel alternately ate and wove between ankles, rubbed against shins, or pressed herself gently against the baby's back.

"See?" Noel was uncertain, his fingers trembling. He stared at Jimmy as if his life hung in the balance. "See, Uncle Jimmy? She was lonely."

"It's okay, Noel. It's fine. You did a good thing." Jimmy went over and stroked the cat.

"How did you know Jimboh swiped a cat?" Savannah asked suddenly.

"Mom told me," said Rob.

"When?"

"I'd phone her. Not every week, or second week, but when I could, sort of. She told me Jimboh came home with a Siamese cat. He said it followed him but she knew he had stolen it. Said it had kittens and he was going to sell them to pay for the cat food."

"I didn't know you phoned. You never talked to *us*."

"No. You'd have said something to your mother." He shrugged. "It seemed easier the other way."

"Easy," Seely muttered, but she didn't say anything else. It was none of her business one way or the other. He wasn't *her* dad.

Kitty had seen the flare of anger, the way the two boys moved toward Noel, as if to protect him. It told her all she needed to know. Myrna didn't seem to notice any of it. Or maybe she was used to it. Old lay-down-the-law, do-as-I-say-not-as-I-do, good-swift-kick-up-the-arse. The big I-am, the head of the house, the boss of all he can find to boss.

He'd spanked each and every one of them within a couple of days of coming home from camp. Glen, in particular. Thrashed his backside with the belt. Lots of pushing and shoving too.

Would it have wrecked his life to talk to them on the phone at Christmas time? No, just take the easy way out, find an excuse, then feel sorry for himself. Just let the old bastard try to warm Noel's arse! Or any of the other kids.

More people arrived, none of them invited, all of them sure of a welcome. Several were Seely's customers, and when they looked at the cake, she knew they wanted one just like it. The answer was no. There would never be another one like that. But she knew she could charge damn near any price and they'd pay without blinking an eye.

She could plant roses all up the driveway, both sides. Singles and groups. A half dozen or so white ones, then a bit of a space and some bright red ones, and so on, and there was a guy south of town who made trellises. She could get them put up all around the bake shop, plant climbers and ramblers and maybe get some hedge roses along the front fence. Then she'd be able to tell people to take a walk around and choose the petals they wanted on their cake. And she was going to make a rule of it: if you took the tower of roses, you did not get the little bride doll and the little groom doll. She was so sick of those damn dolls! As if anything about the plastic image was true, as if it would last, as if it wouldn't wear off before the reception was over.

She couldn't shake the little bit of bad feeling, though. She'd had it stuck in her head for too many years. They'd been married, and then it was just awful, and them going out the upstairs window. Thank God for Kitty. Vic was such a good kid, such a nice kid, such a good-looking guy and he'd have been mush. But Kitty—you just don't find a lot like that, and she had to pee on her head, of course. But they had been married. She didn't get married, Savannah didn't, Glen didn't and Kitty didn't, but Jimboh did. The only one of them to get married. She could not shake the sliver of dread.

Kitty danced with Christie while some of the guests watched sideways out the corners of their eyes. They all knew and they'd known for years, all these nice hometown people. Must run in the family, you know the brother was queer too, and then there's that older one, as queer as they come, that one. Must be genetic.

But it isn't polite to kick up a fuss when you're on the queers' property, attending the wedding of the queer's crazy brother and the town chippie. No, if you're going to eat their roast turkey and potato salad, if you're going to pig out on fresh-baked lemon square and Nanaimo bars, if you're going to guzzle their beer and wine and hard liquor and have yourself a real good time, then you have to be polite.

So they watched sideways, saving it all up to gossip about when they got home. My God, did you *see* them, up and dancing away as if it was the most natural thing in the world? I mean I personally don't care *what* people do, but right out front, with all those kids around! What if those kids get the idea it's okay? Someone should really contact the welfare about it. I wonder which one of them had the little boy, he calls them both Mom and he calls them both by name, either or the other. And did that other one sit by the bed and watch? And who was the dad?

Kitty danced with Deb too. Put that in your pipe and smoke it, McGee. Then, just to stir the pot, Deb danced with Christie. And halfway through, Savannah went over and cut in, danced off with Chris, so Deb went to Kitty, and Lucy laughed and laughed, then deliberately put her cane aside and gimped over to Noreen, who was already handing her beer to Boris and heading out to dance with Lucy.

Watching Lucy dance was something. She sort of lurched to the beat of the music, but it was still dancing, and she was laughing, and if she lost her balance and hit the dirt there would be plenty of people to pick her up.

Gave them all something to take home and mumble about to each other, anyway. Kitty considered delivering the lecture. One in every family, mostly in closets. One in eight, part of the diversity, and by the way, did you know that one in every two thousand babies born is genitally inconclusive? The doctor decides whether it's a boy or a girl, checks the M or F on the government form. Sometimes one or the other is chosen because it would be easier to operate for this than for that, and sometimes because the parents were hoping for an M rather than an F, or vice versa, but very very quickly after being born, snip snip snip and the question is deferred. For a few, the surgery "works," they grow up M or F and seem as content as anyone, but most of them grow up feeling unsettled, and confused and sad, because the one choice was made instead of the other.

Fred and Tony danced, with each other and then with Debbie and Christie. The kids danced, alone and with each other and with various adults. Alan ate too much and had to run into the bathroom and hork it up. But he cleaned up after himself, then went up the slope to brush his teeth and have a bit of a lie-down. After a while he came back, dressed in clean clothes and not hungry.

Rob and Myrna were among the first to leave. Robin and Les stayed. For a moment it looked as if Rob was going to put down his size twelve and insist the boys go to the motel, but Myrna leaned over and whispered something, and Rob shrugged and let it drop.

Kitty stayed until midnight, then found Noel asleep on the back seat of the Caddy, where he wouldn't get overlooked and left behind. Lucy was more than ready to call it a night, Christie was half-hammered and would have stayed longer but didn't resist, and Debbie might have stayed but she was outnumbered and gave in, laughing.

Savannah herded the younger members of her troop up the slope to the big new house. The three wise men went with her to help get their kids ready for bed, supervising teeth, buttoning pyjama tops, cuddling and smooching and talking softly in their own language, the kids answering them in the same musical sounding syllables.

The older kids stayed another hour or so, picking up paper plates and scraping them onto one big paper platter—for Mabel's breakfast, they said. They forgot to take a plate of scraps up for Savannah's cat, but Puss solved the problem by waddling down the hill, tail in the air, belly full of kittens, and she went to the platter of scraps and began to eat. Mabel got up and moved to the platter. She was about four times the size of Puss, who was not a small cat. They looked at each other over the mountain of food.

Mabel reached out, hooked a piece of meat, pulled it from the pile and got it in her mouth. Puss did exactly the same thing with a different piece of meat. Mabel gorped hers down and got another piece. Puss took her time, licking her lips, cleaning her paw. Then she made her silent meow.

Both cats lowered their heads to the food. Mabel wasn't really hungry, she was just making her presence known, but Puss was convinced she was starving, and packed away as much as she could. By the time she had finished eating, Mabel was completely involved in grooming herself.

Jimboh could see Bones over there at the scrap pile, hunkered down, stroking the cats, ignored by both of them. Bones looked up and caught Jimboh's gaze. Deliberately, he lifted his hand from Mabel's back and tapped himself on the chest. Jimmy smiled lazily and imitated the gesture, then pulled his cigarettes out of his shirt pocket and lit one.

Like that, Bones was sitting on Jimboh's lap, leaning into his face. Each time Jimmy puffed, Bones inhaled. Jimmy raised his bottle of beer and sipped. Bones smiled, then puckered his white-rimmed mouth. Jimboh could feel the beer in his mouth but no taste—it had all been sucked away by the Squeyanx. He sipped again and same thing, no taste, just liquid. He wondered how many beer he could drink and still stay sober, and whether Bones would get drunk. No sooner had the thought arrived than the shades of the others did too. They were everywhere, and he could only hope Gran was among them. They hovered over the plates of food, inhaling and swooning. They bunched and gathered around the wedding cake, still ruling over the soon-to-be patio, the rose petals as fresh as when they were picked. Which was probably because of Bones. By this time any ordinary flower would be wilted and turning brown.

Jimmy looked at the wide plain gold band on his finger. Absolutely no design at all. Just exactly wonderful. How had she known?

Just in case Gran was there, Jimmy went to the kitchen and made a pot of tea. He took it outside and put it on one of the rented tables. He filled a mug with tea, added sugar, no milk, and stirred, thinking of Gran, of how she had literally saved them all. Not just the night the gates of hell swung open to admit them, although, for sure she had gotten them safely out to the darkness, to the ditch by the old barn. But all those other times, kicking in the door and taking them back to feed them. No, they wouldn't have starved to death, but something in them would have died.

He went back to his chair. Audrey was deep in conversation with Seely and Gem, who hours and hours ago had said that she could only stay a little while. Patrick was almost asleep. Six beer ago, he'd had too much to drink. Nice enough guy, but soft in ways and places nobody should be.

And the bone people, whoever they had once been, hanging around in two loose groups, one bunch hovering and sniffing at the clear plastic glasses with bits and slurps of wine or gin, the others over by the teapot. Would one of them be Gran's husband? None of the kids had ever called him Grandpa. Why would they, none of them had known him. There were photos, but they didn't mean anything. Was he here? Would he and Gran still be together? Or was all of that finished long before you became a spook?

"You going to fall asleep in this chair?" Audrey teased. Jimmy was startled. He hadn't been asleep, but he must have been wool gathering or spaced right out, because everybody was gone except for the two cats, who lay curled together, purring. And Audrey. And him.

"I'd rather go to sleep in our bed," he smiled at her.

"Yeah, me too."

"Where's the cake?"

"It's in the kitchen. It's fine. You were miles away!"

"Absent-minded professor, I guess."

They showered together, then naked, hand in hand, they walked to the bedroom, closed the door, and lay down together. Both of them sighed at the same time. Jimmy grinned.

"What?" she whispered.

"We both sighed at the same time. That's nice."

"What's really nice is lying here with my head on you, where I can hear your heart beating. I can feel you breathing and almost hear you breathing. And it feels..." She couldn't find the word, but he nodded and stroked her with his free hand. His other arm was under her, fitting around the dips and curves in her body that seemed to have been made just for him.

"I wish I could get madly, wildly passionate," she yawned.

"Damn if I know who you'd be that way with." He yawned too.

They slept together in the heat, their bodies damp, the breeze through the half-open window faint and warm.

Kitty, Christie, Noel, Deb and Myrna went up to the swimming hole with the kids. Lucy and Rob had gone off, saying they were going to drink beer, play pool, catch up on old times, and get drunk as skunks together. Lucy hadn't had a drink in so long nobody could remember when, and Myrna said Rob would probably have two or three, then switch to ginger ale.

"He used to drink something fierce," she told them, out of earshot of the kids, "and then one day he was in the shower and he said he could hear this bang bang bang sound, and it wasn't until it was all over that he realized what he'd been hearing was the sound of his own head banging on the wall. He blacked out, doesn't even remember getting dizzy or anything, just *conk*, and he had a convulsion. Got himself to the hospital and they had to set his broken nose and stitch up both eyebrows. He looked like he'd gone a few rounds with a prizefighter. And he had another one in the emergency, but they had a shot ready and they looked after him. Then they took him off for a million tests, eh, and put him in what they called an induced coma, and when they brought him up out of it, the doctor gave it to him. No frills, no lace, no whipped cream. He was murdering his brain with the booze. He had missed the DTs, because they had him conked out. But they told him, have a few more of the world-famous benders and you'll be lucky if you die, because the alternative is to sit around like a vegetable until you do."

"Jesus Christ," Christie breathed. "I had a neighbour, when I was a kid, that must have been what happened to him. Family had to do for him same as if he was just a little baby. Diapers and all."

"Oh, wouldn't that be fun," Deb agreed. "Bad enough when it's a year-old kid."

"If anything like that happens to me," Kitty said firmly, "would someone please put rat poison in a vanilla milk shake?"

"Swift shot in the head for me," Christie put in. She slipped her arm around Kitty's waist. "I promise you, old girl. But you have to promise me."

"I promise. I'll wangle you away from the caregivers, take you for a ride in the truck. Buy you a soft ice cream, help you eat it. Set you down in some really nice place in the bush, give you a piece of candy to suck—if you can suck on your own."

"You want candy?"

"Yeah. Kraft caramels." Kitty kissed the top of Christie's head.

"You two sure got some weird ideas about what's romantic," Myrna teased. "Now, Rob, he's got some strange ones too, but he doesn't come close to you two."

"So he quit drinking?" Deb prompted her.

"Yeah, he tried, anyway. Did the AA thing and hated it. Went to a residential drug and alcohol rehab and that worked better. But he's got this thing...I mean a real *thing*...about never taking another drink. So every now and again he'll have one or two. Three at most, then cut himself off."

"Well, sure." Kitty seemed surprised that Myrna didn't understand. "If you do what *they* tell you and never have another drink, all the choice gets taken away from you. If you can take just one or two, it's your choice. Each time you switch to ginger ale or tea or whatever, you've just spit in the devil's eye. See, you gorgeous hunk, I *can* control it."

"Gorgeous hunk?" Debbie stared at Kitty. "The devil?"

"Well, sure. You read the Bible. It says he was the star of the morning, the most beautiful of God's creations. He was, like, even more of everything than Michael. They were both archangels. Nobody and nothing was prettier than Lucifer. Would you be tempted by something with horns and warts and fangs? But something beautiful, something that sounded kind and gentle, something that felt gloriously relaxing and tender...bang, you're hooked."

"Pass the collection plate," Christie laughed softly. "The Right Reverend Kit Loose-a-Screw will lead us all in song."

"Kitty," Noel called. "Kitty! *Look!*"

He was standing on Victor's shoulders, balanced unsteadily, wearing a bright red and blue floater vest and a pair of boxers with ET on the front. "You watchin'?" he screeched.

"I'm watching." Kitty stood up so he could see her watching him.

He didn't dive so much as flop off, over Vic's head and into the water. Vic bent over and had him immediately. Noel's legs wrapped around Vic's waist, hanging on like a baby possum, but he was grinning widely. "See? See, I went under!"

They clapped and cheered, and then of course Bobby had to show how he could float face down, and they clapped and cheered some more.

Savannah and the three wise men didn't go up to the swimming hole. They asked her if she would please show them around the place instead.

"Then we can join the others," said Shemp, letting her know that they wanted some alone time with her.

"You should change from your nice pants to jeans," she told them. "Me too. There are burrs and brambles and enough grass seeds to start a hayfield."

They changed, she changed, and then they walked slowly down to the bake shop and had a quick look through the windows.

She took them to where the old barn had been, and they stood, staring at the long grass, but she knew that they were envisioning what they could of that night she had told them about. Moe found the ditch and looked down in it, shaking his head. He reached for Savannah's hand and squeezed gently, and if she'd been one to fall in love she might have done it, but that wasn't what she was and she hoped she never would be.

She walked them up to the bush and showed them the places she'd considered to be her very own. Some of her hideouts were overgrown, but the big fir was still there. Nothing much grew underneath, it was too shady and too acidic. They all sat down and Savannah shared the place with them.

"You are a good woman, Savannah," Larry said. "You are loyal. You are faithful. You keep your children, and two other women's children, all of them our children."

"Even Jason, and he is not an easy child. Even Bradley," Shemp said, smiling slightly. It was as close as she had heard to an acknowledgement that they, like she, had doubts about parentage.

"They're good kids." She leaned on one elbow, her head propped on her hand.

"We wanted to tell you that if you want to find another man, we won't make any trouble for you."

She gazed at them. First at Larry, because she always enjoyed looking at the beauty of him, then at Shemp, and finally at Moe. Small, soft Moe. She really did hope he was Vic's sperm donor. She was as certain as she could be without DNA tests that he was Bobby's dad, but she wasn't as sure about Vic.

"Our mother has won her battle and is quite happy," Moe told her. "We are each of us married now." There was no joy in his voice. "And so it is only fair and right that if you want to marry, we allow it."

"I don't want to get married," she told them, and Moe seemed to relax a bit. "Right now I'm not even interested in dating or even meeting a man, or men."

"If that changes, and if you do, we promise: no trouble," Larry said. "We know that not once in all the time we've known you have you been with another man. You have not even flirted. You are a good, loyal woman."

"Been with another man?" She couldn't help it, she laughed. They laughed along with her, not insulted. "Oh God, guys," she managed. "When would I have found the time? Or the energy?"

"Betty found time, and Carol found time," Larry said. "But never you."

"I had three of the best-looking, nicest, kindest and most gentle horny men anyone could have. I had everything. Too much, if the truth be known."

"So, let us go watch our children being very North American." Moe stood first and held out his hand for Savannah. He pulled her up, then held her. "I miss you, my red-headed woman," he whispered. "I dream of your skin. It glows in the starlight."

"Come on, Moe. Please, darling." She held him, kissed the soft skin on his cheekbone. "You'll make me cry."

He nodded, his neat beard against her cheek. She loved the little line under his chin where the beard was rolled up tidily on itself, completely under control.

"Tell me about your wife," she invited.

"She is very young." He held her hand as they began walking slowly out of the bush. "She has very small breasts and she's very shy about that. She hates to be seen without clothes. I told her it was one area where I was going to be very insistent. And she is obedient. I do not fuck her," he said, without shyness.

"Why not?"

"She is frightened." He shrugged. "She has had no...information, no education at all...she trembles if I hold her."

"Good man, Moe. You're wonderful."

"She goes to school," he went on. "I signed her up. She did not want to go, she was very frightened, but...she is obedient. First I got her a tutor. We all got tutors, I mean we all got a tutor. Maybe I need one myself!" He laughed. "But we got a tutor and told our wives they had to learn."

"They are all obedient," Larry said dryly.

"The tutor is born here," Shemp said. "Some of what she teaches, I don't approve."

"You don't have to," Savannah said. "You weren't born here, you don't know what a woman needs to survive here."

"Larry said that. Moe said that. So...I don't argue."

"That's a change," Larry said.

"Are the other wives as young as Moe's wife?"

"No. My wife is twenty-two. She is very beautiful, she has long, long hair, she has nice breasts and lovely wide hips, and she can sing."

"And yours?"

"My wife is twenty," Shemp smiled. "She has big breasts, the biggest of the three. She has very long legs. She sings too. Some nights the two of them sing together. She cooks, but not as well as you did, and I think she is already pregnant."

"Well, let's hope Bindi doesn't decide *that* kid has no soul." Savannah couldn't stop the bitterness from showing.

"We have told our mother that if she wants any children from these wives she brought over for us," Moe said, "she must acknowledge and be kind to all our children. She was very angry. We went to the temple, all three together, and we talked to the priest and to some of the older men. They talked to their wives. Their wives talked to our mother."

"He told our mother that she must at least pretend to be a grand-mother to all the children," Larry said admiringly, "or he would go to a doctor and get a vasectomy and she would never hold any child of his."

"Moe!"

"Our children have done nothing wrong," Moe said. "And they do so have souls. Every one of them."

"She must have just about shit."

"I'm not sure," Larry laughed. "It is probably packed solid inside her for sixty-three years. Maybe that is why she walks so stiff and straight."

Bobby saw them coming first. The next moment he was out of the swimming hole and running as fast as he could, dripping water, yelling wordlessly, his arms out. Moe ran to him, scooped him up and held him, stroking his back, stroking his legs, talking softly.

Larry stopped and watched, then turned to Savannah. "You must talk to Moe. Please. His wife has told my wife she is terrified he does not even like her. She expects to be fucked. She was brought up knowing she would be fucked. I have talked to him, but you have to give him permission to think of you when he fucks this wife."

"How old is she?"

"Sixteen."

"Dear God. She's a baby!"

They had planned well. Each and every one of them had swim trunks under his jeans. They stripped off and helped each other unwrap their turbans.

"My God, look at the head of hair on him!" Christie blurted.

"They don't cut it," Savannah explained. "Sometimes I wished Moe would, so it would spring up curly all over his head. But I never said anything. If I had, he'd have gone to the barber lickety-split. I didn't want the responsibility—that's a huge thing, like the next best thing to a sin."

"They say they're the hairiest people on earth," Debbie said. "I don't think I could do it, Vannah. That older one looks like an ape."

"You get used to it," Savannah said lazily. "Sometimes they'd let me help them wash their hair, sometimes they'd let me brush it. Moe would sit cross-legged in the middle of the bed, naked as the day he was born, and let me brush and brush. But I never did learn to get it done up the way they do it."

"What about the body hair? Talk about hirsute."

"You're showing off again."

"Do they braid it up before they put on the turban?" Kitty asked. "Or do they sort of do the turban into the hair, twist it together, or—?"

Savannah started to laugh and Kitty joined in, unable to keep a straight face any longer. The others watched them, puzzled.

"Is this some kind of family joke?" Myrna asked.

"Yeah," Kitty managed. "Yeah, it is."

Bobby had one hand wrapped in Moe's hair and was kicking, kicking, being towed while Moe swam back and forth across the pool. Victoria lay on Larry's chest as he floated on his back, dribbling water on her from his fingers. But Victoria wasn't interested in the water. She was soaking up the feel of her daddy, snuggling in, squirming as if to get right under the skin, to become a part of him.

Noel watched. He had climbed out of the water and stood, shivering, watching as Elaine climbed up on Shemp's shoulders, then dove off, landing in a cannonball, splashing the other kids.

Kitty sat down beside Noel. She didn't say anything, she just reached up and touched his back. He looked around and sat down between her legs, leaning against her.

"What's wrong, my guy?" she asked. Noel didn't answer, or couldn't. He shivered harder. Christie tossed Kitty a towel and she wrapped it around the boy, holding him with both arms. "Tell me," she whispered.

Noel turned to her and wrapped his arms around her body, pressing against her, shaking his head.

"Is it because they're men?" she asked. He didn't answer. "Is it because they're almost black?" He shook his head no. "Is it all that hair?" Again he shook his head. "But it's because they're big men." No answer. "And they're almost naked?" He stiffened. "And you can see their hairy bellies? And the lump under their bathing suits?" He didn't move. "And all those muscles in their arms, and their big hands and feet?" Noel began to tremble again, and she heard his teeth chattering.

"Sweetheart," she crooned. "It's okay. These are nice guys. These are good guys, not dangerous guys. Don't you know these guys are your uncles?"

Noel shivered silently and Kitty stopped talking and held him. Christie looked as if she was about to ask a question and Kitty shook her head, short, fast jerks. Christie nodded. Myrna was just about coming apart at the seams with curiosity, but when she saw the head-shake she held her questions.

"When I was little," Deb said conversationally, "we had a neighbour guy down the road who had this fat fat *fat* dog. I mean that dog was *fat*. She was mostly white, with brown patches on her. A little bit like a beagle, but bigger, with longer legs and shorter ears. And *fat*. Just about the only thing that dog could do was swim. She couldn't chase a ball, because she'd waddle and start to pant, and she couldn't play tug-of-war with a stick because she was too fat. But in the summertime, the neighbour would take her up to the lake and she'd swim. And swim and swim and swim." She reached into the cooler, brought out a can of Orange Crush, pulled the tab and sipped it, then handed it to Noel, who took a sip.

"Is there a point to this story?" Kitty asked

"No. I just started to think about that dog, is all."

"Did she bite?" Noel asked.

"Nope. Mind you, she did fart a lot." She stood up. "I'm going swimming, want to come?"

"No." Noel gripped the can of pop. "Later."

"Anybody else?"

"Not me," Savannah yawned. "Swimming looks like work today. Most days it looks like play, but today I'm pooped."

"Small wonder." Christie stood up and walked toward the water with Debbie. Myrna hurried to join them.

Savannah looked at Noel, then looked at Kitty.

"He's afraid of them," Kitty said. "He's had some real bad experiences with men."

"Oh." Savannah patted Noel's leg gently. "You don't have to worry about my guys, they don't do sex stuff with kids. You can ask any of the others. They'll tell you. They're like Jimboh."

Noel didn't answer and he didn't look at her. He didn't relax his grip on the pop can at all.

"Damn, that's some cat Rob brought for Jimboh," Savannah said. "I can't even begin to think where he found it."

"I doubt he 'found' it, Savannah. I bet he paid through the nose for it."

"People are funny. I don't really like him, you know."

"Rob, you mean?"

"Yeah. You see that little interplay there, when he got mad at Noel?"

"I saw it." Kitty pulled Noel closer. "You see what those two boys did?"

"Makes you think, eh? They must be used to him throwing his weight around when he gets ticked off."

"He can find someplace else to throw it," Kitty said softly. "He starts throwing it around my kid and he's apt to find himself sitting on his arse with a big lump on his head."

"Better not try it with any of my kids, either," Savannah agreed. "Jesus knows what those three in the water would do. We all got along real good, you know, in spite of the language barrier at first. Then the kids started coming, and the first time I got ready to warm Vic's ass, whoa, Nellie!" She laughed softly, remembering. "I had all three of them up in arms, just like that. Wound up with the interpreter down at the house, no less. Took a while to find a compromise, let me tell you. It's not how we were raised, and what else did I know? I must have taken three or four of those parenting courses. Mind you, when push comes to shove I'll slap an ass and not feel the least bit bad about it. I just made sure it wasn't when they were around."

"I *hate* being beat up," Noel blurted. "I just hate it."

"Yeah." Kitty blew on the back of his neck. He shivered, then grinned. "And I beat you up all the time. Old Cruel and Nasty, that's me."

"I don't feel cold any more," he said. "Want to go swimming?"

"Love to." Kitty winked at Savannah. "Would you feel embarrassed if I went in in my underwear? I didn't bring a swimsuit."

"My mom used to tell me, it don't make no never-mind to me." He handed the Orange Crush to Savannah.

She sipped the pop and watched them enter the water. Kitty must have changed her mind, she walked in wearing shorts and tee shirt. She lay on her back in the water and Noel floated beside her. All around them people were splashing and laughing, but the two of them lay quietly, their fingers barely touching. Noel didn't seem to notice that they were floating in the direction of Larry and Moe. Poor little jigger, he was probably three-quarters of the way around the bend. And on the TV special she'd seen a few days ago, they'd said that it was a growing sickness, an epidemic spread by the Internet, an addiction that fed an industry in which more money changed hands than in the fishing industry. Ah, technology. Ah, progress. And governments still saving money by cutting health and education budgets. Well, it just go'ed to show you, there's more than one way to fuck a child.

Rob and Lucy got back in time for supper, and not a whiff of booze on either of them. Lucy looked tired, stumping heavily and leaning on her cane, but she looked peaceful too. Rob looked as if he'd had to eat a bowl of broken glass and pretend to enjoy it.

They had cold cuts, cold turkey, potato salad and sliced tomatoes in a garlic vinaigrette. There were cucumber slices with a touch of vinegar, there were pickled beets and bread-and-butter pickles, plenty of buns and a platter of sliced baked ham.

"All you need is a wedding and you wind up with a gourmet spread of leftovers," Rob said, forcing a smile. "You kids got enough?"

"Yes, sir," they answered.

"Eat up, now," he said importantly. "Busy as you've been all day you need lots of protein."

"Yes, sir."

"I don't see no propeen," Bobby said. "Don't I get none?"

"It's in the turkey, darling," Savannah said. "You make sure you get a nice slice. You like the white meat best, right? With salt on it, right?"

"I like it better when it's hot." But he didn't object when she put a slice on his plate. "Can you cut it?"

"I can cut it. Any old time-er-ooni, sweet cheeks."

"Baby," Elaine hissed. "Momma's little baby."

"You're jealous," Bobby said confidently. "You're mad 'cause you're not the baby."

"Good guy, Bob." Elaine put some cucumber slices on his plate. "You want some spud salad?"

"No. Maybe a materslice?"

"Okay. One or two?"

"One." He took his plate to his place at the table and sat on the stool and ate his dinner methodically, starting with the cold turkey bits because he liked them least. When he had gotten rid of them, he had some ham.

Noel didn't take any cold turkey, but he did take a bit of just about everything else. He sat at the table eating hungrily, and when Moe sat next to him Noel managed a tiny smile. Moe smiled back, tasted the turkey, nodded approval and began to eat. He didn't speak to Noel and didn't even look directly at him. He left it all up to the boy. Noel didn't say anything, but at least he didn't start trembling with terror.

Jimboh and Audrey sat together and ate from the same plate. Savannah almost envied them. They were so comfortable with each other, so easy, and it was good to see Jimmy showing his soft side. He'd kept it hidden for so long, protecting himself the only way he could.

"From what I read in the papers," Rob said, a bit too loudly, his smile a bit too wide, "you're a real success as an artist, that so?"

"That's what they tell me," Jimboh said mildly.

"So, where do you get your ideas?"

"Oh, they're just there when I need them." Jimmy gave him the surface-only smile he pulled out for reporters and interviewers.

"We went to the art gallery in the city when they had that big showing of your work," Myrna said quietly. "I think Rob was hoping you'd be there in person."

"Nah, I didn't go." Jimmy lifted his mug and drank half the coffee in two gulps, a sure sign he was off balance. Kitty noticed, Savannah went to get him a refill and Seely tried to think of a way to change the subject. "I was working on a piece. I don't like to go to those things anyway."

"Told the guys in camp about it." Rob blundered on into the minefield. "They didn't believe that you were my son at first. Showed them the thing in the paper and all, and they said it was coincidence that the last name was the same."

"You know how people are, eh," Jimmy shrugged.

Kitty relaxed. However upset he was, Jimboh wasn't going to explode.

"Well, I'd like to have one of your pieces. I'll pay, no matter what it costs. I don't expect any special deals. I guess the big ones cost more, eh?"

"No, sometimes the little ones cost more. Depends on how much work went into them."

"Okay, I'd like something around five hundred."

"Shit, Rob," Lucy laughed. "For five hundred dollars you can maybe get some sawdust off Jimboh's floor."

Rob laughed with the others, but for Savannah there was such satisfaction in knowing how totally out of touch he was that she was almost willing to buy him a piece herself. Let him know what he had walked away from, she thought. Let him find out just how much of a stranger he really is.

While the kids filled the dishwasher and put scraps down for the cats, the others took coffee into the living room and sat looking out the huge front window at the place. They could see Jimboh's house, the bake shop, the driveway, a wide expanse of grassy field and the highway, with cars going past in both directions. When Jimmy got up they all thought he'd gone to the bathroom, but then they saw him strolling down the hill toward his own place. Nobody mentioned seeing him, not even Audrey. After a while his pickup fired up and he drove back up to Savannah's house. He parked near the back door, out of sight.

When he walked into the living room, he was holding a carving in his hand, a large platter made from a single piece of aged cherrywood. The centre of the platter was plain, the rim richly carved with the intricate patterns of Celtic design. It was a gallery quality piece, probably worth as much as Savannah's new house. He walked up to Rob, handed him the piece and smiled. "No charge," he said easily.

Rob didn't know what to say. To Kitty he looked like a beached fish, mouth opening and then closing, only to open again.

"I didn't expect . . . I don't know what . . . thank you, son."

"You're welcome, Rob. Hope you enjoy it." Jimmy walked out of the living room and came back with a big, heavy cardboard box. From it he took a mask, which he handed to Myrna. "There you go, step-mommy mine," he grinned. "And this is for Lucy, and this is for Christie, and this is for Deb, and—"

"Jesus, it's Christmas time!" Seely blurted.

"Nah, fool, it's wedding presents," Jimmy said. "Here, guy," he said to Moe, handing him a mask. "Family potlatch."

Moe took the mask and held it uncertainly. His big, black long-lashed eyes blinked rapidly. "Thank you, Jim."

"You're welcome, bro." Jimmy handed another mask to Larry. "This is for you." And another to Shemp. "And you. And I prob'ly should have told you guys a long time ago, but, well, I'm not as smart as I should be. But you're okay."

"You're okay too, Jimboh." Savannah could have stood up and cheered. Not because Jimmy was being generous and including the guys, but because she had just seen Rob get his toilet flushed in the slickest, smoothest move she had ever seen. Yes, he got a signed piece of his son's work. So did every other adult in the place, including the ones Jimboh hardly knew. Savannah could see that Rob had figured it out. But he would never be able to say one word of criticism without making himself look like a total asshole, and ungrateful to boot.

"We're due to pull out tomorrow morning," Rob said, sounding deeply regretful. Myrna shot him a look of surprise that could only mean this was news to her, that Rob was cutting the visit short.

Kitty looked over at Savannah and got a huge grin. "Oh, that's too bad," she said, and Savannah nodded as if in agreement.

"You'll have to take a whack of stuff with you," Seely announced, already on the same wavelength. "There's lots of baking, and I'm sure Robin and Les can pack it away."

"I'd love to," Myrna said graciously, unaware of the currents, the cross-currents and the dangerous undertow. "Would you let me write down your recipe for lemon square?"

"Sure. And I'll give you the recipe for the one Les liked best, the one that's kind of an adaptation of butter tarts."

Noel was tired enough to be on the verge of whiney. Rather than overextend him, Kitty decided to take him to the motel. "Maybe someone could drive us there, then you guys'd have the car and could stay later?"

"I'm ready for my bed," Lucy said.

"Me too," Debbie agreed. She had no idea what in hell was going on in the living room, if anything was going on, but the back of her neck was prickly, as if somebody were looking at her, staring at her. She had checked twice, and nobody was. Odd how that happened sometimes. There you'd be, all alone in a room, and suddenly this absolute certainty that someone was standing beside you or behind you or staring, staring, trying to—what? Figure you out?

In the morning Rob insisted on leaving early—so early that there was no time to go back and say farewells. Christie thought it very odd, and said so, but Kitty just grinned.

"What does *that* mean?"

"It means Rob isn't going to run the slightest chance of not getting the sendoff he wants. This way, he can pretend that *if* they'd gone over, there'd have been a big hug-in."

"I don't think I understand you guys." Christie reached over and stroked Kit's leg. It was something that hadn't happened for so long, they both felt shy about it. But with Noel snoozing soundly in the small single bed in the same room, they both knew there wasn't a chance in hell of things going any further than this, and that knowledge emboldened them both.

"What don't you understand?"

"The potlatch. It was…incomplete. Absolutely everybody got something, even Victoria, and Jimboh could have sold that stuff for more money than you'll see in the rest of your life. But when we did potlatch, we did it for status. What status did Jimmy get out of it? He already ranked as high as a person could in that group. Everybody loves him, everybody's very happy for him."

"Maybe he gained status in the one place he needed to—himself. He put the old man in his place. That platter? I mean Christ!"

"Myrna didn't get to take any of the baking surplus."

"At least she got the recipes. Savannah and Seely gave her a bunch of copies last night. They knew the old fart was going to pull this getaway."

"Well, it stinks." Christie swung her legs over the side of the bed and moved fast. She hauled on jeans and a tee shirt, then almost ran to the door, unlocked it and raced outside. Kitty could hear her talking out in the parking lot.

Kitty sighed, got out of bed, pulled on some clothes and grabbed the key to the unit. Jesus Jesus Jesus, and now, unless she wanted to look as stupid as Rob, she had to go out and say goodbyes. Honestly, sometimes she wished Christie would butt the fuck *out!*

The farewells were short and sweet, with Rob champing at the bit and trying to smile, but not quite making it, although he might place third in a shark-grinning competition.

"You two guys are very welcome to come to Lucy's for a week or so," Kitty told the boys, shaking hands with them rather than hugging them. "I'll take you riding."

"You would?" Les said. "Really? Like real ranch stuff?"

"Promise. We'll be haying the second cut in about three and a half weeks. When we're haying, that's all we do, so phone ahead and make sure you're not going to arrive just in time to sweat, ache and bake. Once the cut is in, hey, it's slack time. We'll have a good time."

"Thanks, Auntie Kitty." Les blushed. "I'm real glad we got to meet you guys. We'd heard stories, but...you know...it was like someone telling you about a TV show they saw. Now we know you and..." He ran out of words. Kitty nodded and grinned, and reached out to touch his arm briefly.

And then it was into the car and they were off, Rob honking the horn, not even stopping to think that there might be a dozen other people in the motel still sleeping.

"Us tomorrow," Christie sighed.

After all the rain, the fields were thick with grass and clover, and as green as an Irish greeting card. The fertilizer had been thoroughly washed in, and Lucy insisted that if you went out on the porch at night and listened, you'd hear the grass growing. Noel tried several times but didn't hear it. He decided it was because his ears were smaller than Lucy's.

"When I'm bigger," he said trustingly, "I'll hear it."

"That's my man," Lucy agreed.

The sunshine established itself and stayed, day after day, and the temperature rose until it was actually too hot to be comfortable. Every afternoon they took Noel to the beach, such as it was. Christie didn't think it was worthy of the name "beach," but she held her tongue. Except to Kitty, who grinned widely, surprisingly agreeable.

"It's not their fault," she pretended to whisper. "Don't tell them, it'll just wreck it for them."

"You'd think, what with a highway and all, they'd take a trip to the coast and take a look at what a beach really is!"

"They'd all get agoraphobia."

"I'm not sure I can live here, Kit-Cat. I'm sorry."

"Yeah?"

"I thought you were making a joke when you said the woodpeckers have to carry lunch pails between trees."

The heat persisted. Lucy watched the sky and rubbed her hip, and worried. Finally, unable to trust God or anything else, she started moving the irrigation piping to the fields. "When I win the lottery," she promised, "I'm going to get that California irrigation installed. You know the kind where the little jigger lifts up out of its hole when you turn it on? Then, once it's up and spraying, it keeps on until you shut it off; and when you do, the little thingamy lowers itself again. I could grow hay to beat hell!"

"It would cost a million dollars."

"Hey, if I won the lottery I'd *have* a million. Maybe two or three."

"And then what?"

"Keep farming until it's all gone," Lucy cackled.

"That won't take long." Deb shook her head, not laughing, not even smiling.

"Now we get to listen to the whupwhup whupwhup, day and night."

"You okay?" Lucy asked.

"I'm fine, Lucy. I'm just tickety-ickity-boo."

By the end of the first week, Christie could only agree wholeheartedly with Deb. Whupwhup whupwhup, day and night whupwhup, like a huge wet heartbeat, whupwhup whupwhup.

"If I don't get to the coast," Chris blurted at suppertime, "and do some shopping or go visiting or see my auntie or something, I'll start screaming and ripping out hunks of hair." She took a deep breath. "I'm not used to just being in the one place." She knew it was a puny excuse, believed by nobody.

"Whupwhup," Deb said. "Is this a solitary escape, or are you open to a co-conspirator? I've never met your auntie."

"Want to go now or wait until morning?"

"It'll take me five minutes to pack. Maybe four."

Lucy and Kitty gaped, absolutely disbelieving and shocked, as Deb and Chris leapt from the table in unison and started moving. The five-minute estimate was off by four minutes, but then they were piling into the old pickup and driving off together, honking the horn and waving out the windows.

"Never did anything like that before in all the time I've known her," Lucy gaped.

"I can hardly believe what I just saw," Kitty agreed.

"Can I stay up later?" Noel asked hopefully.

"Tell you what, old man. You can stay up as late as you want, right up until the first minute you start acting up. That's the sign, guy, that you go back to your regular eight o'clock bedtime. Deal?"

"Deal." He reached out, his baby finger pointing at her. "Pinky swear?"

"Pinky swear." Kitty offered her own finger.

"Pinky swear," Lucy nodded, holding out her own finger. "So here we are, three of us, batching it together."

"Batching." Noel fell in love with the word. "We're batching." He looked at Kitty, then at Lucy, then at Kitty again. "What's batching?"

"It comes out of the word 'bachelor.' That's a guy who isn't married. So he has to do all his own cooking and clothes washing and housework and stuff."

"Batching. I get to batching?"

"You get to batch, sure."

"Cooking too?"

"What do you have in mind?"

"I can make salad." He thought about it "And if you get some at the store, I can make pizza pops in the microwave."

"There you go. I've never had them, but I'll give them a try. Anything else?"

"Mom used to get these little suppers. Lasagna and other stuff. You just hot them up."

"And plenty of salad?"

He nodded. "And ice cream and fruit salad and pineapple stuff."

"Hey, we're smokin' here. I can do steaks and I can do chicken."

"I can barbecue spareribs."

"So we're fine, even if we're batching." Kitty winked at Lucy over Noel's head, as he put samples of his supper on a small plate. Some mashed potato, some gravy, some pork chop, some applesauce. Then he left the table and went to the back door, carefully carrying the little plate. Lucy almost spoke, but Kitty shook her head. She picked at her supper until Noel was outside.

"He's taking it for his friend." She chose her words carefully. "He has this friend he calls Thingy. You can't see him. But Thingy goes everywhere with him. And Thingy really *really* likes to have Noel make him up these little feasts."

"Kids," Lucy said fondly. "Don't they just get the ideas."

With the irrigation whupwhupping and the sun beating down fiercely, the grass grew steadily. Decision stood in his small patch and contemplated the hayfield. Of course it was greener, it was on the other side of the fence. He was afraid of fences. From the day he was born he'd had nothing but grief when he encountered one. But the grass was *so* green, and there was so *much* of it, and whatever else he had going for him, IQ wasn't on the list.

"He's going to challenge it, you know." Lucy watched the bull pace along the fence line.

"It does look better than what he's got in there. I mean he's got lots, but the hayfields look better."

"We could try moving an irrigation section in there. Or do you think he'd just charge it and bust it to hell?"

"I don't know what he'd do. Doubt he's ever seen a rig like that before, and anyway it's hard to predict anything with him. Sometimes he's like a panda bear, other times he's all set to explode over bugger-nothing."

"Well, we won't know if we don't try."

Noel didn't think much of the rules of this job. Lucy and Kitty got to go into the field, and what did he get to do? Sit up on the hay wagon and watch. Lucy told him if he were going to bed earlier he wouldn't feel so grumpy about it. That was a lie. A big fat one. Bedtime had nothing to do with anything. They got to go in, he got sat up on the hay wagon and told he could watch from there or he could go into the house and watch a video. Who wanted to watch a video? He'd already watched too many of them in the basement suite. He'd seen them over and over and over, and they all bored him now. Even brand-new ones couldn't hold his attention. New or not, they were too much like the old ones. You only had to watch them for a few minutes and you knew who was the good guy and who wasn't, and sometimes, most times, you could even tell who was going to get killed and who was going to be lovebirds, and who cared about lovebirds, anyway?

Thingy sat with him on the hay wagon and did his best to amuse Noel, but the nub of resentment was solidly fixed, and nothing was entertaining. Why did they think Buttons would hurt him? Buttons and he were good friends.

He hadn't told anybody the bull's real name. They called him another name but it didn't fit. Buttons was his name. He had these little teeny buttons where his horns might have been if he'd been going to grow any. That other name was for the big black bull who jumped and bucked cowboys off, and even hurt them. Buttons was the one who just lived in the field with his cows. Kitty said he was lovebirds with all those cows and in the springtime there would be calves. Noel had already asked if he could buy one of them. Nobody gave away something that big and that great, you had to buy stuff like that. Kitty had promised to ask Lucy, because the cows belonged to her. And Lucy said that he could buy one. He already had almost five dollars in his jar. He'd had more but he used some of it to buy a goodbye present for Jimmy.

It was the most beautiful knife Noel had ever seen. He didn't know knives could cost so much. But he didn't have enough money to buy it, and this made him feel as if he was going to cry. Then Kitty asked what was wrong, and he told her, and she said, "Not to worry, guy, we've got this thing we can use instead of money." It was a credit card. She said it was a magic thing, but he knew about credit cards because horrible horrible had them.

He asked Jimmy to go up to the bridge with him. Just the two of them. They stood on the bridge together until Thingy shook his head and pointed, and then Noel took Jimmy's hand and led him over to the nice bench he'd built.

"I wish you were coming with us," he said, and he thought he'd cry for sure.

"I wish you were staying here with *us*," Jimmy agreed.

"I know you can see Thingy."

"You mean Bones."

"Kitty says he's the JimmySpook."

"What does she know? He's your spook."

"I got you something." Noel dug it out of his pocket and held it out to Jimmy.

"For me?"

"Yes."

Jimmy took the knife and held it tightly. He didn't even try to open it. He just held it and then he turned suddenly and picked Noel up, sat him on his knee and held him tight, rocking him gently, saying nothing, just holding him.

Now Noel only had the money in his jar. But by the time the calf came he'd have more. Every time he got any money he put half of it in the jar. Kitty was helping him learn how to figure out money. He knew exactly what calf he wanted. He didn't know what cow would have his calf or if it would be a boy or a girl calf, but he knew that it would look like Buttons. Maybe not exactly like him, but whichever one looked the most like him, that was the one Noel wanted. Only nobody would ever tie bells on him to scare him, and nobody would yell at him or cram him into one of those little chutes. How would anybody else like to be put in that thing? His calf wouldn't get treated like that. And when it was big enough, Noel would ride it. Not jumping and hurting each other, just riding around together.

He watched them with their pipes and stuff. It was as boring as videos. After a while he lay down, and looked for things in the clouds. But there weren't many clouds, and the few there were didn't look like anything but clouds.

He thought of going to get his new bike and riding up and down the driveway. Sometimes that was real fun. Sure didn't seem like there was much to do on a farm. Wasn't as much fun as a playground. The closest one here was way down the road, at the school, and it wasn't much fun to go there because you couldn't really *play*, not with Kitty or Lucy or someone sitting on a bench, waiting for you. And he didn't know any of the kids. In fact he had never known any other kids, not very well, because horrible horrible wouldn't let him go to daycare or anything.

He fell asleep without knowing it was going to happen. When he wakened, the water thing was all put together and Buttons was standing in the spray. Kitty and Lucy were sitting on horses, grinning at him. He sat up, befuddled and almost frightened.

They had a third horse with them, with a saddle on and everything. He knew it was for him. He looked at Kitty and she nodded.

"Need help getting up?" she asked.

The horse wasn't as tall as the ones Lucy and Kitty were riding, and it was wider, but it seemed really nice. Kitty led it to the hay wagon and all Noel had to do was grab the saddle horn and jump, landing belly-down. Lucy laughed approvingly. Noel squirmed himself into place, so excited he thought he might pee his pants.

Kitty dismounted and adjusted the stirrups. "How's that?"

"Fine." He didn't know if they were or not. How was he supposed to know? "I guess."

"Stand up in them." He did, and she passed her hand under his bum. "That's good. Okay, here, I'll put your feet the way they're supposed to be...can you feel that?"

"Yes."

"Okay. Try to keep them like that. We've got a lunch packed and lots to drink, and we're off. But you have to wear a hat."

"I hate hats."

"I don't care. If you get sunstroke you'll be sorry and we'll be sorrier. Here," and she plunked his ball cap on his head. "Ready?"

He was ready. He nodded. Lucy didn't look as if she had done anything at all, but her horse moved off easily. Kitty grinned at Noel and winked, and then his horse was moving, side by side with hers.

It was better than a bike—even a brand-new bike. It was the best.

"What's this horse's name?" he asked.

Kitty heard the quivering in his voice and reached out to touch him reassuringly. "Her name is Lady. She's nine years old. She's what we call a cow pony."

"What's that?"

"Lady was born on a ranch, and by the time she was two years old she was a working animal. She can herd, she can cut, she can do anything a person will ever need her to do to handle cows. She's not any particular kind of horse, like a quarter horse or Appaloosa or Arabian or…she's a mongrel, a bit of just about everything with a lot of work horse thrown in. That's why she's so stout."

She knew most of what she had said had gone right over his head. "That's why she's a cow pony. She knows everything there is to know about cows."

"She's real pretty."

"She is so. That colour is called sorrel."

"I like her. I bet she's real fast."

"Oh, she's not the fastest. No way she could run faster than my horse or Aunt Lucy's horse. But she's a good runner, all the same. Where she really shows off her stuff is when she turns. When you know how to ride really well, you can probably learn barrel racing. She'll be real good at that."

"How come she's on a rope and the others aren't?"

"Because today you're learning how to sit on a horse. Some other time we'll start learning the steering."

He didn't mind just sitting—only his bum had to do it. Inside his head, he and Lady were galloping galloping galloping, no saddle, no bridle, no nothing, just flying over cowboy movie country. The rhythm of the hoof beats was hypnotic, and when he dared let go of the saddle horn and reach out to touch Lady on the neck, he felt how soft her hair was, and how hard her muscles were under that sleek hide.

"Is she real strong?"

"She's probably the strongest of these three," Lucy answered. "That's part of what the word 'stout' means. She's heavy, and she's not the least bit fat. That's all muscle. Now, if you were my boy, I wouldn't have put you up on a big strong horse like that, I'd have got you a little pony. A Shetland, maybe, or a Welsh. But Kitty said no, she wasn't getting one of them because they're so damn snipey-headed. She looked for a bomb-proof one."

"What's that?"

"This horse is probably smarter than you are," Lucy laughed. "If something went wrong, like if a plane fell out of the sky or something, while you and me and Kit-Cat were screaming, that mare would be getting you out of the way."

"Is she the smartest horse?"

"Lots of horses are smart. You just have to learn how to see things the same way they do."

Dog ambled along the side of the road, sniffing and panting, her tail wagging steadily in an almost circular motion, and Pup did her best to keep up. But less than a half hour after leaving the barn area, Kitty had to lean over and scoop up the pup.

"Silly little twit," she said fondly. "Listen to you, puff puff puff. Here, settle down." She reached back and put the pup in her saddlebag. For a few minutes the pup rode there with her head poking out, but she was just a baby and she'd been going at full speed for longer than she should. She lay down and settled herself.

"How far are we going to go?" Noel asked.

"Oh, not too far today. Your bum isn't used to this. We'll go along the fence line, just checking things out. When we get to the creek we'll stop for a while and have lunch, then we'll head home again. How are your legs?"

"Fine." He wiggled his toes. "Maybe a bit, like, pins'n'needles?"

"Don't push down so hard on your feet. Can you ride with your arms out, like this?"

"I'll fall off."

"Then just try one arm. It teaches you balance. You can't hold yourself in place forever—your arms will fall off and land in the dust. You have to learn to sit in place. Go ahead, try one arm."

Daisies were growing all along the side of the ditch, and yellow flowers that looked almost like dandelions, but taller, almost up to Lady's knees. Noel could hear creaking sounds from the saddles, and Kitty's horse made a whuffing noise, blowing through her nose. "Is she mad?"

"No," Lucy said, "she's bored. She wants to do something else, like maybe running."

"I could wait." He didn't want to hold them back, to be the reason they didn't have fun.

"We'll be fine for a while yet." Kitty pulled her cigarettes out of her pocket and lit one.

"Hand 'em over," Lucy said.

Kitty handed the package to Noel and he handed it to Lucy. Then he realized what he'd done and his eyes widened. "I didn't even hold on or nothin!" he blurted.

"Sure you did. You held on with your seat."

Tentatively he lifted both arms. It was almost like flying. It *was* like flying. Way up off the ground like this, and Lady moving along and the breeze on his face and the rocking like wingstrokes, and he wasn't even scared any more. Well, not as much, anyway.

"Creek's up ahead." Lucy pointed. "See? We're going to sit under that big willow tree and eat our lunch. And the horses will eat grass, so they'll have lunch too."

When he climbed down from Lady, his legs felt funny. Kitty and Lucy grinned and Kitty pretended to walk all bow-legged and goofy. "You get used to it," she promised.

"It feels like I hardly have feet or anything," he said wonderingly.

"Okay, what you do is loosen this girth...watch what I'm doing, now. One day your fingers will be strong enough and you'll have to do it. This is so she can breathe and eat and be comfortable. She depends on you to see to stuff like that for her. And we'll take off the bit. See? Undo this and see, it comes out and she can eat better. Her bridle becomes like a halter, see."

"Is she happy?"

"I think she's probably having as good a time as we are. She doesn't have to work hard, she isn't chasing smelly old cows all over the place, and she isn't just around in a field, bored to pieces, with flies biting her. Heaven, I bet."

His bum felt funny. Not exactly his bum, but his butt cheeks—almost as if they weren't really there. That was funny.

Noel was so hungry that he ate his sandwich even though it had avocado slices in it. He didn't like those soft greeny things very much. They felt mushy on the roof of his mouth. But everyone else seemed to eat them all the time. There were chicken slices in his pita, and some cheese, and sprouts and tomato slices and mayo. It was a *big* sandwich.

"What you do when you're finished your lunch, you take this carrot with you and go over to your horse. You take a bite off the carrot, then you give that bite to her. If you know how to hold your hand flat, you'll be okay. Bite by bite you give her that carrot. Let her know that she is *your* horse and you are her person. Let her know you'll look after her. Make real good friends with her. You need for her to be happy that she came here to be with you."

"What if she bites me?"

"Keep your hand flat like I showed you."

"But what if she does?"

"Bite her back, Noel." Lucy said.

He looked over at her. She didn't look like she was teasing him.

"Where?"

"On her nose. Their noses are real sensitive. Then she'll learn a lesson."

He was scared, but he wanted to be Lady's friend. If this was what you had to do, or anyway one of an umpty-zillion things you had to do to get a horse for a friend, he'd better try.

When they got back to the barn, Kitty helped him take off the saddle and blanket, then the bridle. "Be careful, you don't want the bit clattering against her teeth. It could hurt her. And you don't want her to think that every time she goes anywhere with you she winds up with a toothache."

"I don't think she likes that thing."

"She probably hates it. When you can ride better we'll get rid of it, put her in a bozel. Give her the grain in the can, that's your thank-you to her. Okay, now I'll lift her foot and hold it and you'll use this to get the dirt and stuff out. Easy, remember how I did it? This thing here, the triangle? That's called a frog, and you have to be very careful of it. That's it...okay, next foot. And when you've got the feet done, you're going to brush her. It helps get rid of the sweat, and it helps her think of you as her friend. If she's going to be your horse, you have to be friends."

"*My* horse?" He stared at her, eyes wide.

"Yeah, your horse. You can't learn to be a good rider until you have your own horse."

He felt as if he were still riding Lady, rather than walking. He got the brush with the blue nylon bristles and did what Kitty told him to do, working carefully, inhaling the aroma of hot horse, loving the smell of Lady's sweat. She stretched out her neck, enjoying the attention, the brushing. Her nose twitched and she puckered her top lip.

"See that?" Kitty laughed. "What she's doing with her lip and nose? You've found one of her spots. They have these places where scratching or brushing feels so good they just about bliss out...see, she looks as if she's almost asleep."

The horse wasn't the only one who was blissed out. Noel was so enthralled by what he was doing that he forgot to be leery of big animals. He even leaned to brush the underside of Lady's belly.

"My horse," he said to her. "You're my horse. My Lady, my Lady, my Lady."

"They love it when you sing to them," Lucy offered. "Even if you don't sing words, they love you to sing."

"La la laaaah," Noel sang. "Hmmmm hm hmmmmm."

"Bet we can just eff off and do chores, eh?"

"Bet we can so," Kitty grinned. "He'll be in this very spot when we come to get him for supper."

With two of them doing the chores, everything went quickly, and it only took the better part of an hour. Lucy liked having Kitty with her. There was no mention of infirmity, no mention of a limp, no keeping track of whether or not it was worse than usual today. And no mention by either of them that it was Kitty who did the heavier work. It just happened, so naturally that Lucy didn't have to feel diminished or insulted, or cheated or resentful.

When Kitty went out to the barn, Noel was sitting up on Lady's back, brushing what he could reach and still singing. She stood in the doorway feeling as if she were peeking into a part of his life that he had never exposed.

The JimmySpook was dancing, not his usual jerky bones-on-a-string hop and jiggle, but smoothly and beautifully. Noel was singing words and singing with an open throat and a full voice, his still-baby voice unchecked by shyness or fear. There must have been a tape player in that basement bomb shelter, and a Tina Turner tape, and something on that tape must have touched the boy. He knew all of the words and he had sung them many times before, but possibly not this freely.

He turned and smiled at her. "Hey," he said, and the JimmySpook took his bows, throwing kisses to a crowd nobody else could see. The crowd must have been there, though, because he didn't seem to be pretending. And when Noel slid into her arms and she carried him in from the barn the bone rack was still bowing and cavorting, and didn't follow them.

The heat became more intense, the berries ripened a good ten days sooner than usual and the corn Debbie had planted was almost a month ahead of itself. Lucy set the drip irrigation along the rows, left it running day and night. The pumpkin and squash plants looked determined to invade the entire garden, and still the heat did not break. By the first of August, the gladioli were in full bloom, the hollyhocks were going crazy and the roses were starting to suffer, the buds not even open before the petals were dried by the blazing sun. The TV weather guy in the crazy shirts was as excited as a sports announcer. This record set in '38 had been broken in this place and in this other town the heat was more intense than had ever been recorded. He had silly footage of people frying eggs on sidewalks, and did a five-minute bit with a guy from the SPCA about how you shouldn't take your dog jogging in weather like this.

"Hear that, Dog? You might as well leave your Spandex where it is, we're not taking you jogging until it cools off."

"That's nuts," Lucy said. "You remember that cattle dog I had? Summer or winter, hot or cold, that animal could keep up to me on horseback, no problem at all."

"Right, and how many city dogs grow up working in all kinds of weather? It's the difference between me climbing into the ring with Evander Holyfield and having Mike Tyson climb in with him."

"Either way Evander would win," Lucy teased. "Mikey's blown it."

"You'll see. You'll all see. And the South shall rise again. And France will restore the monarchy."

"I could become the Tzarina of Russia," Lucy suggested.

"You could. But why would you want to? They're broke."

"That's okay, so are we."

"Yeah, and we make out okay."

Noel loved to hear them laughing. Even when he couldn't for the life of him understand what they were talking about. It was so nice to lie on the sofa, all bathed and shampooed and clean right down to his toenails. You could smell the soap and shampoo in the living room, like perfume. Even old Dog had had a bath after supper. They put her right in the tub, into the very bath water Noel had just finished using, and the good old girl just sat down, mouth open, tongue hanging out. Laughing, Kitty said it was, and looking at Kitty as if she wanted to speak words, like a person. Noel and Kitty had washed her with people shampoo, then rinsed her clean, really clean. Lucy had a long rubber thing like a hose with a ball on the end. The hose fit on the end of the water spout and the ball sprayed. They rinsed Dog off good with that, then put on some conditioner and rubbed it in real good. Dog liked that too. Her tail wagged and everything. They rinsed her again, even better than the first time, then pulled the plug. The water was *so* dirty. Noel hadn't even thought Dog was very dirty, and yet look at all the dirt and grit and sand, and lots of little things Kitty said were dead fleas.

"Open the door!" Kitty yelled.

"She's open," Lucy called back, and Kitty did a thing with her hand, snapped her fingers and pointed, and Dog was out of the tub and racing away, dripping water on the floor, leaving footprints behind her.

They cleaned up the tub real good, and rinsed it over and over, then mopped up the mess of splashes on the floor. Dog was outside rolling on the lawn, making little soft, happy, whiney noises.

When Dog came back inside, she was as good as dry. Lucy had a little bottle of stuff that she'd got from the vet, and she said it would only take a drop of it at the base of Dog's tail and another drop on the back of her neck, and goodbye Mister Flea. Noel hoped it worked. He already had a flea bite on his ankle. One is enough, thank you.

They lifted all the cushions on the sofa and sprayed stuff there, and did the same on the big chairs. Kitty vacuumed the carpet, sprayed the hose thing, took out the bag and burned it in the old wood stove in the living room. It was a little stove, with a door in the front and glass in the door so you could see the flames. Lucy said they used it in the wintertime to make the room cozy. He hoped he got to see that. It wasn't much fun watching a garbage bag smoulder.

Kitty brought in a tray with cups and stuff, and a teapot and some of the cookies Auntie Seely had given them to bring home. She was sure nice. And Auntie Savannah was funny, always making jokes and cuddling the kids. Not just her own, either—she hugged Noel and she even hugged Les and Robin. She'd given them a big container of that sauce, which Noel didn't particularly like, but Lucy sure did. She said she might pour it on her breakfast cereal except she didn't eat cereal for breakfast. Mostly didn't even eat breakfast.

"Apple juice for cowboys," Kitty invited.

"Thank you." Noel sat up feeling safe and loved.

The sprinkler set up in Decision's pasture helped turned the grass green and encouraged new growth, but the biggest advantage of it was that the bull loved to stand in the spray. The flies were bad, real bad. Kitty and Lucy mounted up and went out to move the cows into the barn. Noel pitched a fit when they told him he would have to watch.

"I've got a horse!" he yelled. "You said she knew all about cows. You said all I'd have to do is sit and she'd do the rest."

"He's right." Lucy lit a cigarette and waited.

"He's not even six years old, for Chrissakes!"

"All's he's got to do is sit."

"If he falls off, he'll be squashed to mush."

"Not if he's *behind* them."

"He could break his neck."

"He could do that falling out of bed."

As she helped him up into the saddle, Kitty gave him his instructions all over again. "You promised," she reminded him. "You'll stay at the back of them and all you'll do is move them ahead. And you'll hang on to the saddle horn."

"I know." He was still angry.

"Noel. The reason I said no is that I'm scared stiff something will happen and you'll get hurt. If you get hurt I would cry like a baby. I'm *scared*, okay?"

"I'm not." He wanted to hurt her, make her feel as bad as he had.

"I know you're not scared. But if you got hurt I'd go wingy."

Now he didn't feel so mad. In fact, maybe he liked someone worrying about him. He gave her a weak smile, and then it was like a cowboy movie.

All they had to do was ride up the sidehill pasture and get the cows started down, but to Noel it was as momentous as a TV cattle drive. Lady knew exactly what to do. All he had to do was sit and hang on, and Lady never went faster than a mild trot, but it was so exciting he felt like his pee was up to his ears and it would come out soon and spray all over everything.

The cows moved sullenly, but obediently. They'd been fed and they'd been turned loose, and their inner clock told them it was time to lie down in the shade. Instead, the fools were upsetting everything.

Once they'd been herded into the barn and stood side by side, nosing at the hay in the manger, Kitty and Lucy moved down the row with a gallon plastic jug and a measuring container with a long handle. Each cow got a premeasured dose of medication poured along the spine, to keep away parasites and biting insects. Each cow shifted and tried to move away as the liquid touched her hide, but she was done before she could shift herself, and Kitty had already moved on to the next animal. Lucy brought the jug and measured each dose carefully.

When they brought in Decision and his smaller herd, a minor kerfuffle broke out. There was pushing and shoving as cows tried to intimidate other cows. For a couple of minutes it looked as if Kitty would have trouble or even get hurt, but Decision was the bull, and these were his cows. More important, he was their bull, and the sidehill cows didn't even have one. The status question was settled quickly, if temporarily. Kitty got the new cows done, and then moved toward the bull.

She was not looking forward to any part of the task. For one thing, she didn't have room to manoeuvre in the barn that she had in the arena. Should she send him through the chute and pin him? No. His trust, such as it was, would be shattered. From then on it would be war, and she didn't want any war with him.

The JimmySpook jumped in front of her, waving his arms, shaking his head no. Kitty stopped and began to back up. Decision pulled his head from the hay manger and whirled, and Lucy gasped in fear. The bull glared at her and she stood stock-still, not wanting to make any move that might cause him to get rid of the annoyance. Then he made his silly little high-pitched bull bleat and turned back to the hay. JimmySpook stepped aside and Kitty moved forward, talking softly. She poured the stuff along Decision's back. His skin rippled, but he didn't try to shift out of the way. She was glad she hadn't decided to use the chute. She was also grateful that the JimmySpook had made her wait those few extra seconds.

They kept the cows in the barn for the rest of the day, giving the stuff time to spread out, to soak in. There was no chance of rain, but Decision could very well decide to go stand under the irrigation spray and wash off his dose.

He was fine in the barn. Why not? He had three times as many cows around him. It didn't matter to him that the new ones were already pregnant and there were no intoxicating scents, no signs that his luck was running full. But there were cows, and he'd been born to adore them. Even better, nature had arranged for cows to adore their bull.

"You'd probably get laughed at if you talked about love." Lucy leaned on the rail wall, watching the milling around and now the gentle nudging. "I hate people who get like that about animals anyway. You know, talking about them as if they were people. But look, aren't those old girls proud of him? Isn't he just the cat's ass out there? And watch the babies. See how they all crowd together and gaze at the old man?"

If anybody else had said it, Kitty would have laughed. But Lucy had been doing this for as long as Kit had been alive, so she was sure to have learned a thing or two.

"They behave differently when there's a bull with the herd. Same as chickens. You get chickens with no rooster and they act one way, pecking each other and fighting and squabbling all the time. Put in a rooster and in about an hour everything sorts itself out. The fighting just about stops and the noise level goes down, way down."

"I have to pee," Noel said, turning and walking out of the barn. Kitty went to follow him.

"The kid knows how to pee by himself," Lucy said quietly. "You fuss over him too much."

"Huh?"

"Maybe you've only had him a couple of months, but that doesn't mean he's only a couple of months old. He knows how to pee. If he needs any help he'll holler."

When Noel came back in again, he climbed on the wall to stand on the bottom board and watch over the top one. "How come some of 'ems got blue tags on their ears?"

"Those are the ones that will have calves with Decision. The others, they don't have the tags and their babies won't be his. That way, if we want, which I hope to God we don't, we could keep heifer calves from the untagged ones, and when they're old enough they could have babies with Decision. But he can't have babies with any of his own daughters."

"Of course not," Noel scoffed. "He wouldn't do that, anyway."

"Actually he would, given half a chance," Lucy said.

Noel shook his head.

Christie was always up first in the morning. She was the one who made the coffee, but the glugging noises the machine made toward the end of the drip cycle usually wakened Kitty and she got up too. Often, before she began to get dressed, she sat on the edge of her bed, feeling warm and slightly damp with summer sleep-sweat, and she rubbed herself gently. Even when Christie offered to do it for her, Kitty rubbed herself, arms and legs, slowly, softly, then belly, where the puckered scar was like a second belly button. That was from a goddamn milk cow, if you can believe the bad luck of that. An off-season job, not supposed to be the least bit dangerous—nobody mentioned dangerous, anyway—and the stupid beast tossed her head sideways and whoa, Momma, it hurt. She could reach the small of her back, but the stroking didn't soothe the ongoing ache. And she could reach over her shoulders where the crick often settled itself. But mostly, when Kitty stroked herself, she stroked her breasts. She loved them. Nature and inheritance had been good to her. She didn't know which of her foremothers had contributed the gene or chromosome or whatever it was, but she never failed to say thank you. At one time Christie had practically fixated on Kitty's breasts, but after you've been together a long time, the fixations fade. Compared to Lucy and Debbie, the time Kitty and Christie had been together wasn't all that long, but it was long enough for the unquestioning acceptances to wear thin, plenty long enough for the cracks and flaws to show clearly. And long enough for the flame of passion to become a flickering candle. But even when things between them were hot and they shared sex often, Kitty stroked her breasts. She liked the way her nipples responded, puckering and stiffening. She liked their sensitivity, the soft, smooth skin of the breast. It was comfortable and comforting and feelgood and proof she was alive and well, and upright. And ready—if not for nourishment, at least for coffee. She never stroked herself at night, never when she was lying down, and she never reached between her legs to masturbate. That wasn't what the stroking was about. It was sensual, but not sexual.

And then she was dressed, and going to the kitchen for coffee. If the coffee maker went off at some ungodly hour in the middle of the night, Kitty got up to pee and then went back to bed and plunged back into sleep. She had never had trouble sleeping. If Lucy wanted to sit up chewing codeine pills instead of going to a surgeon and letting him take a slice out of her in the hope of easing the pain, well, that was up to Lucy. She said she didn't like the odds, said there was a chance the pain would still be there after the operation, and that she would have less movement. That was a chance she wasn't ready to take, and it was her business. Sometimes Kitty thought sure she would choose the knife, take her chances, and wear a leg brace afterward if she had to. Other times she thought she'd make the same choice Lucy was making. A codeine pill doesn't weigh as much as a damn wheelchair. Kitty didn't remember Lucy ever being exactly spry, but she had trouble watching Lucy use a mounting block to get up on her horse. Nice of Jimboh to fancy it up, make it less ugly, but Lucy still needed it and that was sad. When Lucy could no longer ride, that would be really sad. And that day was staring them in the face. Even the training rides were hard on her. She took a pink pill before heading out and often another one when they got back.

But at least Lucy didn't get stiff-necked and owly when Kitty suggested she could put Lucy's horse away with her own, and that maybe Lucy could make a pot of tea and have it ready when Kitty got to the house. Sometimes, some lucky times, Lucy would be in her recliner, the tea made and waiting and Lucy sound asleep, her face beaded with sweat. Then Kitty just closed the door to the living room and found things to do away from the house. Even a couple of hours of sleep made a big difference. Several times Lucy had slept in her chair until supper was ready, then the kitchen noises and the scents of cooking roused her enough to eat supper, but she was subdued and her smile was vague. Those nights it was easy to get her to take a bath right after the TV news was finished. Easy too, to fudge the chores in such a way that by the time the bath was done, so were they. Lucy had no excuse then to stay up, or force herself to stay awake, and she would go to bed, almost obediently, and go back to sleep. Once in a blue moon she would sleep through until morning.

Now they were on the sidehill, Lucy driving the tractor and Kitty on foot, setting the chain. Noel was sitting on Lady in the grassy area in front of the barn, bareback, talking to her, visiting with her, stroking her. And, without knowing it, working on his balance and holding his seat.

The small alders and cottonwoods were easy to yard out. Sometimes Kitty would wrap the chain around three or four of them at a time. The tractor would move forward slowly, and with only a slight lurch, out came the equivalent of weeds. There were other bushes and brush needed cleared out—clumps of thorny witch grass, big clusters of sour grass. They had the sidehill pretty well cleared of the mess and the raw earth was already seeded with grass. Yes, the weeds would come back, but not as many of them. The end was actually in sight. Another three or four years and it would be all pastureland, only grass and clover here, good feed for the cows.

The old pickup came down the driveway, horn honking. Noel slid off Lady's back and raced for the gate, waving his arms. Kitty stepped into the bucket on the front of the tractor and sat herself down, and Lucy drove them from the field.

"It's *gorgeous!*" Deb laughed, clambering out of the pickup and staring at the freshly painted house. "Who did that?"

"We did." Noel was puffed with pride. "I helped."

"Did Lucy go up a ladder?"

"Oh, no," Noel assured her, but Deb was already halfway into a fit of fear.

"If she'd fallen off she could have really hurt herself," she fussed.

"No, she didn't," Noel repeated, but Deb could not accept his reassurance. "Her balance isn't very good, because of her bad leg. Oh, God, I wish she'd just wake up to the fact she isn't eighteen years old any more."

"Hey, there!" Kitty hugged Christie. "You look great! You must have had a real good time."

"Wonderful. Just wonderful. We drove all over the place. But everywhere we stopped they had a bookstore, and finally we had to get a couple of boxes from a liquor store to hold everything. And I got you a great tee shirt! Wait until you see it. And—"

"Did you go up the ladder?" Deb didn't even give Lucy time to say hello. "Are you trying to kill yourself?"

"Hello to you too," Lucy said, her smile turning from welcome to ice. "Fine, how are you? So nice to be home, everything looks great, we had a really good time but it's nice to be back."

"She didn't go up the ladder," Noel said in the sudden embarrassed silence. "I *tole* you she didn't go up the ladder. The *guys* went up the ladders."

"What guys?"

"The painting guys."

"You said *you* painted the house."

"I helped. We all helped. We did the stuff around the doors and windows, and we did the stuff on the steps and the porch. The guys had these sprayer things, eh, Auntie Lucy? They put this stuff over the windows, cloth stuff, and they turned on their sprayers and it was way faster than with a brush. Right, Kitty?"

"Right, guy. Hardly took any time at all. Got the sealer on first, then I think it was three coats of exterior paint."

"You didn't go up the ladder?"

"They've got drones you can hire to do that kind of work," Lucy shrugged, grinning at Noel. "This guy was right in there like a dirty bird and he's got the paint-splattered clothes to prove it."

"The paint guys gave me a hat," Noel bragged. "Same as the kind they wear. It's a painter hat. And they said when I got big enough to work on the ladder they'd give me a job. They said I was good."

"You? Good?" Christie hunkered down and held out her arms. "Oh, I can't believe they said *that*. You're never good."

"I am so." He moved into her embrace easily, his arms going around her neck, his small, grubby hands stroking her hair. "I'm the bestest boy in the world."

"The part I like best is how you're so modest," Christie said.

"It looks really nice." Debbie took several steps toward the house, but Lucy made no move to join her. Deb bit her lip, blinked rapidly, then turned and walked toward the pickup. "Maybe if we start unpacking now we'll be done by the end of next week."

Dog barked and Pup ran to stand beside her. She assumed the who-the-hell-are-you stance, and in her high-pitched terrier yap she issued challenge as a bright blue near-new car moved slowly down the driveway.

"Anybody you know?" Lucy asked Kitty.

"Not me. I don't know a soul drives a new car. My friends drive junkers and clunkers."

"You don't *have* any friends," Christie teased her. "Just me, and all I get to drive is the old bazoo. You drive the new one."

"I stole it, I get to drive it."

"I'd have stolen it if I'd been there."

"Well, I *was* there and I stole it."

"I might steal it tomorrow," Christie teased.

"God, you two." Lucy was grinning, her anger and insult faded.

The car stopped. Kitty picked up the pup and stroked her, softly telling her what a good guard dog she was. Dog nudged her, and she dropped her hand to the rapidly greying head to scratch behind the ears. "Good Dog," she crooned softly. "What a good dog. On top of everything else you're a teacher. Good dog, gonna put you in the hall of fame, by golly."

"Excuse me." A young woman climbed from the car, smiling. She was wearing expensive jeans, a plain cotton shirt that must have set her back two days' pay, and highly polished low-heeled shoes with lace fronts. Her hair was short, and at one time in her life, Kitty would have put the hustle on her without delay.

"Help you?" Lucy moved a gimpy step or two closer.

"I'm looking for—" She checked the paper in her hand. "Lucy Scott?"

"That's me."

"How do you do." The young woman smiled and held out her hand.

Lucy reached to shake and, instead, wound up holding the papers. "What's this?"

"It's a notification of intent to make application for expropriation."

"What?"

"It's a legal document." The young woman looked around the place and shook her head regretfully. "Damn."

"What kind of legal document?"

"I work for the government. Provincial, not federal. They want this property."

"Fuck them!"

"I'd rather not, if it's all the same to you," she grinned. "They're planning a four-lane highway, maybe you've heard about it?"

"Yeah, but . . . that's going in over on the far side of the ridge, on Crown land."

"That area is practically solid rock, with maybe two inches of gravel and dirt over top. It would take an incredible amount of blasting."

"Bullshit. You lay your road over top of the rock, is all. Level off the bumps a bit and paint your yellow line right on the rock."

"The engineers say it would cost about two million a mile more to go over there than to come here."

"This is farmland."

"The second paper in your hand? It's notification of exemption of status."

"What does that mean?"

"It means this isn't dedicated farmland any more. It means you're out of the agricultural land reserve."

"They can't do this."

"I'm afraid they can." The young woman sighed. "Look, my name is Sue Hargraves, and my job is to explain this whole thing to you, hopefully in such a way as to avoid any kind of huge explosion."

"They have no idea how huge an explosion there'll be if they try to kick me off my land."

Sue leaned on her car and nodded. She sighed again. "I've got some maps and stuff in the car, and if you'd give me a half hour or so I'd like to go over them with you, show you what they have in mind."

"I don't give two hoots in hell what they have in mind! This is my place!"

"I don't want to sound like I'm power tripping you or threatening you, but no matter what kind of stink you raise, or how much you wind up paying to a lawyer, when they want to expropriate a piece of land, they always win. Always. Whether it's for an airport or a highway or for something they change their mind about later and leave standing untouched and unused, they always win."

"But—" Lucy was shrinking before their eyes, turning into an old woman in a matter of seconds. "This is farmland, it's always been farmland. It was a farm when we bought it. The damn house is a good sixty years old! We just paid to have it painted. This isn't right. You don't destroy good, productive farmland to put in a goddamn road. I don't care how expensive it is to go on the other side of the ridge. Once that money is paid out, the flipping road will be there forever! They're going to blow up the ridge anyway, for fill, which they'll pay to bring here, so they can dump rock on land that's been picked almost clean of rock. It's *stupid*."

"You can look at it that way... or you can take a hard-nosed stand and tell them that it's going to cost them. Then make them pay."

"Pay? If they think they're going to save a couple of million dollars a mile by ruining my farm, then it's going to cost them at least a mile's worth to shift me."

"Only a mile?" Sue smiled encouragingly. "A place this size? I think you could probably hold out for two or three miles. It's what I'd aim for."

"Hold on," Kitty said. "You telling me Aunt Lucy can get four million for this place?"

"Probably. They don't want a big fight here. Let's look at the map, okay?"

"Bring it into the kitchen. I need to sit down, and I need a pill." Lucy moved toward the house, her limp becoming a lurch. Deb ran up beside her and put her arm around Lucy's waist, and for once Lucy leaned against her. She was crying, and Kitty knew she'd given up. She would bluster and rant, curse the beds they slept in, throw any number of temper tantrums, but Lucy had given up.

Kitty put on a fresh pot of coffee and put mugs, cream, sugar and spoons on the counter. The map had been spread open on the kitchen table and Lucy sat watching, her eyes swollen but her tears under control. Deb stood behind Lucy's chair, her hands on Lucy's shoulders, kneading gently to calm her. Christie brought Lucy a pink codeine pill and a half glass of water, and Lucy smiled her thanks, but it was a grisly sort of smile.

"See, your farm is here, and it's pretty much butt up against Crown land. Almost in it. Most of this has been pretty much logged off, and reforestation here is pricey, and not too effective anyway. What does grow easily here isn't what they call commercially viable. Mostly it's pulp wood. The good stuff, like the fir and pine, takes a long time to grow. When it's mature it's top-quality, hard-grained, almost specialty wood, but even for a company it's too long-term an investment to bother with, and the logging company has already taken a cash settlement for their tree farm timber rights. So they're out of the picture. Have been for two, three years."

"But if they bought them out three years ago, why have they said all along that the goddamn road was going in on the other side of the ridge?"

"I only know what they tell me." Sue shook her head. "Is this a non-smoking house?"

"Oh, fuck!" Christie burst out laughing. "We've got so many smokers in this house the tobacco companies should give us reduced rates. Maybe put us in the ads instead of the Marlboro man. Go for it. We might even have a clean ashtray somewhere."

"Oh, it doesn't have to be clean."

They drank coffee and smoked cigarettes while Noel drank juice and packed away a half dozen cookies. Then he announced, "I have to take some out to Lady," and he picked up four more and skipped to the back door. "I'll shut the gates," he promised.

"Nice kid." Sue waited, but nobody made special claim to him. Obviously his birth mother wasn't Lucy, or Debbie. That left two possibilities, and the more likely one, considering skin tone, was actually the less likely if you went by the way she moved. Sue was pretty sure that Kitty, the fairer-skinned one, was playing in an alternative ball park. It would be interesting to find out, but probably a very, very bad idea.

"See, they'll follow the previously announced route all the way to here, over Crown land. That much hasn't changed. Where the change happens...is here."

"It's got nothing at all to do with rock!" Kitty seethed. "It's got nothing at all to do with blasting! Look, if they go on the far side of the ridge they have to put a bridge over the river...here...and again, over here...see? That's two bridges."

"They'd have to be big ones," Lucy nodded. "That river rises something fierce in the springtime. All the runoff and snowmelt from the hills—the river winds up about three times as wide. They'd have to build to allow for that, or it'd just wash out every year."

"Then why didn't they just *say* so?" Deb snapped.

"They'd have to admit they overlooked it first time around," Kitty grumbled. "This way they sound like they're working overtime to try to save the taxpayers some money. The other way they'd have to admit that they had their bureaucratic heads right up their bums."

"It still makes me sick."

"Then they'll come across here. Now that would cut your place right through the heart. You'd be trying to move stock across a four-lane and you'd go nuts. There would be the chance of animals getting onto the road, getting in accidents, all kinds of stuff."

"Couldn't do it," Lucy agreed.

"What *could* happen is that the land they don't actually need ... I mean, if you're interested in a smaller place ... you'd have about a third of what you've got now."

"We could do that." Deb sounded interested, almost approving. "We'd just have to cut back on the number of head and—"

Lucy shook her head. "We'd lose the hayfields. Nobody can afford to raise beef if they have to buy their hay. And one-third of this place wouldn't be this place. It'd be some other place."

"I like the part about the couple of miles' worth of savings," Kitty laughed.

"I'd rather they shoved the highway up their arses and just let us win the lottery."

"Well, you could do that after you've moved onto some huge hunk of prime land."

Sue Hargraves left a half hour later and they stood together silently, watching the shiny new car head back up the driveway. Lucy didn't say a word to anyone. She went back into the house and disappeared into her room. After a while Deb knocked on the door, but there was no invitation to enter, so she went to her room and lay on her bed, feeling miserable. Why did she do things like that? Why did she open her mouth and blurt out her fears as though they were accusations? Why couldn't she just take a couple of extra breaths and think about how to say things without putting Lucy's back up? *When would she learn to shut up, just shut the hell up?* But the mere thought of Lucy up a ladder was enough to send caution and good sense right out the window.

Christie and Kitty went to the barn and saddled up. Then they established Noel on Lady and went for a two-hour ride. Dog and Pup ran alongside for the first hour, then Pup wound up in the saddlebag, puffing and panting and peering excitedly over the top. They went to the stream, crossed it and rode to the gate at the big grazing field. Kitty dismounted to open the gate for them.

"It's a damn shame," she mourned. "Look at this place! It's a waste!"

"Ah, g'wan with you." Christie shook her head. "This place is okay, and it's probably prettier than any other place around here, but it is, after all, around *here*. All that bafflegab about reforestation and rah rah rah. Yes, Kitty, look at this place is right. Really look at it. Summer isn't even half over and the damn grass is yellow except where the irrigation is going. How much water gets wasted trying to grow hay? It doesn't make any sense. This isn't farmland, it's rangeland, and we can't make it something it isn't."

"Whoa, there," Kitty laughed. "It's not that bad."

"It is. You guys, honestly! You think you can just go any old where at all and make it be what you want. This is grazing land for deer and antelope and maybe moose and elk. Forget the rugged cowboy. Forget the brave homesteader struggling against formidable odds. Did the First Nations people try to make this place a farm? No, they didn't. They lived along the rivers and came up here to hunt or to chase wild horses. Other than that they left it to Creation. You guys, hell, as soon as you figure out how, you'll move to the moon and try to plant the garden of Eden."

"You just think that because you're from the coast."

"You're from the damn coast too! Or you were. You don't really love this place, you love Lucy. Not that you shouldn't, but—hell, listen to me. You'd think I was trying to start a fight."

"No," Kitty smiled. "No, if you were trying to start a fight we'd already be in one."

"They're going to put the highway through. They'll probably throw together one of those places where you gas up, eat, pee, buy souvenirs and have your picture taken with the rolling hills in the background. But what they'll mostly do, I bet, is put in some campsites along the creek and advertise it as a ranchland holiday, maybe give someone the rights to run trail rides or something."

"So what would you do, Chris?"

"Sell the fucker in a heartbeat, for as much as I could wrench out of them, and move to the coast."

"But you can't ranch on the coast. The land costs an arm and a leg and it's lousy for hay."

"You don't have to perch on the beach! Look at the Pemberton Valley. A couple hours' drive and you're standing in salt water, but you could still raise good beef there. There must be a hundred places like that."

"Yeah?"

"And nobody but you is going to be able to talk to Lucy about it. Deb will get all emotional and piss Lucy off. Already it's the eighth wonder of the world that they haven't split up yet. Or split open each other's heads."

"Deb nags like hell."

"Kitty, darling, you know full well that if there's a nag, it's me. I nag you all the time."

"Yeah, and I wish to God you'd stop! We'll wind up just like them."

"Don't change the subject."

"Are you guys having a fight?" Noel asked.

"No, darling, we aren't. But we're pretty upset all the same because we might have to move. Lucy might have to move."

"Good," he smiled. "We can go live with Uncle Jimmy. We can live in the trailer and I can go to kindergarten with Bobby. I'd let Bobby ride my horse. And Alan."

Kitty and Lucy sat in the living room watching TV with the sound on low. Lucy was chewing gum and staring at the screen without watching.

"The kid had a great idea," Kitty said. She sipped her coffee. "He said we should all of us move back to the old place."

"What?" Lucy snapped.

"It's a good idea. There's a great whack of land going unused there, and plenty of chance to buy up more."

"As ideas go, you can tell that one came from a five-year-old," Lucy sneered.

"Ah, drop it," Kitty laughed. "You're going to shit on any idea that comes down the pike right now. Fine. Be that way. But *think* about it."

"I'd rather go blow up the legislature, if you want to know the truth."

"You won't be raising much by way of beef while you're locked up in the pokey or the loony bin."

five

SAVANNAH LEFT VICTORIA WITH AUDREY, then drove her kids to school in the van. Darlene and Lizzie wanted to go along but there wasn't enough room, what with the heaps of school supplies and the extra pairs of sneakers. Each kid needed a second pair for use in the gym exclusively. And another pair for "outside activities." Plus whatever it was they were wearing on their feet to go to school that day. Three pair of sneaks each for ten kids, plus two pairs for Bobby. And nobody standing out on the street corner giving them away.

"Listen, Savannah, nobody can reach in the old hip pocket and haul out wads," Jimmy said, holding out an envelope. "Let me help with the school stuff."

"I've got a credit card for the kids," she said softly. "The guys are real good about everything like that."

"Still . . . " He wiggled the envelope insistently.

"Thanks, Jimboh. You're a doll."

"Yeah," he grinned. "I know, stuffed with straw and a head of wood."

"Is that straw? Oh, I'm sorry, I thought it was . . . oops!" and she had him in a mock headlock, scratching gently at his hair. "Hope I don't get slivers."

She opened the envelope at the supper table and counted the money, and her eyes widened. "Okay, gang, listen," she said, managing to sound firm and authoritative in spite of the tears in her eyes. "Jimboh handed me this envelope today, for school stuff for you guys." The kids could see it was a lot of money. "We've already got all the stuff on the list, even the damn shoes. And you're near drowning in clothes, from what I can see. So think about what else you might need. And the word here is *need*, not want or letch for, okay?"

"We could wait until we'd been in school a little while," Elaine suggested.

"Yeah, there's always different stuff... I mean each school is different, so maybe our stuff won't be right, or..."

"Good enough. I'll put it in the bank. I'll put it in my account, but I won't spend it."

"There's going to be stuff like soccer shoes and ball cleats," Alan offered.

"Good for you. Maybe we should make a little list."

"Oh, the *list!*" Brittany groaned. "Not the *list!*"

Savannah had little post-it lists all over the message board. Every once in a while she checked them and updated them. When she went shopping she pulled off a few at random and took them along, in case something that was written there would apply. Sometimes she even managed to pick up what was on the list. But once off the message board, they never went back on again. When the clutter in the bottom of her backpack started to annoy her, she'd go through it, saving the change and the throwaway lighters, and tossing the notes into the burnable trash.

"If we do that," Caroline said firmly, "we're not doing it with a little post-it dealy-bob. We use a real piece of paper."

"We should make a thank-you card for Jimboh," Victor said. "We could make it like a book. Everybody makes a page of their own and signs it. We staple it together and—"

"We could put our picture on our page," Alan said hesitantly. Most of the time he left the ideas to Victor or Elaine.

"Good idea," Elaine nodded. "And the cover of the book could be a copy of the group picture."

"He's not even *our* uncle." Brandon's voice was so low Savannah could barely hear him. She reached for his hand, patted it and winked at him.

"Of course he is, Bran. You're one of us."

"Not really." He shook his head. "Not really."

Savannah didn't debate it with him. Poor little guy felt like an outsider, and who could blame him? If the bitch ever showed her face again, Savannah was going to give it such a slap that the thrushes would be scared out of the trees in the backyard.

On the first day of school, the money was still sitting in the bank. The kids piled into the van with their bundles of books, their packs, their shoes and everything else. Savannah imagined the walls of the van swelling until it looked like a burgundy pumpkin heading down the road.

When they went by Seely's, they saw she was loading Darlene and Lizzie and their stuff into her car. She waved and Savannah stopped the van, waiting for them to follow her. "It's like a private parade," she muttered, "and we're the clown car."

"They'll think they've been invaded," Alan laughed. "By the Black Watch."

All the kids giggled, and Savannah grinned at his reflection in the rear-view mirror. "Sometimes you come out with stuff that just about blows me away."

"I'm not black," Elaine said. "I'm a very *very* deep chocolate colour."

"I have a suntan," Jason smiled. "All year long."

"It's because of our vacation, you see." Caroline got into it too. "All that surfing in Hawaii and sailboarding in . . . where did we go sailboarding?"

"Cuba," Victor suggested.

"Pango Pango," Brit corrected. "Is there a place called that?"

"Sure," Savannah said. "There's a place in Quebec called St-Louis-de-Ha!Ha!, why not Pango Pango? And there's a place called Head-Smashed-In Buffalo Jump, and one called ManyBerries. And up toward where Auntie Lucy lives, there's a place called Horsefly."

"You made that up," Elaine said.

"I did not. Horsefly."

"Tennis Elbow," Elaine offered.

"Swollen Knee, Saskatchewan."

"Nosebleed Township."

Before long they were inventing names for their mayors: Leonard Lunchpayle, Tom Tubtummy. Brandon won the game by acclamation when he named his town Rumblinbum, and the mayor I.B. Farten.

The school was an anthill. Bobby turned pale and clung to Victor's hand with a white-knuckled death grip.

"Hey, Bobbers," Vic whispered. "You're cutting off the circulation, they'll have to amputate my fingers."

"I don't want to go to kindergarten," Bobby declared. "Too much kids."

"Too *many*, Bobby." Savannah pried Victor loose and took Bobby's hand herself. "You just hang onto me so I don't get nervous in this crowd, and we'll get all these other kids registered. Then we'll go get a pop or something and come back again at noon. They're hardly even here today. It's not real school, it's just registration."

"Don't registration me. I'm not going."

"Hey, if you don't want to go to kindergarten you don't have to. But start getting your head around it, because you'll have to go to grade one next year."

"Next year," he nodded. "Not today."

The secretary in the small office looked startled when she saw how many kids Savannah intended to enroll. The look faded only slightly when she opened the big brown envelope and found the transfer forms from the previous school.

"Are they siblings?" she asked, trying to be tactful.

"Okay, kids," Savannah grinned. "By names. Scotts here, O'Neills here, Swensons here. Does that help?"

"I think so."

"Or would you rather have them grouped by age?"

When everybody was signed up, Savannah made sure everyone had their gear, then said goodbye.

"I'll be back in about an hour, okay? I'll park where we are now. If you're out before I got here, keep track of each other and keep an eye peeled for the van. I don't want to be honking and yelling and putting on a show for the neighbours, okay?"

"Okay, Mom," Elaine said. "We'll be fine."

"Great. I won't kiss you because you'll all get embarrassed, so consider yourselves kissed. Love you. Don't let anybody jack you around. Stick together. You're a big enough gang you can hold the Alamo if you have to."

She walked slowly from the office, Bobby still clinging to her hand. The place was bigger, twice the size it had been, but the old smell was as ripe in the newer section as in the old. The walls of the main corridor were lined with class pictures, and Savannah stopped twice, finding herself at different ages.

"See?" she showed Bobby. "That was Uncle Glen when he was little. Cute, eh?"

"Where's Unca Jimmy?"

"He should be over in this...yes, there he is." Even in elementary school, Jimboh looked stiff and worried and far too serious. "He was about nine when this picture was taken. That's about the same age as Alan and Jason and Brandon."

"Where's Auntie Kitty and Auntie Seely?"

"Okay, let's look... Here's Seely. This must be her grade one picture, she was one of the littlest kids in her class. Sometimes we called her Button, she was so small. And here's Kitty. See the big wide grin? That was Kit-Cat, no matter what."

"She gots hair like you."

"She's got hair like me."

He nodded, recognizing again that he had mixed himself up. He had more trouble with words than any of the others, whether it was because he was the baby of the bunch, or if he was just going to have trouble with language the way some people have trouble with math.

"Hey," Seely said from behind them. "Checking out the rogues' gallery?"

"Some of these pictures should be on the wall of the post office, on Reward posters."

Seely sighed, tapping the picture of Jimmy. "They call them the best days of your life."

"Yeah. Look at the poor little bugger."

"What I can't understand is why they didn't foster us out."

"She sure wasn't much," Savannah agreed. "She got full welfare plus what he sent. It should have been more than enough, but..." And she sighed too. "We never saw any of it except what he sent care of Gran. At least he had sense enough not to send that to her. It would have gone the way of the rest of the money. Look at his damn clothes! It makes me mad now. It used to make me—I don't know. Not sad, but I think I was ashamed."

"Scared," Seely nodded. "I always felt scared."

"Come on, let's get the hell out of here before we get so bummed out we hang ourselves from the flagpole."

When they got back to the school, the kids were waiting for them in a group, carefully ignoring the stares of the kids waiting for the school bus.

"Everything go okay?"

"Sure," Victor shrugged. "I got called nigger once and Paki prick twice. But that's nothing compared to the last school."

"Nobody called me any names," Jason said quietly. "Or if they did, I didn't hear them."

"I'm a black bitch," Elaine said calmly. "And a Hindu hooer."

"Is that the best they can do?" Savannah said. "Not much imagination happening here. Hell, I can do better than that!"

"It's a zero tolerance school," Vic told her. "No fighting at all."

"What about black bastard? Is that allowed?"

"No," he grinned. "The kid who called me a nigger has already got a detention. And I didn't get one."

"What did you call him?"

"It was choice, Momma, but I'm not going to tell you. Dear heaven," he said in a shocked falsetto, "you can't talk that way to your poor old mother!"

"Good for you. Anybody else?"

"They've hardly got any computers in their lab at all. You have to sign a paper to show you got told the rules, and there's a list of the rules on each computer, *and* you have to sign up and wait for your chance at them, *and* you can't go on for more than a half hour at a time. Might as well not bother. Bummer."

"We've got one at home," Savannah said.

"Yeah, but the little kids are always on it, playing games."

"So use mine. No games allowed on mine."

"You don't have Internet."

"Why do you need Internet? It's just another way to waste time. Chat rooms and pornography and instructions on how to build a bomb."

"It's good for homework."

"Sure, pull the other leg, that one's getting too long."

Jimboh's cat Mabel lay on her side, purring happily, swatting gently at the tip of her own tail, which Victoria was waving in the air. The kittens were asleep in their box on the porch, because Audrey wouldn't allow them in the house. They promised to be even bigger than their mother, and it's bad enough cleaning up the scat from a small one. Besides, if an ordinary kitten can fray the material on the sofa, one of Mabel's babies could rip it to pieces and scatter them all over the house. Two of the kittens were striped tabby toms and the other was a tri-colour female that Jimboh insisted on calling Split Face because one side was black and the other was orange.

Victoria was used to cats. Puss moved in and out of the big house at will, although the kittens were strictly outside cats. Victor had made a little house for them, like a dog house, with loose hay on the floor for them to curl up in or wrestle with. Most of the kittens Puss had looked ordinary enough, black and white except for the ones that were white and black. But she had one that was as Siamese-seeming as she was, with tabby stripes that were less orange than apricot. Audrey wanted that kitten for a house cat, but she was afraid Mabel would get territorial and that would be the end of the pretty little thing—not even a snack for the big moor cat.

"Might as well be a friggin' tiger," she muttered.

"Cookie?" Victoria said.

"Sure, kid, why not? But you have to sit on a chair at the table. I don't want crumbs all over the house and I sure don't want to be wiping up spilled juice."

"Joos?"

"Up you get." She patted the chair and Victoria got herself up on it and didn't even protest when Audrey wiped her hands and face with a facecloth. "Don't need cat hair on the cookies," Audrey told her. You might get a fur ball caught in your throat."

"Joos?"

"Coming right up, kidlet."

Jimboh came up from the basement and Victoria grinned at him.

"Hey, princess." He sat on the chair at the end of the table, near the coffee machine and his ashtray. Audrey had plans for that damn ashtray, and they included the trash can. First, though, she had to remember to get him a replacement. This one was square, probably four or five inches across the top, and it was the most godawful colour. Perhaps it had been intended as false amber, but it had aged and gone a sort of pale brown. The edges were badly chipped, and there were tar deposits on the inner lip, where hundreds of dollars' worth of cigarettes had burned down, unsmoked and forgotten.

"The coffee is fresh," Audrey said.

Jimboh smiled and got up for a mug.

"How you holding out with the terrible terror?"

"She's okay. A bit fixated on Mabel's tail, but other than that she's no trouble at all. There's something to be said for being part of an entire tribe of kids."

"We've never really talked about it but . . . ?"

"No," she said briskly. "Between the two of us, Jimboh, our genetic pool is a septic tank. On top of which, while I may be an international sex symbol, I am past the age of safety. I don't know what I'd do if I went through the nine months and wound up with some kind of idiot."

"Okay. Just checking in. Coffee?"

"No, thanks. I'm coffeed right out. Here, babe, juice in your funny cup and two cookies."

"Those are cookies?"

"Savannah makes them. They're so goddamn healthy the UN should be handing them out. Funny thing is, they taste great. Try one?"

"You're sure they don't taste like hay bales?"

"I never ate a hay bale so I don't know. Some of these taste like peanut butter cookies and some taste like almond."

"Can you tell the difference by looking?"

"No, you might have to eat six or eight of them to find out."

"When's Savannah due back?"

"Ought to be real soon. They only had to register. Tomorrow's the first full day."

"It feels so weird, Aud. Just the thought of those kids getting onto the school bus and my gut starts to twist, same as it did every morning when I had to get on it. Everybody staring."

"Yeah, but these kids will go in a group, and they're all real well dressed and neat as pins. And nobody's passed out on the floor in the kitchen and nobody else is in jail, with their name in the paper for all to see. They'll be fine."

"Christ, I didn't know you lived with us."

"I hate to tell you, Jim, but you guys weren't the only ones. I'd climb on the bugger with a black eye that went from my forehead to my chin and everybody knew why. And they knew my mom probably had two of them, not just one. And when Phyllis came up pregnant she quit school, but I had to go every day, with everyone snickering about her. Then Jasmine was up the stump too, and it got worse."

"I had an aunt named Phyllis."

"Yeah." She let the dead lie in their graves, and so did he.

Victoria held out the empty spout-cup. "Joos."

"You'll float, kiddo, I'm warning you."

"Cookie?"

"Sure, and you'd better grab 'em before Uncle Jimmy gobbles them all up. Look at him! Munch munch munch, there goes another one."

"You're good with her," he said. "I didn't expect that."

"Why not? I was up to my arse in kids for years. First I had to babysit the younger ones, and then the older ones started having their own and guess who got to babysit them? It was a madhouse."

"What did they do when you hoofed 'er off down the road?"

"Damn if I know. Damn if I care."

"Want to go back for a visit?"

"Not a chance. Not one of those assholes could pull it together to come to our wedding and that tells me everything I need to know."

"We could rent a limo, show up like a pair of rich bitches."

"Not worth the gas to drive there. Here they come."

Seely pulled her once-in-a-blue-moon strict-as-hell trip and made Darlene and Lizzie clean their castle before she agreed to let them go up to the swimming hole for a quick dip. "Everything," she ordered. "I'm going in there afterward and if I find so much as one sock on the floor, start writing up your obituary. Clean sheets, clean pillow slips, the whole nine yards, and no lip about it, either."

"Nobody was giving you lip," Lizzie said. "You always talk about how lippy we are, and we aren't. Are we, Uncle Jimmy?"

"Better not be. I'm real good at breaking people's legs."

"Yeah, right." She kissed him on the ear, swiped a couple of Savannah's cookies and hurried to the castle. "I'm not doing the TV room all by myself," she warned.

"Oh, shut up, Lizzie. Don't try to get something going." Darlene produced her version of a withering look "Really. She's such a *child*."

"Yeah," Seely laughed. "And she's the only one, right?"

"Coffee?" Jimmy offered. "It's just about fresh."

"From you that could mean anything from ten minutes ago to so long ago it's gone green."

"No, really, Audrey made it."

Audrey began wiping away crumbs and spilled juice from Victoria's place. "Here, I'll just take the backhoe to where Queen Victoria was sitting. How'd it go at school?"

"No sweat. I only really had to go because there wasn't room in the van. I mean mine didn't need to register, right? They could have flagged down the school bus, but who needed the grief? The whining would have sent us all halfway up the tilt."

"Punch 'em in the mouth," Jimboh suggested.

"I tried that and I hurt my knuckles. You punch 'em for me."

"Right, okay. Maybe I'll just head me over and do it right now."

"Better have a doughnut before you go, there might not be any left by the time you get back."

Audrey put a cup of coffee in front of Seely, then sat with one for herself. "What I can't understand," she said, "is why anybody who can bake as well as you do still buys these things. They're shit!"

"Yeah, I know," Seely grinned. "But think how good my stuff will taste after the kids have been eating these."

Mabel came in from the living room and rubbed against Seely's ankle. Seely broke a donut into four pieces and dropped one on the floor for the cat. Mabel sniffed it, then ate it, purring loudly.

"Listen to her," Seely laughed. "She sounds like a bloody airplane. One of those weird ones, ultralights I think they're called."

"When she meows, the windows rattle."

"Everybody's always picking on my cat."

"Nobody would if you had a real one."

"Come on, Mabel, finish your doughnut and then you'n'me's going back down to the basement. Hell with 'em all."

"If you're going down to the basement again, you're taking sandwiches with you," Audrey nagged. "Honest to Jesus, the more he works the less he eats. I'm going to invent a new rule. Supper in this house is at five-thirty at night and *everyone* shows up. Especially," and she kissed Jimboh, "you, mister skinnymalink."

"Okay, Mabel, now they're picking on me too. Let's go. We'll be at the table at five-thirty, I promise."

"Not Mabel. I draw the line."

"Because you're mine," Jimmy sang, "I draw the line."

Savannah had two washing machines going and both clotheslines full, so when she heard the phone she didn't bother to go get it. She was on a cleaning binge like the one Seely was on, the annual ritual. Faced with the gloomy prospect of her kids heading off to school and leaving her alone all day, Savannah cleaned the nest. Let the phone ring, the kids or the machine would get it.

She was stuffing a load into the dryer when Elaine came in, frowning and upset.

"What's wrong?"

"Our grandmother has this idea in her head that she's going back for a visit and I have to go with her. And I don't want to!"

"Might be nice, a big trip like that."

"I'm not going, Momma."

"Hey, hey, I'm not the one you have to work it out with."

"Well, I'm not going. I don't care how mad she gets and I don't even care if the dads get mad too. I'm not going."

"Okay. You're not going. Are you going to say why?"

"You know what they do. Those old ladies get their granddaughters to go over there and the next thing you know they've got you married to some old fuck who wants an immigration ticket."

"Christ, Elaine, why don't you run for head of the KKK?"

"It's true."

"You're way too young for that."

"Not too young to be shown around. Looked at and gaped at and gawked at and then the next thing, in a year or two, it'll be let's take us another trip back, we had *such* fun last time, and poof, that's it. I'll wind up like what's-her-name did. You know the one, her dad had to go over and get her and bring her back with him, they'd locked her in the house or something."

"That was an extreme case. Her mom and dad were halfways split up even before that happened."

"I'm not going."

That night Savannah phoned the guys and talked to them about it. Moe got as upset as Elaine right away. Larry said not to worry. Shemp said it wasn't a problem, they'd talk to her.

What they wound up doing was coming up for a visit. Savannah met them at the airport, and when the kids came home from school, the dads were waiting for them. Savannah had made an enormous meal and invited everyone else to come and eat it. Audrey brought an enormous black cast-iron pot of her paprika chicken and Seely provided cakes, pies and cookies.

Savannah was worried, and wasn't used to it. None of the kids had ever before openly defied anyone except her, and she wasn't sure how the guys would take it. You read stuff in the papers and you hear stories, and you never know. The family feast went on into the evening, everything was smooth as silk, except Elaine hardly touched her food. Savannah knew that sooner or later it had to come to a head. Elaine opted for sooner.

"We will go home as fat as pigs," Larry grinned. "Savannah isn't the only one in her family who can cook like, how do you say it, go-to-hell."

"That's it, Dad," Victor smiled widely. "Or billy-be-damned. We'll have you talking white-trash workie yet. But you're never going to sound like you were born here."

"I'm not going," Elaine said flatly.

Larry's grin vanished.

"I thought we were going to talk about this after supper, quietly, in the living room," Savannah said.

"I'm going to talk about it here, in front of everybody," Elaine announced.

"Do not talk to your mother that way," Moe said.

"Your mother deserves your respect," Larry chimed in. "Behave yourself."

"I'm sorry, Momma."

"It's okay, sweetheart, I know you're real upset."

"Well." Jimmy smiled angelically. "We're all kind of upset. Vic, would you pass the creamed spuds, please."

"Why are you upset?" Shemp asked.

"The thing is, we all know your mom is a pretty stubborn woman. She says something and that's *it*. Which is fine with me. She's worked hard all her life and raised her kids and it's time things went her way. Fine. But she's living over here, now."

"Please pass the excellent chicken," Moe said.

"Audrey makes a fantastic chicken," Savannah agreed, passing the platter.

"What is this?" Shemp poked with his fork.

"Baked beans," Jimmy said. "No pork in 'em, though, you can't get good pork any more, not the kind you need for beans. I used some of that spicy eyetalian sausage."

"Different." Shemp ate a bit more, but kept the same distance as Jimboh did from the rice dish Savannah had made.

"See, Elaine isn't interested in going over there. Which means, to us, that she doesn't have to go."

"She would possibly enjoy herself."

"She might. But we have to make it clear to your mother that Elaine is *not* getting married over there."

"Ah," Larry nodded. "We have already told her."

"Yes, but your mother don't take a telling," Jimmy said. "So what I'd like you to do, seeing as how I don't speak the language myself, is tell your mother that if she pulls any kind of fast one and whether now or later on marries Elaine off to some guy, I will kill her."

"You want me to tell my mother that..." Larry stared. "Would you really kill her?"

"Yeah."

"Then I would have to do something about it."

"You could try."

"Oh, God, let's not start a feud!" Seely exploded. "Can't we all get along?"

"There will be no problem." Larry said. "I will tell my mother what your brother has said. Now, would someone please pass me the big white bowl? Thank you. Elaine, go to the bathroom, wipe your eyes, blow your nose and come back again when you've stopped crying. This is too dramatic."

"Daddy—"

"Did you hear me, my darling?"

"Yes, sir."

Elaine had the sense to drop it, but Savannah knew her kids. As far as her eldest daughter was concerned, round one might be over but the championship bout had barely begun. How could someone who looked so gorgeous, and who was a different height, weight, colour and age than Gran, Lucy and Kitty, manage to look so much like them? It was right there, even when she was being polite and seemingly obedient. Her back was up, and the compostable barnyard animal organic fertilizer was about to hit the air conditioning system.

Moe spoke up, surprising even Larry. "If it is agreeable," he said, "we would prefer if the adults in the family were part of the discussion we are about to have now that supper is done. Elaine, please make coffee for us and join us. The young ones can clean up the kitchen, and then the older ones can assist the young ones in getting ready for bed."

"It's a bit early for bed, Dad," Victor dared.

"That won't hurt you. Perhaps you would want to move the TV into a bedroom and quietly watch a suitable program together."

"Yes, sir." Victor sounded like another person, as polite and formal as his fathers were. Well, Bindi had said the children would either have no souls at all or too many of them. You never know. The old tartar could just as likely be right as wrong.

They took their coffee into the living room and sat down quietly. Savannah would have committed an obscenity for a cigarette, but the guys hated to see her smoke and she didn't want to tip the mood. Shemp, bless his heart, grinned at her and said, "You are in your own house, sweet one. I'm sure you know us well enough by now."

"Thank you." Her uneasiness slipped away. Of course she knew them! In every sense of the word. She got up and opened two windows, turned on the overhead fan and went back to her chair.

"Elaine, would you try to explain why you are so upset?"

"Our grandmother has never been a grandmother to us," Elaine began, obviously having rehearsed her speech. "I didn't even know I had a grandmother until she moved over here. And even when she was living right next door she didn't bother with us. She walked past us without speaking, and if we spoke to her she ignored us. We gave her Mother's Day cards and presents and she didn't even say she got them, let alone say thank you. Then suddenly the phone rings, and it's her and she's all sweet and nice and wants to take me on a trip."

"Perhaps she has changed her opinion?" Shemp suggested.

"Poppa, please."

Savannah could easily guess what Shemp was thinking. Where was their little girl? This person was someone new, and she was appearing years too soon.

"Perhaps you would enjoy the trip," Larry said softly. "There are some very beautiful places to see. You know the languages. You won't find the food strange. You have aunts who would be glad to see you."

"I know, sir. If it was you, I'd go in a minute," Elaine smiled at him. "But if it was you, it'd take hours to get ready because you'd be taking all of us. That's part of it, see. She didn't invite anyone else. Just me. And she didn't mention any one of you going with her, and yet when she came here, she said it wasn't right for a woman to travel alone, and she made someone travel with her."

"When we first decided to work for ourselves rather than someone else, we went to a lawyer," Larry said. "I remember your mother was very impressed because this lawyer could speak what seemed to her like two languages. Actually, he speaks seven or eight. I used to think that when you finished school you would make an excellent office manager or accountant, but now I think we will send you off to be a lawyer, you present the facts so clearly and well."

"I don't want to be a lawyer," Elaine whispered. "I want to be a doctor."

"Dear me, nothing but defiance on all sides," he teased her. He turned to Jimboh. "And you promise to kill our mother if she arranges to marry your niece to someone."

"Elaine's a kid," Jimmy said. "She's a good kid, she's going to make you guys very proud. She doesn't need to be married at all, not until she finds someone, and not until she's at least twice as old as she is now. I don't want any trouble with any of you guys, and yes, she's your daughter, but she's my niece too. If your mother wants to marry off little girls to grown men so that they can get into the country, let her wait a bit. The way I hear tell, all three of you will be starting new families, let her bargain them off. But not Elaine, and not any of the other girls, either."

"Or the boys," Moe added.

Savannah felt as if a goose had walked over her gravesite.

"We will explain to our mother that Elaine is a scholar."

Larry looked at Elaine and then at his cup, and she jumped up to refill his cup and take the coffee pot around the room, quiet and obedient.

"We will also explain that her mother doesn't want her to go. And I will tell my mother what you have said about killing her."

"I read this thing in the paper about this guy up in the Interior," Jimmy said, "whose daughter married someone of her own choosing. The guy mailed them a wedding present, an electric kettle, and when they plugged it in, it exploded and blew them and the rest of the house to hell. Be a shame if anything like that ever happened. It's a two-way road, if you know what I mean."

"I read that same account," Larry nodded, sipping his coffee.

"Have you heard anything at all from what's-her-name, Caroline and Jason's mom?" Jimmy asked. "Or that other one, the twins' mom?"

Larry blinked. Moe looked at the floor. Shemp looked at Larry and waited.

"No," said Larry, still blinking. "Not a word."

"Strange," Jimmy smiled. "I guess it's one of those things. You never can tell. Now me, I'm not one to just hoof 'er off. I don't have much of anything except my family, and I can't imagine anything that'd be so much fun I'd just up and vanish over the horizon."

Savannah's coffee turned bitter in her mouth. She swallowed it, then studied her cup, unable to bring herself to look at any of the guys. The china was so thin she could see the shadow of her fingers through it. This was one of the special "good" set that had been a present when Alan was born, a present from the guys. There had been a card too, she still had it in her album.

"Easy, here." Kitty stepped forward and took Lucy's arm. "Come on, let's you and me go for a limp before things get heavy."

She looked at Christie, who gestured toward Deb.

"Don't bother," Deb answered coldly. "I'm not going for a limp. I'm taking a hike." She stomped off, back toward the house.

"Are we having a fight?" Noel quavered. His face was pale, his lips were dark and his hands shook.

Christie scooped him up and sat him on her hip. "Not a really fight," she lied. "Not a really one. They're both sad because we have to move, and so they're snarling at each other. You know about snarling. Sometimes Kitty and I snarl at each other. Sometimes you and Kitty snarl, and sometimes you and I snarl."

"Not like that." But he accepted her embrace. Christie carried him to the swing they had set up for him and held him on her lap, swinging gently. She decided not to take him into the house, so that Deb wouldn't feel hounded.

She was still on the swing when Deb walked out of the house with her backpack riding on her shoulder and two suitcases, one in either hand. Noel started to cry. Christie held him and watched silently as Deb threw the luggage into the back seat of her little old car, then slid behind the wheel and started the engine, without acknowledging Christie and Noel. She backed up quickly, changed gears and took off up the driveway, driving quickly, gravel spurting from her back tires.

Christie carried Noel into the house and laid him on his bed, then lay beside him, not speaking, not telling him there there now, don't cry. Why shouldn't he cry? She felt like crying herself.

When Lucy and Kitty came back, Christie and Noel were in the kitchen starting dinner. Christie told them what had happened.

"Oh. Okay," said Lucy, and she gimped off to the living room to sit in her chair and stare at nothing.

Kitty started after her but Christie shook her head no, so Kitty stayed in the kitchen, helping to make supper. Noel washed lettuce leaves for the salad, one at a time.

"I guess everybody is mad," he said.

"I'm not mad," Kitty told him. "I'm just upset."

"Me too," he agreed. "I cried."

"I haven't cried yet. But I might."

"Yeah." He indicated the heap of lettuce. "Is that enough?"

"Maybe two more leaves." Kitty didn't feel like eating anything, let alone lettuce, but she couldn't let the boy think he'd done all that work for nothing. "I'll get the spinner and you can spin it dry."

Kitty took a plate of supper in to Lucy and handed it to her silently. Lucy took it without speaking.

"You okay?" Kitty asked.

"I'll be fine," Lucy answered. "I don't want to talk about it right now."

"Sure. But it you start to be not fine, don't keep it to yourself."

Lucy didn't answer.

After supper, and after dishes and cleanup, Kitty went to the living room to watch TV with Lucy. Noel climbed up on Kitty's knee, then Chris came in with tea and fixings.

"I guess as long as I don't have to live *on* the place." Lucy sounded calm. "I don't feel right when I'm there even for a visit."

"Are you serious?" Kitty gaped. "It's a great place."

"Your memories of the place and the old biddy are different than mine," Lucy grinned sourly, like someone with a bad taste in her mouth who has just heard a joke. "Everything about me griped her guts. Robbie was her sugar pie, and then he started going off the rails and she was so worried about him she went a bit wingy. And then there was the old fart. Ten pounds of shit in a two-pound sack, and that was on a good day. She got scared that I was going to go the same route as Robbie. Or maybe she never liked me. I don't know, we never talked about it. She probably died thinking I'd made her life hell, and I don't think it was me at all. I'll die knowing that she was a rambling bitch with a mean-on toward me. And when we go back to the old place, whether it's for a funeral or a wedding, it's as if we're all waiting for something huge to come down on us."

"I feel fine," said Kitty. "I feel as if all the ghosts are quiet, and settled, and at peace."

They both looked at Christie who shrugged and laughed. "I don't much care one way or the other." Her tone was somewhere between bitter and bored. "I'm just along for the ride. My place is where my auntie lives, and we sure as hell aren't going to move there."

"You want to?" Kitty was astounded.

"If I wanted to be there, I'd be there." Chris refilled her teacup. "I'll probably go back there to die. But I don't have to be there because I carry it with me all the time. I think you guys can't do that yet. Okay, so they're going to put a road over this place, and probably a gas station and a tourist attraction and a campsite. Maybe make part of it a little park or something. You two act like it's the destruction of Eden, or some personal insult. Well, what makes you so fucking special and what makes this dust bowl so marvellous? They've done that all over our place. They built towns and cities and ran the shitters into rivers where our food came from and everything else. I'm not holding you guys personally responsible, but, like, give it a rest. I know this place matters to you but from where I'm sitting, it's not much."

"Not much?" Lucy looked ready to go for the throat.

"No, it's not much. There's hardly any topsoil, and the grass goes dry in a week if you don't damn near drown it, with water hauled up from a river that can't spare a drop if you guys ever want to eat fish again. Anyway, you'll take the best part of it with you when you go. If you get smart and learn how."

"I still don't see how you can say this place isn't much," Lucy said. "Deb used to say the same thing. She'd tell me to get my eyes tested so I could see, and my head so I'd know what it was I was seeing."

"There's something you should remember, Lucy. Hay is just dry grass."

"There isn't even a house on the place."

"A house is easy to build. Tell Savannah to phone the three wise men. Don't they have a construction company? Didn't they build her place?"

"We'll have to be in two places at one time," Lucy sighed, sipping from her cup. "I don't know how you can drink your tea so hot."

"And I don't know how you can choke it down lukewarm. I bet you even like it iced."

"Don't you?"

"Gack. What's the use of that? Tea should be hot. That's why you use boiling water."

"We could concentrate on the fences and a barn," Lucy said, planning out loud. "We could move the stock and put the furniture in storage and stay—hell, I don't know—somewhere, until the house was done."

"What about your hay?"

"Neighbours'll be glad to buy it. Most of the stock too. They know my critters, they know it's good blood and thrifty growth."

"What do you have in mind?"

"Not much. You?"

"Well, I do like the idea of having a dozen cows or so. Maybe twenty. But not some huge friggin' herd like you've got. That is *work*, woman! I'd like to try raising rodeo stock. I mean, *if* old man Farnsworth is really going to retire, although I can't picture that. I always figured he'd just kind of fade away on the job."

"I'd let Bobby ride my horse." Noel was sleepy, worn out by the emotions of the afternoon.

"And that's something else, isn't it?" Lucy said. "There's got to be a dozen damn kids on the place, and who knows, maybe more heading there even as we speak. Noel's got *his* horse. You know how it is, one kid gets a pair of roller skates and the whole heap want 'em."

"I don't mind horses," Kitty grinned. "You know what they say, some of my best friends..."

"We could raise 'em, you know."

"That's a fun way to lose money."

"But you wind up with the happiest vets in the country. All their kids get to wear braces and go to Hawaii for school holidays."

"You two!" Christie laughed.

Noel brightened. He climbed out of Kitty's lap and into Christie's.

"Honest to God, you two are too much! Get you steered in the direction of raising horses and the next thing it'll be a riding stable. Because as soon as a few of those kids have horses, your phone is going to start ringing with people who want to rent some and take a little trail ride. And then there will be people who want riding lessons, and then the poor dog food company will have to start a line of vegetarian dog food because there won't be any plugs available. Ninety acres won't be half enough for what's going to happen when the witless wonders get themselves in high gear. Come on Noel-de-bowl, I'll start your bath."

"I'm too tired."

"Fine, then, I'll just take you to bed. You want jammies or you want to sleep in your gauchies?"

"My gauchies. But I want clean ones."

"Fine by me. Come on, you have to walk. I can't carry you, big lump that you are. We have to stop feeding this kid, he's twice the size he was when you brought him home."

"If we move could I have a cat?"

"Why do you want a cat? You've got two dogs."

"Yeah, but Dog is going to die soon, and Pup will be lonely."

"You get one of Mabel's kittens and she'll *eat* Pup."

"I don't want one of Mabel's kittens. I want one of Puss's kittens. I want one like Puss, with orange decorations."

"Decorations. Now there's a big word, where'd you learn that?"

"I don't know."

"I know a *really* big word."

Noel sat on the bottom bunk as Chris undid buttons.

"What."

"Cream of mushroom soup."

"That's not one word."

"Is so."

"Is not."

"Is so."

"I know a bigger one."

"What?"

"Six frogs on a log."

"That's not bigger."

"Is so."

"Is not."

"The log is a hundred and thousand ten fifteen feet long!" he shrieked with laughter.

"I'm going to rip off your ears."

"I'll rip off your bum."

"I'll rip off your jaw."

"I'll get your eyes."

"I've got *you*," and she grabbed him in a hug.

He latched on with arms and legs, clinging like a baby possum. "I've got all of you," he said, "and you're bigger, so I've got more."

"Love you, Noel. I really, really do."

He pulled away from her and crawled between his sheets. "Do you *really* love me, or do you just say it?"

"Hey." She reached out and laid her palm against the curve of his jaw, holding his face gently. "Listen to me. I'm First Nations, eh? We don't just say we love people. We only tell people that when we mean it. All of me, inside and outside, loves all of you, inside and outside. And because I love you, so does everyone in my family love you. All the ones who are alive, all the ones who used to be alive and all the ones who someday will be born. Love, man."

"I love you." He knelt down suddenly and put his arms around her neck. "I love you *so* much." He patted her face and stroked her hair. "I even love you more than I loved my mom. I don't hardly remember her anyway. I love you, and I love Kitty, and I love Lucy, and I love Debbie, and I love Uncle Jimmy and . . . " His eyes widened with glee. "I love *so many* people! I never loved that many people before!"

"I've loved lots of people. I still love lots of people, but it was all just practice for the way I love you."

"You should have your own kid. A girl, maybe."

"Oh no, I'm going to wait and let you do that."

"Listen, you two," Kitty said from the doorway. "All this yapping and gabbing has to stop, see? He's tired, see? And I'm here as the Enforcer, see?"

"Oh God. Quick, Noel, get into bed, it's the Terminator!"

Noel slid back into bed, pretending to be terrified. Kitty sat down on the edge of the bed and stroked his hair, and Christie took Kitty's other hand.

"We was talkin' about love," Noel said seriously.

"Love? Like lovebirds?"

"We didn't talk lovebirds. Just love. Christie loves me."

"I know. And you love her, right?"

"Yeah."

"Noel said that he didn't use to love many people at all, but now he's got a whole list."

"I only loved my mom." He pressed against Kitty's hand, like a cat rubbing against a chair leg or someone's slippered foot. "And I don't hardly remember her. I didn't see her very much, she was gone lots of the time. I didn't love *him* at all. Horrible horrible. I hated him. I still hate him. And them." He looked at Kitty shyly. "You know who I mean, eh?"

"I know. I hate them too."

"Did they hurt you?"

"No, but they hurt *you*. And I love you. Buckets and heaps. So I hate them for hurting you. I don't want anyone to ever hurt you again. You are my dumpling. You are my darling."

"You are my sunshine," he hinted.

"My only sunshine," she sang softly. "You make me happy when skies are grey..."

Lucy stood in the doorway, leaning against the jamb, balancing with her cane. Where did they learn how to do it? Sure as hell nobody had shown them! The old biddy had been as good to the kids as she could be, and Lucy knew she and Deb had both tried their very best when Kitty arrived to live with them, but Kit was older, and long past wanting or needing or being able to accept what Lucy saw happening with Noel. So where did they learn how? She knew some of what had come down on the little boy and guessed a lot of the rest. And she knew all too well what had happened by way of life for Kitty and the others, living with that wandering twat Robbie got hooked up with. Much as she loved Robbie and always would, it had to be said that he'd taken the easy way. Sure, he sent money. Sending money was easy for a logger to do in the days when there was still mile after mile of first-growth timber and no end of demand for it. Loggers went into camp for months at a time, then came out and went on drunks where they lit their cigars with five-dollar bills, just for the fun of watching them burn. The money Robbie sent the old biddy was pocket change to him. Seely wasn't "his" and everyone knew it, but how many of "his" had he left scattered up and down the coast, unknown and/or unacknowledged? Seely was his excuse. And off he went, leaving his kids to the tender mercies of a dedicated and committed boozer, who was what she was for the same reason that so many others were swimming in hooch.

So—where had they learned it, and could a person take lessons?

Lucy went in and kissed her fingertips, then placed them on Noel's cheek. He smiled, his eyelids heavy, as Kit sang "Teddy Bears' Picnic." Lucy went to the kitchen and took a pink pill, then went back to the living room, sat in her chair and picked up the TV listings. Fifty-two channels and nothing on but junk. An entire channel dedicated to shopping, another to golf. What did they really have in mind for those spaces? There must be a scam, a new form of chess, with bribes and behind-the-scenes manoeuvring and still she couldn't find the pieces she needed to finish the puzzle. What were they really vying for, anyway?

Deb was gone gone gone for good. There would be some negotiating. She hadn't taken any of her furniture, or all of her clothes, or her pictures, or much of anything else. Sooner or later she'd come for it or send for it. Well, she could have it. Every stick of it.

The place was officially Lucy's. It was Lucy who had bought it, paid for the improvements, done most of the work. But still, there were all those years of Debbie's work and involvement. Even when she had a full-time job, she'd been there when the calves needed to be castrated or moved from one pasture to another, or when a cow was down unable to deliver. It was always understood that the place would go to Kitty when Lucy packed it in or died. But it was also understood that there would always be a place for Deb.

There were laws about common-law domestic arrangements. If Lucy remembered rightly, if you were together as a couple for two years or longer, then it was split-down-the-middle-half-and-half if you broke up. Did that mean that half of the expropriation money was Deb's? Good palimony, that. Lucy realized that it was a long time since she had thought of the place as *hers*. By the time Deb had lived there with her for two or three months, it was theirs. Year after year, it was theirs. Right up until that car had roared up the driveway, going too fast. Then—*poof*—it was her place again. And even then the fuckers were working overtime to take it from her. Deb had left. Deb had headed off, abandoning it all. Turned her back on it. As good as chucked it away.

What in the name of God was the preoccupation with the place, or with the things? None of that was anything but stuff. Even the damn farm was just stuff. Deb hadn't turned her back on stuff, hadn't rejected stuff, hadn't dumped stuff. She had dumped Lucy. The stuff was incidental. But you can't always bring yourself to holler, Hey, what about *me?* So you yammer about stuff.

And what about her? Could she get past the insult, could she stop feeling as if the person who knew her the best in the world had just said, You aren't good enough, I'd rather drink Drano? But there wasn't much left anyway. If you can't be honest with your own self, what does that say about you? Not much left at all. They lived in the same house but not really together. They spent almost no time together, and most of the conversation was more like verbal fencing, nag nag, flare flare, then stung silence. Were they even friends any more, or just a habit to the other? How many people kept living more or less in the same place just because it was too damn much work to change? All that friggin' packing and moving!

Don't think that Lucy hadn't noticed that when the packing and moving were inevitable anyway, the car had gone off up the driveway. They'd stayed together through worse patches, and Lucy was no longer sure why they had.

The truth of it was that she was tired. There, she'd said it. She was tired of the flare-ups, tired of the rollercoaster emotions, tired of the ups and downs of Deb's menopause, tired of being treated like a witless baby, tired of being told to eat when she wasn't even hungry. In fact, she wasn't sure what she would do or say if Deb walked back in the house right now. She would probably be too tired to say anything.

Was this depression? Clinical depression? Or just fatigue? Lucy didn't feel as if a huge weight had been taken off her shoulders, but she did feel more interested in setting up a new place. This place had been pretty much decided before she bought it. Had the choice been hers, she wouldn't have put the barns there. It's stupid to have barns at the foot of a hill, even a slight hill. Water flows downhill, everyone knows that. So the animals wind up walking through mud up to their bloody knees. Put the barn up, let everything drain away. Same with the house.

Next time she could do it the way she wanted. Ninety acres wasn't much, not alongside this place. But down there on the coast, maybe you wouldn't need as much room per critter as you needed up here. Making hay might be tough, but look at the Fraser Valley, they made hay there, damn good hay. Anyway, you can buy it by the eighteen-wheeler. And for that matter they could eat the damn cows and keep Decision for a pet. Old man Farnsworth might even want him back again.

What next? Phone the real estate guy, first thing in the morning. Phone him and then go there. You never know, there might be other bits and pieces of land for sale right tab-on to the ninety acres. Five or ten or who knows how many other acres. They'd told the guy first crack off the reel that they weren't interested in anything less than a hundred. He'd shown them several places and they'd dismissed them all. Too rocky, not enough water, too much water, too close to town, too far up a back road. Maybe they should all go together and take another look, instead of phoning and saying yes to the ninety. That land was too close to the highway. They'd hear traffic noise all day and all night—who needed that? Besides which, all kinds of planes flew right over top on their way to the airport.

"So, how you doing?" Kitty asked.

"I'm fine," Lucy said. "Hey, I had a pink pill about twenty minutes ago. You could cut off both tits and I wouldn't feel it. I been thinking."

"Jesus, if that doesn't hurt, nothing will," Kitty teased.

"You got 'er. How fast do you think we could haul arse out of here and go have ourselves another look?"

"Depends how fast you want to go. Take me maybe fifteen minutes to get the canopy on the new truck. We have to take Dog and Pup this time, though."

"Why?"

"Because we do. Because the old girl is fading. Because she's not going to die without me there to hold her paw. I don't want to go anywhere without her. Last time was the pits."

"You shoulda said something."

"Couldn't take her in the damn limo! They'd have pitched fits when we got back."

"Stuff 'em. Okay. Need a hand with the canopy?"

"Nope. And let's get one thing straight. You don't drive. I'm not winding up in the ditch with a crushed spine just because you took another pink pill, okay?"

"I don't give a toot if I never drive again. Queen of England gets chauffeured around, why not me?"

They left the next morning. It took that long to get the dimwit lined up to look after the stock. Noel fussed Lady and made promises to be back soon, and was moderately endless in his instructions to the hired hand about how to treat her and feed her and brush her.

"Hey, guy," Lucy said finally. "This man has been around stock all his life, he knows what to do."

"Maybe he doesn't know Lady."

"He knows her. And she knows him. Come on, or we'll still be here tomorrow."

The dogs went in the back, under the canopy. Noel and Christie got in the crew cab seat, Kitty drove and Lucy sat on the passenger side with her cane between her knees.

"The thing of it is," she said, "that when I finally drive away from this place, I'll leave my goddamn back behind too. This is where I finished wrecking it."

"Well, you silly bitch, that should tell you something," Christie said. "Why you think you need the Ponderosa, I don't know. And there's another just like you driving the damn truck!"

"I thought you'd driven off yesterday," Lucy snapped. "But here you are, looking a bit younger and a lot darker, but sounding the same."

"Don't bother trying it with me," Christie said easily. "It won't work with me. I learned with Kitty, and you're two of a kind. Except she can keep it up longer than you. You don't need a hundred damn acres, and you don't need twenty cows and a bull, and you don't need sixty-eleven horses, either."

"So what do we need, oh she who must be obeyed?"

"You need maybe ten acres. You keep three or four of the best cows. I know the damn bull will be with us until he dies of old age. I fully expect to be pushing his wheelchair for him. Your horses, Kit's horses, Noel's horse and the dogs and that cat Noel's pestering us about."

"Ten acres?"

"Jesus, you people! Fat eaters."

"I *hate* charming bungalows with picket fences!" Lucy moaned.

"Nobody's saying you have to get one. But if you've left your back here, what have you got left to leave at the next great notion?"

"Are we going to have another fight?" Noel asked.

"You bet we are. I'm going to reach down her throat, grab her liver and rip it out."

"Can I watch?"

"You can have the liver, if you want it."

"I don't want it."

"Then we'll cook it up and feed it to Dog."

Lucy grinned over her shoulder and winked at Noel. He winked back, scrunching his face to do it. "Sounds tough, eh?" Lucy said softly. "Little does she know."

"Yeah," he nodded.

"It won't be a pretty sight," Lucy intoned.

Noel laughed. He wished Debbie were with them, though. He liked Debbie. He hoped she got over being mad real soon.

Right next to the ninety-acre piece, sharing a fence line, was twenty acres with a two-storey house built back in the days when they actually used wood. Lucy knew that house and she had played in the backyard as a kid. There was a pathway through the bush in those days, where she could ride her bike safe from traffic and play on the swing with the kids who lived in the house. They had a purebred German shepherd, the first real one Lucy had seen. Their dad took the dog to obedience trials and won ribbons and trophies.

She stepped in the house and felt at home right away. The place had been empty for more than a year, and it had that closed-in smell that bit at your nose and throat, but it seemed to be in good shape. The real estate agent had a certificate from someone who claimed to be an inspector, saying that the place was well built and sturdy, that the roof didn't leak and that if the basement did, there were two built-in sump pumps to take care of it. A three-hundred-foot drilled well, a four-year-old pump and two concrete septic tanks—one for toilets, the other for drains, bathtubs, washing machines and such.

There was a fenced-off area that had once been a garden and was now gone to grass and weeds. That would be a challenge. But she could always hire some of Savannah's older kids and get them to dig out the sod and stuff. Lucy hadn't had a real garden for years—the ground was just too far away at times. But she hadn't been on leritine at the time, either. Maybe a foamie to sit on, that might work. Or she could just take the fence down and mow the bugger. No law against not having a garden. They'd passed a half dozen vegetable stands within five miles. She could buy fresh stuff and not even start with the digging, weeding, watering, patrolling for slugs and bugs. "What do you think?" she asked Kitty.

"What I was thinking was I've got some money saved up. I could toss it in the pot and we could get both places."

"Dear God in heaven," Christie sighed.

"We need a barn. Be nice to have a separate one for horses, set them up so they could in-and-out as they wanted."

"Pretty mild here in the wintertime. All's they really need is a place to get in out of the rain once in a while."

"The entire herd, I suppose," Christie muttered. "There'll be more than one back left behind on this place!"

"Be kinda fun, putting in riding trails."

"Yeah. It could be. How many cows were you planning on?"

"Me?" Kitty looked amazed. "None. Decision's leg is fine now. Better than it ever was. The old man is going to want to put him back on the circuit. I thought you wanted—"

"What about those Santa Margaritas you talked about?"

"I've lived my entire life without one, I can finish off my life the same way."

"Still and all, be nice to have both places."

"Yeah, it would be."

"They aren't making new land, you know? And the price is probably never going to be any lower than it is."

"Probably not."

"I can't believe this." Christie walked from the kitchen to the living room, trying to get a sense of the place, get a feel of it. Noel and the real estate agent tagged along, the agent pointing out some of the features. "Two bedrooms downstairs," he intoned, "and three more upstairs, with a big bathroom up there. Laundry facilities in the basement. Which bedroom do *you* want?" he smiled at Noel.

"I don't know. I didn't see any of them."

"Your bedroom would be upstairs," Christie told him. "And you can be sure it won't be the biggest one."

"Can I go look?"

"Sure." She peered out the picture window in the living room. Two huge pastures, invaded by alder trees after a couple of years of disuse. "Did anybody ever farm this place?" she asked.

"I think someone had horses at some time," the agent admitted.

"So where's the stable?"

"It was dismantled several years ago."

"Why?"

"The, uh, family felt, uh, felt it would be best."

"Am I right in assuming you're under no obligation to tell me anything unless I ask you right out?"

"Well, basically... uh, yes. That's true."

"So I'm asking. Why did the family think it would be best?"

"There was an... incident in the stable."

"What happened?"

"The gentleman hanged himself."

"My God! No wonder they wanted it to be taken down! Then what happened?"

"The, uh... younger people didn't live here. They're in the city. And the lady, well, she couldn't really manage the place. So she has moved to the city with them. Has her own apartment and all. But... " His voice trailed off and she nodded, hearing the unspoken.

"Might as well go look upstairs," she sighed.

"There are three bedrooms upstairs, and—" He was all set to go back into his pitch, but Christie held up her hand.

"You said," she reminded him.

He fell silent and followed her up the stairs.

One of the bedrooms was huge. The other two were bigger than the bedrooms being put into new houses. Noel was sitting on the floor in the one nearest the stairs, his head tilted to one side as though he were watching TV or listening to music.

"What do you think?" Christie asked.

"I like this one," he said. "Look." He got up and went to the window. "If this window opened up, I could go out on the roof, see, and then go into that tree. But I can't get the window open."

"Just as well, you'd probably break your neck."

"No I wouldn't."

"Yes you would."

"Would not."

"Would so."

"Would not."

"Look, you can open it at the top. But not enough to climb out of, just enough for fresh air. I don't think the bottom is supposed to open, it doesn't look as if it was built to be lifted."

"I like this room. I could put the bunk bed there and sleep in the top bunk, and then I could see out the window and watch the stars."

"You could so."

"The bathroom's smelly, though."

"That's probably because the septic tanks haven't been used for a while. We'll get them working again. They say if you put a dead cat down them—"

"Not my cat."

"You don't have a cat."

"I will, though."

"No you won't."

"Yes I will."

"Will not. You'll see. No cat for you."

"No cat for *you*, you mean."

"That's right, no cat for me. Maybe we'll have to use some hamburger instead."

"What for?"

"The septic tank, you dope."

"You're the dope."

"Am not."

"It's pretty here."

"It is, for sure. Kind of nice how the house sits up on the slope like this and you can look down on the fields from one side of the house, and at the bush from the other side."

"There's a stream runs through the bush," the agent chimed in, "and a previous owner brought in some machinery and had a big pool dug. I believe it's been stocked with trout, so there should be good fishing for the young fellow."

"I'm not the one you have to sell it to," Christie grinned, teasing him. "Go downstairs and make your pitch to those two, especially the old girl with the cane. Me, I just do what I'm told, go where I'm told."

"Do not," Noel laughed.

"Do so."

"I'm on his side," the agent said. "I don't think you ever just do what you're told."

"Do so," she answered.

"Do not," the agent responded. Noel giggled. "And you're another," he added.

"Am not."

"Are too."

Savannah thought it was outright lunacy, but nobody was asking her opinion so she decided to keep it to herself. A hundred and ten acres, for crying in the night! And crazy Lucy already had her eye on still another place, one that wasn't even listed for sale. Fine, let her buy up the whole world if she wanted to.

And Jimboh, wasn't he cut from the same cloth. Talking about how if they got the strip just behind them they'd wind up side-by-each. "All one place again," he said, as if he'd ever known it when it was one piece of land. It had been split off and bits of it sold long before Jimmy was born, even before Lucy came along.

Crazy. The whole flipping lot of them. There'd originally been over three hundred acres. Surely to God they didn't plan on trying to buy all that back again! God, Savannah, don't even ask them, you might give them more crazy ideas.

First, up went the barn. You'd think they'd have brought in one of those metal prefab things, the ones with a domed roof. No, it had to be wood. Why not just build it out of gold bricks? And Lucy arguing against plywood, as if it harboured bubonic plague. Just have to cover it with siding anyway, she'd snapped. Why? Slap on a coat of paint and call it done. But no, oh no, let's dig in our heels, let's believe that business about animals gnawing at the plywood and getting slivers caught in their throats or getting sick on the glue. Go for it, Luce. Do everything the hard way. No skin off my nose.

And the kids, the whole bunch of them, yammering for horses. She'd ride to hell herself before she'd spring for a horse for each of them! Most of 'em would get tired of it all inside of a few months, anyway. She could see Brit sticking it out, but small chance Elaine was going to be interested in shovelling poop and all the other folderol that went with it. Bobby, now, he was all set to go go go, and he had Noel to get excited with. But Alan? Or Bran? Oh, they wanted one. One each. They loved the idea of it. But they wanted dirt bikes too. And mountain bikes. And this and that and two of the next. Caroline would be more apt to get involved than Elaine, but wouldn't get into it up to her eyebrows like Brit was sure to do. Maybe Lizzie, but Darlene's attention zipped from here to something else in a flash, and she was congenitally allergic to anything that remotely resembled work. And just whisper the word "share" and all hell broke loose. I want I want I want.

"No," Savannah said firmly. They stared at her, as if she'd betrayed them to the enemy and caused them to be hung from hooks on the dungeon wall.

"Not a one. Wait until you've tried out the ones they already have."

"I want my own!" Alan flared.

"Save up your money, then, and buy one. And your own saddle, and your own bridle, and your own halter, and your own damn horseshoes. I am *not* buying a horse. The word is *no*. Anybody here who doesn't understand that word?"

"I'll ask Dad," he muttered.

"Go ahead. He'll ask me and I'll say no."

"I hate you."

"You're entitled. Hate all you want. Hate overtime if it'll make you feel better. It won't change my mind, though. *No*. Not until everything has calmed down, and each and every person who says they want a horse can ride well enough that both Kitty and Lucy say they're ready. It isn't a fur-lined bike that you can drop beside the driveway. These things eat, they breathe—they even, as I understand it, think. So stop it."

Just to be sure, she phoned the guys and told them.

Larry laughed. "A *horse*? He wants a *horse*? He thinks he is the son of a rich man?"

"What he needs is his arse warmed good."

"We'll talk to him."

"He'll threaten to hate you."

"If he does, he will be a very sorry boy. Perhaps it is time he was reminded of his place in the world. He should not be talking like that to you."

"Maybe I'll just go bang him on the head with something heavy."

"How is school?"

"They're doing well. They seem to have settled in. We've got kids on volleyball teams and soccer teams and ... you should come up for some of the games. I'll get a schedule and send it to you. Oh, and I've continued the tutoring. Noreen comes twice a week. If nothing else it gets the damn homework done."

"You sound tired."

"Larry, I'm worn out. I mean, the laundry alone is ... "

"Find someone," he said firmly. "Find someone to come in and do the work. You should never have been doing it, anyway. I have told you, we have all told you and ... now you listen, Savannah! You are their mother, not their slave. If you do not arrange for someone, we will."

"It's expensive, Larry."

"You are not to worry about that."

She was going to run an ad in the paper, but then Audrey caught wind of the plan and spoke up. "I do maybe nine hours a week selling bread with Seely," she said, "and I'm just about chewing nails and spitting tacks with boredom. I was going to go see if I could get a job in the new mall, but hey, I can do laundry and stuff."

"That doesn't seem right."

"Don't see why not. Seely'n me's got her two girls just about trained. They actually vacuum the living room and keep the bathroom clean. The rest of it we get done together, lickety-split. You're looking pale, I should have noticed before. You sleeping okay?"

"Yeah. I just feel tired."

"Small wonder. Christ, just driving Bob in and out to kindergarten each day is a whole job. Why don't you go lie down for a while, I'll finish off the laundry."

Savannah didn't want to, but she was tired. Not really sleepy, but deep-down tired. She leaned back on her pillow to read for a while, and the next thing she knew the kids were home from school. She sat up fast, feeling almost frightened, then she heard Bobby's voice. Someone had collected him. The surge of fear faded and she could breathe again. She slid off the bed and reached for her clothes.

Out of the blue, with no phone call or other warning, a cab pulled off the road and drove to the front of the house, and Carol was back.

Savannah almost fainted when she saw her. For a few minutes she wasn't sure that she was seeing Carol. She had got so used to the idea that Carol was dead, that it was like seeing a ghost.

"My God!" she blurted.

"Yeah. Who you see when you don't have a gun, eh?"

The shock gave way to anger. "Where in hell have you been?" she demanded.

"Now don't you be that way." Carol brushed past her and went to the kitchen and looked around for a cup of coffee.

"Who are you?" she snapped, seeing Audrey.

"Pardon me, madam. The same question might well be asked of yourself." And that was it. Audrey was finished for the day. She folded the dishcloth, hung it over the handle on the oven door and left by way of the back door.

"You know damn well who she is!" Savannah raged. "That was a shitty thing to say!"

"Leave me alone, Savannah, please. I've had about as much as I can take of people snarling at me."

"Where were you?"

"I've just spent eight months in jail, if you must know."

"You *what?*"

"You heard me. Don't you read the papers? I got busted."

"For what?"

"Possession for the purposes of trafficking. I wasn't trafficking and didn't have no intention, either, but I did have a whack of it in my purse. You'd think they'd'a had sense enough to know that if I was trafficking, I wouldn't be sitting around half-blasted with all that in my friggin' purse, right? But no. In comes Johnny R-for-Righteous Law, and holds up my purse and says, Who owns this? And like a fool I said I did. I said I was half-blasted, didn't I? And . . . eight friggin' months."

"Why didn't you phone?"

"What would you have done? Baked me a cake with a file in it? You think I wanted my kids to know I was in the Crowbar Hotel?"

"Did you phone the guys?"

"Why would I do that? They'd just come to visit me and nag until I volunteered to be the first woman executed in recent memory."

"So what now?"

"Nothing now. Same as before."

"No," Savannah said coldly. "*Not* same as before. This is *my* house. The guys built this house for me. And I'm not picking up after you like before, or putting up with snarly shit, either. You can stay here for a while, but then you figure out something else."

"Jesus," Carol sighed. "Welcome home, Carol."

"You aren't at home," Savannah yelled. "You're in my house! You didn't want your kids to know you were in jail? You could have let me know what was going on and where you were, and we could have figured out some other story for the kids. But no, you just vanish into thin air. I thought you were dead! And now what? You show up, just poof like that, and what are you going to tell the kids? Oh, sorry about that, it slipped my mind? You as good as dumped them, and I got to look after them. And do all the work too. And now I guess you'll just take them away again."

"If you don't get off my case, I'll take 'em with me tonight, soon as they get home from school, and that'll be that."

Except the kids let it be known that they had no intention of going anywhere.

"You aren't my mom anyway," Brit said loudly. "And I'm not going anywhere with you." She stomped out of the kitchen, and when she came back she was wearing a look on her face like the one on the German general when he realized Paris was his.

"The dads say I don't have to go anywhere at all with you."

"You talked to Dad?" Jason blurted. "What did he say about me?"

"Go phone him your own self. I just asked about me and Bran. And the dads said we can choose."

"I'm staying." Brandon looked at Savannah. "Is that okay, Mom?"

"You know it is." She held out her arms and he walked into them. "It's okay, Bran. It's a mess and it's noisy and there's going to be one helluva fight, but it's okay. You're okay."

"You kids get your stuff," Carol shouted. "We're out of here."

"I'm not out of here," Jason shouted back. "I don't have to go anywhere!"

"I'm not moving again," Caroline wept. "You didn't even tell us where you were, you didn't say when you'd be back, you just went. We thought you were dead."

"Why in hell did everyone think I was dead? Do I look dead? Do I sound dead?"

"You don't quit yelling at me and these kids, you'll *be* bloody dead," Savannah snarled. "Count on it. Why don't you just fuck off into town and get a hotel room for the night and give us a chance to get used to the idea you're back?"

"A hotel room? I got my own room, right here."

"No, you don't. We rearranged rooms. And I'm not going to shift kids at this hour of the day."

"Fine." Carol reached for her cigarettes and lighter. "But I'll be back, and when I get here, you'd better be in one helluva better mood."

Savannah let her go off thinking she'd had the last word.

Jimmy felt so bad about it all that he insisted on going in to the airport to pick up the guys. "You're all going to be as busy as one-legged tap dancers," he said, "and I'm not going to be able to do any work today anyway."

"You're a doll." Savannah kissed his cheek. "You really are."

"Anything you need in town?" He didn't feel like a doll, he felt like an idiot. He'd been so sure they'd offed her! You heard about it all the time, the exploding kettle, the midnight fire, the prowler who panicked. There were all kinds of stories. They were forever going after each other with swords, or those ceremonial knives they all wore.

The plane was late, but not by too much. And if their smiles faded when they saw it was Jim waiting for them and not Savannah, they stayed pleasant and polite. Jim shook hands with them and led the way to Audrey's car.

"Listen, I owe you guys an apology."

"You thought we had executed her," Larry guessed.

"I was sure of it. What with her whoring around and all."

"Would *you* have killed her?"

"Me?" Jimmy was dumbfounded. "Nah! What makes you think that?"

"You know how it is," Larry grinned. "We read the papers. You people are forever killing each other. People shot in front of nightclubs, people beaten to death with baseball bats. Every night, are three or four articles in the newspaper about you people killing each other."

"Okay," Jimmy laughed softly. "I figured you'd cut her in two with one of those swords, eh."

"Ah, the sword. Yes. And a woman like Carol would stand there while we got it out of the trunk, unsheathed it and ran at her with it."

"I'm sorry."

"I'm sorry too. Now you have insulted me and I will have to use the sword on you."

"Want me to pull over so's you can get it out of the trunk? That'll give me time to find my six-shooter and cowboy hat."

"It isn't easy to apologize," Moe said from the back seat. "I find it very difficult to admit I have made an error."

"I don't mind making an error," said Jimmy. "It's when I'm right out to lunch I start to get shirty."

"Shirty?" Shemp asked.

"Shirty. Antsy...uh..."

"Ah, antsy. Yes."

"Antsy and sort of...ticked off."

"Ah. So when I am sitting here and wishing to all the heavens that my life wasn't in such turmoil, I am feeling shirty?"

"Probably. Unless you like turmoil."

"I pray for boredom," Shemp sighed. "But I doubt it will be given to me. No man with as many wives and children as myself is going to find boredom."

"It's the screwing you get for the screwing you got," Jim agreed.

Shemp sat back, puzzled. He whispered something to Moe, who shook his head. They spoke softly together, then leaned forward to talk to Larry.

"What does that mean?" Larry asked Jimmy. "The screwing you are getting for the screwing you are getting?"

"No, no. It's the screwing you are getting now that pays you back for the other screwing you got before."

"I do not understand."

"Don't worry about it, Larry. It's sort of a joke."

"A sort-of joke? Your sister used to drive me mad the way she described measurements. A dab of this, a dribble of that. A touch of something else. Finally I realized they all meant the same thing. All those English lessons."

"Yeah, well, you speak it real good."

"I ought to, I was born here," Larry said.

Jimmy gaped at him and Larry smiled angelically.

"A sort-of joke," he said slyly.

Carol sat at the supper table looking defiant and pathetic. She smiled, she listened to the conversation, she spoke when spoken to and her table manners were impeccable. Still, she looked as if ritual suicide would be an option if only she knew how to go about doing it.

"I am not sure about the protocol," Moe said. "I do not know if it would be more proper to discuss this now, at the table, or if we should wait and go elsewhere."

"Here," Brit said bravely.

"Brittany?"

"This is our business too." She looked to Victor for help. He just smiled at her and nodded. "This is all of our business. If she leaves again, that's going to come down on us, and if she stays, we have to live with her, and so that's our business too."

"And you are frightened because you spoke up?"

"Yes, sir."

"Do not be frightened. You were polite. That is what counts." He looked at Carol. "You?"

"I didn't want them to know. The kids, I mean."

"Do you deny it would be their business? How did Brit say that, come down on us? It came down on them when you disappeared."

"I'm sorry." She made it sound like Fuck you.

"Caroline?" Larry smiled at her. "This comes down on you. Is that the correct term?"

"Yes, Daddy."

"What do you have to say?"

"She said she was leaving and we had to go with her and—"

"Excuse me, who is 'she'? Are we discussing the Queen of England?"

"Mom. Mom said she was leaving and we had to go with her. And I don't want to go with her. I want to stay here! I *will* stay here."

"You have something else to say, I can see it in your face. Your very beautiful and very frightened face."

"We didn't know where she was . . . Mom was, I mean. And if we have to go with her . . . what if we don't know where YOU are, or . . . and anyway—"

She looked over at Jason. He stiffened and his face paled, but he spoke. "We want to stay here with the family. We don't want to move away."

"I only said I was leaving because Savannah was being such a bitch!"

"Me, a bitch? Carol, you come in here like an invasion and you fill the place up. You're a whole crowd when you've got yourself in a mood. Me, a bitch!"

"Hey, Shemp, did you enjoy your trip?" Jimmy grinned. He passed the big yellow bowl to Shemp.

"Oh, indeed," Shemp said, "and it is so nice to unwind after a busy day at work and just enjoy the peace and quiet of the country."

"Yeah, well, I hope it was worth it."

"What?"

"The screwing you got back then. Because the screwing you're getting right now is—"

He didn't get to finish. Savannah started laughing, the kids joined in, Carol forgot she was angry and threatened, Audrey poked Jimmy and told him he was just *awful* and Seely got the giggles. Victoria crowed happily.

Larry spoke to Shemp, who nodded, and as he turned to Moe to speak, the penny dropped.

"Ah! Ah, yes!" Shemp shouted, and then he was laughing with the others, explaining the joke to the other two.

"Ah," Larry breathed. "Of course! Yes, certainly," and he laughed softly.

Lucy couldn't watch when the stock truck came and loaded the bulk of the herd to take it to the neighbouring spread. The foreman of the big ranch looked as if he wanted to go to the house and say something reassuring. Finally he shook his head, pushed his hat back and said, "Helluva shame."

"It's a kick in the teeth, for sure," Kitty agreed.

"We lose a twenty-acre pasture, but nothing like this."

"Yeah. If I was you, I'd get the boss to write a letter right now, putting dibs on the hayfields. They aren't going to cover the whole thing with pavement, you know, and if you go on about how the long grass might be a fire danger, what with tossed-out cigarettes and all—well, it's worth a try. I know a guy cuts hay alongside the airport. You never know."

"I'll tell him. Good idea, thanks. You tell her we'll try not to let it go to waste, okay? Tell her..." He shrugged. "Hell, what can a person say?"

"Not much," she agreed.

They hauled up the irrigation system and took it apart carefully. There was so much to move! The stuff in the barn alone would have filled a moving van. Lucy paced and fretted. She limped to the barn and saddled her horse, then rode off by herself, her cane stuffed into the rifle holder. Either she didn't talk at all or she went on long verbal riffs about the conspiracy to hand the entire world over to agribusiness and control politics by threats of famine.

When the haying crews arrived and people she didn't know drove out to mow the hay she had tended so carefully, Lucy was so upset Kitty feared she would have a stroke. But halfway through the cutting, Lucy suddenly came to terms with something. Dan Conrad, the neighbour who was taking the herd, drove into the yard to check on things and Lucy got up out of her chair, grabbed her cane and headed outside to talk to him.

Kitty, who was helping replace some blades on one of the mowers, saw Lucy stump up to Conrad, thrust out her hand and start talking. After a while she heard Conrad laughing.

"There you go," Kitty said, wiping her hands on a piece of cloth and stuffing it in her back pocket "I think that's got 'em all."

"Should flag that damn boulder," the driver snapped. Kitty looked at him and shrugged. "Why? We knew it was there. What do you care anyway, you get paid by the hour."

He dismissed her with a flick of his eyes and she moved away, laughing. Lucy called to her and Kitty walked over.

"I feel one whole helluva lot better now," Lucy smiled.

"Yeah?"

"Yeah. Dan and his boys are going to come over after we get booted off. Anything we leave behind, they'll take over to his place."

"Gonna take the barn apart," he grinned. "Take about a week to get it down and a coupla months to figure it out, then maybe three days to get it back up again."

"Is it worth it?"

"Ma'am, that's one aitch of a barn. You can't find support beams like those ones any more. Don't you worry, there won't be a gate or a fence post here when those yutzes show up. I can get what's-his-name in town to come out and put jacks under the house and we can take 'er up the access road and set 'er up in the off pasture, run electricity there no problem, coupla poles is all's we need. Give 'er a septic system and hey, it's going to be fine."

"House too?"

"Waste not, want not."

"Yeah, and leave not behind when you go." Lucy looked content for the first time in weeks.

"Foreman told me your idea about leasing the haying rights. Got a lawyer workin' on it."

"I appreciate what you're doing," Lucy said, her voice suddenly choked. "I don't feel quite so much like some beautiful animal just got its throat slashed and has to lie down and bleed to death. I feel like she's just moving over the hill there."

"Remember when those damn kids turned the beef loose in the hay-field?" Conrad started to laugh. "Whole lot of them needed their backsides blistered. Now my boy's gonna wind up livin' in your house. How's that for a switch?"

"How's he doing?"

"Good. Real good. Got him a real fine wife and two kids. Little girl nearly three and a new baby boy. They're both of 'em vets now. They got a big practice, office in town. I tell him the hours are just as bad as if he'd taken up ranching the way I wanted." He smiled at Kitty. "Been seeing you on the TV. That's some hat, lady."

"Isn't it a doozy? Got her in a junk store in New Westminster. She was perched on the head of one of those mannequins. I looked at those red-painted wooden balls of cherries and I said Damn, I have to have that hat."

"Is that the old bugger over there? He looks like he's watching the whole hay show, maybe judging who does what better than who else."

"He's something else again, I tell you."

"He going with you?"

"I guess." She shook her head. "It's a comedown for him, though. I thought the old man would decide to rodeo him after all, but he says no. The bull had this little—well, not a limp, but he'd hesitate a bit with that right front leg, and Farnsworth has decided it was all the travelling. Standing on a metal floor, bouncing and jouncing, then standing in a small pen. Says he'll just cripple up again if he gets treated that way again. For sure he's had no trouble at all in the time he's been here making time with the girls."

"Had a horse like that. Got her for next best to nothing. Beautiful mare. You must have seen her, great big red, one of those European breedings. Looked as if a tall man would need a ladder to get up there. She'd been trained for a show horse. Guess she did real good at it for a while. Then she started coming up lame. No reason they could figure out, she'd just come up lame. Had her to more vets than made any sense at all, took her to this place where they do rehab, with swimming pools and all. She'd be fine and then she'd come up lame. So finally they decided to off-load her. Friend of mine worked on the place. It was one of those places in the Valley. You know, white-painted fences, the whole trip. I figured if nothing else, I could use her for brood. Even if I only got one or two foals out of her I'd be ahead. Went down, trailered her back. She came out of that damn trailer on three legs. I was just about to get the rifle. She never looked that bad when I loaded her in! I put her in the small field south of the house, where I could see her and check on her. Three, four days she's limping again. I couldn't see a hint of any reason why that mare would be limping. Hoof was beautiful! Hard as slate. So I stretched the leg. That's all I did, had the wife hold the lead rope and I just moved that leg, the whole length of it, and I mean I moved it. Didn't hear a thing. Two days later, she's walking fine. Must have been a muscle or a tendon. So every morning, first thing, we'd go out and we'd stretch that leg, whether she was limping or not. Had her on pasture for oh, hell, month, month and a half, and then we started riding her. No trouble at all. Not a sign of trouble. We figure what it was, they had her in a paddock, like a big living room. So most of the time she stood around there waiting for them to put one of those pancake saddles on her and take her to the ring. Ride her around, lunge the hell out of her, keep her in top condition for the show ring, then cool her off and put her back in the paddock. That mare needed to walk and trot and run on grass. Just like your bull, eh? Into the trailer and trying to keep his balance, everything hard and shifting all the time. All's we did was treat her like a horse, and after a bit we didn't even have to stretch that leg any more."

"They didn't want her back? Once they knew she was fine?"

"They never found out she was fine. My buddy, he didn't tell them that part. Now, that bull of yours is one aitch of an animal. Should you decide not to move him, well, I've got lots of open pasture for him. And cows. Lots of cows."

"That's decent of you."

"No, it's not. It's self-serving and devious and stingy and taking advantage of your good nature."

"There's the old man to consult. He'll prob'ly want some rodeo stock out of him."

"No problem. He can just slide his cows in with mine. Come pick up the calf when he wants it. I'm easy. Is the bull hard to handle? I heard he killed a fellow."

"He's easy to handle. The fellow he killed was trying to ride him." She told Conrad about the leg giving out and Decision stumbling. "He didn't do it on purpose. But you know what people are like."

"How do you move him around? He okay with horses?"

"He's okay with horses, but mostly when it's time to move him I just open a gate and call him."

"You're kidding me."

"Come see."

She got some treat biscuits from the barn, then moved to the fence and called the bull. He turned and she called again.

"Come see," she invited him. "I've got something real nice for you."

Decision ambled over, no sign of a limp. Kitty was used to him, and it wasn't until she saw the look on Dan Conrad's face that she remembered all over again what the white-faced black bull looked like to other people. "Big guy, eh?"

"Man, he is something. Boxcar on four feet."

"That might be part of why he had trouble with that leg. Him being so big. I've heard those giant people have leg troubles too."

"How's his heart?"

"Better'n yours. Get Buddy to check him over."

"Well, don't know as I want that black son to stomp my son."

"Just tell your son not to try to ride him."

"The only one who can sit up on him," Lucy added, "is my grandson Noel, and you're not supposed to know he does it."

"Damn." Kitty's stomach tightened. "You're kidding, I hope."

"Nope. I got no sense of humour at all, you know that. I caught the little guy. He cried and made me promise not to tell you."

"What did Decision do?'

"Stood there eating grass. Kid sat there and waved off the flies. Just sitting up there, talking away, soft and easy, happy as a fly at the manure pile."

"Be okay if we came over tonight or tomorrow night, whichever he can manage, and take a look?"

"Give a phone call before you head over and I'll have coffee waiting."

Lucy didn't ask any questions. She understood exactly why Kitty was willing to leave her baby behind. She wanted to think that she'd have done the same thing. But no denying it was the best kind of life for the bull. Miles and miles of grassland and more cows than he'd ever be able to service alone, no highway traffic, no tribe of kids. No treat biscuits and no adoring little boy, but everything else he could want.

The first truckload of stuff arrived just before dark. Rather than try to unload anything, Kitty parked near the new barn, then climbed into the crew cab with Noel and Pup.

"How you doing?" she asked.

"I missed you."

"Hey, you were fine in here. Better than you'd have been in that crabby old thing. It isn't set up for a guy to take a snooze, okay?"

"I know all that. I still missed you."

"I don't know *what* we're going to do about that." She put her arm around his shoulders and pulled him tight against her. "I mean, what are we going to do when you head off to kindergarten? I can't very well go with you."

"I'm not going to kindergarten. The only way I could do that would be to stay with Bobby and then I wouldn't be with you, so I'm not going to."

"I know. For now, anyway. But *if*, and if and if . . . we might get our stuff moved by maybe Easter time, and if we do—"

"If," he nodded. "If and if, and if."

"Right. Always an if. Life is an if."

"We could make a song. Life is an if . . . "

"You got it. Life is an if, don't get your neck stiff."

"Or I'll give you a biff, if you do."

"Listen to that noise in the back seat there," Lucy laughed. "Sounds like fingernails on a blackboard."

Kitty would have preferred to stay at the motel, but Savannah had her mind made up, and when she did, the best thing the rest of the world could do was just go along with it.

The headlights of the pickup swept over the small cottage, still under construction. Carol would live there and the kids could go back and forth as they wanted. But from what Kitty heard, they weren't in any mood to do much to-ing and fro-ing. And could a person blame them? Just left off like that, not even a Sorry but I'll be a bit late phone call? She wished she could see Carol's point about not wanting to tell the kids she was in jail, but there are limits. If she was so worried about what her kids might or might not hear, why was she hanging around with a crowd that gets unexpected visits from the cops?

"Bobby said Auntie Savannah was going to make pizgetti."

"Yeah? Lucky us. Bet she makes two kinds of sauce."

"Yeah?"

"One with meat, one without. Bet ya."

"Bobby said she was going to put cabbage in the sauce."

"Oh, yum yum. You know what that means? She's going to make lions' heads. She takes meat, real good meat, and she puts in her special secret spices and stuff, some grated onion, lots and lots of garlic, and rice. Then she puts cabbage on the bottom of the pot. Lots of it. And then she makes balls out of the meat stuff. And then," and she poked him in the ribs to make him giggle, "then she cooks it and the rice all swells up and looks like a lion's mane. And good? Oh, boy, wait until you scoff it down! You put the lions' heads on the side of your plate, and then you put some spaghetti in the middle with sauce over top of it, and you make sure you get some of the cabbage, and slurpo slurpo until it's time to burpo burpo."

"We're going to have lemon squares too."

"Did Bobby tell you that too?"

"No, I just know. Thingy told me."

"What can I say, it must be true."

"They sure were careful that she wasn't smack up Savannah's nose," Christie said quietly. "She's way to heck and gone over the far side of Jimboh's place."

"Maybe it's just as well."

"I hope she doesn't get out of line around Jimmy. Audrey'll pull her face off if she does."

"Or borrow one of those ceremonial swords, right?" Lucy offered, and they laughed.

The pickup stopped, the front door opened, kids poured out and Savannah stood in the brightly lit doorway, smiling and waving. Noel squirmed and wriggled.

"Hey, hey," Kitty protested. "Hang onto yourself, guy. Can't rush the ones in the front seat, remember?"

"Try to rush me and I'll whap you with my cane so hard you'll feel it back to when you were a baby," Lucy promised. She swung her legs out of the truck and Victor was there in a flash, holding out his hand. "Thank you, sir," she smiled at him. "You're a gentleman and you've got a good strong arm."

"Love you, Auntie Lucy." He hugged her and waited until she had her cane settled. As she made her way toward Savannah, he caught Noel on his way out of the truck, held him face-to-face and kissed him on both cheeks, then on the chin. "Hey, cousin," he said softly. "I've missed you something fierce."

"I missed you." Noel kissed Victor several times. "Is Bobby here?"

"Bobby's in that crowd. Look, he's waving. Off you go." Vic turned and moved forward. "Auntie Kitty. How are you? You're looking wonderful. And Auntie Christie, it's so good to see you! Got any packs, suitcases, whatever you need carried in?"

"We've got them, Vic. We're fine."

"Hey there, Dog! Come on, old girl, come to Vic. I'll get you down. Yes, I will so, I'm not like these other ones, leave an old girl in the back of the truck all night, as if she didn't count for anything. Come on, babe."

"She's getting awful old and stiff, Vic. She's not going to be with us much longer."

"There you go, get your legs under you. What a fine dog. Yes, she is so."

Dog was happy on the porch until bedtime, then she wanted back in under the canopy. Kitty lifted her in, climbed in after her and made sure her blanket was in the right place and smoothed down. Dog circled several times, then lay down and sighed.

"Yeah. Nice to know where you belong, eh?"

But Pup was in the house, the centre of attention. From the youngest on up to Victor and Elaine, the kids pampered her, spoiled her and took her outside for purported pees. And when it was time for the littler ones to go to bed, Pup wound up in Bobby's room. Rather than look like a hog, Noel climbed into bed with Bobby so they could share Pup.

"No chattering and giggling and tickling," Savannah warned, "or that puppy will be right back out in the truck with the big one."

"We'll be good," Bobby promised. "Won't we, Noel?"

"Very good."

They actually were very good, probably because Pup was so tired from all the jumping and ball chasing that she curled up between them and went to sleep immediately. They were so busy petting and stroking her that they didn't see the sandman slip through the window and toss sleep in their eyes. Noel yawned, Bobby yawned, and that was it for the night.

The next day was eaten up by the unloading of the truck.

"What's that?" Brandon blurted.

"Part of the water sprinkler." Noel felt ten feet tall. Bran was older than Noel, and yet there was something he knew that Bran didn't. "When it's all put back together again it waters the hayfield. It can make a huge spray."

"Can you run under it? Like with a regular one?"

"Not if it's in the hayfield. Auntie Lucy won't let you play in the hay. She's real crabby about her hay."

"And what's that stuff?"

"It hooks on the back of the tractor. You can do all kinds of stuff with it. I bet we can watch Kitty get it out of the back of the truck. She has to bring it down that ramp. We had to get the ramp specially made. The other one was just wood and Kitty said it would break."

Bran watched, and when Kitty hollered for them to get back from the ramp, he took Noel's hand and made sure they were well clear. The tractor came down the ramp, the mower following, and Kitty took it to the equipment shed that the construction firm of the three wise men had built adjoining the barn. Bran watched closely as Kitty unhitched the mower, then he ran back to the truck to watch the tedder come down. Noel was bored, having seen it a zillion times already, so he went to the house to check out his room. The windows still didn't open. He'd been hoping that someone had told the construction guys to fix the window while they were building the new barn. But no, he would have to figure it out himself. Or maybe Uncle Jimmy could get it to open.

"You have to make a decision, Noel." Christie put some mashed potato on his plate, next to the two slices of chicken breast. "Kitty's going to drive back for another load of barn stuff. She's going to be real busy and she won't have a lot of time for fun stuff with kids. So you have to choose. Are you going to go with her, or are you going to stay here, with Lucy and me?"

"Why are you staying?"

"Some guys are coming to put in the fences, and Lucy needs to be here to make sure they go exactly where she wants them and the gates are in the right places. And I'm going to stay here because the inside of the house has to be painted and those old carpets have to be lifted up. If you go with Kitty, you've got a real long drive and then she'll be busy and then you'll have that real long drive back. If you stay here, with us, you can go to kindergarten with Bobby."

"I'll miss you," Noel said, accusingly.

"I'll miss you too, Bubba, but ... " Kitty shrugged. "Sometimes we have to eat a little plate of yuck, eh?"

"You'll like kindergarten," Bobby promised. "I'll share my stuff with you."

"I might cry," Noel warned.

"Go ahead," Kitty smiled. "Come on, guy, don't put me through the hoops on this. I'll be gone tomorrow and tomorrow night, that's one sleep. And I'll be two days sorting and loading, that's another sleep, and maybe another, so that's three. Then I'll drive back here, and I'll try to get back before bedtime, but if I don't make it, that's four sleeps."

"That's a long time!"

"Yeah, I know. But look at it the other way. If you come along, you've got all that time either on your own, bored stiff, or in the truck, bored even stiffer. I won't have time to play or go riding or anything."

"You want me to stay!"

"Yeah, darlin', I do."

"Tell you what," Jimmy said suddenly. "If you go along with this, and make it easy on everyone, then each night before you have to get ready for bed, you and Bobby can come to my place and I'll take you down into the hell hole and you can work with me."

"Spoiled brats," Elaine said pleasantly. "It's always the little ones, isn't it?"

"Always," Victor agreed. "Spoiled babies. Nobody ever said I could go into the hell hole."

"He likes us best," Bobby said placidly. "You know he does. 'Cause we're nicer, is why."

"And much, much cuter," Audrey added. "Those other ones are handsome and beautiful, but you two are cute. Makes a difference."

"Four sleeps?" Noel looked stricken.

"Four, but not five. And I'll give you the phone number for the new phone I got."

"What new phone?"

"Wait till you see it. It's in the truck."

"I got it for her while you guys were unloading equipment," Christie winked at Noel. "It means you can phone her at night, when you've had your bath."

The tractor rode back to the farm and Kitty used it almost steadily, moving the last of the equipment into the truck, going from pasture to pasture to load the old bathtubs that had been used as waterers. She had a garage full of tools to box and load, she had gear and whatnot in the sheds and outbuildings. The hired hand helped her, and what she didn't take, he loaded into Conrad's three-ton—anything he didn't keep, other neighbouring ranchers would be able to use. At noon, three of them showed up to help Kitty dismantle the weight-chute and load it.

"Missus sent over some lunch," one of them said. "She said to tell you to slow down to a fast gallop and get some grub into you."

"Thank you. Aunt Lucy said these planter boxes of hers were to be shared out with her friends and neighbours. I can put the forks on the tractor to get one into your truck, if you think you can get it back out when you get home."

"No problem. She'll be real glad of it. Probably set me to work making another one so's she's got a match."

"Aunt Lucy's got a zip-top plastic bag in each one. She's written down what all kinds of stuff grow in the boxes and what kind of fertilizer she uses. And she said now's a good time to move the rose bushes, while they're dormant. Said if you dug 'em up and put the root balls in sacks you could store 'em in the root cellar until the ground was thawed enough you could dig good holes for them. She wrote instructions, just in case nobody else in the world knows how to dig rose holes."

"Appreciate it."

With their help the work went quickly. Noel was getting ready to go to bed for his third sleep when Kitty drove the heavily loaded truck up to Savannah's house and honked the horn. Wearing only his pyjama bottoms, Noel raced to the door. He was halfway down the steps when Kitty grabbed him, lifted him, and hugged him tight.

"I missed you, my Christmas boy," she told him.

"I was good," he bragged. "I didn't cry or anything. And guess what, Christie and Aunt Seely got me my own stuff for kindergarten and I get to sit next to Bobby."

"You're a marvel, you know that? A miracle."

"And we've got lemon squares. Auntie Savannah and Auntie Seely made them together. They made lots."

Kitty didn't mean to sleep late in the morning, but she did. When she finally wakened, her back was stiff and sore, her shoulders ached and her hands were swollen and stiff. The house was empty when she got up, so she made coffee and took it into the living room.

The truck was gone. The pickups were gone. The cars were gone. Not a soul to be seen or heard. No sign of Dog, no sign of Pup, just the giant cat and two of her half-grown kittens, sitting on the front steps. The kittens were already bigger than full-grown house cats, obviously capable of pulling down and eating a rabbit.

She had a second cup of coffee, then filled the tub and sat in it for a good long soak. She hoped the stiffness would go away in the hot water, but when she got out and pulled on clean clothes she still felt as if she'd been stretched on the rack.

She was sipping her third cup of coffee and thinking about watching TV when the JimmySpook appeared on top of the set. He looked as sleepy as she felt. He grinned at her and pointed his finger, and she stiffened, expecting to be hit by a wave of raw energy. But he shook his head, teasing her, and vanished as suddenly as he had appeared. She looked for him and finally found him sitting out on the porch, stroking Mabel. Her kittens, not yet ready for ghosts, spooks or ghouls, were streaking away from the house.

Seely came back first. She parked down at the bake house and went inside. Kitty pulled on her jacket and boots and walked down to find out where everyone was, and why, and who had her truck.

"Hey." She hugged Seely. "You're sure looking good, Seel."

"I feel good. I feel happy. It's nice to have us all back together again. Well, almost all. Some of us, anyway."

"Yeah. Where is everyone?"

"Up at the new place. I came to pick up lunch—you can help me load it. We were going to take it when we went, but what with mops and pails and brooms and God knows what, there wasn't room. Here, you take this."

"What's in it?"

"Soup. Don't slop it. Oh, and this. It can heat up in the oven of your brand-new stove."

"Brand-new stove?"

"Lucy insisted on deep-sixing the old one. We moved it over to the cottage. It still works—just fine, in fact, but you know Lucy. She got a new fridge too. We moved the other one over to the cottage. By the time she's got that place the way she thinks she wants it, the cottage will be so jammed we'll have to build another one for people to sleep in!"

"Kids in school?"

"Yeah. They wanted to stay home. Said they'd help! The best help from them would be to go into hibernation so we could stack 'em on a shelf until we're finished."

The truck had been unloaded and the bathtubs were in place in the new fields. A backhoe was parked near the barn and new ditches ran to the tubs. Kitty moved to the closest one and looked in. Pipes. Fine. Wonderful, in fact. She hadn't been looking forward to dragging hoses around behind her.

"You're not going anywhere until Monday," Lucy greeted her. "You're staying put and catching some rest. Don't argue with me! I know what a kidney-smasher that damn truck is, and even professional drivers have to take breaks."

"Hey, am I arguing with you?"

"Don't, then. Just use the boot jack and go upstairs and have a look."

"Yes, ma'am." Kitty winked at Seely, who winked back.

"Don't think I didn't see that," Lucy said.

Kitty was wide-eyed. The big bedroom was totally changed. Freshly painted, with scatter rugs on the floor, it looked bigger and brighter. Brand-new furniture stood gleaming, a brand-new bed had been installed and made, with new sheets, blankets and quilt. Christie was standing on a chair, hanging new drapes.

"My God," Kitty breathed, "it looks like a hotel room."

"Or a high-class hooker's workshop."

"I don't know," Kitty teased. "I never hired a high-priced hooker, nor worked as one either."

"I did," Christie said easily. "This would be your two-hundred-a-go room. Thousand a night."

"Darling, believe me, you're *worth* a thousand a night."

"Thank you. I take that as a real compliment." She climbed down from the chair and put her arms around Kitty. "Lucy says all the furniture at the other place is to go to the Sally Ann. Says if we're going to start over new, we'd better start over all new. Even her chair!"

"What about Debbie?"

"She hasn't been in touch. Not a word. If she shows up before the stuff goes to the Sally Ann, fine, she can have the whole thing. But Lucy says she doesn't want anything at all."

"Boy, she's stubborn."

"Yeah. The whole family is like that."

"Not me."

"No, Kitty, not you. You're the exception to all the rules," Christie teased.

"There, see? Finally. Some appreciation."

"If this house wasn't full of people I'd show you appreciation." Christie snugged against Kitty, holding her, stroking her back, her flat ass. "Oh, you just bet I'd show appreciation. I'd wear you out with appreciation. I'd exhaust you with it."

"I'm going to remember you said that. I'll get my chance. Either that or I'll foreclose the mortgage on the farm, little Nell."

Lucy was limping, but she seemed brighter and happier.

"She was born to give orders, is what it is," Savannah decided. "She's got a whole whack of people she can boss around, so of course she's as happy as a clam in deep water. Do this, move it there, set it up exactly like this."

"The place sure looks different," said Kitty.

"Blame that sweet darling of yours," Savannah smiled. "There's another one designed by nature to make decisions and give orders. She's had workers coming and going the whole time you've been gone. Paint this room this colour and that room the other colour and get that carpet hauled up and bring in a big sander and get the floors done and do it now. We'll be worn to nubs, I tell you. I didn't know you could get so much done in a couple of days."

"I had to make it happen fast," Christie said matter-of-factly. "Or else this one would be back and Lucy would have the outside done the way she wants it and then I'd be up against the both of them and we'd *never* get a decision on what colour to do the kitchen. I know them. They're bossy."

"And you're not?"

"Me? Hell, no, I'm devious. It's the only way to survive with those two bossy ones around."

Savannah made sure she got a moment alone with Kitty. "The guys said I was to be sure to tell you that they really appreciate this chance. They've hired local, even a foreman's from here, but the overseer, well, he's from one of the crews in the city. They know he's totally loyal, eh, and nobody's gonna pull a cute one with him in charge. They're gonna open an office locally, expand the business. They're trying to talk Aud into running it, but you know Aud, she's full of Oh but I never did that before."

"Tell them if she says no they should talk to Christie. She could run the world and have everything organized before coffee break."

When Kitty got back to the place, Debbie was there with a moving van. They looked at each other and then Kitty was holding Debbie in a tight hug and Deb was weeping.

"What you ought to do," Kitty said firmly, "is send that moving van down to the Sally Ann and come back with me."

"I can't," Deb sobbed.

"Of course you can," Kitty snapped. "Don't cut off your nose just because you're mad at your face. It's halfways set up, we're more than halfways moved. There's new stuff there, everything brand new. And Lucy must have hopes and dreams because there's two bedrooms downstairs and she's got furniture in both of them. And not spare room furniture, either."

"I can't stand to watch her abuse herself any more."

"I know all about that. You think I like seeing her all wore out and hurting like hell? You think anybody does? But that's her. She's stubborn, she's hard-headed, she's her own worst enemy. And she isn't going to change."

"She bought the ninety acres, right? And now she'll kill herself trying to whip it into a replica of this place."

"No. Not that at all. Not really. She bought it, but . . . Come on, let's see if the coffee machine is still available. There's a whack of stuff you need to catch up on."

The coffee pot wasn't packed. They had to get mugs out of the box of kitchen gear, but the movers didn't mind, they got paid by the hour. If people wanted to sit around drinking coffee instead of moving, well, they'd drink coffee. It wasn't often a guy got a chance to get paid for resting his tired body. And then, when the coffee was finished, didn't the tall, slender one toss over the keys to the empty truck.

"You guys go get yourself something to eat," she said, her tone gentle, her eyes anything but. "Take a couple of hours. Phone your boss, tell her there's been a holdup."

"Yes, ma'am." They didn't argue with her. Customer is always right.

"I want the old clocks," Debbie said. "And that doorstop, I got it when we were on holiday. It was in an antique store and when I saw it I almost flipped so Luce went in and got it for me. I have no idea what she paid for it, but I'll bet it wasn't free."

"You take a look around. Take your time. Think it over. If it doesn't work out, I promise you'll get everything you need to set up on your own."

"I'll have to phone the manager, tell him I won't need the place after all."

"Fine. We can do that."

"The house plants. I want the house plants."

"No problem."

"The freezers are just about full."

"That's fine. Lucy hasn't got around to buying new freezers. Even if she has, these'll fit somewhere. No problem."

Lucy was supervising the building of the new planter boxes when Kitty drove the truck up the driveway. Lucy saw Debbie before she opened the truck door and stepped down. They looked at each other, and Kitty had to turn away, suddenly shy, overwhelmed by the charge of emotion coming from each of them.

"Kitty says my room is downstairs," Debbie said.

"You get your pick." Lucy's voice trembled. "Come, have a look. I've been staying in one, but I'll take the other one if you want."

"Oh, you know me. I'm easy," Deb dared.

"Yeah. I've noticed," Lucy smiled wryly. "Come on, have a boo." She held out her hand and Deb took it. They walked slowly to the house together.

Kitty turned her attention to the house plants. They were wrapped in quilts and stored in styrofoam boxes, but the ground had been frozen when they drove from the farm, and she could only pray that the plants had survived.

"How did you manage *that* minor miracle?" Christie whispered. "Here," she said in a normal tone of voice, "let me take that, you've overloaded yourself."

"You know me," Kitty whispered back. "Miracles I can do immediately, the impossible takes a bit of time."

"There, that looks fine," Christie nodded, smiling. "Those window sills were made for plants. But I'll let Deb decide which ones she wants where, I'll just put some water in the bathtub and sit these in it to soak and recover. Going to have to prune back the big begonia. I bet you packed it. Deb would have given it a box all to itself."

six

KITTY DROVE BACK TO THE FARM in the new pickup truck with Dog on the seat beside her. Pup was happy to stay at the new place with all the kids to play with and all the new scents to sniff. But Dog pined when Kitty wasn't near her.

At eight that evening she had checked into a motel. She had supper, phoned Noel to tell him nighty-night, then climbed into bed. Dog was asleep on the rug, undisturbed by the sound of snow plows and sand trucks. In the morning Kitty had breakfast in the motel dining room. Then, with a fresh thermos of motel coffee, she drove to the farm.

Just after she finished the last no-longer-hot cup of it, Conrad and his crew arrived with their stock trailer. It didn't bother Kitty to load cows and calves and send them on their way, but she knew it would have ripped Lucy to pieces. She got some idea of how much that ripping hurt when Decision was loaded. "You behave yourself, now," she told him. "It's not bad work and it's not hard work. You've got it made, you old fool."

The stock truck arrived just as Conrad's crew was leaving. The remaining dozen cows were easily loaded, all of them pregnant with Decision's calves. When the cattle were in the truck, the horses were loaded.

"Nice stock," the driver commented. "Someone's been paying attention."

"My aunt," Kitty said. "She's fussy about them. Shows, too."

"Does that. Well, if that's the lot of them, we're on our way."

"Here's your map. Follow the highway until here, then . . . got it marked, and got it written. This is the phone number at the house, and this is the one in my truck. Phone me first. I'll either be just a bit ahead of you or just a bit behind."

She stood in what had been Lucy's driveway and took a last look. The house was already up on jacks and looked as if it was ready to move. Dan intended to move it across the fields, but if he didn't do it soon he was going to have to wait until the snow melted in the spring.

She wasn't sure she'd come back in the spring. She wasn't sure she'd ever see this part of the country again. So many days and nights of her life, so many memories, and already it looked like foreign territory.

The JimmySpook sat on the corral fence, watching quietly.

"No use you staying here," Lucy said to him. "You might as well ride in the truck with Dog and me. Keep your bones warm."

The JimmySpook was waiting in the front seat when Kitty opened her door and slid behind the wheel. Before she started the truck, she poured thermos coffee in the cup that sat in the special holder between the bucket seats. "Here," she offered, "a little something to bring a smile to your face." The Squeyanx grinned, then leaned over and gently tapped the cigarette package in the front pocket of her work shirt. The touch was feather light, but even through her shirt, her tee shirt and her winter undershirt, Kitty felt the buzz. It was almost like grabbing an electric fence. This wasn't electricity, but it was some kind of serious energy. With it, this spook was deadly.

She lit a cigarette, turned the key, popped the truck in gear and headed up the driveway. She had just turned onto the road when she saw the house-moving truck coming toward her, turn signal blinking. She honked and waved at it, and at the several pickups following it. She wasn't the least bit tempted to go back and watch them get the house up onto the huge flatbed. It was finished. She'd arrived here a numb, frightened, lonely kid and now she was leaving forever, a different person but still frightened and, in some nubbin of a place inside her, still numb.

She stopped for gas and stopped at the usual place for coffee, a hamburger for Dog and a good pee for herself in the warm, thank God, women's washroom. Her favourite chatty waitress wasn't there, just a tall, thin teenager with bad skin who looked so sullen and pissed off Kitty wondered if it was safe to give the hamburger to Dog. She ordered a piece of lemon pie to go, and went back to the truck.

The JimmySpook grinned when Lucy dumped out the cold coffee and half-filled the mug with hot fresh from the thermos. Dog ate the hamburger greedily while the JimmySpook inhaled the scent. When Kitty unwrapped the lemon pie and put it on the seat beside him, the bag of bones looked hard at her, his eyeholes shining.

"Enjoy." She started the truck, checked in both directions, then pulled back onto the highway. "The only other pie they had was raisin. I figured you could handle this one better. No lumps."

She had no idea how he did it. He was just bones, without any stomach to put it in, but in a moment the pie had turned to nothing but damp pastry and the Spook was leaning back, eyes closed, bone feet up on the dash.

"Go for it, Dog." Dog sniffed the pastry, then slowly ate it. "Yeah, you're a good dog. You're a fine old dog. I'm going to bawl like a baby when you go, because I'm a selfish bitch and I'll miss you. But I'm not so selfish I'm going to make you stay. I'm not dragging you off to the vet every week, getting vitamin injections and who-knows-what. When it's time for you to go, you just go. Just ignore it if you hear me bawling and slobbering and generally acting like a fool. And when you want to come back, you know where I'll be. I promise you, any stray dog that shows up at my door is going to be fed and fussed. It might be you, come back again. We'll know each other, won't we, huh?"

The snow fell steadily in little flecks, and the wipers made a steady, almost hypnotic sound. The snowplows and sanding trucks were out, with their orange warning lights flick flick flicking, easy to spot even in the snow. Kitty turned on the CD player and Itzhak Perlman's violin filled the cab. How come none of Savannah's kids played violin? How come the whole bunch of 'em took piano lessons instead, or took band at school and tooted on flutes and clarinets? Violins came in small sizes, maybe Noel would like to take lessons. Darlene played the guitar pretty well and Lizzie could sing like crazy and she played guitar too. But so far there wasn't a fiddler in the litter. How many hours of Perlman's life had gone into playing the violin? Had he ever rebelled, refused to practise? Or was he one of those kids who love their instrument from the minute they touch it? Even something you love can get to be a drag. He had trouble walking. Had he been a polio kid or something? Wouldn't that be a bugger, to be a kid in a wheelchair, especially back then.

What about her own little boy, Noel? What was waiting for him? He'd had enough already. He didn't need any more disappointment, didn't need any more fear or pain or sorrow. If it was true that the first eighteen months made a kid what he or she would be, what did Noel have that would stand him in good stead? It was official: traumatized kids had trouble with schoolwork, their brains were overloaded, they couldn't sort things, they couldn't remember because their circuits were full, or cut off. And it would be more obvious with Noel because all of Savannah's kids were so bright. Kitty didn't remember being especially bright, and not her sibs either. They could barely scrape through each grade. But there you have it again, the traumatized kid. Whereas Savannah's kids were like goldfish gulping at their flakes of dried whatever. No chewing, no choking, just gulp gulp gulp, huge hunks of learning taken in and digested. In fact, they had just moved Victor another year ahead. At this rate, the kid would be finished high school and on his way to university before he was sixteen, with Elaine only a half step behind him. And wasn't *she* something.

"You know my nieces and nephews?" she asked. The Squeyanx nodded. "They going to be okay?" He stared at her, but she couldn't tell what he was or was not saying to her. "Reason I ask is we've all had about a gutful where rotten luck is concerned. Especially Noel."

The JimmySpook turned his head away from her, his way of telling her to go fuffle up a gum tree. He was keeping an eye on the highway, watching the snow. He had no time for silliness.

"You warm enough?" she asked. He nodded. "Keep me awake, would you please?" He reached out and gestured to the coffee mug in its holder. Kitty reached for the cup and tested the brew with her tongue. "Lukewarm," she said. She eased off the accelerator, wound down her window and tossed out the coffee. Then she refilled the cup by holding the thermos between her knees. "We're fine," she assured Dog. "But you're right, next time I'll pull over to the side of the road to do this."

The hot coffee helped and the snow thinned out. The road ahead was black now, not white with a layer of frozen snow. She wondered how Conrad was making out, moving the house in this mess. He'd been born here, he knew this weather, but there was no way they were going to be able to take the house over by way of the back access road. Even in good weather that road wasn't easy. It had never been graded or maintained. The most that had been done to it was that Lucy had taken the tractor over it, bucket down, scraping the top in a mostly futile attempt to level it off and fill some of the holes.

The phone didn't ring and the stock haulers had no trouble finding the place. When Kitty finally got home, Noel was awake and waiting for her, along with Bobby, who was every bit as excited as Noel.

"Can we watch?"

"You bundle up warm, now. We don't need two boys with bad colds."

"Jackets." Christie held them out. "And muddy-buddies and gumboots. And if you don't hurry, it'll all be over and done with before you're ready."

The horses came out first. One by one they stepped down the ramp and into the corral. They were sweated up and nervous, and they milled around stupidly, snapping at each other, kicking and shoving. Kitty coaxed them into their stalls with food and closed them in while they ate.

The cows came out in a scrambling swarm, bawling and complaining. They lumbered into the corral and rambled foolishly, amid incredible noise. Kitty finally got them into the barn, but by the time the last one heaved its shit-bedrizzled arse through the door, she was just about ready to kill them all and hang them upside down from the support posts.

"That's my horse," Noel told Bobby as they stood in the horse barn. Bobby was anxious and uncomfortable. He was used to Pup, to Mabel and Puss, not creatures this big. "That's Lady."

"You sit up there?"

"It's fun, Bobby, it really is. She smells good! And sometimes she licks my face, and her tongue is real real smooth, like a person tongue, not a dog and *not* a cat's, all rough and scratchy. Lady's tongue is exactly like mine, only bigger."

"Does she bite?"

"Nah."

"She's way too big to take for show and tell."

"We could take pictures. You sitting on her, me riding her, and we could take them to school."

"Yeah." Bobby's fear had already begun to fade. His eyes flashed with excitement. "Yeah, and you could take that poster from your bedroom, the one with Auntie Kitty on it in her clown stuff. Nobody has an aunt or a mom who ever did that!"

"We've got bideos."

"Really?"

"Yeah. When everything is unpacked we can watch them. We've got a bideo of Auntie Kitty riding a bareback horse, and one of her on a saddle bronc, and she didn't get thrown off, either, she made the whole ride. She got thrown off the bareback horse, though. And we've got bideos of her riding bulls, too. There's one from the time she got hurt real bad but Auntie Christie won't let me watch that one. I only got to see it because Auntie Lucy was watching it. It made me cry. And we've got bideos of Auntie Kitty being a clown. She's real funny! There's two different ones of her being a clown with Decision. Nobody ever rode him, he was too tough."

"Could we take a bideo to show and tell?"

"Prob'ly. Want to pat my horse?"

"Are we allowed?"

"I'll ask."

They got carrots from the fridge and found the brushes in the tack room. Noel showed Bobby how to hold his hand flat and feed bites of carrot to the mare. "When you brush her," he said, "she's got tickle places. And she pooches her lips, like this." He demonstrated. "Sometimes she makes noises, but don't be scared. They're just happy noises."

"My mom said to be careful because horses step on your feet."

"Lady never stepped on me. Aunt Kitty says if she steps on you, you step right back on her."

"You're sure she won't bite me?"

"Lady, don't bite Bobby, okay? Bobby's my cousin. He's nice." Noel turned to Bobby and smiled. "See, you're okay now. She knows you aren't a stranger. Kitty says they can tell from smells. And you're wearing my old jacket so you'll smell like me. You're fine."

By the time the stock haulers had taken their pay and gone, Kitty was ready to eat a horse and chase down the rider. When she lit a cigarette, her fingers trembled. "I don't care if I never have to make that trip again," she said hollowly.

"Brace yourself," Lucy grinned, "because I changed my mind and we're moving back there tomorrow."

"Yeah, right." Kitty arched her back and twisted her shoulders. "Jesus, someone left the Tin Woodman out in the rain last night."

"You know what they say, even a barrel of fun can leave you aching."

"Who says that?"

"I don't know. They."

Deb had scrambled eggs with melted cheese on top waiting for Kitty.

"God, I'd be just about ready to kill for that, it smells so good."

"And here's the hot sauce. The red and the green. Two slices of toast okay?"

"Plenty. Thanks, Deb."

"You've had enough coffee." Christie kissed Kitty's cheek. "Your hands are shaking. Have a pot of tea instead."

"It was snowing on and off and on and off right up to about sixty miles out, then it was rain. I *hate* driving in snow! After a couple of miles or so it starts to space me out, those flakes seem to float or something. When I design a pickup truck I'm going to heat the windshield so the snow melts off instead of building up just past the wiper blade tracks. You wind up feeling like you're driving through a tunnel, and it's getting narrower by the minute."

"Maybe they do that on purpose, so you have to stop every now and again and clear it off. That blast of cold air probably gets the cobwebs out of your brain."

"My who?"

"Exactly."

"Kiddleys, you say? Where do you keep those kiddleys?"

"They say silly things," Noel explained to Bobby, "because they love each other."

"Yeah?"

"Yeah, they're lovebirds, eh? They sleep in the same bed and they cuddle each other. Sometimes I climb into bed with them and we all cuddle."

"My mom used to sleep with my dads, but not any more. My dads all got new wives. My mom says she doesn't want a new boyfriend."

"My mom had boyfriends. My really one. She had lots of boyfriends."

"Do you got a dad? I got three."

"No. I never had no dad. Just horrible horrible."

"Who?"

"His name was Jerry but I call him horrible horrible, because he was. He's dead now, though, and I'm glad."

"How'd he get dead?"

"He wrecked his car and got all burned up."

"Were you scared?"

"Kitty was there. She was holding me. And I was scared, but not of her and not of the fire. There was something else I was scared of, but I don't remember what it was. Did your mom have lots and lots of boyfriends?"

"Just my dads, I think. But Carol, she has boyfriends. My dads said they don't care. They said she's just going on with her life. But my mom said she doesn't want to go on with her life with a bunch of boyfriends getting in the way."

"I don't want no boyfriend."

"Boys don't have boyfriends, boys get girlfriends."

"I don't want one of them, neither."

"I got a girlfriend."

"You do not."

"Do so! Leah Carter."

"She is not!"

"Yeah, she is. She trades me her yogurt for my dessert snacks. She doesn't like yogurt."

"Me neither. But Christie says I have to eat some every day because it keeps your stomach sweet."

"Sweet like candy?"

"I never asked. I just eat it. I can eat a yogurt in eleven spoonfuls."

"I don't know how many it takes me."

"Want to find out?"

"Sure!"

"Can we?" he asked Christie.

"What's that?"

"Have yogurts, please?"

"Sure, but you get it yourself. I'm having tea with Kitty."

"What kind do you want?"

"Berry. I like the berry kind."

"Me, too. I *hate* the banana one. It tastes like soap."

"I wonder if you taste like soap," Kitty murmured.

Christie looked up at her and grinned slowly. "Depends on whether or not you like the taste of soap. If you do, I'll make sure ... "

"Ssshhh, they're coming back."

"As long as someone comes we'll be fine."

"Okay, first you lick off the stuff on the silver paper lid. That doesn't count. But don't spill it and don't choke, because if you do, it gets in your nose and that's gross."

They might have managed to eat their yogurt in eleven spoonfuls, but Bobby got the giggles. Which caused Noel to get them too. Somehow they managed to keep most of it in their mouths without spraying, dribbling or spitting anything on the table, but it was the end of the big heaping loads. It took fifteen spoonloads each. But they scheduled another try the next day.

By Easter, they were all beginning to make order out of the chaos of the move. The boxes and barrels of bits and pieces were unpacked and the work shed was set up, with tools hanging from nails and hooks on the walls and drawers under the counter full of nuts, bolts, screws and connectors for things that might one day need them. The horses had the bigger pasture and the cows grazed in and between the trees, nibbling on salal and Oregon grape. All the animals were fed grain morning and night and hay whenever they wanted it.

To everyone's surprise except her own, Debbie had a coop and a hen yard built. She got a dozen twenty-week-old chickens from a hatchery, and a big naked-necked rooster from a farm on the far side of town.

"That thing is ugly!" Lucy laughed. "I have never seen anything so ugly before."

"Some people call them turkens, as in cross between chicken and turkey. Other people say they come from Transylvania and that's why their necks are bare, so Dracula can take a drink without getting feathers caught in his fangs. But they're just chickens."

"Ugly. Butt ugly."

"Not in the eyes of this beholder."

Some of the hens were laying when they arrived, and others began producing a week or two later. The eggs were so good Jimmy asked for two dozen a week and Savannah said she could use all they could spare. With a demand like that, Debbie sent away for another dozen birds. These birds were huge and flecked with grey and black. They looked like barred rocks, only much bigger.

"Lakenvelders," Deb said. "I think they're Dutch, or maybe German."

"They're no prettier than the others," Lucy said. "Don't they grow pretty chickens any more?"

"You want pretty, you get bantams. You want eggs . . . "

"Maybe I will. They could keep down the flies at the barn. Just set 'em up there, let them wander."

"If you're talking banties, you might as well make it your idea that they wander, because you'll never keep them confined."

They hired the kids to dig out clumps of grass and sod, then Lucy took the tractor and rotovator into the garden area and turned it over and over and over again. When the earth was tilled to her satisfaction, she went to the manure pile and brought bucketload after bucketload of manure, and dumped it. Then she rotovated some more, mixing the fertilizer with the soil. "Might as well," she said, still in the habit of defending her actions. "Some lettuce is always nice, and a few green onions. Nothing much, just a few fresh things. You know how it gets sometimes, you'd fight the cows for the greens."

"Some beans," Kitty suggested. "Pole beans."

"Bush beans," Deb put in. "Yellow ones."

"Maybe some squash?"

When the first of Decision's calves was born, Noel got to watch. He was fascinated. He hunkered down near the labouring cow and gazed, wide-eyed, as the calf came out. When the cow lumbered to her feet and started licking the calf clean, Noel could barely believe what he was seeing.

"How does she know what to do? You said she never had a calf before."

"Isn't nature wonderful," Deb agreed. "And you watch, that brand-new baby knows what to do too. First she has to get herself up on her feet. And then she has to find the taps and drink. And she already knows it."

"Can I phone Bobby? Could he come over to see?"

"Sure. All the other kids will want to come too, and they'll all want to see. So you and Bobby will have to share."

When the second calf arrived, Elaine was on hand, equally fascinated. "Hey, Babe," Kitty said softly. "See how the feet come out first? They're soft, real soft. You can go closer and touch them if you want. The cow isn't going to bother, she's busy and she won't even notice you. Sometimes the calf gets in the wrong position. You can tell the front hooves from the back easy enough. If you see back feet coming, or if there's a back and a front, well, you have to get involved. Take off your shirt, put Betadine all over your hand and arm, rub it until it foams like soap. Then you reach in and get things straightened out. Sometimes you even have to help pull the calf out."

"They *are* soft. How can it stand on soft feet like that?"

"They manage. See the bottoms? They look like gills, don't they? That'll wear off inside of two days. I'm not sure why but I think the bottoms of their feet are ribbed like that so there's some kind of traction for the baby until its hooves harden."

"Oh, look! I can see its nose!"

"What I do is take a clean fresh rag, like this one, and dip it in rubbing alcohol, like this, then clean out the nose before the calf comes all the way out, because they usually get mucus in their noses."

"What do they do in the wild?"

"They lose a lot of calves, actually. Nature never intended every animal to duplicate itself every year. Lots of them are born dead because the cord gets wrapped around their necks, or they're in the wrong position inside and get their necks broken as they come out. You think of how many things can go wrong and they all happen. But there's a place for the ones that don't make it. Food for the birds and the little critters, I guess."

"How do you know if the cow needs help?"

"That's the tricky part. The only way to learn is to pay attention, and after a while you know what's supposed to happen and how long it's supposed to take, and then if it doesn't, you help. Just like now. That calf has been presented too long. She should be at least halfways out by now. She's got both feet out, she's got her head out to the eyes, but she's not coming out any farther. That means she's probably got big shoulders. So what you do is grab hold here, at the ankle, see? The way I do it is to sit, and I put my feet against the cow's backside with my knees bent, like so. Some people use ropes but I don't like to do that. I wrap dry cloths around so's my hands don't slip too much, because the baby is soaking wet and slippery. She has to be slippery to slide out of her momma. Watch the mom's belly. See how it tightens up, bunches up, and...okay, now she's pushing so I pull...steady, hard as I can. Push with my legs, pull with my arms and back...there, we've got the entire head out. Next push, or the one after..."

"Could I try?"

"Sit in front of me, between my legs. Okay, get your feet on the cow's butt. Move up closer if you have to. You need your knees bent so you've got some leg room to push. Okay, grab on, put your hands just below mine and watch her belly. When you think it's time to pull, you say so. I'll wait for you."

Kitty could feel Elaine trembling with excitement. The cow gasped for breath, made a soft sound, and then the belly bunched up.

"Now?" Elaine asked.

"Just a few more seconds...wait...wait...okay, now you can actually feel the baby moving a bit. So right now is when we pull like hell."

Two contractions later, the calf's shoulders cleared and it slid out as far as the back legs. Kitty stuffed a clean cloth in the calf's mouth and swabbed. The calf didn't move.

"Pull it out, Elaine, it's in trouble."

She and Elaine hauled together, and when the calf was completely out, Kitty had it by the back legs, lifting it over her knee, head hanging. She thumped the ribs several times, then lay the calf on the floor and sucked at the nose and mouth. She brought out a mouthful of mucus and spat it on the concrete. She pushed the rib cage, then blew in the calf's nostrils, keeping the mouth shut with her hand. She pushed, counting, then breathed again. Two minutes later the calf jerked, coughed, spat out more mucus and gasped wetly.

"You saved its life!" Elaine looked at Kitty as if she had just demonstrated how to walk on water.

"Okay, let's us get the hell out of the way. Momma's going to get to her feet, and you'n'me'll just be in the way."

"You're all wet, and you've got blood all over your face."

"There isn't much that's messier than being born," Kitty agreed.

"It would have died, wouldn't it? If it had been wild."

"Probably."

"So you saved its life. And probably the cow, too."

"We should phone the vet, I suppose. Get that cow checked over, maybe she needs antibiotics. She was open for a bit longer than she should have been, and that's when you got your infections. No matter how clean you keep your barn, it's still a barn, right?"

The vet was there when the third calf was born. He had just finished checking over the second calf and her mother when Bobby came running into the barn from outside.

"Come see," he shouted. "Noel's got a calf!"

The cow was licking the calf, cleaning it, making soft mooing sounds. Noel sat with the calf's white head on his lap, stroking it and talking softly.

"See?" he smiled. "This one's mine. He looks just like his daddy. See?"

The cow arched her back and lowed, then sank to her knees and lay on her side, panting.

"Looks like you're about to get you another one," the vet laughed.

"Will it be mine, too?" Noel asked hopefully.

"I don't think so." Kitty shook her head. "I think one calf is enough for one boy."

"What about me?" Bobby asked. "Could I have it?"

The second calf was also a bull, and also had a white face. "Tell you what," Kitty told them. "You go get the wheelbarrow and we'll move these fellas and their momma into the barn. We'll keep them inside for a couple of days, because they're smaller than they would have been if they'd been born singles, and because that way you guys can make friends with them. How are you going to know which is which?"

"Because mine has some white hairs in his tail and Noel's doesn't."

"Okay. You go get the wheelbarrow."

They moved the calves and got the cow up on her feet and following.

"She's some worn out," Kitty worried. "Are they always this worn out with twins?"

"No. Keep an eye on her, see how she makes out."

The cow let the calves suckle for three days, then she wouldn't let them near her. Kitty had the vet back out again, and he checked the cow but could find no reason for her distress. Her bag was swollen, but he could express milk. Her temperature was elevated but nothing that should have caused concern. She just wouldn't let either calf anywhere near her. When they persisted, she kicked at them.

"Well, they've had their colostrum," Lucy said. "All's we can do now is bucket-feed them. Leave them in with her and she's apt to kill them."

"But why? They're her babies, why doesn't she want them?"

"It doesn't always work that way. Maybe one of them hurt her when he was sucking, or maybe she's just not a good mother. Some aren't."

"Mine is," Bobby said firmly. "My mom is the best."

"Mine wasn't," Noel admitted. "Not like yours."

The bucket-feeding was easy. Lucy made them wait until the calves were bawling and howling. Then she and Kitty held one of the calves and Christie got the rubber nipple into the wet mouth. The calf tried to shake out the strange thing. But when its jaws closed, it tasted milk, and that was that. And when the second one smelled milk and saw and heard the slurping and gulping, he pushed in and wanted some, too.

"The thing is," Lucy warned, "you have *got* to keep watch. If you see any white-coloured poop on the floor, you come get me right away."

"Poop isn't white," said Bobby.

"Let's hope not."

Audrey went down into the basement to get a jar of bread-and-butter pickles for supper, not to eavesdrop. But when she heard the sound of weeping coming from Jimmy's workroom, she naturally went and opened the door to see what was wrong.

He was sitting on his chair, sobbing hopelessly. In one hand he held a razor-sharp carving tool. Audrey was terrified he was going to slash himself with it, and this time do a real job. She went to him and laid her hand on his shoulder.

"I can't do it," he blurted. "He hardly ever even comes to see me any more!"

"Who?"

"Look at this fuckin' thing!" He gestured at the piece of jewellery he had been making. "Look at it!"

"Jim, it's gorgeous. The Queen herself would be happy to wear it."

"It's clunky! It's a big lump. I hate it. I'm going to take it apart and melt it down! It's ugly and *this* isn't working." He gestured dismissively at the piece of wood on the bench. "I could do better than this when I was twelve years old. Jesus, I'm going nuts here. The only thing I ever know how to do and I've messed it up!"

As he flung his arms out angrily, the carving tool grazed Audrey's arm. Anything else might only have left a scratch, but the tool was sharp and tore a sizable gash in Audrey's arm.

Jimmy stared, horrified, then jumped to his feet, grabbing for a clean towel. "Oh fuck!" he screamed. "Oh fuck!"

Bones danced like a mad fool on the workbench, pointing his finger and cackling silently. "You, you bastard!" Jimmy yelled. "Now you show up! Where in hell you been? Look what you made me do!"

"Jimboh, there's nobody there," Audrey managed. She held the towel to her arm, pressing firmly to stop the bleeding.

It was too much like the night they'd had to take that damn kid to Emergency when he cut himself farting around like he always did. Except now it wasn't the kid, it was Audrey, and it wasn't her hand, it was her arm, and she wasn't wailing and snuffling, she was the calmest person in the car.

"Savannah should drive race cars," Audrey smiled widely. "Or getaway vehicles for bank robbers."

"The guys paid for driving lessons," Savannah said, her eyes focussed on the road ahead. "Then, before I drove Vic anywhere, I had to take the lessons all over again. And when it snowed, didn't I have to take winter driving lessons. Good, the cop is pulling out ahead of us. Seely must have phoned ahead."

"Usually the bastards aren't around when you need them." Audrey leaned against Jimboh. She could feel him trembling, hear his rapid, shallow breathing. "Jim, if you don't calm down you'll have a heart attack."

"Oh Jesus, I'm sorry, I'm so sorry—"

"It's okay Jimboh. It was an accident."

"It was me being a klutz!"

The police car ahead cleared the road and the Emergency attendants were waiting in the parking lot. Savannah pulled to a stop, someone opened the door, Audrey stepped out and was whisked into a wheelchair. Jimmy stumbled out after her, his clothes smeared with blood. Savannah drove to the parking lot, found a space, and turned the car off. She sat there a long time, smoking cigarettes and waiting until she was calm enough to walk. When she finally headed toward the brightly lit Emergency entrance, her legs felt wobbly, too long and too insubstantial to hold her.

"Dear sweet Lord," she said aloud. "If it isn't one thing, it's another."

Jimmy sat on a bench in the hallway, his hands clasped between his knees, his shoulders bowed, his head bent. He looked as forlorn and pathetic as he'd looked when he was eight years old, waiting outside the principal's office.

"Hey, guy." Savannah sat down beside him and put her arm around him.

He leaned against her and sighed, a ragged sound that made her feel like crying.

"They're sewing her shut," he choked. "They want her to stay overnight but she said no, she wanted to go home. They stuck her with needles to freeze the arm, and other ones to ward off shock and others full of antibiotics, and she said if she took a drink her butt cheeks would spray it out, like in the cartoons."

"So you blame yourself. Even Audrey says it was an accident."

"I don't care what it was, Savannah. I should have put the bugger down. But no, I had it in my hand, and the awful part of it is, I didn't even know I had it in my hand. I hold those things for so long it's like they're part of my hand, like another finger or something."

"I know."

"You don't know, Savannah."

"Okay," she nodded. "I'm not here to argue with you."

A cop came in from the Emergency ward where he'd been talking to Audrey. He stood in front of Jimboh, his notebook in his hand. "Would you care to tell me what happened?" he asked.

Jimmy shook his head, then got up suddenly, brushed past the cop and headed outside.

"Did you see the incident?" the cop asked.

"What incident?"

"Were you present when Mrs. Scott was injured?"

"No. I live pretty much next door and we have an intercom on the phone because the kids go back and forth, and I heard Jimboh hollering through it, so..."

"Has anything like this happened before?"

"Well, Jimmy's cut himself quite a few times. That's his work. No, not *cut* himself, but he's a carver, so... What, you think he sliced her on purpose?"

"We got a call, ma'am, we have to account for it, make a report."

"Oh. Well, no. I didn't see the... incident."

The cop wrote in his book. "Your name, please."

"Savannah Scott."

"You're related to Mr. Scott."

"Jimmy's my brother."

"Thank you for your co-operation," he said formally. Then he went outside to try to talk to Jimmy.

Moments later Jimmy came back, smelling of cigarette smoke. He paced, chewing his inner lip, whispering to himself, looking nuttier than he'd looked in a long time. The cop followed him in, notebook in hand. Jimmy stopped pacing, stopped whispering, seemed to be listening and watching intently. Then he whirled.

"I was upset," he blurted. "And Audrey was talking to me. My work wasn't going well, I didn't like the result. We both moved at the same time. I had the carving tool in my hand, I think I was about to set it down. Aud moved over to give me a hug. She got cut."

"Did you intend to cut her?"

"Jesus, no." Jimmy shook his head.

"It's routine, sir. Man cuts his wife, there's a lot of paperwork." He put the notebook in his pocket. "I guess carvers get that same thing writers get; the block, you know."

"I don't know. All's I know is, year after year I worked in wood. Even when I did those bronzes, they started out as wood, and once I got what I wanted, all's I had to do was copy it, bigger and bigger. Then I started feeling... I don't know... and someone said maybe I should try jewellery, and I did, and..." He sighed, walking toward the front door. The cop walked with him. Savannah, trusting nothing in uniform at all, not even a dog-catcher, was on her feet, following. "I had fun with it, applied to the art school in town to take some courses. And I got myself scrambled. I don't know enough about jewellery to do what I want, and now I'm losing my touch with wood."

Jimmy turned to look at the cop, and stopped in his tracks, his eyes widening. There was Bones, perched on the cop's head, pointing his finger.

The cop pushed the door open. "Come on," he said, "let's get some fresh air." He held the door open for Jimmy and Savannah and joined them outside.

"We see some of the most unbelievable things," he said. "Sometimes I go home and I stand under the shower and I soap and soap and soap myself, trying to wash it off. I've got two kids. Two boys. I don't want either of them to be cops."

"Yeah?" Jimmy was listening intently. "You don't want them to be carvers, either, man. Take my word for it."

"There's stuff that isn't bad and some of it's even good. Like last week we got a call about a kid, five years old, missing for several hours. That can mean something so awful you puke, and we were all geared up for it, they called in the detachment psychologist, the whole nine yards. We get assigned our areas, out we go. I get paired with a dog handler. Personally, I don't have much use for dogs, but did what we were told, and not fifteen minutes later we find the little guy. He's sitting under a bush. He's found a litter of wild kittens, barely old enough for their eyes to be open, and he's visiting with them, he says. Man, when we took him home to his momma, she was so glad to see him she didn't even argue about those three mutt kittens he took with him. That was a good one. But I've been there when it's gone the other way. So what we do, we try hard to remember the good stuff, like the look on that kid's face sitting there with those kittens. And the look on the mother's face when she saw him."

"Right."

"Nobody except you expects you to be able to be an expert overnight, you know."

"Yeah?"

"Now me, I play at the banjo. Notice I said *at* the banjo? I've been playing at it for ten years. Another ten and I might be able to play it. I get these tapes, videos, step-by-step, how to play chords, how to improvise, how to, I don't know, jump in the air and kiss yourself on the foot. But I guess there's no tapes for guys like you."

"Guess not."

"It was my uncle—we call him Crazy Larry—who told me the word 'seer' was originally 'see-er', someone who sees."

"You been seeing long?"

"Yeah. You?"

"Yeah."

"So I'm off to the station. You need us, you call us, okay?"

"Okay," Savannah said.

One of the many shots in the backside they gave Audrey must have had something in it besides antibiotics, because she was sound asleep before they finished stitching the gash in her arm.

"I really would prefer she stay here tonight," the attending physician said. "She lost a fair bit of blood and refused a transfusion. Not that I blame her, but I'd like her under observation. I want to have a look at that arm tomorrow morning, too."

"See you about ten tomorrow morning," Savannah agreed. "Come on, Jim."

"I'll stay here with her."

"In a pig's eye. You think these people got nothing better to do than step over your feet? Come on, damn it!"

Savannah drove five miles under the speed limit all the way home, and she didn't even try to strike up a conversation. Jimmy sat in the passenger seat, staring at nothing, his lips moving as if he were talking. She wondered just how nutbar he really was. What would they decide if he was to go to one of those places where they give you all kinds of tests and ask questions and poke and pry and then hand out a diagnosis? And who would pay attention to it once they'd done it? He was Jim. He was James Robert Scott, Jim, Jimmy, Jimboh, her big brother. He was the one who had held her hand when she first learned to walk, who had stood between her and Glen, who had coaxed her into the shallow end of the swimming hole and sat with her while she splashed and got used to it. He taught her to hold her breath and put her face in the water.

He had never seemed particularly crazy to her. He was Jimboh, and he had his own ways about him, but that didn't mean crazy. Other people said he was. Other people had started saying that when he was about ten years old. Oh, he's a deep one, they said, he's an odd one. What they meant was that he was crazy. But who had he ever hurt except himself? She wanted to tell him she loved him, but he wouldn't hear her now. He was having one of his Jimmy-things, no use trying to talk to him. Gran had said he was listening to the angels, but maybe they were imps from hell. They didn't seem to be bringing him any peace of mind.

Jimmy was still muttering when Savannah took him by the arm and led him to his bed. She didn't have to tell him to lie down, he just flopped. She pulled off his shoes, then put the comforter over him. He nodded but didn't speak, so she didn't either. She patted his shoulder, left the room and closed the door.

"He looks awful," Seely whispered.

"He's upset. So'm I. You got coffee?"

"Fresh pot. The kids are all in bed. Bobby stayed over at Kitty's, he's sleeping with Noel tonight. That okay?"

"Those two. You'd think they'd been born Siamese twins and were never going to forgive anyone for separating them."

"Victoria's sleeping in my bed. She fussed up so . . . " Seely blushed. "You know me, the original prisoner of love."

"That's why she fusses up, silly you. I should sign her over to you, like when you get a dog from the SPCA and they make you sign the form."

"She's wonderful."

"Yeah, she is. Except when she fusses up. But I think maybe she has to fuss once in a while, or she'd wind up totally overlooked. All the baby stuff she does is so cute, and it was real exciting when it was Vic and Elaine doing it, but let's face it, the novelty has worn off." Savannah sipped her coffee and sighed. "I should pay more attention, spend more time with her."

"If you did that, I wouldn't get the chance." Seely looked around, almost guiltily. "She's a lot more fun than Darlene or Lizzie were," she whispered.

"Hey, when you had Darlene you were a little kid! You were terrified you'd drop her on the floor or drown her in her bath, remember? Then— *pop*—no time at all and you had Lizzie, and I have to tell you, even back then I was glad she was yours and not mine. I never saw such a kid for squirming, fussing and wriggling. And Darlene with her nose out of joint, and then *he* had to do his number and she wasn't getting any better and you wound up having to stumble along under the load, and God, babe, all this when you should have been in high school decorating the gym for the Sadie Hawkins dance."

"We sure all tried to get where we are by way of the hard places," Seely agreed.

"Not me. I moved into the lap of luxury," Savannah teased. "Lived the good life, no muss, no fuss, no bother, just endless days of leisure and pleasant experiences."

"Yeah? With three hubbies? Hell, I can't face the thought of life with one of them."

"Life with Larry and Moe was fine. It was Shemp was kind of hard to put up with. He's moody. Most of the time the other two kept a lid on him, but he could get—overbearing, I guess you'd say."

"You'd say overbearing, because they sent you off to school all the time. Me, I'd say fuckin' mean."

"Yeah. He has that streak in him. He's the boss. He stands up to pee. But he isn't the oldest, so it wasn't too bad. Along about the fourth or fifth time he got rough, I just made sure Larry saw the bruises. I wasn't scared of Shemp, but I knew it was best if Larry thought I was."

"What did he do?"

"I don't know. All's I know is the next time Shemp walked into my room he had a better attitude. Not a lot better, but there were no more bruises. And he wasn't so...kinky."

"Shemp? Kinky?"

"Oh, yeah. Not as kinky as Moe, mind you. Now there's a kinky guy! But nice kinky, if you know what I mean."

"No." Seely shook her head. "No, I don't know the first thing about kinky. Just ordinary fucking, and that all stopped when I got pregnant with Liz. I didn't enjoy it, Savannah. I wouldn't have bothered at all except you have to if you want kids."

"You got any idea what you're missing?"

"I'm not missing a thing. For me, this is fine."

"So, what do you do, look after yourself? One of those riggins from the sex shop, or—?"

"No. Nothing. I went to a doctor about it one time. Lizzie was three or four. I'd seen this thing on TV about genes and chromosomes and the differences between gay guys' brains and straight guys' brains, and I thought maybe that was it. They had this one part about women who have no male stuff at all, not a titch of it, and they look like the ultimate woman, but they never get pregnant and they aren't interested in sex. That wasn't me because I've got kids, but the other thing, hey, you never know. So I went to see this specialist. Jesus, the tests and all I got to do. I tell you. In the end she told me I had all my bits and pieces and they were all functional, and she didn't have any idea why, but not to worry about it." She smiled. "So I stopped worrying about it. For a little while I wondered if I was, you know, like Kitty and Glen and Lucy, but no. Just not interested. You?"

"Used to be. It was high on my list. I used to tease myself that it was a good job I found three guys who could get along with each other so well, because I'd'a killed one guy."

"And now?"

"I'm fine. I've come to this place I ought to have started out at, only I didn't. If I was to meet someone who was special and nice... but unless I do, this is fine."

"Do you think people can really fall in love? You know, like in books and movies?"

"Yeah, it's out there. Jimboh really loves Audrey, no doubt about that. And she's nuts about him, you can see it in everything she does. But I'm not sure it's all that common."

"You think Kitty loves Christie?"

"Yeah, but I'm not sure Christie loves Kitty in the same way. Lucy and Deb—well, that isn't my cup of tea, but they've been together a long, long time."

"I heard sometimes people decide to fall in love, without even thinking about it. You think that's true?"

"Scary thought, that one. I don't know. I'm fond of Larry and Moe, and yeah, I think I love Moe. He's a sweet guy, lovable and cuddly. But decide? I decided to move in with them. I wanted out—oh, yew, tee. And I did. I went up by the swimming hole and I sat there and I went over a list of different ways to hit the road. Any job I'd'a got would have been for slave wages, and I'd met them before, been with them, you know. And so I decided. Just, yeah, decided. Went to the motel, waited for them to show up after work, invited myself inside and while they showered and everything, I made them tea and some supper. They had this little bit of a stove in the motel—Christ, what a pain in the butt that thing was—and I did rice, because I figured that's what they ate, and I did stir-fry because that's pretty safe no matter what you like to eat, and they really liked it. They probably would have anyway, after so much café food. So we were just kind of sitting around, and nobody really knew what to do, and at the time I couldn't have a real conversation with any one of them." She shrugged. "And I just never left. Except to help them move into a different motel unit. A two-bedroom. One of the bedrooms was mine, and that place had a decent stove."

"As cold-blooded as that?"

"Yeah. It started out almost like a business arrangement. But then Vic came, and he changed everything. Nothing would do but we settle down, you know. Had to have a place for Vic, had to have the best for him. And then for Elaine, and now here we are, all these kids later."

"Did you *decide* to have the kids, too?"

"Oh no, I'd'a still been having them except for a few changes and alterations along the way."

"Carol? And what's-her-name—Betty?"

"Nah. That part never bothered me. Changes like...oh, maybe growing up in my own head, for starters. And then the old lady arrived and I knew that was *it* for me. But it wasn't her. She was the excuse, the catalyst, I guess you'd say."

"You'd say. I'd say last straw."

"Tell me my kids got no soul."

Audrey was waiting for them when they went to collect her the next morning. "I hope you brought clean clothes," she griped. "These ones are stiff and bloody and they're starting to smell."

Savannah handed over a plastic shopping bag.

"Where's Jimmy?"

"He's still asleep. Seely said to leave him. That okay with you?"

"Poor guy. It really was an accident, you know."

"Hey, I know that. He'd never, I mean *never* deliberately hurt you. He might do a rack of other stuff, but hurt you? It's not in him."

"I'll need help getting dressed. They've got me wrapped up like a mummy."

"Yeah, I figured. That's why I brought an old shirt, we can cut off the sleeve if we have to. How's it feel?"

"Like a toothache. But I can move my fingers okay. No nerves or muscles or anything like that. He says I'll have a dilly of a scar, but I wasn't due for any pin-up photo sessions. But right now I can't really close up my fist or pull on things. Like socks, and that's a hint, okay?"

"Sure. Shove out your foot and I'll give you a hand."

"You tryin' to be funny?"

"Nah. Okay, give me the other one. Need help with the underwear?"

"I think I can manage one-handed. But not the jeans. My God, I'm as useless as Victoria."

"I brought you a bra."

"Leave it in the bag, it'll be easier. I can't do up this button one-handed. Damn jeans are getting too tight."

"They don't make 'em right any more," Savannah agreed. "You notice how the pockets are getting tighter all the time? Hardly get my hand in them now."

"It's the zippers get me down. Even when the jeans fit, the zippers stick. Practically need to call in a crew to get them done up. Maybe I'm going to have to lay off some of Seely's desserts."

"I thought of that once, then I decided I'd rather go up a size in jeans."

"You can afford to go up a size or two. Me, I'm about at my limit. I get any porkier I'll have to go to Omar the tent maker for my clothes."

"You're fine the way you are." Savannah eased the shirt over the bandaged arm and nodded. "There we go. Won't even have to rip out the sleeve."

"This isn't my shirt, that's why. You brought one of Jimmy's."

"Well, why not? After all, he cut you. If anyone's going to wind up with a one-sleeved shirt, it should be him."

Audrey sat down on the side of the bed. Jimmy opened his eyes, saw her and sat upright.

"Ah, Audrey."

"Hey." She put her good arm around him. "Don't do this to yourself, okay?"

"I never meant to—"

"Jim. Look at me. *Look*. I know you would never, not ever, hurt me on purpose. But you have to stop beating yourself up or you'll hurt me worse. This on my arm is a cut. You feeling so awful is like a knife in my throat."

He wriggled over so that he was close to her, his arms around her, his cheek against hers.

"Careful," she whispered. "The door's open, there's people in the kitchen and I, sir, am a wounded woman."

Lucy had almost forgotten how wet springtime could be this close to the chuck. Up-country, spring came a good month or month and a half later and was a matter of snowmelt filling the ditches and seasonal runoff channels. She had forgotten about liquid sunshine, and about early green grass.

It was nice, though. Nice to be greeted by masses of snowdrop flowers she hadn't even known would be there. Crocus, too, carpets of them, no longer confined to flower beds, spreading from the house out as far as the driveway at the front and heading determinedly up toward the bush at the back. Daffodils grew even along the fence lines of the pastures, and just to one side of the walkway to the kitchen door, iris were sending up sharp swords.

But there was work to do. Everything was overgrown and almost choked by grass. A cow person didn't want to curse grass, but it was needed in places other than the iris bed. Lucy bought a little spiral notebook and started making notes of things to do in the fall. If she dug up the iris beds, broke the rhizomes apart and got rid of as much grass root as possible, she might have a chance of keeping the stuff under control. She could see places where entire clumps of sod could be dug out and moved. There were areas around the watering troughs that could use some fill—already the cows had made bald impressions in the earth, so that the troughs stood up on little islands above the compressed dirt. Only to be expected, what with each cow weighing in at eight hundred or more pounds, and all of them pregnant again.

And hadn't that been fun. For a while it had looked as if the AI guy was going to move in, bag and baggage. Breeding worked fine with dairy cows. You're right there with them twice a day, you aren't going to overlook telltale swelling or nervousness or standing heat behaviour. But beef, well, that's a whole other story.

Funny, too, how Noel was the best of them at knowing when it was time to phone the AI guy. Who'd have thought a kid who had just turned six years old would be able to tell a thing like that before adults with years of experience caught on? Kitty said it was because kids hadn't yet caught on to the fact that they weren't supposed to know, and that if grownups had sense enough to leave kids alone they'd get the answers to a whack of stuff that was puzzling them. Instinct, she said. Just plain old-fashioned unvarnished instinct.

Well, maybe.

She left it up to Kitty to decide which semen to use. All of Decision's bull calves except the twins had been left whole. The twins were rubber-ringed before they were twenty-four hours old. If Noel and Bobby were going to make pets out of them, best they never feel even the first surge of bully energy. The others they separated off, and old man Farnsworth, who hadn't retired and apparently never would, was due to come pick them up any day now. The heifers they were keeping. That would make seventeen head, more than enough.

Kitty decided on shorthorns. Small heads, small front shoulders, easy births. Lucy wasn't sure she'd have made the same choice, but none of it mattered enough to bother discussing, let alone holding out for something else. When it was time to breed the heifers, which Lucy insisted wasn't going to happen until they were at least two years old, Kitty wanted to try her idea about using Santa Margarita blood. That was going to mean two totally different bloodlines. Oh, well, variety is the spice of life. It all seemed a bit much to Lucy. Beef was beef and should wind up on the table. But Kitty was interested in a cross that would throw bull riders to the moon.

Lucy hadn't protested and wouldn't, but she did question the Santa Margarita plan. "You've thought out this thing, eh?"

"Yeah. I've even checked bloodlines and narrowed the choice of stud bulls down so I only have to fuss and dither about which of six instead of the whole herd of 'em. I'll have to buy an entire tube, eh, and that's enough for maybe twenty or thirty. And I'm not sure we could store it safely, so it wouldn't be good the year following. What I figure is, Dan Conrad'll have some Decision-whiteface cross heifers ready by then, and maybe he'd want to use the extra. Those Santa Margaritas are pretty incredible. Crossed with a whiteface, it ought to be extra beef, which is extra profit."

"Might be there'll be trouble with the birthing. If they're all you say they are, the calves are probably huge."

"I think they'll be longer in the back, but no bulkier. We'll find out, though. And at least there's some of us know what needs done until the vet arrives."

"The vet here seems to have more experience with Shih Tzus than with shorthorns, I have to tell you."

"Yeah, but you've been teaching Elaine. If the vet's no good we'll hand her a butcher knife and let her do the Caesarean. What a kid!"

And any worry about birthing problems evaporated in a happy, agreeable discussion about the splendour of Savannah's first daughter.

Dan Conrad was pretty pleased with the use he'd had of Decision, and he'd have him back again after the season was finished. Personally, Lucy was glad to see the black bastard gone. Just a bit *too*, if you asked her. But it was hard on Kitty, who was a bit goofy about the bull. Maybe he was a fine critter, but there are lots of fine critters to choose from and few of them have put someone six feet under.

Kitty was out spreading fertilizer in the pastures, which she now insisted were hayfields. Lucy doubted any of it was worth the damn trouble, but she wasn't about to debate the issue. She'd known since they were forced to move that her real farming days were done. She just didn't have the interest in turning this place into a working farm. Kitty, now, she was brimful of ideas, up and at it every morning. You could almost see the energy zinging off her. And Christie, too. Right out there, jeans, work boots, work shirt, leather gloves, stringing farm fencing with the best of them, using the come-along to tighten the wire, hammering in fence staples, the whole thing, day after day.

Now the cows could graze in the bush, cleaning up the underbrush, doing their bit to make it look like a landscaped park. The horses had a five-acre field that was still too rough for a hayfield, but inside of a few years, that fiend Kitty would have it worked into shape.

Lucy sat on the back step and looked at the rose roots in the box. Hard to believe these dried-up things were going to send up green shoots. But there you have it. She checked the sketch in the back of her notebook. Maybe she wouldn't put the climber up the side of the new greenhouse after all. What if it pulled the fibreglass panelling loose? It would look nice at the front. She could use a length of farm fencing, put a good two-by-four under the frame of her bedroom window, fasten the fencing to it, then hang it down to the ground. She should find a way to hold it tight, maybe another two-by-four at the bottom, so it didn't flap in the wind. Maybe dig a bit of a trench, bury the two-by-four and five inches or so of the wire. Plant the climber and let it grow up. Sooner or later it would hide the wire.

She'd get Alan to dig the hole for her. He'd done a good job digging the others. And the hole alongside the greenhouse—no problem. She'd put a tree rose in it, something that would hold itself upright. Maybe that one they said would have greeny petals. Who would have thought they'd develop a green rose? What next!

Alan had done a good job on the bed along the greenhouse too. Strange sort of a kid. Prickly as hell, but get him interested and there was no stopping him. He not only dug the bed, he sifted the soil, said he could find the grass roots easier that way. Good for him for thinking of it.

Kitty took the tractor back to the tool shed, parked it and used the bucket to lift the bulk sack of 18-18-18. She fastened the holding chain to it, then released the bucket and turned the tractor so the fertilizer sprayer was under the spout of the bulk container. She untied the spout and watched the granules fall into the big red cone. When it was just about full, she started twisting the spout, working hard to shut off the flow.

"Here," said Christie, appearing with a length of strong nylon rope. "Let's tie it off before you pull a muscle or something."

"It's the something had me worried, the muscle is no problem."

"There you go. How are the fields?"

"Wet. But that's okay, this stuff will dissolve better. I'm using a lot of it because I think it's been ages and ages since anybody fertilized out there."

"I'm just about finished in the other field. Got the clumps of swamp grass dug out and plenty of new seed in the bald patches. That little garden tractor thing works fine. I don't think they designed it for this, but there you have it. What piece of farm equipment ever does what they designed it for? And it always winds up being used for something else. Like using the bucket to hammer in fence posts." She laughed softly. "I'll just get me another sack of canary grass seed, and by the time you've finished where you are, well . . . come on over and see me, why don't you?"

Kitty's hand was sore. The big lump on the back of it was swollen and pinkish. Too much clenching, too much lifting and squeezing. But she was more than halfway through. Jimmy had said his friend would have the clamp ready by tomorrow. Wasn't that the way? Get the thing about two hours after there'd be any need for it. At least it would be here for the next time. That's pretty well what farming was all about, anyway—next time.

The JimmySpook was sitting in the bucket of the tractor, happy as a kid, and he didn't look as bony as he once had. Sometimes there was almost the hint of a real face, not just a skull mask. Noel insisted Thingy had eyes but all Kitty had seen were holes. Sometimes they sort of glowed, but they were holes, not eyes. Noel said eyes, though. He said Thingy smiled a lot. The only way Kitty could tell whether the spook was in a good mood or a bad one was by the way he moved. The angrier he was, the jerkier were his movements. Right now he wasn't the least bit jerky. And why should he be? She was smoking an Old Port cigar for him. What more could a woman do to please a ghost, pray tell?

She saw Mycat streaking across the yard, tail in the air. It must be just about time for Savannah to bring Noel and Bobby home from kindergarten. She'd heard of dogs knowing things like that, but Mycat was the first cat she'd known that could keep track of time. He looked like his mother, only the markings giving any sign of the Siamese in his background. Nice round face, not one of those sharp, triangular ones. And cream-coloured with reddy-orange markings. Bigger than most cats, although nowhere near as big as those damn monster cats of Jimmy's. Didn't even *look* like cats. But people were lined up from here to Halifax and back, money in hand, hoping for a kitten. A kitten? By the time they were a month old they were almost the size of spaniels, or so it seemed.

She looked up at the sky. Greyish clouds coming in from the west. She'd known it was going to rain, that's why she was fertilizing today. The weatherman had promised a week of rain. As if anyone needed to listen to the weatherman in the springtime, when rain was about all it did.

When Kitty got to the house Noel and Bobby ran to her, bringing her up to date on the latest doings at kindergarten. Teacher said this and teacher said that and teacher said something else. Did the conversation go the other way around at school? My mom said this, my mom said that?

"Hey." She knelt down and presented her cheek. "Gimme my smooches before I get insane."

"You're wet."

"You bet I'm wet. I'm wet on the outside and probably on the inside too. That's real rain out there."

"Auntie Debbie said to tell you she's got your bath started."

"Three cheers for Auntie Debbie. Can someone help me off with this wet boot? Ah, I don't know what I'd do without you two to help me. Look, my sock is wet. Now isn't that something? And I greased up those boots just two days ago."

"Can we go to the complex after supper?"

"What?" She pretended shock. "To the *complex?* You two? Who'd want to take you to the complex?"

"It's Friday night. No school tomorrow. We can stay up late."

"Oh yeah? Who said so? Not me. I say you're going to bed right now. Both of you. No supper, straight to bed, and stay there until it's time to go to school on Monday. You better phone over to Auntie Savannah and tell her, there's probably a bunch of other kids will want to go, too."

Savannah was worried about Moe and didn't have anyone to talk to about it. Even Jimmy wouldn't understand, and there was no use going to Larry or Shemp about it. That would only upset Moe even more. He phoned her a couple of times a week, never from home, always from a pay phone, or from the office. Sometimes he wept.

"I would leave here and move there," he told Savannah. "I don't even ask to be allowed to live with you. Just let me live near you."

"I don't know what to say, Moe. I'm not mad at you, nothing like that. If you want to move here, that's up to you. And you can see the kids any time you want. You can live right here in the house."

The problem was his wife. She didn't know up from down or push from shove. She was the most innocent sixteen-year-old a person could imagine. Moe hadn't told his mother he wasn't being sexual with the girl, but Bindi found out. Bindi could find anything out. Sooner or later, Bindi found out everything. And when she found this out, she blamed the girl, which made the girl's life miserable.

"How can I?" Moe mourned. "She isn't much older than Victor! She doesn't know as much as Elaine does."

"If you don't feel right about it, don't do it."

"My mother thinks it is foolish to send her to school. She says school is part of the reason why she is so ... so much a child."

"Fiddle. Does she enjoy school?"

"Who can say? She is so quiet I cannot tell what goes on in her head."

"Okay." Savannah gave in and said the words Moe had been praying to hear. "Jesus aitch Christ, bring her here with you. She can go to school with her step-children. I wouldn't do it for anybody else in the world."

"I love you, Savannah. That too is why I cannot be a husband to this wife. I only want you."

"Moe. Stop it. I'm a habit you got into, that's all."

She knew an uproar would get kicked off when Moe announced he was moving, but she had no idea how big an uproar. Larry phoned her, Shemp phoned her, someone she didn't know phoned her and said he was the family lawyer.

"I don't know you," she said firmly, "and I have nothing to say to you. If you're Moe's lawyer, put Moe on the phone and let him talk to me."

"He is not here right now."

"Then phone back when he is." She hung up.

The man didn't phone back, and Moe was as puzzled about it as she was. "It may have been my mother's lawyer, or a friend of hers. Or someone from temple."

"Yeah, it could have been a door-to-door salesman, too."

When Moe brought his wife, she took one look at the girl and shook her head. "Someone's been lying to someone," she said. "This kid isn't sixteen going on seventeen. This kid probably hasn't had her fifteenth birthday. Did she tell you she was nearly seventeen?"

"Yes. She said the date of birth, the place, everything."

"Tell her that as her husband, you insist she tell you the absolute truth. Tell her if she tries to lie you'll... oh, I don't know, cut off her head with your sword."

Moe didn't have to threaten. He merely said he was her husband and she was never to lie to him. The girl began to weep. She spoke in a whisper, and Moe listened, nodding gently.

"You are right," he told Savannah. "She is younger than Victor. All her papers are lies. She replaces her sister, who died two years ago."

Savannah didn't know whether to laugh or to scream. "Well, look on the good side, you got married to the sister. She's dead, you're a widower, and this kid is now your underage sister-in-law. You're a free man, Moe."

"If I send her back, she will... she will suffer."

"She'll die, you mean. Well, she's not going back, she's not going anywhere except to school. She can move in with Elaine. But we need a real name for her. I'm not calling anyone by her dead sister's name. It would be like calling Jimboh 'Glen,' a lie every time you opened your mouth."

When Moe and the girl moved, Savannah felt like the houseman in some bizarre poker game, shuffling kids and rooms instead of cards. If Moe expected to slide into Savannah's bed he was disappointed, but he said nothing, just nodded and smiled and set about turning what had been intended as a garage into his bedroom.

"I will build an addition," he told Savannah, "so the freezers and washing machines will have a place and you won't be crowded when you're doing the laundry."

"Listen, guy." She kissed his cheek, "Maybe I'll just take the laundry as far as the doorway and leave it there for you to do."

"I can do that," he agreed.

One of the very first things Moe did was go to the municipal hall, get a business licence and rent an office on Commercial Street.

"You have never used our family name," he said to Savannah at suppertime.

"No," she agreed.

"These children are known by their mothers' family names."

"Yes." Savannah felt a stab of fear. Was Moe about to come down heavy about it? People change, they do it every day.

"Would you mind if I used your family name?" he asked politely. "For the business."

"Excuse me?" she gaped.

"My name would not be an asset to the company. Not at this time, not in this town. But your family is well known here."

"The thing is, darlin'," she said, flooded with relief, "is that the reasons my family is well known might not be an asset to you."

"So you would object?"

"No. It's fine by me."

"I will ask Jim," Moe said, continuing to feed Victoria.

The little girl was totally in love with her daddy. She didn't even play coy with him, she just did whatever she thought he wanted her to do. Her bouts of terrible-two nastiness had begun to diminish in frequency and duration, for which Savannah and everyone else was grateful. Bobby didn't seem as impressed with the new circumstances, but who knew what went on in his head? He was so emotionally glommed on to Noel and Kitty that he behaved like a visitor when he spent time with his mother and siblings.

The child who had been passed off as her sister was shy, but Savannah figured that would pass. Already she was settled into Elaine's bedroom, with her own dresser for her clothes, and with Elaine's permission to use the sound system any time she wanted. Sometimes Savannah listened to the two of them chattering away together and wondered at the almost tribal bond the kids seemed to share. All the fuss and go-round meant nothing to them, not even to the one who was part of the mixup, they were just two kids forming an alliance against a world of inscrutable adults.

Savannah got the younger ones bathed and into bed and supervised the older ones as they settled in with their homework, and she watched Caroline and Jason trudge off sullenly for a brief visit with Carol. She had come back again from one of her almost regular trips to the city, and Savannah had given them a raisin pie to take with them because Carol didn't bake and would have forgotten to pick something up at Seely's shop.

"Be sure to tell her that she's expected for supper tomorrow night," Savannah had said.

"Mom!" Caroline protested.

"Hey." Savannah kissed Caroline's forehead, then her nose, then chin, and finally her lips. "Come on, store it away for some other time. Your dad's moved in, your mom is entitled to at least see his face, okay?"

"Why can't he just go over and—"

"Caroline." Savannah's voice was firm. She didn't have to say anything else.

Savannah had a bath, then went to her bedroom. Moe was at the table with the kids, watching them, drinking in the sight and sound of them as they frowned over their work or teased each other. She wondered if he'd ever get enough of it. And she wondered what he saw when he looked at them. What she saw, except for her suspicion about Betty and the Irish door prize, was a bunch of kids who were East Indian, in polite talk, and Paki or Hindu or rug rider or buddha-eyed mutts in not-so-polite talk. Dark hair, big dark eyes, dark skin, not what you'd think of as white kids. Did Moe see them the same way, or did he see the opposite? They were human: clean, neat, well dressed, loved, even pampered and indulged. Did the difference show as clearly to "them" as it did to her, only from the other side of the fence?

She pulled on her flannelette pyjamas and sat on her bed brushing her wet hair, trying to get some control over it before it dried and headed off in all directions. If she could get it pulled back and held down, it would dry without turning into a cloud of curls. If she didn't, it would do what it wanted, and then wherever she went, her hair would call attention to her, like a big neon sign blinking and flashing Look Look Look Look.

There was a tap at her door and before she could open her mouth, the door opened and Elaine entered, smiling nervously. "You busy?"

"No, pet, I'm not busy. I'm having a fight with my hair."

"I could help." Elaine took the hairbrush and Savannah relaxed into the gentle pull of the bristles through her mop. "Let me know if I pull, okay?"

"You pull and everybody'll know. They'll hear the noise up at Kitty's place."

"It's funny how the other farm was always called Lucy's place and this one is . . . you know what I mean?"

"Yeah. And it's Jimmy's house but it's Seely's shop, right?"

"Yeah, but it's not Darlene and Lizzie's bunkhouse. That's just the bunkhouse, or no name at all."

"Sometimes it's called the girls' bunkhouse."

"Sometimes."

Savannah enjoyed the brushing so much that she didn't even bother asking whether Elaine had finished her homework. It wouldn't matter anyway. Elaine was so far ahead of the others in her class that the principal wanted to move her a grade ahead. Noreen was against it. She was sure Elaine could get all the enrichment she needed with the extra tutoring. Besides,

Noreen said, the last thing Elaine needed was to feel any more different than she already did. Because all the kids were doing so well with the tutoring, Savannah was more than willing to listen to any suggestion Noreen made. She had a way with them, no doubt about that.

"Momma," Elaine said, "she can't go to school with that name. The kids will make her life hell. She has to have a *name* name, something they can pronounce, something they'll believe."

"Yeah?"

"They've given up teasing us. So we look different, what the hell, there's lot in the school look different. They've got Asian kids and kids from the reserve and kids with red hair and fat kids, but they've all got names. Real ones."

"I expect her name is real enough."

"Not here. Here it's a noise. They'll call her Shoe Shit, just for a start. Then it'll get worse."

"So?" Savannah took the brush, turned Elaine around and began brushing her long, wavy black hair. "We'll find her a name, okay, but I'm out of names. There are so many kids in this house that I had to use up all the ones I had. What do you suggest? Something exotic? Yasmin, or..."

"Something very plain and ordinary, something here and now. Nothing old like Abigail or Rebecca, nothing off the wall like Sheena or Carmen or Peony. Something everyday ordinary and blah. Something like...Susan."

"Susan?"

"Susan. Susan Jane."

"Okay. I guess she'll have to use your dads' last name. All those papers and immigration forms."

"That's okay. We'll just say she's the dads' youngest sister. No way we can say she's our stepmother."

"She isn't really. It was her sister's name."

"I know, Momma. She told me. And Dad didn't...you know."

"I know, but do you?"

"Yes, Mother." Elaine rolled her eyes. "Really! You'd think I was an infant!"

"Sweet darling, as far as I'm concerned, you are. I know it ticks you off. It would have ticked me off, too, had it happened to me, but you're my baby. The oldest you will ever get in my mind is to be my kid. I am *never* going to be able to think of you as my grown daughter. You might have grey hair and a face full of wrinkles, but you'll be my kid."

"No, Momma, Victoria is your baby."

"Listen to you. I look at Vikki and I see you. Except you were very very *very* much prettier than she is."

"Nobody could possibly be prettier than Vikki is! Momma, she's gorgeous!"

"Not a patch on you. So it's Susan Jane, is it? Okay. What else has she told you?"

"She's terrified of our grandmother."

"Who isn't? I have to tell you, the next time the Ayatollah or one of those guys gets out of line, I say we pack up your grandmother and ship her off to deal with him. Having a spot of trouble in Bosnia? Send Bindi. They won't abide by the treaty in Ireland? Won't even have to send her there, just threaten them and they'll fall in line."

"She's afraid of her own mom and dad, too."

"Anybody she isn't afraid of?"

"Me. Vic. Us. All of us, I think. She's fraidy around Carol, but then Carol'd had a few beer before she met Sue and that's enough to scare anyone. She's scared of Uncle Jimmy, but she's scared of all men, pretty much. Except Dad. She's not quite scared of him. She's just scared he'll...you know."

"Well, he probably won't."

"I know. He's in love with you. Do you know he never, not once, with Carol?"

"You're kidding! And how do you know that?"

"Carol told me."

"Carol told you *that?* The woman needs her mouth washed out with soap! I'll have something to say to her about that!"

"She won't care. She thinks it's funny. She says mostly it was Shemp who...you know."

"Stop saying 'you know.' If you're old enough to come in here and talk about it, you're old enough to call it what it is."

"I can't say that word. Unless I'm mad."

"Well, if you can't say 'fuck,' try saying 'have sex.' Or 'being sexual'."

"Some people say make love."

"Yeah. Some people do. I don't."

"Why not?"

"I don't know. I guess for me, love didn't have a lot to do with it."

"Don't you love the dads?"

"Sure I do. Well, not Shemp. He's a horse of a different garage, as my Gran used to say."

"That doesn't even make any sense."

"I know, isn't it wonderful? But Larry, I'm fond of Larry. I'm not in love with him, but I respect him and I admire him and I'd do just about anything for him."

"And Moe?"

"He's a sweetie," Savannah smiled.

"How come you never use their real names?"

"Because when I first got to know them I was an ignorant small-town racist bitch, and I insisted that I couldn't pronounce them. Of course I could have, I just didn't want to try. And I made jokes about them because I felt embarrassed, or shy, or ashamed, or I don't know. And then the names stuck, and they never complained."

"How did you wind up with all three of them?"

"Oh, darling, that story is so long and so littered with old shit that it's hardly worth telling any more. To start with, I was Susan's age. But I wasn't shy and fraidy like she is. I was angry, defiant, tough, nasty a lot of the time. You wouldn't like me if you met me the way I was back then. I was a tramp."

"Momma! You are not."

"Not now. Mother Superior Mary Chastity, that's me. But not back then, hon."

"Which one did you ... have sex with first?"

"Larry. Then a week or so after I'd been getting it on with Larry, Shemp showed up in my room one night. Moe didn't make his move for a month or so. He was so shy."

"Maybe he'd never ... "

"If you say 'you know,' I'm going to pull your hair."

"Maybe he'd never had sex before."

"I don't think he had. He sure didn't know much. I had to teach him how to kiss. Then again, Larry didn't know squat about kissing either. The rest of it he was fine, but not kissing."

"Some of the kids at school are having sex. Two of the girls are pregnant. I'm glad it's not me!"

"That's two of us, believe me."

"I'm not even interested. Maybe I won't ever be."

"Maybe not."

"What if I'm like Kitty and Lucy?"

"What if you are?"

"Some of the kids at school make jokes about them. Victor almost got in a fight over it."

"One of these days we'll all sit down and all us old soaks will give you young soaks a rundown on some of the dirt under other people's rugs. Then, if any of those pizmires gets lippy you can just say Oh, yeah? Zat so? If I had *your* family history I'd be careful what I said. Or hasn't anybody told you your dad went to jail for statutory rape?"

"Who was that?"

"Heh heh heh."

"Heh heh who?"

"Who did Vic almost fight?"

"George Harper."

"Well, it wasn't George's dad. The skeleton in George's closet is his grandpa, old George. That old fart was a diddle-hand. Cops put him on some kind of list, so if he moved anywhere—which unfortunately he didn't—they'd warn the cops in the new place about him. He wound up in court about it, but it was closed court because the kids were so young, and the judge said he wasn't allowed to go anywhere near the school playground. Dirty old bugger. It wasn't in the paper, though. Because of the kids, and because the paper here tries to pretend nothing nasty happens, we're just a nice quiet little town."

"Good. I'm going to tell Vic."

"Anybody else?"

"Phyllis Carmichael. She's always teasing Caroline about how she's not really my sister, and her mom is always going off to the city, and...you know."

"Phyllis Carmichael's father got fired from his job for stealing from the road crew. He was the one who drove that mower contraption that cut the long grass and brush at the side of the road. He drove other things, too, trucks and stuff, and he cut the grass on the sports field. But then they canned him for swiping stuff. He'd take jugs of oil home in his lunch bucket, or let's say you needed a new whup-diddle for your car and it was going to cost you a hundred and ten bucks. Well, Phil would swipe one from the repair shop and sell it to you for fifty. But he finally got caught and that was it, he was fired. Union didn't even try to stick up for him."

"Wow! That wasn't in the papers!"

"'Course not. Phyllis Carmichael's mother is a Norton. None of *them* ever wind up in the paper."

"So why does Carol go to the city so much?"

"Because she isn't a small-town person, that's why. Nothing more to it than that. We've got one movie theatre, and sometimes it's a couple weeks before they change the movie. And when was the last time you went to a concert? I don't mean a school Christmas concert, I mean a real one. You can go to a hockey game if that's your bag, or you can go to the curling rink and watch people sliding rocks along as if it mattered or made sense, but how far would you have to drive to hear live music?"

"Well, some of the pubs—"

"Yeah, right. And just guess what the old biddies would have to say about that! They'd be teasing Caroline that her momma was a barfly."

"Is she lonely?"

"Carol? Oh, yeah, darling, she's real lonely. Been lonely most of her life, I'd bet. It's not easy for her."

"So you're okay with Susan?"

"Yeah, it's an okay name. Are you okay with having her share your room and all?"

"She's nice. None of it is her fault. She just did what she was told to do, because she was brought up to be like that."

Every Thursday evening Audrey drove to the college and sat with ten other people in the Creative Writing course. Ward Gregory, the instructor, was well past middle age, and he had the face of a petulant baby and a round, hard belly that rode above his belt buckle. He obviously felt the job was beneath him, his talents wasted, and some of his purported constructive criticisms seemed to Audrey more like carping and bitching than help. She went faithfully to class anyway, because of some of the others who attended.

"You're progressing nicely," Gregory smiled at her one evening, showing crooked, less-than-clean teeth. She wondered why someone who was so over and above everything and everyone would have ignored the invention of braces for teeth, or even toothbrushes.

"Thank you."

"Obviously you're working hard at it."

"I try," she nodded. She had begun to feel the unease so familiar to her, from dealing with customers at the two-four and any of the restaurants or pubs she had worked at.

He moved a half step closer and she felt the sudden lurch that signalled it was time for her to take two steps back. But she didn't want to offend him. She'd wait a moment or two, then just saunter back, not leap like a scalded cat. "Perhaps you might benefit," the old goat said, "from working on something a bit more...personal. More...revealing."

"Beg pardon?" She moved gracefully, picking up her notebook and opening it, giving every appearance of being ready to take notes, while actually having got the table between them.

"A writer has to dare," he pontificated. "Finding the personal voice is very challenging and too uncomfortable for some people—most, in fact— to accomplish. Right now you are doing very good work as a detached observer, which is excellent for a journalist but not for a novelist or poet."

"I see," she nodded, making no pretence of writing anything down.

"If you wish," he smiled again, as she resisted the impulse to look away, "I would be quite willing to give you some private instruction. Some tutoring."

"Thank you." She didn't smile back. "I'll have to discuss it with my husband."

"Your husband? Ah yes, the sculptor." In his mouth the word was trivial, a child pounding a piece of rock with a hammer.

"I have a job, you see." She hoped Seely would forgive her the fabrication she was about to make. "And on top of that, I'm taking some lessons from my sister-in-law, learning the secrets of baking and cake decorating. So that takes a couple of evenings a week, and then I'm helping Savannah set up her business, and frankly, between my practice writing and this course every Thursday, time is in short supply. I'm sure you know how it gets, you must be very busy too. And then you have your own writing..."

"I always have time to help promising students."

"Who does he think he is?" she griped to Jim later that night. "What do people see when they look in a mirror? Does he know what he looks like? Maybe the reason he hasn't had any work done on his teeth is that no dentist will wade in there! I mean, they're almost fuzzy. Stop laughing, James!" But he chuckled happily, holding her close, stroking her shoulder with his calloused scar-crossed hands. "And then there's that belly. Did you ever look at people like that and wonder how they manage to do anything? You can't tell me his prick is long enough to poke out past that ponce."

"That what? What in hell is a ponce?"

"I don't know. It's what my granddad used to call the bellies of very *very* pregnant women."

"How can a woman be *very* pregnant?"

"How would you like it if I bit your nose?"

"I'd like it just fine. I've got some other things you can bite too, if you're of a mind."

"Oh, James-my-boy, how could I have any mind left after snuggling up with you like this? Or like this. Or...how's this?"

"Careful," he whispered. "Watch out for the ponce."

"That is not a ponce."

All thoughts of the writing instructor were dispelled.

But the harassment continued in class, until finally one of her classmates, Doreen, spoke to her about it.

"It's none of my business," Doreen said uneasily, "but I guess you know Ward's trying to put the make on you."

"Yeah," Audrey nodded. "I don't know what to do about it. What I'd like to do is give him a quick knee to the slats, but I really like this course, you know? Not him, but the chance to meet with the rest of you, listen to what you're working on, get feedback."

"Yeah. Well, last year it was someone else. Every semester he zeroes in on someone, usually a first-timer, someone who's feeling off balance and uncertain about her writing. I don't know that he's ever managed to dip his wick, but he sure gets off on his little game."

"Christ, I can't even begin to imagine..."

Doreen laughed. "Come on, be honest, don't you wonder what scientific experiment is going on in his mouth?"

"Oh, God."

"See, you *can* imagine it!"

"Has anyone ever, like, reported it?"

"You've got to be kidding. The thing is, what has he actually said or done that you could report to someone, and not look like a damn fool?"

They started meeting on Tuesday evenings, one week at Doreen's place, the next in Audrey's kitchen. After a few meetings with their work, a teapot and a plate of Seely's best, they were joined by a third, then a fourth woman.

"If you want," Jimmy murmured as he snugged to her back, curled himself around the warmth of her butt, "I can make sure you've got the place to yourself every Tuesday. Seel wants to join in. I can take the girls to the pool or something. Or just tie 'em up in the woodshed."

"You wouldn't mind?"

"Hey." He kissed the space between her shoulders, feeling the soft, fine peach-fuzz of hair. "Downy as a baby duck," he whispered. "A person needs their own time and space, eh?"

"It would be great, Jimboh. Really great."

"Okay. No problem."

But there was one. Somehow Ward Gregory caught wind of the Tuesday night meetings. He didn't say a word to anyone about it, but his attitude toward Audrey changed completely. She knew he was stung that she had said she didn't have time for private tutoring, then turned around and found time every Tuesday night for something that didn't include him. She braced herself for his anger, waited for him to rip apart every piece of work she did. But instead, he acted as if she wasn't even in the class.

"What a relief," she told Jim. "If I'd known it would work out like this I'd have jumped into it even faster."

Seely didn't dare share any of her own writing at the first half-dozen meetings she attended. Who was she to intrude? They all had more experience than she did, and some of them had been writing for years. What did she know about it? When she finally did dare, she knew her work was feeble compared to everyone else's.

"I'm not very good at this," she whispered.

"Ever see me smear icing on a cake?" Doreen replied easily. "And I make cake-mix cakes, too. You practise at this as much as you did at the other and you'll do just fine."

Seely didn't believe her until the night she read them the story she had written about supper-with-the-rellies. The gales of laughter surprised her, then thrilled her.

"I don't know why you're all laughing," Audrey said. "It's a slice-of-life journalistic rendering, all she's done is transcribe from a tape recorder."

"Someone invite *me* for supper, please," someone said.

"Me too."

"If it's potluck, I'm coming too."

Jimmy actually enjoyed the party. He had so much fun he almost suggested they do it again the following month. But years of experience with his particular affliction, the name of which he had never found although he'd read all the pop-cult articles on health that he could find, had taught him that intentional repeats are seldom as good as occasional accidents. So he held his tongue.

Still, it was tempting. The kids had brought out their musical instruments and joined in with two men who had brought guitars and women who brought Celtic drums, a violin, a mandolin and a banjo. Some of the music they made was fun, some was actually good, and quite a bit of it was downright awful. There's something about "Tom Dooley" played off-key, off-beat and accompanied by a nine-year-old on a coronet that can simultaneously offend the ear and fill the air with laughter.

"All's we need is a parade," Alan said. "We could come after the kitties and just before the old old fire truck. Instead of us throwing candy to the crowd, they'd throw stuff at us."

"Wonderful idea," Noreen agreed. "Let's just make sure we come before the horses or you know what it is they'll be throwing."

"How does that thing work?" Noel was drawn to the violin. The young woman playing it had carrot-red hair and a wide grin. She demonstrated how to hold it, then tucked it under his chin.

"It's too big," he complained.

"That's okay, I've got one at home that will fit you. I used it when I was your age. I'll bring it out and show you some stuff."

"Would you? I'd like that. I'd pay you."

"Would you really?"

"I'd pay, too." Bobby had a tambourine that didn't play well because half of the little tin clatterers were bent or missing. Still, it was better than nothing.

"Would you? That would be wonderful!" She didn't tell either of them that she made her living on lessons, for which she charged more than either of them probably had in the piggy bank. "Would you pay me enough that I could buy a kitten?"

"What kind of kitten?"

"You see that one over there? The sort of Siamesey one with the tabby-cat markings?"

"I've got one like that," Noel said. "I call him Mycat. But he's older and he's bigger. Christie said I had to get him fixed but we didn't yet. But she says if he sprays anywhere in the house he has to go toot sweet."

"Maybe you should take him in *before* he sprays instead of after."

"That's what Kitty says. But I don't want them to hurt him. Getting fixed might hurt a whole lot."

"Oh, they give him something that puts him to sleep for a while. I had my old cat fixed when he was eight months old. I took him in before I even had my breakfast and I picked him up after work. He was sleepy that night and in the morning he was fine. He walked kind of funny for a few days, but he didn't seem to hurt at all."

"Where's the fiddle?" someone called.

"Gotta go." She grinned at them and Noel handed her the violin. He watched her walk away with it, then he picked up the two spoons and waited for the music to start so he could clatter along, somewhere in the vague vicinity of the rhythm.

The roses took hold and began to show green swellings Lucy was sure would become twigs and leaves. The repaired greenhouse was ready for cucumber and tomato plants, for peppers and the cantaloupe vines Noel had started from seed. Lucy wasn't sure how well they'd do. They were too big to keep in the kitchen any longer, but some nights were colder than she thought the plants could tolerate. She solved the problem by putting a heat cord in the ground, encircling the vines. They were spindly and pale when she eased them out of the margarine containers in which the boy had planted them, but inside of two weeks they had not only taken hold, they were doing their best to take over.

"Do you suppose you're supposed to pinch the tips or cut them back or something?" she asked.

Noel shrugged, his interest in the vines waning. "I didn't even grow anything before."

"If it's all right with you, I think I'll stake them up and treat them the same as if they were tommy toes."

Noel watched while Lucy set up the stakes and got her foot-long lengths of binder twine.

"Can I help?" he asked.

"That would be great. Some jobs need three or four hands. You could maybe hold this for me? Careful, now, the way this vine is growing it might lift you off the ground, like Jack's beanstalk."

"Yeah," he giggled. "With a giant at the top."

"And treasure," she reminded him. "There's always treasure."

Noel listened carefully and tried to do exactly what Lucy told him. Sometimes, not often but sometimes, Lucy could get real crabby. Kitty said it was because she wasn't used to having a kid around, and that she'd get over it. Kitty said when she had to go to live with Lucy it was the same thing, but after a while it worked itself out and Lucy became a good friend. But there had been lots of water go under the bridge since then, she said, and Lucy got out of the habit. Noel wasn't sure which bridge she meant, but if it was the one over Eagle River, there sure had so been a lot of water go under it! They went there on his birthday.

He had never had a birthday like this one! Kitty said he'd have lots of good birthdays, but this one would always seem special. He woke up early, because of the tree and the hoping to see Santa, and that was real great. He had neat stuff in his stocking and a Christmas orange in the toe, and it was just like he'd seen on TV.

He got videos, and not just little kid ones. Other ones too, about places you could visit, and a couple of great ones about the olden days when the people owned everything. That's what Christie called them, the people. She said not to call them Indians because none of them had been born in India. India was where Uncle Moe came from, and he sure wasn't an Indian. It was very confusing. And clothes, lots of winter clothes, and Adidas tee shirts, and a No Fear tee shirt and a pair of Adidas pants. It didn't matter that they were a bit too big, because Debbie just stood him on a chair and said Hold on a minute, darling, and she marked stuff with pins. Before breakfast was over, she had the pants fitting him just fine. Room to grow, she said.

They were just finishing breakfast when the door opened without any knocking. When he thought about it later, he knew they'd all been in on it, because Pup barked a couple of times and Deb said Oh that dog, I'm not putting up with that this morning, she can just go outside and turn the snow yellow, and she carried Pup to the door. No more barking. Someone had snuck up to the door, probably Uncle Jimmy, and Pup must have been too busy wiggling and licking his face to make noise when the rest of them got there. They said they parked by the mailbox and walked up so he wouldn't hear the car or anything.

And the door opened and everyone came in yelling Happy Birthday! They didn't even bother about Christmas, it was Happy Birthday. He was so excited he couldn't finish his breakfast and nobody cared. Presents and jokes and a cake. He'd never seen anybody get a cake like that. It looked like a great big pig all covered with whipped cream, only coloured whipped cream, and he didn't even know you could do that.

And it went on and on. The whole house was full of people, and they were all there to have fun for his birthday. Auntie Audrey took five rolls of pictures, and they ate and ate, and then Auntie Savannah said everybody put on their jackets and snow boots and off they went.

Uncle Jimmy took them way up a logging road, way way up where there was snow, all the snow you could possibly want. They built forts and snow people, and they rolled in it and slid on it and had real fun. There was snow at home, but only a little bit of it, and it was wet and slushy. Up there the snow was white, except for some that looked blue, and it wasn't all soggy. You could play in it and only get damp, not soaking wet.

And on the way back they stopped and walked from the road to what Uncle Jimmy called The Lookout, and there was Eagle River. Uncle Jimmy had a bag of rocks, real nice ones, black and shiny. And there was a rock for everybody. "So hold it tight, and then put that fist against your forehead, like this, and *think*. Think real hard about all the things that bug you or hurt you or make you sad. Think about the things you worry about and the things that make you feel like you're being picked on. Okay, now pick the worst one, the very very worst one, and *think* that you're putting that in the rock. Ask the rock to take that worry or that upset, or that nasty. Please, rock, take this with you . . . now *throw!*"

Noel threw you-know-who. It didn't work all the way, he couldn't throw away *all* the stuff, but he threw a whole bunch of it. He still remembered, but it didn't make him scared any more. And he didn't remember anywhere near as much, either. He knew what had happened, but not the same way, not each and every awful hurty thing jumping up to scare you real bad and make you feel like it was all happening all over again. Not like it had been. What he remembered now was like one thing, like a slide-open matchbox, and there it was, this thing you could open if you wanted to or you could leave it shut. You could know what was in there but leave it shut and not have to think about it.

He felt better as soon as that rock left his hand. And Thingy, with a party hat on his head, following the rock down, pointing at where it went into the river. Noel cheered and cheered and yelled and yelled and the other kids joined in, as if they could see Thingy too.

And when they finally got back to Auntie Savannah's house so all the kids could change into dry clothes, Noel was almost asleep. And Kitty had dry clothes for him, too, and all of it brand new, either Christmas stuff or birthday stuff.

You could smell turkey all through the house, and smell other things, too, good things. All the plates were piled up for people to take one, and the knives and forks were out on the table, and there were all kinds of pickles and olives. Noel was so hungry he had to swallow or the spit-drool would dribble out of his mouth.

"There, that's as good as we can do." Lucy nodded and so did Noel. The cantaloupe vine was securely tied to the stakes, looking like a decoration. "See here?" Lucy pointed. Noel didn't know what she meant but he nodded. Maybe she'd tell him what he was looking at, just a lump as near as he could tell. "That's going to be a flower. And there's another one. And another. When the flowers are ready we'll take a feather and we'll pick up dust from this plant and put it on that one, and pick up dust from that one and put it on this one, and then maybe we'll get a cantaloupe."

"I don't know," he said doubtfully. "It looks . . . well, it looks . . . " It definitely did not look like the picture in the seed catalogue.

"Yeah," Lucy agreed. "Yeah, it does, but . . . "

"Yeah."

She reached out and took his hand, gave it a soft little squeeze and winked at him. "You're a good friend," she told him. "I'm sure glad you decided to come and live with us."

It was so unexpected that he burst into tears and cried like a little baby, reaching out his arms to her. Lucy pulled him against her and he clung, gripping her jeans with his fingers. Thingy was there suddenly, leaning down, and he put one arm around Noel and the other around Lucy and hugged them both. Sometimes, when Thingy touched people they went stiff and flopped over, and that one gross guy died, but Lucy just smiled. And how did he know, with his face buried against her belly, that she had smiled?

"We make a good team," she told him. "All of us."

He was asleep and yet he wasn't, not all the way. He was lying on his right side with his knees drawn up, and he knew that he was dreaming, but he could see the window across the room from his bed, see the moon in the sky and some stars, he wasn't sure which ones. Thingy lay in bed with him and he must have been asleep too, because there was no shine in his eyes, no glitter, no warmth, just dark spots like holes. Mycat was curled on the pillow just above Thingy's head, purring. Noel could see it all, just the same as if he was awake, but he knew he must be asleep and dreaming, because he couldn't make any part of himself move.

And you-know-who was there, with a bunch of other guys, the gross one who died, the other who had laughed and held Noel too tight and then hurt him so bad Noel couldn't even cry, or breathe, just gasp and tremble. Other guys, and Noel didn't know them, had never seen them, but they were there and they acted like they were at a party, except they didn't have any drinks or smokes, or food or music or anything. But they were talking to each other and standing around and walking over to talk to someone else and then they all turned, all at the same time, and looked at him in his bed and he knew, he just *knew* they were going to come for him. Except there was an old woman there. She wasn't Lucy but she looked like her, and like Kitty, too, only older. She looked just exactly like the woman in the picture on Savannah's piano, the woman sitting on the front steps of Uncle Jimmy's house, holding Victor on her knee. Victor was a baby and all he had on was a disposable diaper, and the old woman was looking at him as if he was the first baby she had ever seen in her life. She was smiling, though, and this one in his room wasn't smiling. She looked mad, and when she frowned it was like Uncle Jimmy's frown when he'd had enough. "Had enough of this," he'd say. "Had more than enough of this," and he'd walk off. But this old woman wasn't walking off. She was standing by his bed, staring at you-know-who and the other guys, and they were scared of her. It seemed like she had others with her, only he couldn't see them, he just felt as if they were there.

The room was gone, and he knew he was all the way asleep, or at least moving toward that know-nothing place. In the morning he could remember it, like something he'd seen on TV. He almost said something to Kitty about it, but then he didn't. Maybe because she'd try to explain it to him and he didn't need it explained. None of them were going to get past that old woman, not without making so much noise they wakened Thingy, and if they did that, too bad for them. Too bad for all of them. Just point the old stick and good night nurse. That's what Christie said sometimes, "Good night nurse." Sometimes she laughed and said Tell mother I love her, and it meant the same thing.

It was Darlene's idea, but Lizzie was in on it from the get-go. Jimmy had been so busy learning how to make rings, bracelets, belt buckles and stuff, and busy being married, he'd paid scant attention to the many times great-grandchildren of old Patsy-Ratsy. He'd managed to pull it together long enough to separate the males and females so that no more babies arrived, and he still fed them every morning and made sure they had lots of clean drinking water, but he didn't seem to care about them any more. Some of the old ones died, not of neglect but because they were old, and the guy from the pet store had come out twice to catch some and take them, but there were still four females and two males left.

"Can I have the rats?" Darlene asked.

Jimmy looked at her across the supper table, and you'd have thought he'd never seen her before. "What for?"

"Because there's no jobs I can get, and we live too far from town in either direction for me to get babysitting. I went to the café and to the two-four and they both said I was too young, come back when I was older. And I want to make some money."

"You get an allowance."

"Five bucks a week," she said. "I'd have to save for years to get enough for a pair of jeans."

"Your mom buys your clothes."

"You know what I mean. It's five bucks to go into the movie house. There isn't a place in town you can buy a hamburger for five bucks."

"Okay," he nodded.

"Just like that?" Darlene was flabbergasted.

"Just like that. Only thing is, if Lizzie wants in on it, you have to give her a chance."

"Oh."

"Lizzie, if you go in on it now, and if you do half the work, and if you listen to Darlene and don't argue and bitch and fight and everything, you can have one-third of the rats out there. If you don't go in now, and help with everything even-steven, then if you do decide to join in, you'll get two rats as a startup."

"Is that fair?" Lizzie asked.

"It's fair," Audrey said. "After all, Darlene had the idea. If she wanted to be a bitch she could have talked to Jim about it sometime when you weren't around. Squeezed you out altogether."

"If it's fair it's fine by me," Lizzie shrugged. "But one-third is still only two rats."

"It'll work out better, you'll see. You'll get one-third of the money no matter what your two rats do. The other way, all you'd ever see would be money from them."

Some of the preparations were pretty gross, as far as Lizzie was concerned. First off, Auntie Audrey went on a kick about something called hanta virus, and she insisted they had to wear those masks that drywallers use.

"It's in the poop," she told them. "It's a virus, and it can live for who knows how long, and then you go to sweep things out or something and the poop is all dry and it turns to dust and you breathe it in and then the next thing you know you're so sick you're on the verge of death."

"I thought the verge was alongside the road," Lizzie puzzled.

"Don't be so damn literal," Darlene snapped. "The verge along the road is the edge of the road, right? The verge of death is the same thing. Right at the very edge."

"Oh. Like at death's door?"

"Exactly." Audrey hid her smile, certain Lizzie wasn't anywhere near as dense as she was making herself out to be. But it was a great way to get a rise out of Darlene. "Or, as your Auntie Christie would say... good night nurse. Now put on the masks, okay?"

They used the wheelbarrow, two shovels, a rake, and the garden pitchfork. The empty cages were taken down and moved, then wire-brushed, washed with disinfectant, and finally the wire was burned by the flame from the butane torch. Then the ground was levelled where the new setup was going to go, and wheelbarrow loads of cedar sawdust were spread. When the site was ready and the cages almost clean enough to use for storing food, Jimmy set up the frames and helped them install the cages. Then he helped them move the cage of females. All they had to do was line up the doors, and the rats moved into the clean one. They practically raced into it, rushing immediately to the food dish.

"Told you," Jimmy said quietly. "You can get them to do damn near anything for food. I know you thought I was being gnarly this morning when I said don't feed 'em. But now you see why."

"We should get a book," Lizzie said. "And write down all this stuff. You know, like Hints from Heloise, or something."

"God," Darlene sighed. "Can't you remember so simple a thing as they'll do anything for food?"

"There'll be other stuff, too, you'll see."

Once the males were moved into a clean cage, they had to go through the whole scrubbing and scorching routine on the dirty cages. That was really gross because of the wet pee and the rat smell. But worst of all, they had to go over and clean up the stuff that had been under the cage site. That's where the wheelbarrow got a real workout.

"What are we going to do with this stuff?" Darlene asked. "What about that virus?"

"We'll burn it." Jimmy pointed at the trash burning site. "Dump it over there with the stuff that's piled up and waiting. I'll set it on fire while you guys are getting fresh sawdust to put down. I'll get a load of topsoil tomorrow, and put that over the sawdust, then maybe the grass'll do its thing."

Moving the roof dealy was too awful to even talk about. Neither of them had any idea how to go about it, and for more than two hours Jimmy ignored them and pretended to be too busy with the trash fire.

"Uncle Jimmy, we don't know what to do now. We got the roof off, and we took down the supports, but half of 'em are punky. We're stumped."

"Bring the punky stuff over here, put it on what's left of the fire. I'll have a look."

He seemed to know what to do before he even got to the rubble. The actual roof was still in reasonably good shape, so he put them to work pulling nails and stacking sections of the sheet metal roofing. Then he took apart the rest of the roof frame and discarded much of it, getting them to drag it off to the fire. Finally he got new two-by-fours from his shed, and his round saw. By suppertime the frame was in place over the cages, and before bedtime the sheeting was on it and nailed in place.

"We want to put tarps up," Darlene told him. "Can you tell us how?"

"Tarps for what?"

"When it rains the wind blows the water sideways and it'll go under the roof and they'll get wet. If we put up a tarp—"

"The wind'll blow it to bits. What we'll do is plank in along the side. Maybe use a coupla sheets of plywood. Didn't have to worry about it before because it was butt-up against a shed wall, but you're right. Except for one thing. If you plank it in, or put up a tarp or whatever, they aren't going to be able to see what's going on in the world. What if they go stir-crazy, like convicts do?"

"But they'll get wet."

"Most of the rats in the world live in sewers and swamps and stuff like that. As long as they've got a dry place to get into they're okay, and they've got that with the nesting boxes."

"Are you sure?"

"Hey, you want to plank it in, you go right ahead, we've got lots of recycled planking in that pile behind my woodshed. I don't happen to think it's needed, but if you want to do it, do it. There's some do-it-yourself books in the living room. You'll need two-by-four supports coming down from the roof frame. They'll have to be level and even, and make sure you've got 'em all facing the right way. And—"

Darlene went into the house, sat on the floor in front of the bookcase and leafed through the manuals. A half hour later she came back out and spoke briefly to Lizzie. Instead of planking in around the cages, they started cleaning up the site, putting the tools away, parking the wheelbarrow in its place, leaving the rats to figure things out for themselves.

The work didn't end with the setting up of the rats. The second day they moved two females into the cage with the males, then moved one of the males into the cage with the other two females.

"What about giving each female her own cage and then just letting them visit with the males when it's time?" Darlene asked.

"They'll spend all their time and energy trying to get back in with each other."

Jimmy stood with his hands in his pockets, watching the girls as they fed and watered the rats. They seemed easy with them, easy with each other, already the rats seemed to sense that food was coming not from Jimmy, but from Darlene and Lizzie. They moved to the doors of their cages, crouched, waiting. None of them tried to escape, or tried to defend territory, or bite.

"You be sure to wear those heavy gloves each and every time you have to put your hand in there," Jimmy nagged. "You get bit by a rat and you'll know you've been bit! And fast? They can score three or four times in the same amount of time a dog could only get you the once."

"Why would they bite me?" Lizzie demanded. "I'm feeding them."

"Because they're rats."

"Patsy-Ratsy never bit Momma."

"Patsy-Ratsy was a special case. The goddamn thing woulda bit holes in every one of us, given a half a chance. You have to remember these aren't pussycats, these are Norwegian rats. Look at the size of 'em! That black male is as big as most alley cats."

"His name is Caesar." Darlene put carrot chunks in the metal food dish, on top of the measure of rabbit feed. "And the girls are Alice and Annabelle."

"Mine is George," Lizzie offered. "And the girls are Betsy and Bertha. Darlene got the As and I got the Bs. And we can keep track of the babies, so we'll know who's brother or sister to who. For as long as we have them, anyway. And that probably won't be long."

"Rats start having baby rats when they're only six weeks old," Jimmy warned. "So when they're a month old you have to split 'em up."

"That's what the other cages are for. And the guy from the pet store wants them when they're still small."

"Is he buying them by the numbers or by the weight?"

"He wanted to buy by weight but we said no, if he wanted to do that he'd have to find someone else with rats for sale. And we told him they were the same price brand new as they would be when they were two months old. He didn't like that idea, but Darlene told him it was to protect him, said if a baby was going to die it would die when it was small, and this way, he only paid for the ones he got alive and healthy."

"Send her out trading horses," Jimmy laughed. "He'd have bought 'em small, fed 'em next to nothing for three weeks or so, then sold 'em for two, three times what he'd paid you."

"That's what Darlene said," Lizzie nodded. "She's pretty smart, you know."

Lizzie wasn't exactly a dim bulb herself. She talked privately with Carol, and the next time Carol came back from a few days of what she still called R&R in the city, she brought three white rats with bright red eyes, two females and a male.

"People like white ones best for pets," Lizzie grinned. "Anyway, I can put the girls in with Caesar or George and get patchy ones. People will like them."

"We're going to have some all brown ones, some black ones, some all white ones and some patchy ones," Darlene grinned. "It's Lizzie's idea. Her other idea is good too. She brings Mabel over every couple of days and walks around the cages with her. That way the rats know they're better off where they are, and they know if they do break out they'll be lunch."

"Good job Mabel's as big as she is, or those rats would eat her!"

Carol no longer isolated herself. She gave up nagging Caroline and Jason to move in with her and seemed willing to accept that the bond the kids had with each other was too strong to be stretched, let alone broken.

"If any one of 'em gets married," she pretended to grumble, "the whole clanjamfrie of 'em's gonna go off on the honeymoon. What surprises me is that Kitty's managed to keep Noel up the road with her. I'd'a thought he'd'a moved in with the rest of 'em."

"Other way around," Savannah chuckled. "Bobby spends almost as much time over there as he does here. And that's fine, he gets lost in the crowd too much of the time."

"Doesn't it...bother you to see him handing out smooches to them, and not to you?"

"Yeah. Sometimes. But I figure he's better off learning to hand 'em out than he'd be if he was overshadowed by the whole bunch and feeling like he wanted to give a hug but couldn't be seen to give it. You up to joining us for supper tonight?"

"What can I bring?"

"Would you mind going down to the farm for whipping cream and making up a whack of it. I mean a *whack*. They've got fresh strawberries in, and Moe's bought up prob'ly half the supply because he wants a shortcake. Jimmy'n'Audrey's bringing her chicken dish, the polish or Ukrainian or something one. Seely's doing the cake and making a pineapple square, a new twist on an old favourite, she says. Whatever. I've got a grown pig's worth of spareribs baking in the oven, and thought I'd do up a big pot of rice and some oven-browned spuds."

"I'll do the spuds. You know Jimboh isn't going to eat any rice."

"Oh, I don't know. He ate it on Tuesday."

"With your Chinese pork."

"He eats it in rice pudding too."

"I'll do the spuds with Greek spices. That should go okay with Audrey's Hungarian chicken."

"Is it Hungarian? I'm never sure."

"Personally, I think it's *her* chicken. I can't believe people in those starve-to-death countries ever managed to steal enough chicken to make it the way she does. And whoever heard of any of them using ginger for anything, except maybe cookies?"

"Jesus, Carol, were you always a racist or did it just sort of sneak up on you in later life?"

"The O'Neills have always been racists. Hell, we were racists back when it was considered a scientifically proven fact that only Anglo-Saxons were put together properly."

"Kitty and Lucy and that lot will be over in time for dessert. They're bringing something, I'm not sure what. Christie wouldn't tell me. I told them we were okay for berries, and she laughed and said whatever it was, it wouldn't be strawberries. So who knows."

Kitty almost wished the twin steer calves had been born with black faces. That way Noel wouldn't have claimed the first one as his, neither of them would have been ringed and both of them would have stayed complete bulls, equipped for breeding. As it was she had two of the finest young steers she had ever seen, when with only a bit of luck and black faces, she could have had a matched pair of top-grade breeding bulls.

Well, might as well store that away with the rest of the might-have-beens. They were steers and they were pets, so make the best of that and get busy training them. Anyone who can train a horse can train a steer, especially if you start when they're only a week old and still trusting you and getting increasingly bonded by the milk bucket. Every day Noel and Bobby brushed their calves and every day they fussed them, even washing their hooves clean of manure. And every day Kitty walked them on a lead rope, teaching them exactly the way she would teach a foal. She got them used to having a blanket on their back while they ate, then she left the blanket on when she walked them, and eventually, when they were bigger, she put harnesses on them. It wasn't easy adapting a horse harness to a steer, but by the time they were six months old, Pete and Repeat were not only responding to the reins, they were pulling a cart.

"When they're older and stronger, you guys can ride in the cart," she promised. "But right now we have to take it easy. We don't want to strain them or overwork them, it wouldn't be good for them."

"I saw a thing on TV," Bobby piped up, "about the olden days, and they had cows pulling covered wagons and then later on they pulled logs out of the forest and stuff, too."

"That's what we'll do with these guys," Kitty agreed. "We'll teach them to haul logs, then we won't have to worry about the tractor tipping over on bumpy ground. We can clear land with the steers."

"When?" they asked eagerly.

"Next year. By then these guys will be just about full-grown, and we'll have them in tip-top shape. Maybe by then we'll have the right kind of gear for them, too. There's someplace in Nova Scotia where you can still get oxen yokes made up. Steers need their own kind of harness, I guess because they're built different than horses. Horses kind of pull with their chests, see, and an ox, he seems to pull more with his front shoulders."

"The cows in the TV thing had horns, and they had big shiny balls on the end of them. Ours don't have horns."

"No, and they won't get any, either. Their daddy didn't have horns and neither did their mom."

"So no shiny balls."

"But we could get bells," she said. "When we get the yokes made for them, we can get things put on that we could dangle jingle bells from, then they'd go jingle-jangle as they hauled the logs."

"That'd be a better name than Pete," Bobby laughed. "Jingle and Jangle."

"Tick and Tock."

"Art and Fart," Noel giggled.

"Yours is Fart."

"No, mine is Art."

"The pair of you are fartsacks," Kitty told them. "Just a pair of fartsacks."

When Lizzie presented her research at the supper table, Seely just gawked. Whatever she had been expecting of her younger daughter, this kind of nose-to-the-grindstone business sense wasn't part of it.

"We've been winging it," Lizzie said, reading from the small stack of looseleaf paper in front of her. It was rumpled, it was stained, it was the work and property of a kid, but there was something non-kid-like about the way she was talking. "We just kind of went on with what Uncle Jim had been doing. He was just making sure he didn't wind up buried in rats and ratlings, and what he got for them went into more rabbit food and maybe a bit of repair wire from time to time. But if we want to do this properly and make some money, we have to make some changes."

"We're listening." Audrey lifted her teacup and sipped, hoping to hide her indulgent smile.

"So there's a place near the city that rehabilitates owls that have been hit by a car, or got tangled in electric wires or whatever. And just about the only thing owls will eat are rats and mice. This place just can't get enough of them. The owls will eat chicken too, but that's expensive. Then there's another place that takes in birds. They get hawks and eagles and blue herons and ravens and like that. They grow a few mice and feed them live, but they need more rats. People who own snakes need food for them, and a lot of people keep snakes as pets. Why anybody would, I don't know."

"There's people would say the same thing about rats," Seely said mildly.

"These aren't pets," Darlene corrected her. "Patsy might have been, but these are an investment. Anyway, most people raise what they call domestic rats. They're smaller than the Norwegians, more the size of the white pet ones. I can't see any reason for us to get rid of the Norskis. But if we want to make money, we'll need to do better than the few breeders we have. There's one place in the Cariboo where the woman has nine hundred breeders!"

"Nine hundred?!" Audrey was close to going up like a helium balloon. "We can't have nine hundred rats here. People won't come to get their cakes and pies and stuff."

"Right. But Kitty and Lucy have a shed they aren't using, and they *are* a farm."

"Something tells me they aren't going to jump up and down at the chance of having a couple of hundred rats on the place."

"I asked, and Lucy laughed but she said fine. So we're moving. The only ones we're going to keep here are the pet stock ones, and we need to be near them so they'll get used to people and be tame and affectionate."

"Patsy was affectionate." Seely smiled at the memories. "She'd crawl into bed and get under the covers, then she'd go exploring. I'd watch the covers moving, this little lump like a bubble tunnelling around. When she'd checked it all out and was sure everything was the way it was supposed to be, she'd snuggle against me, right under my chin. Sometimes she'd make little patting motions with her front paws, and she'd make these noises. It was like she was convinced I was a rat too."

"You should write a story about Patsy," Audrey said. "How you got her, why you kept her, how she behaved. The group would love it."

"You think so?"

"Yeah. I think so. I would, anyway."

Kitty did the same thing Lucy had done. She burst out laughing.

"Are you serious?"

"Look at it this way," Lucy said. "How much a pound do you get for your beef? If you're lucky, and if it's a good year, and if and if and if, you'll get a dollar a pound live weight for a six- or eight-month calf. Figure it out. An empty heifer costs you anywhere between eight hundred and a thousand dollars. Figure in another fifty or so for A.I. And that's only if it takes on the first try. Then for nine months you feed that cow, with hay that's worth anywhere from five to ten dollars a bale, and you know they'll eat a bale a day given half a chance. And how much land do you need, three acres per cow? Five? And a barn, Jesus, let's not forget the barn. Then you've got the medicine, the vet, the ear tags, the de-louser you pour down their backs.

And after nine months, you get a calf. Right away you have to figure in the cost of disinfectant and antiseptic for the navel. And if they get scours, you've got electrolytes, and nine times out of ten the vet, and then there's the castrating, and if you do it yourself you still have to figure in your time and what that ought to be worth, and..."

"Stop it," Kitty howled.

"And then, for the next six or eight months you've got that calf drinking milk and eating grass and chowing down on hay, and if you want him or her in real good shape, you grain them as well. It all costs. And then you get your buck a pound live weight. Well, these kids have it figured out that they're going to make about seven dollars a pound for their rats."

"Okay, okay, but if the damn things get loose—"

"If they get loose, I'm sure Mycat can handle them. And Pup isn't going to sit there with flies crawling on her head if there's rats running around. They wouldn't last three minutes."

The shed in question was emptied, and Jimmy and Moe brought in a pickup load of old windows and began installing them.

"Moe got them when he did a renovation job on the old dance hall," Jimmy grunted, lifting his end. He and Kitty slid the window into place. "Jesus Christ, they're heavy."

"What I don't understand is—"

"It's the girls. They don't want the breeders to get bored, you see. Their big argument is along the lines of how would *you* like to be locked in a shed all the time, with nothing to look at but more others just like you? Can you see the bubble in the level, Kit?"

"Needs a skinny shim at your end. Here, try this."

"Bloody window weighs a ton."

"Here." Moe stepped in and took over with the window. Jimmy slid in the shim and Moe checked the bubble. "You are a couple of experts," he laughed. "Any time you want a job, just show up with safety toes and a hard hat and you're hired."

After the windows were installed, the inside of the shed was walled in with salvaged wallboard.

"God, someone paid through the nose for this stuff once upon a time." Lucy sat on a block of wood, smoking a cigarette and drinking coffee from a thermos, her cane propped against the outside wall of the rat shed. "Twenty-five, thirty years ago, this stuff was all the rage for fixing up houses. This piece here, that's supposed to be birch, and that's probably mahogany over there. Then you've got your knotty pine. What it is, is a thin layer of real wood over top of an eighth-inch or so of trashwood. Later on, those ones over there, it wasn't even veneer, it was just a photo of the kind of wood it was supposed to be. And now..." She shrugged. "Makes you wonder what we're going to do when gyproc goes out of style."

"Pretty swank for a packa rats."

"The rat," Moe said quietly, "is a sacred animal. Rats are very clean. Rats are the best mothers on the face of the earth. They even adopt each other's babies. If a rat has more babies than she can feed, other rats with small litters take one or more babies and raise them. Rats look after their old, they take care of their cripples, they set a good example for the rest of us if we only take the time to pay attention to how they live."

"They spread disease."

"So do we," Moe smiled.

Jimmy laughed. "I heard about how rats will take a piece of wood, or a twig, or a long piece of grass or something, and use it to lead blind rats to where the food is. You think that's true?"

"It's true," Moe said firmly. "And male rats help look after the young. They even have a kindergarten. The young rats are taken to a particular place and left there with the old rats while the healthy adult rats go out looking for food."

Kitty shook her head. "That one goes too far. Can't swallow that."

"I am serious. The girls said they wanted the cages placed so all the rats could see outside. My question is, why cages?"

"They considered aquariums, but the cost of one aquarium is more than the cost of the wire for a half dozen cages. And they figure the cages will be easier to keep clean."

"I thought rats could go in and out of the smallest holes."

"Baby rabbit wire," Jimmy said, as if that explained everything.

Kitty let it go. No need to ask a whack of questions. She'd soon enough see the stuff. Meanwhile, she couldn't help worrying.

In fact, she was doing a lot of worrying. She could see all the small beef producers being steadily squeezed out by agribusiness interests. She could keep her stock until it was fully grown and sell it directly to the customer, but that involved a lot of work and expense, and a growing number of stupid government rules and regulations. It would mean phone calls and people driving up to ask questions and then, sure as hell, some dickering.

People who wouldn't hesitate to drop fifty, sixty bucks on a bottle of fair-to-middling Scotch would argue and complain over the price of the food they were putting in their kids' mouths. They'd drive up in a car with more chrome and gadgets than anyone would need, park and get out in their L.L. Bean clothes, then grouse about the cost of a side of beef. Everything Lucy had said was true. The expense was rising and the hard work was endless. And growing hay wasn't going to be anywhere near as easy here, near the coast, with month after month of rain leaching the nutrients from the soil. The harvest would be a total gamble.

Sometimes, she still thought fondly of the rodeo. She missed the excitement, missed the charge of adrenalin, even missed the travel. But usually, before the missing grew strong enough to turn her thoughts toward going back to it, something here would show itself and she'd be unwilling to risk what she had now. Looking over at Lucy sitting on a block of wood, rolling a fresh cigarette, brought a lurch of emotion. Lucy was the first crush Kitty had ever had. Yes, Kitty had loved Gran. Gran might have been brusque, she might have had a thick hide, she might have been strict and stern and sometimes disapproving. But she had bent over backwards to do as much as she could to improve the lives of Kitty and her siblings. Gran had grown ten times as much garden as she needed for herself, and done all that work to ensure there were fresh vegetables for the kids. Sure, she had made the raggedy lot of them pull weeds, made them help with the watering, threatened to pull their ears or tan their arses if they didn't get out there and pick beans, pick peas, pull carrots, thin beets. She was quite prepared to carry out her threats. But when the beans were picked and the new spuds dug and scrubbed, there was supper, with mint sauce for the spuds and garlic-in-margarine for the beans. She made meat loaf, stretching the hamburger with crushed cracker, with chopped onion, with eggs, with chopped fresh tomato when they had one, then stuffed the mix into a vegetable marrow or a squash and roasted it in the oven. If the meat loaf bubbled grease and drippings into the pan, Gran added spuds and baby carrots and cooked them in it. And when it was all done she made a big deal of serving it up, urging them to eat more and even more. Then she brought out the chocolate cake or the blackberry pie. Sometimes the kids practically staggered away from the table, packed full and burping.

Then, horribly, it was changed and Kitty was living with Lucy. At first that's all she did, live with Lucy and Deb, feeling alone and lonely, and totally off balance, faced with culture shock. Lucy was so much like Gran in some ways. She expected everyone to share the work, and God knows there was more than enough of that. She also expected everyone to make it possible for a kid to be a kid—never any question that she would drive Kitty to softball games, or take her to some essential team practice at the pool or at the soccer field. Now that Kitty knew what the workload really was, she was newly impressed with what Lucy had done. Chores had to be done early and the schedule had to be speeded up, the same work done more quickly to make room for the two or three or four hours it took to get the kid where she had to be and bring her home again. And never a complaint.

Now Lucy was obviously past it. She included Noel in everything, but someone else would have to drive him to Friday night skating. Someone else would have to take him fishing, clean his room, make his bed. The hands rolling the cigarette were large-knuckled from years of hard work, the face was lined, the skin on her throat was sagging and the short-cropped hair was past grey and almost white.

Whatever else happened around the hay, it would have to happen without Lucy. The move had stolen something vital from her. The move, and whatever she had gone through when Deb had hit the road and disappeared for all that time, had tipped Lucy into another and very different stage of life.

If the kids could figure out a new way to make a few bucks, if they could turn the rat business into an efficient and profitable enterprise, maybe Kitty was going to have to take another look at the whole problem of hay. Maybe instead of thinking about new ways to grow, harvest and store the damn stuff, she should think of ways to get enough money to buy it. She would need more, maybe twice as much, of the nutrient-poor local coast hay than she had needed when she was feeding them the rich crop of the dry interior. She'd probably be better off turning her hayfield into a money maker and getting the hay trucked in. Everyone said that Alberta hay was so rich you needed to feed less than half the amount. They grew so much of it that it wasn't too expensive, and they shipped it in ultra-compressed bales, so that a little pillow of the stuff went as far as a big bale. Weighed like hell, but when you're buying by the tractor-trailer load, it's bulk you worry about, not weight.

So what could she grow that would sell for enough to make it worth her while to import her hay?

"You going to stand there all damn day staring out at nothing, or are you going to grab the other end of this thing and hold it in place while I pound nails?"

"I'll pay you fifty cents to pound sand up your own nose," she offered.

"Pound sand up *your* nose, sister dear."

"Up yours, brother darling."

Every rat had a view. The lucky ones had their choice of windows through which they could watch the comings and goings on the farm. In with the pile of farm gear and equipment moved from Lucy's place were several large ventilating fans, left over from the days when there had been pigs in the back barn. Moe overhauled them, then cut squares in the wall up near the ceilings, built little boxes and fitted the fans in, bolted the boxes in place and wired them to the main power source. Just flick the switch and the fans sucked out the stale inside air, replacing it with fresh. "In the hot of summer," he said, "we can reverse the direction of the fans, bring air in, put containers of water here beneath the fans, and cool it off."

"Thinking all the time, aren't you?" she teased.

"Even better would be to freeze the containers, pull air over the ice."

"You going to install TV for them?"

"If I can find a free TV. Everything here except the cage wire is salvaged. You people!" He teased her right back and she enjoyed it. "You throw away the most useful things."

"Throw you away," she threatened. "Just toss and chuck."

"I am full of ideas," he bragged. "I am what they call an idea man."

"Well have an idea for me, God knows I need one." She told him about the hay.

Jimmy listened, but with only half an ear. He was sitting with his back-side on the ground, his back against the outside wall, busy with a pencil and a small notebook, working on an idea he had for a figure. Not a fright mask but a figure of Foam Woman, she of many breasts, who nourished the children lost to the waves. He also wanted to do a sealkie, and maybe find a way to have the two figures fit into each other. If they did, the combination of the two mythological women should make a third figure, he just wasn't sure who, or what. A whale? And what if Foam Woman's hair actually looked like the tentacles of a squid? Or maybe when the two of them fit together they made a clam shell, or an oyster shell. The more closely he concentrated on his growing vision, the fainter the voices of the others became.

"Hemp," said Moe, testing the fans.

"You mean pot?"

"No. Commercial hemp. We grow it back there, you know. It is used with cotton to make clothes. It is used to make paper."

"I'll be go to hell," she blurted. "If it had been a dog it would have bit me. The biggest cash crop on the coast is pot. The growing conditions are ideal."

"See, I told you. I am an idea man."

"I owe you," she said simply.

She was so excited by the idea that she could hardly wait for the rat palace to be finished. By the time it was, and the first of the breeders had been installed, Kitty had her government-issued permit to grow hemp.

"You could smoke an acre of this stuff and not even get a buzz," she laughed, "but it's still a controlled substance."

"They'll keep a close eye on it," Christie warned. "There'll be spot checks, unnanounced. They'll be in the field with sniffer dogs, making sure you haven't hidden a few of the real thing out there."

"Fine. They can come any time they want. Won't find a thing."

Kitty had her crop sold before she even got it planted. That was encouraging. She'd never had that kind of guarantee when she was growing hay. Not that she'd grown much hay. Lucy was the one who had ruined her back harvesting the stuff.

Not this time, though. Lucy had her flowers, her greenhouse, the vegetable garden she shared with Deb and Christie. It was Kitty who hitched up the groundbreaker plow and turned the grass under, Kitty who disk-harrowed, Kitty who spike-harrowed and Kitty who planted row after row after row after row of little round black seeds. And when the first of the hemp plants sprouted, it was Kitty who drove between the rows with the tines carefully placed to leave the crop alone and till the spaces between the rows, trying to kill off the grass that kept popping up.

"It's like blasphemy," Lucy sighed. "All those people, all those years, trying to get a good root system for hay, and look what we're doing."

Each female rat produced a litter every eight weeks, usually a dozen young ones but often as many as a dozen and a half. The one Savannah called the Goddess of Fertility had one litter of twenty, and the all-time record litter of twenty-two. She couldn't possibly feed that many, so Darlene marked the extras by snipping off the ends of their tails and placed them with other newly whelped females.

"Don't process the snipped-tail ones," she told Lizzie. "We might want to keep some of them, if they're as good as their mom."

They got twenty-five cents each for the three- or four-day-old pinkies, fifty cents for the week-old hoppers and seventy-five cents for the fuzzies, which were two to two and a half weeks old. The teenagers, a month old, fetched a dollar and a half, and the full-grown adults brought two dollars each if they were dead and two-ten if they were alive and not Norwegians.

"The Norskis are too big when they're full grown," Lizzie explained to Savannah, who pretended deep interest. "Only the very biggest snakes can choke 'em down, and they might fight the hawks and even hurt them."

"Then why do you keep them?"

"Because those are the ones we started with. From mom's pet rat. We just won't use any as replacement breeders. Well, maybe one of them we'll keep. She's brown with black and white patches, and she's real smart. I open her cage door, and she jumps onto my shoulder and rides up there while I do the chores. But if I'm going to process 'em, she starts to squeak and chitter and I have to put her back in her cage."

"Careful, she might bite you."

"She hides when it's processing time. Soon as I get out the bucket, before I even start, she goes into her nest box and shoves her nose in the corner and crouches down in the wood chips, like she's pretending she isn't even there."

"If you call her Patsy I'll brain you, you know that, eh?"

"Sure you will. And I'll just stand around while you do it."

Noel liked the rats. He understood why they had to stay in their cages, but he was allowed to go into the shed and move from cage to cage with offerings of clover, bits of bruised cherry or windfall plums, shreds of apple or salmonberry. He had to leave Mycat outside, though, because the rats went nuts if they smelled or saw him.

He didn't like the idea of the rats being killed. The adults had explained it to him—even Uncle Jimmy said it was like a modern improvement on the natural order of things. Noel liked the part about the hurt owls being fixed up, and how if they could fly and look after themselves again they got let go, and if they couldn't fly again they went to places where kids could go and see them and learn about owls. He liked the part about the hawks and eagles and blue herons too. Christie said in the old times there had been lots of them, that you could go to almost any beach at low tide and see big families of herons wading back and forth, cleaning up the mess.

But he didn't like the idea of the rats being killed. He tried to talk to Bones about it, but Bones just shrugged. When Bones wasn't interested in something, that meant Noel hadn't figured it all out and was being silly.

Noel had to think it through for himself, because everybody else he asked said the same things Uncle Jimmy had said.

There were three chairs in the rat palace and a little short-legged table Deb said she was going to swipe one day because she could fix it up and it would look great in the living room. Uncle Moe had salvaged it and given it to Noel, along with the chairs. Darlene and Lizzie had said sure, put it in the rat palace, just don't get careless and let any of the rats loose.

He'd like to. He'd like to walk over and start opening cage doors. But what good would that do? Mycat and Mabel and Puss and other cats, wild ones that lived in the bush, would hunt them down and kill them. Darlene had told him the rats didn't have all their instincts any more. Instinct was what made birds know when to fly away in winter and when to come back in the springtime.

Deb said she would get him a different table so he'd still have his own. That would be okay. Noel wasn't in love with this table, and it would be nice to have it in the living room. Deb said that when people said things like oh, what a gorgeous old treasure, she'd say, "That's Noel's table." That would be something.

He knew the table she was going to get, too. They'd seen it in the recycling place. The only reason they hadn't brought it right home was that it wouldn't fit in the car. If they'd had the truck, the different one would already be set up and this one would be in Deb's place in the basement, with the other stuff she was fixing. She and Uncle Moe were going to have a business together. Already his office had fixed-up chairs in it so that when people saw them and said how great they were, Uncle Moe could say yes, my friend did them. Then people would have something to think about when they looked at brand-new stuff and saw how flimsy it was. Uncle Moe would say how that kind of workmanship was almost impossible to find these days, or that the attention to detail was first rate, notice this or that. Christie said Moe could sell the country back to the Europeans and this time collect the money for it. When she said that, everybody laughed, even Bones, but Noel had no idea what it meant.

The spotted momma rat had pulled the nesting material back, exposing her pinkies. Auntie Seely said that meant the nest was too warm and she was giving her babies some cooler air. Auntie Seely said when the pinkies got too warm they started panting, which made them thirsty, so they started squeaking and the mom had to go back and feed them again. She said that was hard on the mom because she had to make extra milk, but if she didn't feed them, all the other rat moms would get upset, same as people do when a baby person is howling and wailing. So she pulled the nest stuff aside, the babies cooled down and quit panting and the mom got a rest. Pretty neat!

The pinkies were growing fast. Some of them had the first fuzz down their backs, and by the weekend they might be different colours, not pinkies. Sometimes you could tell when they were brand new that they were going to get dark, because they had blotches or streaks. The one Noel wanted for his very own was pink with a dark line up its back and dark feet. He'd already given Lizzie a dollar and she'd said the rat was his, but then he saw her give the money to Deb. That didn't make much sense because Deb didn't have anything to do with the rats. Kitty had started building a cage and he thought it might be for his rat, but he wasn't sure because it was big. It had one big cage room, then a tunnel made out of baby-wire, then another cage, and in that one there were swings and a slide-down-into-a-basin thing. He hoped it was for his rat, which he intended to call Bunny. Bones liked the joke, a rat named Bunny. If and only if either of the girls was in the shed to help him, Noel was allowed to sit with Bunny on his lap, stroking and talking and even holding him up to his face and sniffing at him. Bunny was too baby to sniff back, and anyway his eyes were still shut. By the time they started crawling out of the nest, their eyes would be open. They might even recognize Noel when they saw him. Especially Bunny.

On those days when Noel had been smooching up Bunny, Mycat would jump on his lap and sniff sniff sniff, and sometimes he would lick the place where Bunny had been lying. Lizzie said the cat was tasting tasting and getting ready to munch munch. But Noel started crying and Lizzie grabbed him and cried too, and said I'm sorry, I didn't mean to upset you, I was wrong. And then Seely told them to stop it, and said just sit down here and eat these cream puffs. "Mycat won't eat Bunny," she told Noel. "He's just giving kisses. Just giving kisses." Noel ate the cream puffs but he didn't believe her.

Then Bones took a hand. Mycat was sniffing sniffing, licking, and Bones laid his hand on Mycat's back. The cat froze, not even breathing. And when Bones took his hand away, Mycat wasn't interested any more. Oh, he still sniffed, still licked, but now he purred. Maybe they'd be friends. Maybe they'd get along the way Noel and Bobby got along.

But he still wished they didn't have to die. Why couldn't they feed those eagles on something else? Fish, maybe. Christie said there wasn't enough fish left in the ocean to fill a good-sized aquarium. Anyway, she said, the fish don't want to die any more than the rats do.

The table had gold tubes for legs, and crisscross bars that went under the thick piece of glass to help hold the weight of it. Noel thought it was gorgeous. Deb agreed with him, said it was exactly what a little guy would fall in love with. Nice and garish, she said. Whatever that was.

The hoppers in the cage in the corner were learning to play with each other. They had a game that was a lot like tag and a lot like catch-me. Noel and Bobby played that. When you caught the guy you were supposed to wrestle him down to the ground and he was supposed to let you. Not really play fighting, because of the letting it happen. Sometimes Bobby sat on Noel's belly and tickled him. You couldn't really feel it if you had a jacket on, but just the idea of being tickled could make Noel laugh.

Kitty got interviewed four times by the local newspaper. The first time, on the occasion of the permit being issued, they'd come out with a camera to get pictures of her planting the seeds. The second time they came, the hemp was six or eight inches high, the rows showed clearly and the article explained the cultivation and harvesting process, the uses to which hemp fibre could be put and the fact this was not—repeat, *not*—the kind of hemp people smoked. They not only interviewed Kitty for that one, they interviewed the staff sergeant and two of the constables, and the article was filled with warnings that the police would be increasing their patrols in the area of the hemp fields.

She knew that some kids would have to find out for themselves. Several of the plants closest to the fence had been stripped of their leaves and two plants had been hauled out of the dirt, roots and all. But she had plants growing in peat pots, ready to be brought in as replacements. When she found a clump of the real thing in one corner, she called the police. "They aren't mine," she said firmly. "Someone's come over the fence and put them in here, probably hoping nobody would notice and they could come back before harvest and nip them back again."

"How did you notice them?" The cop was suspicious. Why not? He got paid to be suspicious.

"I could try to impress you with my expertise," she grinned at him. "I could yammer on about the slightly darker shade or the scent from the leaves, or say that they vibrated and hummed with a different tone, but the truth is I noticed them because they aren't lined up with the others. They're a good foot to a foot and a half out of true and they're in a clump. An untidy one. The machine doesn't make mistakes like that."

"Appreciate the fact you called us instead of just dealing with it yourself."

"Constable, I'd like to get one thing clear. I don't want trouble of any kind. My motives here are purely selfish. I want the police car seen. I've phoned the newspaper and they're sending someone out. I want everyone to know this stunt isn't going to work. There aren't going to be eight-foot-tall pot plants just waiting for someone to come and collect them."

It was a front-page story, complete with photos of cops, plants and even a dog. The article suggested the dog had picked up the scent of the people who had planted the illegal crop and would recognize it if he smelled it again. Kitty doubted that anybody would believe that part of the story, but you never know. Anyone dumb enough to come over the fence and dig in pot plants without even trying to camouflage them was just about dumb enough to believe almost anything.

Christie lit the barbecue and cooked up a mountain of her not-quite-but-almost world famous ribs'n'sauce. Savannah and her crew arrived with bowls and platters and a big stainless steel pot of chili. Uncle Jimmy and Auntie Audrey brought Hungarian chicken, Auntie Seely came with cakes and pastries and pies and Carol had actually done some cooking—she brought a great big huge thing she called a hot salad, with all different kinds of beans in it and sliced raw onion and even some Ichiban noodles. She had put the flavour pack from the noodles into the dressing. Noel could easily have sat down and pigged out on that alone. But you weren't supposed to pig out on just one thing, you had to share with the family. Besides, the ribs'n'sauce were so good. And the chicken, he didn't know what Hungarian was, but if it was a place to live and people ate like this, he'd move there. If everyone else came with him, of course.

He sat on the top step with his plate on his knee, feeling very very lucky. This was the first outside meal they'd had in a long time. Mycat sat next to him, waiting hopefully. Noel finished picking the meat off a rib bone and dropped it where Mycat could get it.

"Good stuff, eh?" Uncle Jimmy sat down next to him, put his glass of wine between his feet and balanced his plate carefully on his knee.

"Real good," Noel sighed. "I wish my tummy was as big as yours. I'm almost full but I still feel hungry. It's so good! I wish I could just eat and eat and eat."

"So what's your favourite?"

"It's all my favourite. When I'm eating the chicken I think it's the very best, but then I eat some ribs and I think they're the best, and I don't have any room left in my belly at all! I probably won't even have room for cake."

"You still upset about the rats?"

"Yes."

"You remember how cute Pete and Repeat were when they were babies? Remember how they sucked your fingers and followed you around when you went over to visit with them? This barbecue you like so much is from a steer your Aunt Lucy raised, and when that steer was a baby, he was just as cute as Pete and Repeat. And the chicken? That used to be a cute little fluffy baby peep. That's what life is, sweetheart, everything eats everything else."

Uncle Jimmy tossed a wing tip to Mycat, who grabbed at it as though he hadn't had a bite to eat in days. Pup was so full she lay on her side, eyes closed, pretending to be asleep. She wasn't, though. Noel could tell she was awake because her ears weren't folded, they twitched in the direction of whoever was talking. Dog was so old now that she had to be helped up and down the stairs, and when she had to pee Kitty had to help her balance.

That's what this party was for, a goodbye to Dog. Kitty was taking her in to the vet tomorrow, and when she brought her back, Dog wouldn't hurt any more, she would be gone to spiritland. They were going to bury her empty body under the apple tree in the front yard, the place was ready. Deb said not to think of it as a hole in the ground. It wasn't a hole at all, it was a resting place. He'd cried at the thought of the dirt being put on her, but Deb said it wouldn't bother Dog, she wasn't even going to be there. Anyway, it wouldn't go into her eyes or nose. She would be wrapped up in her old blanket, the one she'd had in the back of the pickup. The new one, Kitty promised, would be washed, then dried, then washed again, and when it was dry the second time, Noel could have it. He wasn't going to put it on his bed, though. He was putting it over the big old soft chair that stood by his window. Sometimes Pup liked to curl up in that chair. Dog was so old she wasn't even interested in the treats everyone was trying to give her.

"How's kindergarten going?"

"Good." He nodded for emphasis. "Real good. The teacher lets me'n'Bobby sit at the same table and she doesn't even ask questions."

"What kind?"

"People ask how come my paper says one name and I say my last name is Scott, like everybody else. Well, most everybody. And people ask how come Bobby'n'me's got the same last name, and are we brothers and stuff like that. Mrs. Hobson doesn't ask any of that."

"What does she ask?"

"She asks did we have a good sleep, and she asks oh, did you see the moon last night, and she asks, how is your cat doing. Bobby'n'me told her about Dog, and about how she was going to pass on and so we were having a party, and she asked how we felt about it, and were we sad, and would we be okay, and did we need the day off school and like that."

"And do you? Need the day off school?"

"No." And then Noel dared himself. "Bones will look after her." It felt like the time Bones said to jump out of the car and he did, even though he didn't know Kitty would be there to catch him.

"He speaks to you?"

"Sort of. Not like you. Not words with his mouth, but like a voice, only it's not words in my head."

"Lucky you. He's never said a word to me."

"Oh. But he shows you things. Faces in the wood and stuff. He doesn't show me that. He tells me things, sometimes he tells me stories." He looked over at Dog, and at Bones, who sat beside her, stroking her in long, soothing waves, starting at her head and moving the length of her body, smoothing the black fur, paying no attention to Noel or Jimmy or anybody, just to Dog. Bones hadn't even come over to get the food Noel had put aside to share with him, and Mycat had eaten it. Maybe there were so many good smells and tastes in the air, coming from the platters and bowls and the barbecue, that Bones wasn't hungry. Maybe he'd already had enough.

Jimmy looked in the same direction the kid was staring. His appetite vanished and his throat tightened. He put his plate to one side, and stood slowly. As he moved toward Dog, Bones did his thing—*zip*—and he was sitting next to Noel, glaring at Jimmy. No, not glaring. Something else, because he wasn't angry at all. There was none of the bugs-under-the-skin feeling Jim got when Bones was angry.

Jimmy hunkered down and stroked Dog's head.

"Kitty," he said, just barely loud enough for her to hear.

"Ah, no." Kitty moved quickly, and as she knelt, Jim put his arm around her shoulders. "Ah, Dog, you old bitch, you. I was going to let you ride in the front of the truck. I was going to stop at the two-four and get you a brick of ice cream and all the chocolate bars you wanted." She turned to Jim and her eyes were bright with tears. "She always wanted chocolate, the smell of it, and she was mooching. But you can't let them have it because it screws up their liver. One chocolate bar can be fatal for some dogs. I figured that since it was her last day anyway... and now she won't get any." The tears spilled and Jim sat on the weather-bleached porch, holding her and rocking her. "What kind of rotten break is that? To live your entire long life without even once tasting a chocolate bar!"

Then Bobby was there with a piece of black forest cake on a small plate. He put the plate on the porch beside Dog's dry black nose. He didn't say a word, just hurried over to sit next to Noel. Jimmy noticed Bobby didn't try to sit where Bones was. He walked to the other side, moved the empty plate and sat there. It might have been coincidence but Jim doubted it.

"Maybe she traded in her chocolate bar for the chance to die with all her friends around her," he murmured. "Think about it, Kitty. She knew we were here. She got patted and stroked and told she was a good old girl, and everybody fussed her. She could smell all the good smells and so she just... went to sleep."

Kitty sobbed for a long time.

"Well," she said finally, and Jim released his hold on her.

"Yeah," he agreed.

They wrapped her in her blanket and Kitty carried her to the grave. She gave Dog to Jimmy and jumped down into the hole, then he handed her the limp bundle. There was just enough room for her to lower Dog carefully into the ground. "Good old girl," she whispered. She leaned over, removed the worn collar and placed it in the blanket. "You run free, now. You probably won't have to come when you're called, either."

They buried Dog silently, all of them remembering Glen and Sandra's funeral. It seemed like years had passed since they had all gotten together, Deb and Lucy, Kitty and Christie, Jimmy and Seely and Savannah and Carol, and all those kids and everyone else in the whole clanjamfrie, to mark the passing of two of them. And years more since they had all been shaken up and tossed around, then landed again in different places. Kitty figured that there would be more shaking and tossing, and more landing. Maybe they had always lived on the edge of Hardscratch Row and maybe they always would, and maybe that was fine. She looked over at Bones, the Squeyanx, the JimmySpook. He sat quietly and almost respectfully at the side of Dog's grave, but every once in a while his bony, shadowy form gave off a tiny spark of light. It was as if he was full of energy, and just waiting to see what would happen next.

The Fiction of Anne Cameron

"Anne Cameron's fictional voice is unique in Canada. She can cuss like a logger or set down words as tender as lullabies. Her West Coast, small-town characters, like her prose, are rough and tough, sweet 'n' tender."

–Ottawa Citizen

"The anger and passion with which Cameron writes lift the ordinary into something stronger."

–Quill and Quire

"Cameron understands the way a woman's work affects every other sphere of her life."

–Feminist Bookstore News

Daughters of Copper Woman
Legends • 5¼ x 7½ • 200 pages, paperback • 1-55017-245-X • $19.95 Can, $14.95 US

Since its first publication in 1981, *Daughters of Copper Woman* has become an underground classic, selling over 200,000 copies. This new edition includes fresh material added by the author.

"Oral traditions, once committed to print, lose something of their intrinsic quality. Those passed on by the Nootka published in Anne Cameron's Daughters of Copper Woman *however, manage to preserve their simplicity of theme and directness of expression. They lose nothing of the sense of inherent wisdom, courage and foresight characterized in the society of women from Vancouver Island."*

–Guardian

"Daughters of Copper Woman is something of a marvel, certainly an enchantment, an uplifting revelation... Cameron's voice is prophetic, her talents mature and powerful."

–Ottawa Citizen

"Cameron's work compels attention, calling out for social justice and spiritual healing."

–Quill & Quire

Sarah's Children
Novel • 5½ x 8½ • 288 pages, paperback • 1-55017-274-3 • $21.95

This is a story about one woman's slow and painful recovery from a serious illness; a story about a family taking an honest look at itself; a story about the power of love. "It takes a whole community to raise a child," as the saying goes, and this lucid, startling novel shows that it also takes only one middle-aged woman to change a whole community forever.

"Cameron, with this and her other books, has carved out a place in literature... A very good read."

–Lower Island News

Those Lancasters
Novel • 6 x 9 • 398 pages, paperback • 1-55017-227-1 • $21.95

A novel that puts the fun back in dysfunctional—a light-hearted look at the trials and tribulations of a family that defines disadvantage.

"The Lancaster brothers and sisters exemplify the importance of love, fierce loyalty and tolerance for personal idiosyncrasies in maintaining strong family ties."

–Vancouver Sun

Aftermath
Novel • 6 x 9 • 400 pages, paperback • 1-55017-193-3 • $18.95

An examination of the child-welfare system through the lives of hauntingly memorable characters.

"Finally an author who tells it like it is. In Aftermath, *Anne Cameron writes brilliant, funny and sometimes overwhelming social commentary on the ins and outs of abusive families and the child welfare system in Canada, and presumably, around the world."*

–amazon.com

"Cameron's book is a testimony to the underprivileged, the abused, the vulnerable children of Canada and to those who daily struggle to break out of the cycle of degradation and humiliation."

–Winnipeg Free Press

"Cameron gives us a complex swirl of a story, weaving one life into another. The novel is a testament to the human spirit, to the resilience of survivors and to writing that keeps Fran and Liz in sight long after the novel ends."

–Prairie Fire

Selkie
Novel • 6 x 9 • 192 pages, paperback • 1-55017-152-6 • $17.95

One morning it starts raining in Cassidy's house, and nobody can get it to stop. Like everyone else, Cassidy figures it's just a problem with the pipes. She doesn't know that she's about to embark on the ride of her life.

"These are stories of loss and reclamation. Designed like a fable, Selkie *begins at a point of extreme despair and works steadfastly toward enlightened resolution. Anne Cameron's tale may be simple in form but it is nevertheless moving, testifying to one woman's unequivocal victory over adversity."*

–Vancouver Sun

The Whole Fam Damily
Novel • 6 x 9 • 264 pages, paperback • 1-55017-134-8 • $17.95

This story is told in Cameron's signature style—direct, smart and very funny, with the undertone of anger that marks the most provocative fiction.

"Beatings, sexual abuse, arson... all of the sickness that spins out of a family as it swirls in its own destruction from generation to generation... The Whole Fam Damily *rings powerfully and disturbingly true."*
–Ottawa Citizen

"Theirs is a world where children learn that beer and violence are as much a part of life as TV and Kraft Dinner."
–Regina Leader Post

"...an absolutely riveting cacophony of voices that will stay in your head long after you've put the book down."
–Halifax Daily News

DeeJay and Betty
Novel • 6 x 9 • 264 pages, paperback • 1-55017-112-7 • $16.95

A story about two women who overcome their pasts to forge strong futures for themselves and each other.

"No doily or decorative language, no fancy postmodern structured techniques, just a straight-from-the-heart story."
–Vancouver Sun

Kick the Can
Novel • 6 x 9 • 160 pages, paperback • 1-55017-039-2 • $15.95

Rowan Hanson refuses to get involved with "the ex, the kids, the house, the car, the boat or the lawyer who's apt to wind up with it all, anyway." But in the end she has to take the advice her grandmother gave her twenty years earlier: "When it's your turn to take your kick at the can, kiddo, you do 'er."

"Cameron knows how women talk to each other."
–Province

"Cameron's women aren't whiners. Their problems are believable, their triumphs small but fulfilling. They feel real enough, likable enough, to want to call one up to go out for coffee."
–Coast News

Escape to Beulah
Novel • 6 x 9 • 236 pages, paperback • 1-55017-029-5 • $16.95

Their story is a tribute to the strength of women everywhere and a passionate statement about human freedom and dignity.

"A feminist fable for our times, told with a dispassionate, fascinated vigour."
–Province

South of an Unnamed Creek
Novel • 6 x 9 • 200 pages, hardcover • 1-55017-013-9 • $26.95

This novel focuses on five women from diverse backgrounds who find common ground in the dance halls of the Klondike Goldrush.

"...joins courage to comedy with a light, sure touch."
–Ottawa Citizen

Women, Kids & Huckleberry Wine

Short stories • 6 x 9 • 258 pages, paperback • 0-920080-68-5 • $16.95
With clear-sighted realism and wry humour, these stories enchant, move, disturb and provoke.

"Witty, entertaining and strangely uplifting."
–Edmonton Journal

"...easy-going, direct, funny, cynical and full of incisive curses and wisdom."
–Diversions

Available at Better Bookstores or

Harbour Publishing
P.O. Box 219
Madeira Park, BC, Canada V0N 2H0

Phone (604) 883-2730 • **Fax** (604) 883-9451
Toll-free order line 1 800 667-2988
Toll-free fax order line 1 877 604-9449
E-mail orders@harbourpublishing.com
Website www.harbourpublishing.com